ORCHARD BOOKS
338 Euston Road, London NW1 3BH
Orchard Books Australia
Level 17/207 Kent Street, Sydney, NSW 2000

First published in 2015 by Orchard Books

ISBN 978 1 40833 425 6

A CIP catalogue record for this book is available
from the British Library.

1 3 5 7 9 8 6 4 2

Printed in Great Britain by CPI Group (UK) Ltd, Croydon, CR0 4YY

Orchard Books is an imprint of the Hachette Children's Group,
and published by The Watts Publishing Group Limited,
an Hachette UK company.

www.hachette.co.uk

TERI TERRY

ORCHARD

In memory of Joan and Eric Terry

Truth is the cry of all, but game of the few.

George Berkeley
1744

1
CHANCE

*Earth has its boundaries, but human
stupidity is limitless.*

Gustave Flaubert

1

A school shouldn't be this quiet. I slip down the stairs, Hex a shadow behind me, matching my exaggerated careful, slow steps. Sound or sudden movement trigger the cameras, and I fight to breathe slowly, in and out, silent as I can, though my heart is thudding so loud I'm sure it will set the cameras off all on its own. But they stay still.

We pass the final year students' rooms, one by one. They are silent as graves with a red light over each door marking them as occupied. I glance back at Hex, an eyebrow raised, and can see he is worried. Could we be that unlucky that this is the one day of the year that every single student is in attendance? But at last there is an empty room. Hex pulls a face: it's Jezzamine's. If they trace the hack to here, retribution will be harsh. But as good as his word, he fiddles the lock and is inside and plugged in within seconds.

Now it's up to me. *Come on, Luna, you can do this.* I continue my slow progress to the next corridor, and wait. Through the window in the door I can just see the green light of the camera. Security is higher through here, cameras on all the time and not just sound and motion. There is no point in continuing if Hex can't—

And the green light goes out.

I grin, and remember just in time to move slowly until I'm through the door and out of range of the hall detectors. Once the door shuts I dash across the room to the next door just as the lock clicks open. *Hex, you are brilliant.*

Remembering he wasn't sure he could keep it unlocked for long, I look around the office for something to jam in the door, then end up shoving one of my shoes in it. I step into the room.

So this is the centre of evil.

It looks much like any other PIP, but hooked into this Plug In Point is the Bag herself – Beatrice Annabel Goodwin OBE, Head of Learning and Chief Torturer of Students. Her usually disdainful face is blank; her body is here on the PIP sofa, the rest of her in virtual assembly. We picked the one moment of the week that every single one of the regular students and teachers would be there, occupied and unable to unplug.

Nervous to be this close to her, I can't stop myself from waving a hand in front of her face: no reaction. *Don't be an idiot, Luna. You're wasting time.*

I pull the gloves and paint out of my backpack, and get to work.

When I'm done, I back out of the room. The camera light is still off. I stoop to pull my shoe out of the doorway; the door clicks to and locks. I hesitate, staring at the shoe in my hand. They're purple, and I hand-painted the butterflies on them myself. The only pair quite like them.

I push the shoe just out of sight behind a plant in the outer office. This time, there will be no escape.

*

12

Rachel raises an eyebrow as I slip into my seat next to hers. 'Where've you been?'

'Nowhere.' But I can't stop myself from grinning. Our minder, Anderson, is still slumped on his desk asleep, and our class of Refuser misfits in its usual chaos.

She shakes her head. 'That look means trouble is in the air, and *nowhere* is somewhere you weren't supposed to be. And where is your shoe?'

I glance down: one purple butterfly shoe on the left, barefoot on the right. 'I seem to have misplaced it.' Good idea, bad idea? Time will tell, but my stomach is clenching in knots. I didn't really think that through, did I?

Hex slips through the classroom door a few minutes later as planned, and sits at the back. I turn and glance at him, like I'm not supposed to do. He's all nonchalant, but *he* didn't leave a shoe behind.

'I don't suppose you've got spare shoes with you?' I whisper to Rachel.

She shakes her head. 'Even if I did...' She shrugs, no need to finish the sentence. Rachel is an RE: a Refuser on Religious Exemption. Her church refuses technology, and fashion: her plain chunky black shoes would scream *wrong* on my feet. 'How about your gym shoes?' she says.

Can I get out to the lockers and back again before—

The door opens. No. I can't.

It's Mrs Goodwin, but not like we've seen her before. Her face is serene, unaware. As serene as you can be with elaborate face paint: a clown face, but not just any clown. A nightmare

13

clown. A giant, manic red smile and red nose are stark against chalk-white cheeks, and even better: snakes reach down from her hair, like some sort of mad Medusa. Somehow they add up on her face to pure evil. *Genius*. At last: her exterior matches her interior.

When Rachel looks up she draws in a sharp gasp, and I can feel Hex's eyes burning into the back of my skull. All we'd talked about was spray-painting a few comments about the school around her office. But semi-permanent body paint is a much better way to get a point across, isn't it?

Careful to show no movement above the desk, I kick my other shoe off, and tuck it and my feet under my backpack.

Goodwin turns to the teacher's desk at the front, and raps her hands down loudly on it. Anderson jumps out of his nap, starts to apologise, then looks at her. His words die away.

'What is it?' she snaps, but he just stares at her, mouth opening and closing like he can't breathe. When he doesn't instantly answer, she shakes her head and turns away from him. His face is baffled – he probably thinks he is still in a sleep dust-induced dream. Not that he knew there was sleep dust in his tea. Even though he often naps through the morning after giving us our assignments for the day, this time I couldn't take any chances.

She faces us. The more familiar long-suffering contempt with a veneer of gentle condescension takes over under the clown face.

'Good morning, class. As you've missed assembly *again*, and we don't want you to miss out on anything important, here I am. *In person*. No matter *how* busy I am, every student's learning is important to us.'

Her voice drones on with school news and equipment upgrades, and I cast a careful glance about at the other students. In our high school of over 600, the class of Refusers has dwindled down to about twenty, covering all year groups. Others have been browbeaten over time to accept Virtual Education. There are a few, like Hex, here involuntarily – excluded for a short time for virtual misdemeanours. In his case he hacked into eighteen-plus games and bypassed the password net; the whole school was into virtual worlds that parents and teachers most definitely did *not* approve of. Most of the rest are REs like Rachel, and now that the initial shock of Goodwin's appearance has passed, they are composed, gazing back at Evil Clown with equanimity – the same way they react to anything interesting. The danger points are the MEs, six of them in a cluster across the room. The Medical Exemptions are unpredictable. Most of them are staring at her with fearful wide eyes, but worse: a few of the younger ones are whispering and struggling not to laugh.

'Quiet!' she suddenly snaps at them, and all noise in the room ceases. 'I insist on your full attention.' She moves further into the room, staring every student in the eye in turn. She stops by my desk.

'Luna, you're looking pleased with yourself today,' she says, and raises an eyebrow. One of the snakes painted across her forehead splits with the movement. She hates all Refusers, but especially me because, in her own words, I have no excuse for it – no religious or medical grounds that preclude me from Virtual Education. No matter that it is part of NUN's International Bill of Rights of the Child that anyone can decline educational feed Implants. That students can insist on an old-fashioned non-virtual education. Even she can't ignore New United Nations directives, but she makes sure the standard is as low as is legal, and torments us every chance she gets. Especially me, as she is convinced I Refuse just to spite her, to waste time and resources.

That'd be a good reason. If only it were true.

She won't lay into me with this many witnesses, but I manage to say nothing, to return her gaze calmly. Careful to keep myself from looking either too angry or too happy, the two expressions she can't bear to see on my face.

Eventually she breaks gaze, and looks around the room. 'I'm required by New United Nations directive NUN-92 to emphasise that your continuing refusal of PareCo's Virtual Education opportunities doesn't bar you from entry to the PareCo tests.' Her teeth are gritted, as if saying the words causes her physical pain. 'All final year students were entered by the school, and those successful at obtaining Test appointments will be notified by school feed tomorrow morning.'

The two boys at the front are giggling again, hands over faces, trying to stop.

She spins round, leans forward and puts a hand on each of their desks. 'What. Is. It. Already?' she demands, voice raised.

One of them looks across the room for guidance, and

she smacks a hand down on the desktop in front of him.

'*You*: answer me!'

He swallows. 'You…you've got something on your f-f-f-face,' he answers.

'What?' She backs away, and nervously brushes at imaginary crumbs. Then Mr Anderson stands up. Convinced he isn't seeing things now because of what the boy said? He pulls a mirror out of a locker of science equipment, and hands it to her.

At first I think she won't look; she'll smash it on the floor or fling it back at him. But curiosity gets the better of her, and she holds it up. The room is so silent I can hear my heart beating for the second time today.

She wordlessly puts the mirror down on the desk, and leaves the room.

Everyone breathes out at the same time when the door swings shut. The lunch bell goes seconds later: she won't make it back to her office in time. *Everyone* will emerge into the halls and see her.

Anderson faces the class. Is that a smile twitching behind his moustache? 'Well, now. I don't suppose anyone here knows anything about that?' The room stays silent. 'No? Well, if you do, I expect you'll be hearing about it soon. Go. Off to lunch.'

My gym trainers don't go with the purple dress I modified, but being a Refuser has its advantages: you can wear what you want. Even if it is always wrong. The final year students' lunchroom is crammed with seventeen-year-olds in jeans and red tops. There is no uniform in test year, but apart from Hackers who do their own thing, somehow the rest of them always dress the same. I used to be mystified until Hex told me they confer in Realtime before school.

By tradition Refusers have our own section of the lunchroom, and despite the crowded room none of the jeans-and-red-shirted others venture too close. Hex comes in late, but instead of heading straight for his Hacker friends as usual, he pauses next to Rachel and me. He raises an eyebrow over his tattoo-encircled left eye: has an extra black swirl been added? That was quick. 'So. Is art one of your best subjects?' he asks.

Rachel gets up. 'Somehow I don't think I should be listening to this conversation.'

She goes to fill a water glass, and I shrug.

'You should have told me,' he chides.

'Angry?'

'No.' He grins. 'Considering that wasn't virtual, it was brilliant.'

I smile back. We'd been arguing that very point. So used to spending his life plugged in, he didn't get the power of the personal touch in the real world. Hex had been convinced virtual means were the only way to get revenge for his exclusion.

'But she will be trying very, very hard to find someone to blame,' he says.

'Are your tracks covered?'

'Oh, yes. She won't be able to prove anything. That doesn't mean she won't work it out. She'll know somebody hacked the cameras and door, and there aren't many here who could do that.'

'Modest, aren't you? What if she notices the new mark by your eye?'

'Damn. You noticed? I thought it was subtle.' He grins, clearly pleased he earned another Hacker's mark – the Hacker equivalent of bragging about something that cannot be admitted to without risk of prosecution. 'Anyhow, she'll know it was more than one person. So are *your* tracks covered?'

I stare back at him, a shoe-sized knot of guilt uncomfortable in my stomach. 'The deal was if one of us gets caught the other says nothing, and I never will. So you have nothing to worry about. Now push off before anyone notices you're slumming it.'

Rachel returns to her seat. Conversations echo around me: the whole year saw Goodwin's face, and it is all they can talk about. I push my lunch about a plate, unable to even think about eating. Will my plan work?

Lunch is nearly over when it finally happens. Rachel nudges my arm. I look up, and her eyes are fixed on the door. Conversation dies away.

Robson, head of school security, marches across the room, and stops behind me. A meaty hand clamps onto my shoulder, and pulls me out of my seat.

2

Both my purple shoes are on Goodwin's desk when I'm marched into her office. She is in a desk chair behind it, her head and face swathed in a scarf.

'Leave us!' she snaps at Robson, and he exits the office. Not good: no witnesses.

She holds up my right shoe. 'Exhibit A: found at the scene of the crime.' She holds up the left one. 'Exhibit B: found in your locker.'

I say nothing, stare back at her.

She yanks the scarf away: her clown face shows signs that she tried to wash it off, but it is still stark – that semi-permanent paint will take *days* of scrubbing. 'Would you like to confess? Or should we make like Cinderella, and see if the shoe fits?' Her voice is strangely calm.

'They're my shoes,' I say, and hate that my voice wavers.

She nods her head. 'Sit down, Luna.' I perch on the edge of the chair opposite her desk. 'I suppose you think you're very, very clever. You are, and that is part of both the problem, and the mystery.'

'I don't know what you—'

'Be quiet.' She stares back. 'I've been looking at your records. You had straight As in primary. In secondary, when you started to Refuse, you've been average across the board. Every now and then you get a good grade in maths, almost like you can't help yourself, but soon follow it up with a fail to make it all very *carefully* average.'

'No! I always do my best in all my subjects.' The lie hangs in the air between us, heavy and visible like skywriting.

She smiles. Raises an eyebrow. 'I don't need to tell you the chief NUN directives, the conclusions reached after human stupidity and the third world war nearly destroyed the planet. And you know the dual nature of the NUN tests run by PareCo?'

I nod, no point in denying what everyone knows.

'Tell me.'

'There are two tests. The first is intelligence quotient. And the second, rationality quotient.'

'But that is only half the story. I'm going to tell you something you haven't been taught in school, but you, my dear, are so *clever* you may have worked it out. Your very average grades suggest this to me.'

I stare back at her. 'I don't know what you are talking about.'

'Then listen. The stated purpose of the tests, IQ and RQ, is to select the best applicants for university and PareCo placements, yes? The ones who are not only brilliant, but rational. The unstated purpose – the duality! – is to identify dangerous individuals. The *clever* ones, my dear, who are also irrational, and have to be watched, *not* given responsibility. For the safety of us all. And the reason, of course, is to avoid having the intelligent but irrational in charge of *anything*, ever again. Not even their own lives. The New

21

United Nations has enforcement powers well beyond any previous UN, solely to prevent this. Because the clever-stupid, as I like to call them, like *your mother*, are a danger to themselves and society.'

I won't react; I won't. When I was younger Goodwin could make me cry. Not any more. I struggle to hold the pain inside, to keep it from my face, but she knows it is there.

She smiles, and picks up my right shoe in her hand. 'And then we come to this interestingly decorated object, casually left behind in my outer office. Placed behind a plant where it wasn't immediately seen, but easily found on a search. No doubt with your fingerprints all over it. Why?'

'I dropped it. That's all!'

She shakes her head. 'Don't bother, Luna. So. My first thought: that isn't clever. My second thought: it is irrational. *Or is it?* What would leaving evidence of your identity behind at the scene of your breaking and entering, and assault upon my person, actually achieve? And I've come to one conclusion. *You wanted to get caught.* But why?' She pauses, as if waiting for an answer, but I'm too stunned she worked it out to come up with anything.

'The answer is obvious. I'm not giving you what you want, Luna. Your elaborate plan has failed. You won't be expelled.'

'*What?*'

'You heard me. But that doesn't mean you won't be punished, oh no. Once the tests are under way next week, we'll find some interesting extra lessons for you to do for the rest of the school year. I haven't decided quite what yet, but they will be very…*interesting*. You can alleviate your fate, in part, if you identify your accomplice.'

'I acted alone.'

'Oh, really? You, a Refuser, hacked into the school security system? And not only that, you did it at the very same time as entering my office?' She shakes her head. 'Even *you* aren't that clever. Now get to class.'

She has Robson escort me to my classroom door. When I open it, every face looks up with shock. It seems consensus was that I'd never be seen again. I sit down, and Rachel squeezes my arm.

I'm a minor celebrity. Even though I don't confirm or deny anything, everyone put Goodwin's clown face and Robson hauling me off at lunch together, and by the end of day came up with the right answer for a change. Students who've ignored my existence for years break into spontaneous applause when we go down the stairs.

Despite being totally weirded out by what Goodwin said, worried about what will happen next week and, most of all, upset that I didn't get expelled so I could spend the last pointless months of school before work placements away from this place, it is kind of fun.

Until I get home.

3

My stepmother Sally is waiting for me as soon as I walk through the door.

'Bea tells me you were trying to get expelled. Are you insane?'

There is a very big disadvantage to having my stepmother going to the same virtual gym as my head teacher. I walk through to the kitchen to get a drink, and she follows.

'What were you thinking?' she says. 'I've a good mind to get your father in here, and—'

I look up. I know an empty threat when I hear one. 'Please do. I haven't seen him in weeks.'

There is a giggle from the corner, and I go and slip an arm over Nanna's shoulders. She switches back to humming, rocking back and forth slightly in her seat.

My stepmother flops down in a chair in front of us. 'Luna, I just don't understand. *Why* would you try to get expelled?'

And she looks genuinely distressed, and worried, and I'm contrite.

'I'm sorry, Sally. I don't want to upset you. But what is the point to finishing the year? I'm well out of the grade bracket to get a Test appointment. The rest of the year is just all the failures marking time, before whatever dire work placement headed our way begins.'

'If she'd expelled you, that'd be on your record forever,

Luna. We've got enough problems in this family without you adding to them more than you have already.'

And I stiffen. Now and then I think she is human, but it always comes back to that: her shame at being associated with our gene pool, that her son is tainted by it forever – by a half-sister who is a Refuser, a grandmother who is away with the fairies. And then there is my infamous mother.

Sally stands up again. 'Whatever your reasons, you're grounded. Forever.'

'Well, since I have such an amazing social life, that'll really hurt. Got anything else? Deny me virtual access, maybe?'

She stomps off. Nanna sticks out her tongue, and I stifle a giggle.

Dinner: no Dad as usual, and Sally is giving me the silent treatment, but Jason doesn't notice. How such a cute kid came out of such a miserable woman is one of life's great mysteries. Jason babbles on about Virtual Harry Potter World: at ten years old, a few months ago, he finally got access to more levels. And he was SO excited to meet Luna. My namesake. He can't understand why I won't plug in and play with him.

'Couldn't you, just this once…' Sally says, finally breaking the wall of silence.

'No. I can't. In case you might have forgotten, that is kind of what being a Refuser is all about.'

'But it's so much *fun*, Luna,' Jason says, and starts telling me all about playing Quidditch, before disappearing to plug in and play some more.

Before heading up for the night, I go to Dad's office. Check his life support. His skin is pale, too pale. How long has it been since he's unplugged? I check a screen log – weeks. I consider an emergency unplug, but what would my excuse be this time? Being pulled from whatever game he is guiding newbies through this evening would make him as grumpy as imaginable. These evening hours are prime time for paying customers. I blow him a kiss, and turn out the light.

That night it's the same nightmare, but knowing what it is doesn't make it stop. There is no escape.

I'm lying still. It's warm, soothing; I want to sleep, to drift, to both plug in and disconnect at the same time. To be part of the Game at last.

Click. The interface shimmers, my vision goes soft. But I'm not in; at least, not properly. The screens and room around me are all still here. But the virtual hallway beckons. My stomach lurches, and I fight to make reality disappear. I hate it.

I stand, and enter the hall. One step; two. And stupidly, I start to hope. This time, it will be different. This time, I will belong. I hear voices, laughter through doors that beckon and tempt in the hall, and I reach to push one of them open.

Then the floor shimmers, and disappears.

I grasp wildly around me but everything turns to smoke, vanishes, and I fall. Hurtling down, faster and faster. Screams rush past me as the virtual world collapses, is gone, turns to nothing. And I know I will fall, gain speed, faster and faster

26

until veins and skin and organs stretch out and burst apart;
until I'm not a person any more, but a blur, a smudge.

But then a hand reaches out.

It grabs my arm tight, in a claw grip. My arm almost
rips from its socket, but somehow it holds, and I stop: like
slamming into a brick wall. From freefall to no movement at
all, in an instant.

The pain is so intense... I wake up.

Not a dream, at least not that part of it: there are hands
clenched on both of my arms now, digging painfully into
my skin.

Early morning casts enough light through the window to
show wild, panicked eyes. Dark grey-streaked hair in wisps
about a drawn face.

'Luna, you're in danger.' A hissed whisper. 'You must
hide. You have to live; so much depends on you.'

My heart thuds painfully in my chest from the fear of the
fall, the abrupt end to the usual dream. I breathe in and out,
try to steady myself so I can steady her.

I reach my hands to hers, gently ease her fingers one
by one from my arms until they release, and then hold her
hands in mine.

'Nanna, everything's fine. Don't worry.'

'Don't let them notice you, Luna, or all will be lost.' Her
eyes are bright, penetrating and focused. She is so rarely
present this way, that even though I know it isn't really her
any more, that she doesn't know what she is even saying most

of the time, I can't help myself. I *hope*. That she'll come back to me, be the woman who made up mad adventures with me as the hero; who taught me about the beauty of numbers, and made every day add up to magic. Who told me I must keep my secret, hold it close and dear like life itself.

Who held me, night after night, after my mother died.

She starts to tremble, and I sit up and pull her next to me, slip an arm over her shoulders. She is so small, so slight now. It is hard to know where the strength came from to grip my arms so tight that the imprint of her hands is still felt on my skin. Interesting hand-shaped bruises are probably on the way: that'll give school idiots something else to laugh about.

'Did you take your meds last night?' I ask her, but she is gone again. To wherever she usually goes. She starts to hum, smiling, rocking back and forth to music only she can hear.

'Come on, Nanna,' I say, and stand, pull her to her feet, and lead her back to her room. I help her into bed, pull the covers up. Soon her eyes close; her breathing evens. I walk back across the room, then hesitate by the door controls.

The doctor says we should keep it locked at night. That we should tell him if she has any more 'episodes'. That he can increase her meds.

The ones that make her hum and drift in her own world more and more, until she almost never comes out.

Stuff the doctor.

4

Today I feel conspicuous in jeans and a long-sleeved top that covers the bruises on my arms. The other girls are all in black skirts with outrageous animal-print tights and tops, and the boys are hunters, complete with fake bows and arrows. Some not-very-subtle Friday theme dreamed up this morning in Realtime? Though something is up. There is none of yesterday's applause, and hostile glances are cast my way. I start to walk past them, and head for the stairs.

'Heh, Lunatic. Wait,' one of them says. I keep walking.

'Luna?' Another voice, one I know. Melrose. We were friends when we were younger, but not any more. Now she generally treats me like I'm contagious, like the rest of them do. As if crazy could be catchy. 'Luna, please,' she says.

For some reason, some soft note in her voice, I stop. Mel is smiling. The others aren't.

'What do you want?'

'Haven't you checked the school feed?'

I shrug. Not stating the obvious: Refusers don't plug in before breakfast like the rest of them. 'Why?'

'The Test appointments are up today.'

'So?' I glare back at her, sure what is coming but even though I shouldn't be, hurt that Mel would stoop to that, to mocking my failure in front of them all. Did Jezzie, the one smirking at her shoulder, put her up to it?

'You've got one.'

'What?' Now my face is as shocked as the rest of them. 'There must be some mistake.'

'That's for sure.' Jezzie this time. 'There's no way a nutcase like you could possibly—'

'That's enough, Jezzamine,' says a voice beyond the crowd. It parts to admit Mr Sampson, School Test Coordinator. 'You have expressed an unsubstantiated opinion. You'd do well to remember to leave bias behind in the rationality quotient phase of the Test. *If* you make it that far. Now, everyone, get to class. Except you, Luna. Come with me.'

He walks towards Goodwin's office, and I follow. What is going on? My head is reeling. Has Goodwin found something even *worse* than the interesting classes she threatened me with? Has she somehow got me a Test appointment so I can fail in a public and spectacular way, be branded irrational and locked in a loony bin forever? *No way.* I can't believe even Goodwin has that kind of power. This must be some kind of sick joke.

I follow him to her office. He opens the door. Goodwin is there; a few other teachers. He points at a chair opposite the row of them, and as I sit in it the bell goes.

Goodwin is less clown-like than expected. Her hair is combed forward to hide the snakes. She scowls and her face moves strangely, and appears to almost crack: ah. Heavy concealing make-up.

'Luna.' She spits out my name. 'Explain yourself!' She's

30

not in calm control like yesterday, and I'm glad the others are here.

'Explain what?'

'This Test appointment.'

Baffled, I look back at her. 'Is it true? I thought they were joking.'

'Of course: you won't have seen the school feed this morning,' Sampson says. He taps on a handheld screen, turns it to show me:

PareCo Test appointment: Luna Iverson. Monday 9 a.m. at NUN test centre 11, London.

I stare until the words start to throb on the screen. Real words, not something they made up. Goosebumps walk up my back.

'This is for real?'

'It is,' he says.

'I don't understand. Only about the top third get appointments, and I'm nowhere near.'

'There have been a few *discussions* about it,' Goodwin says, and the Medusa snakes I painted on her forehead are still in operation, despite being covered up: her look could turn the unwary to stone. 'But you tell me now if you've had anything to do with this, or so help me—'

'How could I?'

'Your Hacker friend, maybe?'

'What: hack into PareCo? Are you kidding?' I look back

at Sampson. 'I don't understand how this happened.'

'Neither do we. Checks have been made. You really do have an appointment.'

'But my grades aren't—'

'Grades aren't the only factor. There are algorithms and analysis of a host of factors, environmental and genetic potentialities, and—' He stops abruptly when he realises what he said and who he said it to, and I flush. Sympathy crosses his face.

Goodwin snorts. 'On every measure, you're a failure, Luna. So are you denying any involvement in tampering with PareCo protocols?'

'What? I'm denying any involvement in anything.'

'Get out. But you haven't heard the last of this.'

I head for the door; Sampson follows me out. 'Come with me a moment, Luna.' In another office, he gestures at a chair. The final bell goes.

His eyes unfocus, then come back again. 'Don't worry, I've messaged your teacher. You won't get a late.' He grins, and I'm unsettled.

'So, Luna, you've got a chance. A Test appointment.'

'I can't take this in; I don't understand. How'd I get an appointment?'

'Maybe there's been a glitch somewhere.' He grins again.

'A glitch? In PareCo's latest and greatest protocols? No way.' I can feel my mouth hanging open.

He winks. 'Incredible it may be, but anything is possible. But listen to me, Luna.' All trace of humour leaves his face.

'No matter how or why this has happened, don't waste this opportunity.'

He doesn't have to say any more: I *know*. All the top university and training places are taken by those who do well on the Test. Part of me grasps at it: could there be a chance? *One* chance, and one only. One was Nanna's favourite number: *one is action, new hope, and new beginnings*. But most of me quashes the hope down.

'Mrs Goodwin will never let me—'

'It's not in her control. Ignore her sputtering and raging: she can't do anything about it. Who gets an appointment is decided by PareCo, and PareCo alone. When she found out about your appointment she even tried to have you expelled for yesterday's mischief, and it was refused. One more thing.' He hesitates. 'I know you aren't an RE. Or an ME.'

I raise an eyebrow. In my class of REs, MEs and the excluded, there is only one Unclassified: Lunatic Luna.

'So?'

'Doing the test with pen on paper is harder. With the virtual test you can manipulate patterns, give instant answers, get through the questions quicker. And scores have time bonuses or penalties. Think about it, Luna.'

It's harder with him than Goodwin. With her, even if there wasn't good reason to keep silent, sheer contrariness is enough to make me refuse to give a reason. To hang it on my rights and let her seethe about all the wasted resources. But with him I wish there was something I could tell him, some way to make him understand. But then we'd be well past *potential* genetic issues, and into something else entirely. Some secrets are better kept.

I say nothing, and head for class.

That night, Sally is out. So her good friend *Bea* didn't tell Sally about my appointment? If Sally knew, there's no way she wouldn't have been here when I got home. I guess Bea only passes on the bad news.

I make dinner for Nanna and Jason, but don't dare eat myself. Nanna goes to bed and Jason plugs in to play Quidditch. And now it is time to *try*, for the first time in *so* long.

There is still a PIP in my room. I haven't got an Implant, so have to plug in the old-fashioned way. When I sink into it, the moulded sofa adjusts to my body – I was smaller the last time I used it. I close my eyes and try to relax as the warm fuzz of the neural net closes around me, to let the sensory and neural connections happen, not fight it. My room is as dark as I can make it: I even unplugged the vid screen so there is no little light on the bottom of it, and stuffed a towel under the door to block any stray light from the hall.

Click.

The interface shimmers, my vision goes *wrong*. The dark room is still here, but I can almost ignore it.

Dizzy, hesitant, I step into the Realtime hallway. Being here is all kinds of *wrong*. I can make my feet take me forward, but it all feels detached and jerky, like I'm half here – half moving by remote control. There is nothing *less* real to me than this place. Was it some sort of sick humour that made PareCo name their social portal to the virtual worlds *Realtime*?

I walk past doors for every group I belong to, unread message numbers flashing above them. Most of them are things like the school feed and the library, where as a student I'm an automatic member, whether I ever go there or not. There are several unanswered group invitations also, from fan clubs of my mother; I flick *no* as I go past and the doors disappear. How these nutcases find me with all the privacy locks on I have no idea. And there are a few friend groups from years ago, like Melrose's: her door is still there, no locks, and I can hear laughing voices through it. I'm surprised she hasn't blocked me by now, but I suppose there's no point when I'm never here.

And the one door I'm heading for.

I breathe, in and out, deep and calm as I can, and walk to the door slowly, trying to keep nausea at bay. For years I'd thought it was like this for everyone. When I found out it wasn't, that for everyone else the physical world vanishes and this is as real as anything in it, I almost let it slip. But Nanna told me it it had to be a secret. I didn't understand *why* at that age – what was I, six or seven? I did years later. *Different* isn't good sometimes.

There it is: Dad's door. I knock, open the door and walk in. No one is here. I almost cry with relief to see that the sofa is still there, though the colour has changed from red to blue. I sink down on it and close my eyes. This is the best place in here: this sofa is enough like the one my body is on for the two – virtual and real – to not jar so much.

'Dad?' I call out, tentative. 'It's me. It's Luna.'

Moments pass, and I'm not sure how long I can stay. The intense dizziness and disconnection seem even worse than the last time I was here: inside I'm spinning, falling, looking over a precipice and about to throw myself over the edge. Like in my dream.

'Luna?'

I risk opening my eyes: it's Dad. I mean, he looks like Doctor Who no. 32 just now, but I know who he is. As if he knows I won't be here long, he rushes over and gives me a big hug and kiss on the cheek.

'Dad!' I protest.

'Sorry. It's just so good to see you.'

'There's an easy answer to that. Unplug and join the real world now and then – I'm usually there.'

'Is something wrong?'

He knows how much I hate being here, though not the real reason. He always assumed it was because of how Astra – my mother – died. Nanna said not to tell him, and I never set him straight. Maybe that was a mistake? But it seems far too late to tell him the truth now.

'No. Something is right for a change.'

'What is it?'

'I've got a Test appointment. Next week.'

His eyes widen. 'Really? No way!'

'Yes *way*.'

'I'm proud of you.'

I blink my eyes hard. 'Don't be. I bet me even getting an appointment was a mistake. I'll probably flunk the lot of them.'

'I doubt it. You're as brainy and beautiful as your mother.'

I shake my head. 'I wish. Maybe you could come for dinner on Sunday?'

His eyes unfocus, then come back again. 'I've got some appointments, but make it lunch, and I'll see what I can do. That is one of the perks of being a Time Lord.' He winks.

'Did you hear Jason is playing Quidditch?'

'Oh, is he? I might see if I can show up as Dumbledore a bit later.'

I laugh, but then the world lurches one time too many and my stomach is coming up. 'Gotta go, Dad; see you then?' I'm unplugging already and he shimmers, waves. Then is gone.

I'm breathing in and out, in and out. Hyperventilating. And trying to calm it down. I put the lights back on to see my real room. Touch things that *exist* – my books, the vid screen. The framed picture of Astra that I keep putting in a drawer and taking out again. And gradually my breathing goes back to normal, but the world still spins and spins until I give up trying to stop it, and vomit in a bin.

Five minutes of Realtime, and it is nearly two hours before I stop being sick. That's a pretty good reason to be a Refuser, isn't it?

5

The doorbell rings again. Where is Sally? I tear down the stairs, run across the front room and whip the door open.

Melrose?

'Hi,' she says and smiles. I stare back at her, mouth hanging open. She raises an eyebrow and I snap my mouth shut.

'Aren't you going to invite me in?' she says.

'Uh, OK. Sure. Come in.' I stand back from the door, and she walks through it. When I don't, she pushes it shut behind her.

'Didn't Sally tell you I was coming?'

'No. Why would Sally…?'

She half frowns. 'I messaged her, as there didn't seem to be much point in messaging *you*. You haven't answered any of my messages in about five years.'

'Mel?' Nanna says softly, looking up from her chair. 'Melrose,' she says, her voice stronger this time.

Melrose walks over to her, kneels down and puts a hand on hers. 'Hello. Good to see you, Mrs Iverson.' Nanna smiles, then her vision fogs away; she's gone again.

'She remembers you,' I say, surprised. Nanna's memory comes and goes, and significant people she should recognise, like Sally, or her doctor, she often doesn't.

'I did kind of half live here for years,' Melrose says. And she did, with dinners and sleepovers several times a week, and when she wasn't here it was usually because I was at her house.

But that was then, and this is now. 'Why are you here?'

'The Test? You may have heard of it?'

'Once or twice.'

'But do you know what is happening next week? Where you have to go, what to take with you?'

I stare at her blankly.

'I didn't think so. Sampson said that—'

'Ah, I see. He's put you up to this, has he?'

'Don't be such a dys. I went to see *him*. And I'm here because I want to be.'

'Forgive me for being sceptical. If that is true, where've you been for the last five years?'

And Melrose pulls back, as if she'd been slapped. 'I can't believe you just said that. I called you again and again; *you* blanked *me*.' She shakes her head, and starts for the door.

'But you *ignored* me when we started high school, completely brushed me off. You had that whole group of brain-dead fashion clones as your new friends. How was I supposed to take that?'

She turns, faces me. 'Not everyone can get by with just themselves, Luna. You were impossible. You deliberately alienated everyone – you were so prickly. Still are. Look, it's fine you wanted to Refuse and do your own thing, not go along with the crowd. Even though you wouldn't talk to me about it. But *you* went out of your way to avoid *me*. Not the other way around.'

She stares back at me and somewhere inside I start to get an uncomfortable feeling. Was it really like that? I'd felt like a camel with two heads that first year at high school, segregated into the freak show others pointed at in the hallways. But was that because of me, not them? And then I remember something else. I *had* avoided talking to Melrose about all of this. Because I couldn't tell her the reasons. Maybe I'd avoided her altogether without realising that was what I was doing.

'I... I...'

She half smiles. 'You haven't changed, Luna. Your face looks like it is going to crack because you can't say *I'm sorry*, can you?'

'I'm sorry.' I manage to get the words out. 'I didn't see things that way at the time, but I'm sorry.'

'I'm sorry, too. I knew things weren't right with you, and I should have tried harder. I gave up.' She holds out a hand. 'Friends again?'

I swallow. There is part of me that doesn't believe this. That wonders if she is just here because now that I have a Test appointment I've crossed the line from socially unacceptable to OK to acknowledge in public.

Then Nanna pushes me from behind. I ignore Melrose's hand and give her a hug.

'Aw, sweet. Have you two made up at last?' Sally stands in the doorway, and we spring apart.

'You didn't tell me she was coming,' I say, blinking furiously.

Sally raises an eyebrow. 'Thought things might work out better this way. Are you staying for lunch?' she asks Melrose.

'Yes, if that's OK. We've got a lot to talk about. Come on.' She pulls me by the hand to the stairs.

'Did you tell her?' I whisper on the way to my room.

'What?'

'Did you tell Sally about my appointment?'

'No.' She frowns. 'You're not telling me she doesn't know about it, are you?'

'It kind of hasn't come up,' I admit, as I open the door to my room. Shut it firmly behind us.

'Luna, honestly. You think she might notice when you're away next week?'

'I'll tell her. Eventually.'

'When?'

'Dad said he'd come for lunch tomorrow. I wanted to leave it until then. She'll be all over me if she knows. This way gives me some peace and quiet until then.'

'Really? You're not just keeping it from her because you know it would make her happy? She's not that bad.'

'You don't have to live with her.' Sally had always liked Melrose, so she didn't get the sharp side – Melrose's dad is in the House of Lords and a NUN representative, and that put her in a more-than-acceptable-to-Sally social range. 'Actually I'm surprised she even let you come over: I'm supposed to be grounded.'

'I'm not surprised. That you're grounded, I mean.' Melrose looks disapproving. She was always one for following the rules, doing what everybody else did, but she still used to see the funny side. On the quiet.

'And? Your thoughts on my…misplaced artistic abilities?'

She muffles a laugh. 'That, was BB, babe. *Beyond brilliant*. Now. Before we get distracted, what are you going to wear tomorrow night?'

'Tomorrow? But my appointment isn't until Monday.'

'We have to go the day before, and meet the other candidates at a big formal dinner – there are a number of schools at this one centre. Ours and three others, so about 200 of us all in.'

'Formal?' Horror must be etched on my face; Melrose smirks.

'Yes.' She hesitates. 'I can tell you what we're all wearing. If you want me to.'

My stomach is churning already. 'A big formal dinner with candidates from four schools?'

'It'll be fine.'

'Has Jezzamine got an appointment?'

'Of course.'

'Then this could be some other version of fine: *not fine*.'

She shrugs. 'Just ignore her.'

'And that's just the start of it. What about the Test? I think I'm going to be sick.'

'You'll do fine, Luna. You were always smarter than me. Your grades were miles better when you bothered to try. Anyhow, you can't study for an IQ test. And nobody knows what the RQ test is.'

I cross my arms over a churning stomach that is doing a good impression of a Realtime reaction even though I'm resolutely in the here and now. Am I smart? OK, I am quicker to work things out than some people, but that is only half of it. No one has ever accused me of being too rational. What the consequences would be of being branded clever-stupid, like Goodwin said, I don't want to think about.

I shake my head. Nanna might have been having an episode in the middle of the other night with her warnings, but they echoed what she told me when she was totally with it years ago. *Don't let them notice you.*

I can't do well at this even if I'm able to, can I? *Don't let them notice you're different.*

There is only one answer: I have to fail the first test.

By the time Sally calls us to a late lunch we've managed to catch up on the last five years, and the very surprising fact that Melrose is v-dating Hex. *Hex?* A Hacker? Not sure what her dad'll make of that, even if it's just virtual. And we've worked out that I have nothing that fits our school's agreed long midnight blue off-the-shoulder dress for the formal, and desperately need to go shopping. Melrose has persuaded me that there is only one way to make that happen.

'Sally? There's something I have to tell you.'

'What is it this time?' Her face is a picture of alarm.

'I...ah...that is to say...' Some devil inside makes me draw it out.

'You tell me right now.' Sally is starting to freak out; Jason stops eating to hear what it is. Even Nanna stops rocking in her chair.

Melrose laughs. 'Spit it out already, or I'll do it for you.'

'I've got a Test appointment. Next week.'

Whatever Sally was expecting to hear, this wasn't it. 'A Test…?' She looks to Melrose for confirmation.

'It's true,' she says.

'Why didn't you tell me?' Sally demands.

'I just did. Tell you.'

'You idiot girl. You clever thing!' Sally says, gets out of her chair, and then her arms are around me for a too-tight hug. I roll my eyes over her shoulder at Melrose, who coughs to hide a laugh.

'Mum?' Jason says and a note in his voice makes Sally release me and us both turn instantly. Nanna's arms are wrapped around her head. A high-pitched keening moan starts inside her.

I put an arm around her. 'Nanna? Everything's fine, OK?'

But my words and touch don't soothe her like they usually do; she suddenly lashes out with both hands, swiping dishes off the table that crash onto the floor. She starts screaming.

'Take Jason,' I say to Melrose. She's frozen. '*Do it!*' And she pulls Jason into the other room. I wrap my arms around Nanna and try to rock her back and forth, but she struggles. Sally is on the phone to the doctor before I can say *wait, see if she settles*, but she's not settling: she's screaming louder and louder as if she is being tortured by my touch, and tears are starting in the back of my eyes and spilling out.

The doctor must have been lurking in the bushes, he is there so fast. He makes me hold Nanna tight while he gives her an injection. She struggles, and I feel like a traitor.

She gradually slackens; her eyes start to close, then flutter open. She stares into mine. 'Eleven,' she says, and then she's gone. Unconscious.

Unease walks up and down my back with cold feet. *Eleven is a warning: danger, or treachery.*

Sally and the doctor talk in low voices by the door; some of their words penetrate. *Psychotic episodes. Delusional. Safety...*

Sally and I help Nanna to bed.

'She's getting worse,' Sally says.

'I know.'

She doesn't say anything else, but it is all there on her face. Nanna should be in an institution where they can look after her: that's what the doctor said at her last review. Calling him today will raise that all over again.

She touches my shoulder. 'Don't forget your friend.'

Melrose: she's been with Jason all this time. They're both silent and pretending to watch a vid when I get myself together enough to go back downstairs. I sit next to Jason, and he slips a cold hand in mine.

'Thanks,' I say to Melrose. 'I'll take over now. I think the shopping trip is off.'

'No worries. I'll lend you something.'

'Sure. Whatever.' She gets up to go. 'Don't tell anyone about Nanna. Promise?'

She looks shocked. 'You don't need to ask. Of course I won't. Do you want a lift tomorrow?'

'Are you sure that's OK?'

'Of course. We'll come at four.'

'Thanks. See you then.'

Later, I watch Nanna as she sleeps. Is she really psychotic and delusional? *Away with the fairies* – that was the expression I liked. When I was little she used to whisper that she believed in fairies, that they lived in sunlight and shadows. That they told her the secret numbers of the sun, the moon and the stars: that mine was the most magical of them all. But numerology is totally dys, isn't it?

Jason doesn't really remember her as she was. He's just afraid of her. This time, I lock her door when I leave.

6

'Come *on*. Before she changes her mind,' I say, and hold out Jason's bicycle helmet. Sally's get out of jail free card could be pulled if she thinks about it too much; she's only let me go despite being grounded because she's still happy about my appointment, and that Dad is coming for lunch.

Jason yawns. 'Can't we go later? It's practically the middle of the night.'

'The sun streaming through the door says otherwise, lazybones. And, no, we can't go later. I'm going away for the whole week, leaving this afternoon. Remember?'

He relents, finally takes his bike helmet, puts it on and starts to follow me out the door. There used to be a time when Jason would plead with me to go on safari every weekend: our bicycles were our 4x4 jeeps, Richmond Park our game reserve, and squirrels and deer our lions and elephants. But now that they've lowered the age of consent for Implants from twelve to ten he's been plugged in every chance he gets since his birthday. Park adventures have been left behind.

Just as I'm about to pull the door shut behind us, Sally appears in the hall. 'Stick to the Els,' is all she says.

We have a way to go before we reach the closest El. The streets are quiet. There are no Sunday morning ball games in front gardens, even though the sun is shining

47

and no April showers are in sight.

We pass a local primary school, and I'm surprised to see a chain across the fence, a closed sign. I slow down to let Jason catch up.

I gesture behind us. 'Didn't some of your friends go to that school? When did it close?' I ask him.

He shrugs. 'I dunno, a few months ago.'

'Do you know why?'

'They said it was surplus. All the students from there are going to my school now.'

A surplus school? I frown. 'They all fit into your school?'

He nods. 'Classes fuller now, can get away with more.' He grins.

'Excellent. Come on.'

We reach our branch of the Richmond El. *Safe Cycle Elevation* is emblazoned on gates that swing open when our registered bicycles are detected. Our wheels link securely to the moving track, and I sigh. I can get why Sally wants us to take the Els: it's safer. No cars or collisions or falling off possible. I can also get why Jason likes it. Less effort, good views as it soars over the streets below. At maximum speed the whole thing is a bit like a rollercoaster. But somehow it still feels like cheating to me.

'Wow,' Jason says.

'What?'

'I've switched on *London Now and Then*. It's cool. You can see St Paul's without the dome. And how it was before, too: not so white as it is now.'

I stare into the distance at St Paul's Cathedral, the NUN towers beyond it. The round white dome has always been as it is now in my lifetime, a landmark you can see from the El in recent years, and also from King Henry's Mound in Richmond Park. I know from history class that it was destroyed in the third world war, then rebuilt, that this isn't the original dome. But it's the only one I've known.

Jason twists on his bicycle to look behind us, his eyes moving around at things only they can see with his Implant.

'What are you looking at now?'

He shrugs, makes a small gesture and his eyes refocus to here and now. 'You miss so much stuff, Luna,' he says, not answering the question. 'Why don't you get an Implant?'

I look at Jason in surprise. 'You know. We've talked about this before.'

'That you'd rather see what is real all the time. But that's stupid. And boring!'

'Gee, thanks.'

'And you can still see what is real, and what isn't. With Implant stuff it's just like an overlay on things, you can switch it on or off. It's not like being plugged in.'

The El drops to street level again, and then abruptly ends at a gate, one that wasn't there the last time we came this way. We wait, but the gate doesn't open.

Jason unfocuses, checks out the delay. 'You need a pass code now from someone in the Queens Road community.'

Melrose lives there. She never mentioned they've extended

the gates to cut off the El, but with five years to catch up on yesterday, it obviously didn't rate with all the gossip and boys. I could ask Jason to message her; I *should* get him to do that. But needing my little brother to communicate for me rankles inside.

'Let's exit,' I say, instead.

Jason grins. He likes doing things Sally says not to as much as I do; at least that is still the same.

Once off the El we have to go around the whole gated community. Jason takes off in front, and when he turns right at a crossroads, I call out for him to come back.

'The park is the other way, isn't it?' I say when he reaches me.

He gives me a look, shakes his head.

'I don't know this way. Check your Implant map.'

He sighs, and unfocuses to switch it on, then looks back at me. 'It *says* to go right.'

'Are you sure?'

He crosses his arms. 'There is an arrow on the ground in front of my bike that says where to go. If you had your own Implant, you could check it. You'll just have to take my word for it.'

I roll my eyes. 'OK, fine. You're in charge.'

Jason heads off in front again. The road loops back around, so we are indeed going in the right direction for the park. As we go there are more and more houses that are closed up, dark. Shutters drawn or boards across windows, and for no reason I can identify, I start to feel uneasy.

I catch up to Jason and cycle next to him. 'Maybe we should go back,' I say.

'Why?'

'It's kind of creepy around here.'

He gives me a look again. 'We're nearly there now. Come on.'

He picks up speed, and I follow. There are more empty buildings, others run-down. Rubbish on the street. We pass a house with a garden so strewn with junk that it looks like a tip. A movement flicks near the ground: a cat? I look again, and beady rodent eyes stare back. There are figures lying on sofas in the midst of it all, unmoving beyond twitching. Implant Addicts? Here, in Richmond?

Even as my legs pump the pedals faster to leave this place, my eyes are unable to look away. There are five of them. Two men, three women, and then with shock I see that one of them is actually a girl. She looks younger than me. But Implant access is restricted until age eighteen: it shouldn't be possible.

At last we reach the park gates. There is a moment of disquiet inside when they don't swing open, but then, seconds later, they do.

Once through the gates the park is as always, and gradually I relax. Here, there are no Els: the park has been maintained to be the same for centuries. There are crisscrossing cycling and walking trails, a road down the centre. All is peace and order. A few walkers push baby strollers; a bicycle goes past with a toddler in a seat behind the rider. We spot deer through the trees grazing on grass. Fawns will be born soon.

We head for the adventure playground but it is almost empty, and we soon move on. When we go past the under-five playground it is busy with toddlers, parents and nannies. Nowhere do we see any kids near Jason's age; no wonder he doesn't want to come here any more. He doesn't want to hang out with babies.

It didn't used to be like this here, even just a year ago. I frown to myself. Why the change? *The Implant age*. That's it, isn't it? I'd tried to argue with Dad and Sally about Jason having Implant surgery at ten, just months ago. Sally threatened unspeakable things if I tried to infect him in any way with my Refusing. But she didn't have to. I want him to be happy, to fit in with the other kids his age. To not be a freak like his sister. But at *ten*? How could he make such an important decision at that age?

When we leave the park we divert without discussion to the nearby cemetery. Jason stops, leans his bike against the fence. 'Now for a survey of the latest late,' he says. And I nod, pleased this is one ritual he wants to keep.

And we walk along, searching out the new graves, noting the names. We always did this, to imagine the recently dead in our zombie adventures. Jason has always liked his stories scary, the scarier the better. Back then he was imagining being able to play *Zombie Wars* version 12. Now he's playing it, for real – virtually, that is – version 14.

'Alexander J. Munch: zombie or vampire?' I say.

'*Definitely* a vampire name,' he answers. 'But kind of old

for killer status.' The carved dates have Munch at over a hundred years old. 'Though that could be creepy. Next?'

'Here's one. How about Rory Middleton-Smith?'

'Zombie,' another voice says, so quietly I wasn't sure I heard or imagined it, but Jason has turned sharply at the sound. I reach for his arm to pull him back, but he's sprung out of reach and is around the other side of the gravestone.

I dash after him. A man lies in the grass on top of a grave, his face blank. Body wasted. His glassy eyes are moving back and forth so fast they must be unaware of their surroundings, but then he swivels his head to Jason.

And his eyes still, and focus.

'Zombie,' he says again, more clearly. Then his head slumps back, his eyes start moving again.

I grab Jason's shoulder, pull him back.

'What's the problem?' Jason says. 'He's harmless. He can't even move. See?' And he twists away from me and pushes at the man's leg with his foot. He doesn't register, just twitches, his eyes darting and dancing at things only he can see.

'Jason!'

Jason shrugs, steps back again. 'Don't freak out, he's not dangerous. He's always here.'

By the looks of him, not for much longer. I'm shocked. I've seen Implant Addicts before, like on public service announcements of how to spot early signs of overuse in the mentally deficient, or from a train window, sprawled on railway benches, but always distant, removed. The ones we cycled past in front of that house today were the closest I'd been before now. And although his clothes are almost rags, I can still see the Hacker design. The swirls of tattoos around his left eye – his are white, to contrast against dark-as-midnight skin – mark him out. He was a *Hacker*? And not just any Hacker: going by the extensive interlocking swirls of his tattoos, he was on the absolute top of the Game. Why on earth be an addict when you can design your own worlds safe and sound in a PIP?

Then Jason's words from before penetrate. 'He's always here? Have you been coming here on your own?'

Jason shakes his head. 'No. Not on my own; with friends from school.'

So they're not *always* plugged in, and while that is good to know, I'm sure this would be news to Sally. If she knew it'd be banned straight away.

'It's perfectly safe,' Jason protests, reading my face.

'Come on. Back to our bikes. We're going home.'

This time we head straight for the El gate at Queens Road, and Jason uses his Implant to message Melrose to let us in. The gates swing open.

'She's out shopping. Says see you later,' Jason relays.

As we ride the El back over all the beautiful, sprawling mansions and gardens of Melrose's neighbourhood, I wonder: what if we didn't know someone here, and couldn't get the gates to open? Unless we repeat the way we went this morning, something I don't really want to do – at least, not with Jason – the whole park is barred to us. My eyes search out the gates and barriers scattered about these exclusive neighbourhoods, the encroaching dying streets beyond.

Though close in distance, our own street is a million miles away from both Melrose's mansion and the dark areas.

But the latter are closer.

7

'Good ride?' Dad asks.

Jason holds up a hand and Dad gives him a high five.

'You should have unplugged earlier and come with us,' I say. 'Get some real sunshine.' Dad is pale, his skin almost waxy: it hasn't seen the sun in months.

'Why not programme the PIP life support to give some artificial sunlight every day?' Sally suggests.

'Clever woman, that's why I married you.' Dad kisses Sally and I resist the urge to mime retching, but then Jason does it for me. I wink at him.

'Maybe the real thing would be healthier. You used to take me to the park.' I mentally add, *you and Astra*, but don't say it out loud. Nothing would send Sally into a grump faster than being reminded of the more gorgeous, smarter and all-round better woman she can only fail to replace. And I don't want to do or say anything to make Dad avoid unplugging for weeks again. Isn't that the real reason why he married her? Once Nanna started to lose it, he needed someone to look after things, so he could hide away from troubling reality with a clear conscience.

'Parks and sunshine are kid stuff,' Sally says. 'Jason is outgrowing them.' Unsaid, but there, on her face: Jason is outgrowing *you*.

I narrow my eyes. 'There were no kids in the park

today at all. Just babies, little ones. None near Jason's age, or mine. Once they get Implants they don't want to play any more.'

Sally frowns and I know I'm verging into her *not-in-front-of-Jason* areas, but I want to hear what Dad thinks about it.

'They're still playing – just not where you can see them,' Dad says.

'It's not the same,' I say.

'Of course it isn't,' Sally answers. 'It's safer. No broken arms or skinned knees. And no passing germs around to each other. Especially at *your* age.'

I roll my eyes. 'It'd be hard to break an arm cycling on an El. And there are plenty of opportunities to catch germs in school, y'know. If one is interested in *germs*.' But she is right about one thing. It didn't take Melrose's updates yesterday, I already knew: the whole boy-girl scene at my school is virtual. Everyone looks better on a v-date than they do in real life; everyone has a designer wardrobe; everyone is a good kisser. If you don't fancy meeting up with someone who exists, a whole range of fantasy boyfriends is available once you pass the under-sixteen blocks, and you can't catch anything or get pregnant. What's not to like?

Unless you happen to be a Refuser. Unless you would like something *real*.

'Though germ opportunities at school may be gone by the time Jason gets to secondary,' Dad says.

'Who'd want germs anyway?' Jason says, it all going over his head.

'Why, what do you mean?' I ask Dad.

'You really miss out on the news by not signing up for feeds,' he says. 'Secondaries are being phased out.'

'Really?' Jason says. 'No more school in another year? Awesome!' He looks very happy, and Dad laughs.

'No, you'll still have to go to school. But as your education post-ten is almost all virtual now anyhow, you don't need to *physically* go there. You can do it virtually at home, right?'

'What about sport? What about actually interacting with kids their own age, at lunch if no other time? What about Refusers?' I say, the questions coming out in a rush.

Dad looks uncomfortable. 'Sport and social stuff are nearly all virtual now anyhow, and the cost savings will be huge. As for the other, not sure if they've worked it all out yet.'

'Hmmph.' Nanna's dismissive noise sounds very like what I was just thinking. What about NUN's International Bill of Rights of the Child? I glance at her across the table, but her eyes have slipped closed.

After lunch I'm up in my room, packing. Sally has passed a message on from Melrose: she is lending me a dress for the formal tonight, and has sent along a detailed list of what everyone is wearing the rest of the week.

Monday: smart black trousers, white shirt. And round glasses? *Really?* Given that all refractive errors requiring glasses have been corrected years ago, this, I'm guessing, is supposed to be the intelligent look. That's the day of the IQ test. And no need to worry about packing beyond that, is there? I'll fail it, and get an early ticket home.

But a half-empty suitcase might raise suspicions. I throw in a few tops and jumpers, jeans and skirts, in a haphazard, random fashion, ignoring the list past the first day.

There is a light tap on the door just as I'm zipping up my case. The door opens; it's Dad. He comes in, shuts it behind him and sits next to me.

'Heh,' he says. 'All ready to go? It's almost four.'

'Think so.'

'Don't look so worried. You'll do well.'

'No. I won't.' I sigh, look at my shoes. I won't do well because I won't allow myself to do well. But I can't tell him that, can I?

'None of that negative stuff, Loony-Tunes,' he says, a name he hasn't called me in years. 'Your mother would be so proud of you.'

Some lump twists in my throat, and I blink. He picks up her photo from my dressing table. Looks at me, then at her. 'You look more and more like her every day.'

'I do not! She's gorgeous.' I stare at the photo of Astra in his hands: the long thick dark hair pulled back in a simple ponytail, the mischief in her pale grey eyes. The Hacker's intricate black swirls around her left eye, more than I've seen on anyone else, stand out stark on pale skin. Was she naturally pale, or was that just from spending too much time plugged in? Like Dad.

'You've got her eyes, her hair. And her smile. Not that you use it enough. You know, Luna, you don't have to keep doing this for her. Avoiding plugging in. She wouldn't want you to limit your chances.'

I stare back at him, and I'm *this close* to telling him that the way she died isn't the reason I Refuse.

But then there are footsteps on the stairs, and Dad hurriedly puts the photo down. Sally appears at the door. 'Car is here,' she says, smiling. 'Wait till you see it!'

'Knock 'em dead,' Dad says. 'Now I'm off to explore strange new worlds and all that.'

'Trekkie Sunday?'

'That's it!' He leans in to give me a hug, and says low in my ear: 'And, Luna? No matter how it goes, she'd still be proud of you.'

I bite back the words, but can't stop them inside: *if she was so concerned about me and my future, then maybe she should have stuck around.*

Out front is not just a car but an official government car: a long black electric limo with the dual flags of the UK Union Jack and the NUN Rainbow. A uniformed driver takes my bag and holds the door for me. I climb in, surprised to find not Melrose, but her dad in the back of it.

'Hi, Mr Asquith,' I say, a bit uncertain. I haven't seen him in *years*, unless you count on the news when he got elected to NUN's executive council. Even when I was in and out of their house he was rarely there except late at night, always off at government meetings. And who knows what he thinks of Refusers.

He smiles. 'Hello, Luna, good to see you again. Hope you don't mind: Melrose has been shopping in the city, so it made sense to collect you first. And I'm on my way in to NUN Towers for a meeting.'

'Of course, it's fine. The meetings aren't all virtual now?'

'The international ones are, by necessity. Moving all national divisions to virtual is under debate. But some of us like to know our private conversatons are still private.' The car pulls away. 'And I'm glad we've got a moment to talk.'

Ah. Is that why he's really in the car? Here it comes. He's not happy with Melrose and me taking up our friendship again. He doesn't want to upset her, so he's warning me off. I'm not surprised.

'Are you excited about the Test?' he asks.

I stare back at him, not sure where he is going with this.

'Or scared, maybe?'

'This isn't about Melrose?'

'She's neither excited nor scared. Daft girl – but I expect she'll do middling to well, and be happy to get into university. It's you I'm worried about.'

'You're worried about *me*?'

'Don't look so amazed.' He laughs.

'Why?'

He shrugs. 'General weirdness,' he says. And I remember the late-night drop-ins he'd have to our sleepovers if we were still awake when he got home. Telling us tales of his day, of trying to juggle UK and NUN interests, and of PareCo's meddling: *general weirdness*. That's what he used to call it. Melrose'd get bored and tell him to stop, to go away, but I was fascinated, and if you asked him a question, about *anything*, he'd always answer it.

'General weirdness…something about PareCo to do with *me*?'

'Do you know why you got an appointment?'

'Teacher said it might be a glitch.' I shrug. 'I shouldn't have.'

'PareCo doesn't have glitches.'

I stare back at him and my stomach lurches. 'If it isn't a glitch, then why?'

'I don't know. They want you there for some reason. But what could it be?'

'You're asking me? I've got no idea.'

'It worries me. Take care, Luna,' he says, and his eyes are on mine, steady and serious.

The car is slowing, stopping. The door opens, and Melrose gets in, bags of shopping in her arms.

'Just a few essentials?' her dad says, and she thumps him on the arm.

She smiles at me as the car pulls up the road. 'And off we go! All ready?'

'Guess so.'

'You got through Queen's Road El OK this morning?' she asks.

'Yes. Thanks. When did they gate the El there? Makes

it hard to access the park.'

Her dad looks embarrassed, shrugs. 'That was kind of the point, I'm afraid. There have been problems.'

'With Implant Addicts? We saw some today when we were cycling to get around the gates.'

He raises an eyebrow. 'Just so.'

Melrose looks shocked as the pound drops. 'You only went one way through the El. Tell me you didn't cycle all those miles round the other way when you got there!'

'OK. I won't tell you.'

'You did, didn't you! And you saw addicts? They're dangerous. Tell her, Dad.'

'Well, I wouldn't recommend getting too close,' he says mildly. 'Not sure about dangerous.'

'More like upsetting,' I say. 'I saw a girl in a group of addicts. She looked younger than me. I thought Implants were limited usage until eighteen?'

'They are,' he says. 'Maybe she looked younger than she was? Addicts are often so malnourished.'

'I suppose it's possible,' I say. 'Why does everyone get Implants if addiction is on the rise? Doesn't it show Implants are dangerous?'

'What makes you say it is on the rise?'

'You're not denying it.'

'Officially, the numbers are declining, though observation seems to suggest otherwise.'

Melrose shakes her head. 'The number of addicts must be declining. It is only the mentally deficient that become addicts, and they're screening them out as MEs now.' This is the official line.

Then I realise what had niggled at me about the addict Jason and I saw in the cemetery. 'Really? So, say, Hackers couldn't be addicts. Could they? They're the smart ones.'

'Of course not,' she says, dismissing the notion with a flick of her hair.

'I saw a Hacker who was an addict.'

'How did you know?' she asks.

'The usual ways. Clothes. Tattoos around his eye.'

'That's crazy,' Mel says.

'General weirdness?' I venture to say, and her dad raises an eyebrow.

A long pause. 'Maybe,' he says, at last, and I'm shocked. What could PareCo have to do with the impossibility of a Hacker being an addict?

Then I can't stop myself from asking one more question. 'What about the school closures? A primary near our house. And I heard secondaries are being phased out.'

'That is still under debate,' he says. 'There are outstanding issues before it can be implemented. There are appeals by religious groups going through to NUN right now. As far as surplus primary closures go, people are having fewer children. So fewer schools are needed.'

The car slows, stops.

'I believe we're here. Do your best, Melrose,' he says, kisses her cheek. He holds a hand out to me, and I take it for a formal handshake. 'Take care, Luna,' he says again, holding my eyes with his a moment, as if he is trying to tell me something, but I don't know what.

The driver opens the door, hands us our bags from the boot. The car waits until we disappear through the front door of NUN test centre 11.

2
TESTS

*An intelligent hell would be better
than a stupid paradise.*

Victor Hugo

8

'Heh, you scrub up OK,' a voice says behind me, and I turn: it's Hex.

I shrug. 'Whatever. I wish I was a Hacker. That'd make dressing easier. Not to mention walking.' I look down at my shoes, and grimace. They match the deep blue of this beautiful dress Melrose lent me perfectly, but teetering across the quad from the girls' residence was both slow and painful. Hex is dressed as usual – black jeans, trainers. Grey T-shirt, black scribbles around the edges that probably mean something but not to me. Hackers stand out because they aren't fashion clones like everyone else: they wear whatever they want. They all have their own variation on a theme and get away with it, boys and girls both.

'Sorry, I'm afraid as a Refuser you don't pass Hacker basic criteria. Plugging in is kind of part of it.' He winks.

I laugh. The room is becoming more crowded, and he is standing close enough that I'm suddenly aware that these shoes make me taller than he is.

'Where's Melrose?' he asks.

'I thought she was with you!' The reason I'd come here on my own. They'd had to get together in person for a change: the whole test centre is Implant blocked, and no PIPs are available apart from for the test.

'She was. She said something about having to straighten

her hair.' He looks pleased with himself, as if he'd had a hand in messing it up.

My eyes hunt around the hall for Melrose. It's a massive space – tables set for dinner, complete with candles, at one end; the rest is a dance floor. Dancing, in public? In these shoes? I sigh. There are stairs that lead up to a second level that overlooks the dance floor; my choice of designated hiding spot for the socially inept. Except for Hackers dotted here and there, everyone else is colour-coded. Our school in blue, one in red, one in purple, one white. Others from my school glance at me, curious that there is someone in their dress code they don't recognise. Then they realise who I am and look away.

Melrose comes through the doors and is surrounded by friends before I can catch her eye. That is when I spot Jezzamine. She starts speaking earnestly to Melrose; both look at me, then back again to each other. Disquiet settles inside.

'Are you all right?' Hex says. His arm curves comfortingly around my back.

I shrug. 'Oh, yeah. I'm feeling right at home.'

'Be like me: don't give a monkey's what the idiots think.'

'Easy for you! Everybody loves a Hacker.'

'What's not to love?'

Melrose walks over. 'Oh, there you are. Do you want to sit with us for dinner?' she says to me, but her voice is strained, and she's looking between Hex and me, an odd look on her face.

I start, and pull away from his hand on my back. 'No, no; you go on,' I say, knowing it is the right answer, but not wanting to say it.

'Then come with me, instead,' Hex says, and pulls me by the arm towards a table at the back. Hacker land.

I turn to look at Melrose, but she's stomping off to the sea of blue dresses and tuxedos.

This is *so* not going well.

'Hex, don't be such a dys,' I snap.

'What?'

'Melrose is jealous.'

His face goes from surprised to pleased. 'Is she? Cool.'

I smack him. 'Go make nice, or she'll be not happy with me.'

'OK, fine,' he says. 'Here, sit.' He heads for two empty seats at the long Hacker table, and pushes me into one of them. A sea of surprised tattooed eyes swivel in my direction as he walks off towards Melrose.

'Uh, hi, everyone,' I say. 'Is it OK if I stay here?'

'Free country. At least, it's supposed to be,' a voice says to my left, on the other side of the remaining empty chair, and I turn. Here's a surprise: no tattoos around his eye. But even though he's not Hacker-pale, he *looks* like a Hacker, in that careless above-the-law-and-don't-give-a-damn kind of way. Too long, dark, almost black hair curls around his ears, and eyes just as dark stare back at mine. There is something *exotic* in the way he is put together: part some interesting mix of parentage, part something all his own. He doesn't need to go

71

virtual to look good. He raises an eyebrow, and I blush when I realise I'm staring.

'Fall out with your friends?' he says, and gestures to the blue tables. 'Should have thought of that before you picked wardrobe.'

'I'll try to remember that next time I'm getting dressed.'

His eyes widen, and sparkle a little. He leans in closer. 'A clone with attitude? Curiouser and curiouser.'

Hex comes back, takes the empty seat between us. 'Jeez, you were right,' he says. 'She's pissed off with me. She thought I was going to sit with *them*.' He shudders.

I roll my eyes. 'Obvious, Einstein, don't you think? You probably shouldn't sit next to me, either.'

'Happy to oblige,' the dark-eyed guy says, and gets up to swap seats with Hex, a knowing grin on his face that says *you just said that because you want to sit next to me, didn't you?* 'I'm Gecko,' he says. 'And you are?'

'Luna,' I say, trying to hide curiosity from my eyes. Who is this guy? This *Gecko*. Weird name, but then Hackers, like Hex, like my mother, Astra, choose their own names as part of what they spin virtually. Astra was the queen of space games; Hex is into magic games featuring curses and spells. What would a Gecko be into?

Waiting staff come in and start putting plates of yummy food in front of everyone, and conversation reverts to *pass the pepper* kind of stuff for a while. I glance at Gecko surreptitiously between mouthfuls. It's not just the lack of tattoos that marks him out; there is something *else*. Others on the table are chatting about meta this and beta that, but keeping an eye on him a lot of the time, too.

'Heh,' he says in a low voice. Leans closer to me. 'Is there something stuck on my nose?' He brushes at it.

'What? No.'

'Or in my teeth, is that what you keep looking at?' He smiles, teeth showing. Like a wolf.

I roll my eyes, sit up straighter, look resolutely straight ahead at the wall over the girl opposite. Whatever he may be to these Hackers, he's a jerk.

When dinner is over, it is announced the dance is about to start. Gecko and most of the Hackers scatter: not into dancing? I wait until Hex leaves to get drinks so he won't try to stop me. I'm getting the hell out of here. I start to walk across the floor to the doors all the way on the other side of the massive hall. I have to go past the sea of blue dresses, and suddenly one of them detaches from the rest and stands in front of me.

'What were you thinking, Lunatic, wearing that? Did you think it could possibly make you one of us?' Jezzamine. Conversations quieten down around us, heads turn.

I don't answer, turn to the side to get round her.

'Honestly. It's hard to imagine what they were doing, letting you in here. Not just a Refuser, but with your *genes*.' She titters.

My hands form fists, and I turn back. 'Excuse me, Jezzamine? What did you say?'

She smiles. With her perfect, swept-up blond hair and blue

eyes, she looks angelic in this shade of blue: bet it was her who mandated it. 'Well, from what I heard you've got insanity on *both* sides of your family. First your mother kills herself, then your dad's mother was screaming the place down and having a psychotic fit, just days ago.' There is dead silence around us. Not just those in blue, but other schools too, are listening, eyes looking to and fro.

My eyes open wider in shock. They hunt for Melrose, and when I finally find her, she looks away. She told Jezzamine about Nanna? She promised she wouldn't. She *promised*. The hurt is taking over the anger, and I push past Jezzamine, and half run towards the door. A heel catches in the hem of my dress and I trip, sprawl across the floor with a painful thud. The whole massive room is quiet now.

I struggle to pull myself up in the narrow skirt, eyes blurring with tears. A steady hand reaches out.

'Let me help you. Come on.'

I grasp it, am pulled to my feet. It's Gecko? The mocking is gone, replaced by kindness, but it's too much. I kick the shoes off and run barefoot all the way to the girls' residence.

I throw the dress on the floor of my room, glad now that Melrose wasn't assigned to the same one. Jezzamine was right about one thing: what was I thinking? How could changing my clothes do anything to make me one of them? I'm still Lunatic Luna underneath.

Even without Implants, gossip as good as this travels at speeds unknown. By the time my roommates return, they all know.

It's in their eyes, in their silences. It's in the one closest to me pulling her bed as far away as she can, and pushing it against the wall.

9

Next morning I empty my suitcase out on the bed. At least I can wear whatever the hell I want to now. It becomes apparent that the black trouser/white shirt thing was beyond just our school. The other three in my silent room are putting on exactly the same outfit, fake round glasses and all, keeping their eyes carefully averted from me the whole time. Fine. I pick the brightest thing I can find out of my randomly packed case: a neon-green top with a pale pink seven I painted on the front, and cut-off jeans. Try to ignore me now.

I head across the quad. I should fail this stupid IQ test and get the hell out of here. Then my life will be the way I always thought it'd be: a few more months dodging Goodwin at boring school. A brain-dead work assignment. A dead-end life.

But I only have *one* chance. Could these two tests really change my life?

Nanna's numbers say yes. *One is a new beginning. Two is a choice that must be made.*

The taunts are still ringing in my ears. Adrenaline rushing through my veins. Somewhere inside are the voices of caution: *Don't let them notice you. Fail. Take care, Luna.* Even Goodwin's bitter diatribe on the fate of the clever-stupid.

But I don't care.

I'll show them. I'll show them all.

The only one who has opted for a pen and paper test, I'm on my own in a small exam hall. Everyone else is in the PIP centre, getting plugged in, waiting for the Test to download at the precise strike of 9 a.m. Here I've got one haughty invigilator with a stopwatch, a paper turned upside down on a desk. The clock outside starts striking nine, but she waits until the last chime before saying, 'You may begin.'

And it's like I've been set on fast-forward, or am in some illegal Implant programme. I race through the IQ questions: sequences; spatial tests; logic problems; pattern recognition. It's almost like there is a part of my brain I don't usually use that has been let out, and it is calmly chewing through the questions while the rest of me is watching, cheering, from the sidelines.

It is only when I hand it in and the invigilator hits the stopwatch, notes the time with a look of surprise on her face, that that part retreats. The rest of me is back in charge, and full of an overwhelming realisation: I'm in serious, serious trouble.

That night I wait until even breathing says the others in my room are asleep. I slip out of my bed, and creep down the hall to the front door.

I'm getting out of here.

I switch off the motion detector light before I step out of our building. There are no other visible detectors, cameras or security devices to avoid, and I'm surprised. Even our school has more security than this.

The buildings of this test centre form a quad, but there are arches between some of the buildings that lead out. Instinct says avoid the main entrance; head for a side exit, away from the halls of residence. There's one by the cafeteria where, apart from that first formal dinner, we have our meals. I head there, keeping away from entrances to other buildings that may have their own motion detector lights. There are some dim energy saver lights on in the quad, but few and far between enough to avoid their thin pools of light.

I think I hear a noise, and huddle along the side of a building, but can see nothing in the darkness. My heart is thudding fast but my skin is cold, clammy. It is colder than I thought it'd be, but there's no way I'm going back for a jacket.

Where am I going? I brush the thought aside. Every instinct says *run*, get away. Don't let them make me do the RQ test. Don't let them label me irrational, and make Goodwin's predictions come true.

I continue on to the exit, and slip into the darkness under the arch between two buildings. Pause, wait for eyes to adjust, step forward, and then—

A hand clamps over my mouth. A scream rises up inside, but I quash it, twist round and ram an elbow into whoever is behind me. The hands let go; there is a muffled cry of pain.

'What'd you do that for?' He straightens up, and I can just make out his face in the dim light.

'Gecko? What are you doing here?'

'Me? What are *you* doing here? Apart from causing grievous bodily harm.'

'I didn't know it was you. You scared me!'

'Sorry, I didn't want you to call out.'

I glare at him. 'If you'll excuse me,' I say, and continue walking the way I was heading. Out and away from this place.

'You won't get far,' he says, and I falter, but keep going. At the end of the passageway, a strange light shimmers in the night air. Weird. I hesitate, then reach a hand out to it, and push against the shimmering. It's vaguely warm, and feels like thick treacle. I can almost push into it, then my hands come out again as if something is pushing back.

Gecko is standing next to me, lit up strangely by the pulsing light. 'How'd you do that?' he asks, curiosity in his dark eyes.

'Do what?'

'Push your hands into the wall.'

I frown. 'There isn't a wall. There's like a funny light, that shifts around when I move my eyes.'

'You can't see a wall?'

'No.'

'Weird. I wonder if…' He pauses, closes his eyes, then pushes at the light like I did, but can't get his fingers into it at all.

He opens his eyes again. Whistles low. 'That's worrying. Clever bastards.'

'What do you mean?'

'What you've described seeing is a force field. So why do I see it as a wall and you don't? I hear you haven't got an Implant. Which means it must be a sensory suggestion placed by my Implant. They're supposed to be blocked here, but it turns out they're only blocked one way. As this wall proves. But I can't overcome it by just knowing there isn't a wall. To me, it is still a wall.'

'That doesn't make sense. I thought Implant images were always obviously not real? Just guides, things like maps and stuff.'

'They are supposed to be. And they always have been to me, before.' He shudders. 'Maybe not, and I just couldn't tell the difference.' He looks about at the buildings as if wondering if they are really there.

I shake my head. 'Either way, so what? I can't get through it, no matter what it is; I can barely push into it at all.'

'The wall goes all the way around. I've tried every possible exit; this was the last one.'

'Why would they put up a force field disguised as a wall? I don't get it.'

'Obvious, I should think. We're prisoners.'

His words sink in. There's no way out? We're trapped? No wonder there is no internal security; they don't need it. No one can get in; no one can get out.

I sigh, deflated. 'Why are you trying to leave?' I ask.

'That is just the question I was going to ask you.' He stares back at me, but I stay silent. He smiles. 'Fair enough: how about we agree to swap stories? But there is a better place we can chat.'

He starts walking out of the passageway, back to the quad. Looks back when I don't follow. 'Well, come on. Unless you want to stay there to be first in the breakfast queue.'

Fine. I follow. Out of curiosity, I tell myself. Nothing more.

He skirts round to the next building: there's another passageway, between it and the grand hall, but this one is open above to the night air.

'There's a balcony above, where we can talk out of sight,' he says. 'I'll give you a leg up. There's a ledge you can use.' He points out the way.

'I don't need help,' I say, and check out the climb. It's easy, really, but it is so dark tonight: no moon, no stars. I climb up, afraid but determined not to let it show. Once up I can see why he's picked this place. The balcony is wide. There are benches against the building, not visible from below. The sliding doors lead into the upper level of the dark hall, empty this time of night. He follows behind and drops easily onto the balcony.

'One thing first,' he says. 'Follow me around.' We walk along the balcony, down the side of the building. At the end of the balcony there is a shimmer in the night air.

'Can you see a top to the wall?' he says. 'I mean, to the force field. What can you see?'

I look up, then shake my head. 'There is a shimmer of light in the air. It goes up forever. What does it look like as a wall?'

'It stops at the top of the building. Shame; I was hoping we could climb over it.'

He takes my hand, pulls me towards a bench. 'Come on. Let's talk.' He takes his jacket off, then pulls his dark hoodie off over his head and tosses it to me. 'Put that on first. If your hand is any indication, you're freezing.'

'What about you?'

'I'll be fine.'

I want to argue but I'm so cold I put it on, still warm from his body, and pull the hood up over my head as well. It's so big it flops over my eyes. I sit down, and he slips close next to me, pulls his jacket over both of us. I try to stop shivering and he pulls my cold hands between his. Part of me is *aware* of his closeness; part of me is scared of what he might ask. What I might say.

'First rule of escaping in the dead of night: dress warm,' he says. 'So, do you want to go first, or shall I?'

'OK, fine. I will,' I say. 'I'm trying to get out of here because I don't want to take the RQ test.'

'Neither do I.'

'Are we all done with sharing now?'

He laughs low, and it is a good laugh. 'But *why* don't you want to take the test? I know some idiots gave you a hard time about your family the other night. But so what? If you got a Test appointment, you must be able to do the tests. Get a placement, get away from them, go to uni or whatever. Start over again where people don't know who you are.'

'You make it sound so simple.'

'Isn't it?'

'No. I don't think I can even go to university without an Implant.'

He shrugs. 'Get one, then. See the walls they want you to see. It's not so bad.'

'I can't. And *don't* ask me why. Now it's your turn. Why were you trying to leave, really?'

He sighs. 'I didn't think it would be as easy as just slipping out in the night, but I had to try.'

'But why? You're a Hacker, aren't you? You'll be in demand. You'll get an awesome computer job, and live happily ever after.'

He laughs again, but this time it isn't a happy sound. 'That'd be great if you don't mind imaginary walls.' He turns to face me and even in the darkness his eyes glitter. 'Is there one thing you want, one thing that is more important to you than anything else?' His voice is intense, insistent, and demands an answer.

My mother back. The thought is unbidden, and silent, and I push it away. Out loud all I say is, 'I don't know. How about you?'

'Freedom.'

'Freedom? It's a free country,' I say, repeating what he said at dinner last night.

'Is it? How free are we, right now? Why is there a force field stopping us from leaving, in a free country?'

'I don't know. Maybe it's to stop people from cheating on the tests. Or to keep us safe, to keep others out.'

'We're not babies; we don't need a playpen with no sharp corners.'

I shake my head. 'Why would the government lock us in?'

'Ah, now that is kind of the important part of this: it's not our government. It's not NUN, either.'

'Who else could do something like this?'

'PareCo, of course.'

I stare back at him, uneasy. They're just a corporation, no matter how huge – global, yes, but they design computer systems and games, they don't run the world. OK, they design tests like the ones we're taking this week, but NUN pays them to make programmes. They're not in charge; NUN is. They can't detain people. But then Melrose's dad's words whisper inside: *general weirdness*. What would he make of this?

I shake my head. Gecko must be wrong: this is crazy. 'Why'd you even come if you don't want to be here?' I ask.

'I didn't. They brought me.'

'*What?*'

He swears under his breath. 'My own stupid fault. I should have gone into hiding. I should have realised they wouldn't accept a *no, thanks*. Not in my case.'

'What's so special about you, then?'

'How many Hackers do you know over the age of eighteen?'

I stop to think. 'I can't think of any,' I admit. Was that part of what was so weird about that Implant Addict Jason and I saw in the park – he was a Hacker, and he wasn't young?

'Hackers think they're the ultimate rebels, playing the system, manipulating it as they want. PareCo *lets them*. They're identifying possible future risks, and taking them in: testing them, appealing to the extreme competitive streak they all have to make them go for it, then praising the winners and offering them dream game jobs where they can be master of their own virtual universe. Safely contained away from the rest of us. And then what happens to them?'

'I don't know: what?'

He shrugs. 'I don't, either. But I'm afraid I'm going to find out.' He's silent a moment, then slips an arm around my shoulders. 'I'm sorry.'

'What for?'

'I shouldn't have dumped all that on you. Forget I said it. Let's go back to *you*: tell me why are you are *really* trying to leave.'

I sigh. 'I don't need to wait for the results of the IQ test – I know I did rather well. But I won't do so well on the RQ. I'll be considered dangerous: smart but stupid. God knows where they'll put me, but nowhere nice, I'm guessing.'

'What makes you think you'll fail the RQ?'

'Did you listen to all that stuff yesterday? My genes say so, for a start.'

'That's not it, is it? There's something else you're not saying.'

I don't know what it is. Something about talking in the night, in darkness so complete his questions are almost like a disembodied voice despite the warmth of his body next to mine. Something makes me want to tell, to say words I've kept hidden inside for so long.

'It's like this. When I plug in, I get really dizzy and weirded out. Always. Five or ten minutes, tops, and I'm vomiting all over the place.'

'Nice. Is that why you Refuse?'

It's not the whole answer, but I nod.

'You really *are* crazy,' he says.

'Heh!' I pull away, start to get up from the bench.

'Calm down; listen for a moment. Have you heard of ANDs?'

'Of what?'

'ANDs. Simple, over the counter anti-nausea drugs for motion sickness: they may help. I've heard of this problem before. It's the disconnect between the sense of motion and the fact that your body isn't actually moving when you're plugged in. Some people can't handle it, but ANDs should solve it. Then you can get an Implant, go to uni, and *you* can live happily ever after. I can't imagine why they weren't given to you when you were younger. Your doctor must be an idiot.'

I stay silent. The doctor didn't know, because Nanna said it was a secret, not to tell. Could it really be that simple? Of course it isn't just that I get sick, it is *why* I get sick. It's the double awareness I didn't tell Gecko about; that I'm still seeing and feeling the real world when I'm plugged in.

The clouds pick that moment to pull back. Stars peek out above us; Gecko is looking up at them. Silver glints around his left eye in an intricate pattern – beautiful, and somehow so *right* on his dark skin. Are they Hacker swirls, but in silver? I couldn't see them before. But now I can, in starshine?

Goosebumps trail up my spine. *I've seen silver marks like this before.* Astra had them. I was so young when she died that I'd forgotten this, somehow – but in starshine, there were swirls and patterns on her skin that echoed the dark ones. Just like Gecko, except he hasn't got the black Hacker tattoos as well. My mind is full of my mother's face, laughing in the garden at night, spinning me round under the stars. Tears start to come and there's nothing I can do to stop them. I lean forward to hide my face under the hoodie.

'What is it? What's wrong?' He turns to me now, stares at me with his dark eyes, one outlined in silver.

'Nothing. I've got to go.' I stand and start to take his hoodie off.

'Keep it. Give it back to me tomorrow,' he says.

I climb off the balcony and run back to my room, not even trying to be quiet any more.

Later the tears subside, but questions are left behind. What do the silver marks mean? There is something about them, something to do with my mother and who she was, but the answer slips just out of reach.

10

I wake up late. Open one eye a crack, and light is streaming into the room.

Melrose is sitting on the bed opposite mine. I sit up fast.

'What are you doing here?'

'I thought we should talk about what happened.'

'You mean how you told Jezzamine about Nanna after you promised you wouldn't?'

'I didn't tell her anything.'

'Sure you didn't. Just like you didn't have a jealous fit when Hex dragged me off to have dinner in Hackerville.'

She crosses her arms. 'All right, I did. A little. It was stupid, and I'm sorry. But why'd you have to stomp off like that after dinner? And I'd spent *ages* getting everyone to agree that you could sit with us at dinner, and then you wouldn't. How do you think that made me look?'

'Sure. Whatever. I suppose *that* is what you were talking to Jezzamine about.'

I get up, head for the shower. Turn back, find her dress. 'Thanks for the loan, but please take it back.' And hand it to her and walk out the door.

I'm actually shaking.

She *said* she didn't tell Jezzamine. But how else could she have known? There wasn't anybody else there. Even Sally doesn't talk about Nanna; she goes to pains to hide her away.

I make it to the grand hall just before the IQ test results get pinned up on boards. Everyone rushes to look; I hang back, wait for the crowd to thin.

Some faces are happy; others are sad. Some are angry, and there are glares directed at me from my school. Jezzamine walks past. 'Did you do OK?' I ask sweetly. She ignores me.

Most have gone when Gecko walks in behind me, and I hand him his hoodie. 'Heh,' he says. 'Ready for the big moment?'

'Yep. Are you?'

He shrugs.

We walk up to the board together. The names are split into ten even groups, ranked in grade order.

I scan the names in the top group, and there it is: *Luna Iverson*. I sort of knew, but shock makes me look again: it's still there. I really did it. Despite thinking it may have been a bad idea, there is a warm glow inside: I proved them wrong. And Hex is on the top list, too. And Gecko. I find Melrose in the fourth group – middling to good, just where her dad said she'd be – Jezzamine is there also. There is a note that the bottom two groups must pack and transport has been arranged: their IQ results aren't good enough, they're being sent home. The rest of us are to assemble in the hall after lunch.

I glance at Gecko; he *so* doesn't look happy. But this can't wait.

'Can we talk?' I say. He nods, and we walk away from the board. Out the door, away from the others chatting and milling about outside.

'I can't believe we're both in the top ten percent,' he says, and shakes his head.

'Gee, thanks.'

'It's just that the others in the top group are all Hackers. So, how'd you do it?'

'Honestly? I don't know. I mean, I know I smashed the test; it was like there was this clever part of me taking over.' I shake my head. He puts his hoodie on the grass, gestures for me to sit on it, then drops down next to me.

'And I *really* shouldn't be in the top group,' he says. 'I failed the test.'

'No, you didn't!'

'Oh yes I did. For every question I put the most obviously wrong answer: I failed it spectacularly, and went way over time, too. Maybe it would have been wiser to just do average on it?' He shakes his head.

'I don't understand. Why would they put you in the top group if you failed?'

'They went to a lot of trouble to get me here, and more trouble, with that force field, to keep me here. Were they going to let me just fail the test when they've so obviously got plans for me? This IQ result *proves* they're up to something. If only I knew what it was.'

I stare back at Gecko, shocked into silence, goosebumps cold on my arms despite the spring sunshine on my skin.

Can they really fake results? But even if they could, why on earth would they?

No way. He's acting in his own play; he *must* be making all this up. And that story about being brought here against his will, and thinking the force field was there just for him. If it were all true, why would he even tell me? He doesn't really know me: how could he know I wouldn't tell anyone else?

His words *feel* truthful, and there is something about him that makes me want to trust him. But if he were delusional, he'd believe what he was saying. Is he sick, like Nanna? Part of me wants to run away from the dark eyes staring at me intently just now; part of me needs answers.

And worse: something in his eyes *waits* – waits for me to say something to his claims. Somehow I can't lie to those eyes. 'Maybe you've got delusions of grandeur,' I say.

Hurt flashes across his face; fleeting, then gone. He shrugs. 'Maybe I do. What is it you wanted to talk about, anyway?'

I search his face for the silver I know I won't see in daylight. 'There's something I need to ask you. Last night, when the clouds lifted, I saw silver around your eye. You've got silver Hacker marks. What do they mean?'

His face stills. 'They're not that usual, and they're kind of secret. But most people can't see them, even in starshine.' He stares at me.

'I've seen them before. My mother had them,' I say, the words dragging out of me, slow and reluctant. I never talk about Astra; I rarely refer to her as *Mother*. Never, ever *Mum*. It hurts too much.

His eyes widen. 'The mother they said killed herself?' he says. The one thing he could say that will *make* me answer.

'She didn't kill herself! At least, not the way it sounds. She was a Hacker; her life support failed. They said it was her fault, that she set it to fail when she died virtually in a game. That she was so convinced it could never happen that she raised the virtual stakes, gambled with her life, and lost.' I say the words that defend her, unable to stop myself. But isn't what happened only marginally better than choosing to take her own life, choosing to leave me? The Game was more important to her than anything else. Including me.

'Who was your mother?' His voice is oddly strained.

I don't want to tell him. He's a Hacker; it always freaks them out when they find out. Even Hex couldn't believe it, and for ages tried to ask me questions about her until he finally gave up when I wouldn't answer.

'Please tell me, Luna. Who was your mother?'

'Astra.'

He stares at me, wonder in his eyes, and I shake my head.

'Don't give me that hero worship thing just because Astra was the best space game Hacker, ever. I've heard it all before, and I'm nothing like her.'

'I can't believe I didn't see it. You've got her eyes.'

Oh, great. Not only is he potentially delusional, he's also one of those freaky fan club Astra-worshippers. He's probably got her picture on his bedside table.

Most of me wants to run, to get away from him, but *I have to know*. 'Please tell me. What do the silver marks mean?'

He stays silent a moment, and I don't press. Finally he looks around and leans in close. Lowers his voice. 'All right. Because of who your mother is, I'll make an exception and tell you something I'm sworn not to tell. But you have to promise to keep this to yourself.'

'I will, I promise.'

'It's like…' He hesitates. 'A different type of hacking. A different level. Undetectable.'

'But you said PareCo lets Hackers in, lets them do their thing so they can observe.'

'Not this. They can't see this; can't control it; can't stop it.'

'So how'd they catch on that you're a Hacker? You've only got the silver marks, no black marks everyone can see.'

'I don't know. Somebody must have sold me out.' And there is cold, controlled anger in his voice.

'Maybe they worked it out for themselves. Marks or not, it is obvious you're a Hacker. You dress like a Hacker, you've got a weird Hacker-name, you hang out with Hackers.'

He smiles. '*Now* I do. I gave up masquerading as a regular student once it became apparent they knew. There was no reason to hide any longer.'

'Why haven't you got any black Hacker marks? My mother had both.'

'I've stuck to silver hacking only. Your mother was particularly skilled in both silver and traditional world manipulation. It's a surprise they left her alone as long as they did.'

'What do you mean?'

'Nothing. Look, I've got to go. Remember: you promised not to tell anyone, right?'

He gets up and takes off as if something is after him, leaving the hoodie I'm sitting on behind.

Well. What does all this mean? I shake my head. This can't be for real. If he is delusional or making things up about the other stuff, *everything* he says must be suspect.

It must be.

But my guts clench cold, inside.

It's a surprise they left her alone as long as they did...

11

'Hello, everyone. I'm Dr Rafferty.' He smiles at the assembled students, eyes twinkling below a shock of white hair. Despite my usual mistrust of doctors, there is something about him that makes me smile back.

'Some students get a little stressed about the testing, so I've been assigned by HealthCo to look after you. I'll be meeting with a few of you for a chat this afternoon. If any others have worries or questions, you can also make an appointment to see me. But don't ask me about the test itself; that I can't tell you. And not just because I shouldn't: I don't know a thing about it. But here is someone who does.' And he introduces Langdon, a test official from PareCo.

Langdon steps up to the stage. Is he an evil mastermind, manipulating test results, installing force fields, and setting Implant suggestions so strong even a Hacker can't see through them? He just looks like a geek, not much older than we are.

He smiles nervously at everyone. 'Hi,' he says. Then looks at a card in his hand, and reads it out. 'Big congratulations to each and every one of you! Your IQ test results show you've been graced with intelligence. But do you have the ability to handle your gift? In many ways this is far more important. The RQ test on Thursday will determine this. Until then you will be assigned to groups and prepare for the test together. In a moment you will each receive a folder with instructions, and you will meet with your group at dinner.'

Then they hand out folders to each of us. Mine has a sticker on top: *meet with Dr Rafferty at 2 p.m.* Any imagined liking I had for him before vanishes.

'Hi, Luna, come in,' he says, and holds the door.

I step reluctantly into his office; it swings shut behind me.

'Have a seat,' he says. 'And stop looking so worried.'

'Sorry, I'm not worried,' I lie. 'I'm confused. Why am I here? Do I look stressed out to you?'

He laughs. 'Perhaps a little, but that isn't why you're here. There were reports of an episode the evening of the formal dinner, and I wanted to talk to you about it.'

An episode. That's what they call it when Nanna flips out. I'm properly worried now.

'Thank you, but what if I don't?' And I know I'm being stupid; I'm pushing him, and there is no logical reason to do that, and any number of reasons why it could be a bad idea.

He laughs again. 'Please relax; you're not in any sort of trouble here. This is purely for your benefit, and completely confidential. Just between us,' he adds.

'I do know what confidential means.'

'I'm sure. Your IQ test suggests you're rather bright. So do you want to tell me what happened?'

I stay silent, and he looks down at some notes. 'Here goes. You came to the dinner in the same colours as your school, but declined to sit with your classmates and instead joined a Hacker friend. Hex, I believe?'

I nod. 'But they're not my classmates. I mean, we're not in any classes together. Because I'm a Refuser.' I say it defiantly.

He nods. 'That is also noted on your records.' He looks down again. 'Then after dinner, you left abruptly, had words with a girl from your school, ran out—'

'—and fell over in a highly embarrassing fashion in front of everyone.'

'I just have it as "tripped".' His eyes are twinkling again.

'Tripped. Yes, that's it.'

'What were the words about? With—' and he looks down again '—one Jezzamine Taylor.'

'Nothing important. Just a little disagreement,' I say. Not wanting to cover for her, exactly; more not wanting to repeat what she said about my mother, or Nanna.

'Reports are that you looked very upset.'

I say nothing, stare back at him.

'This is going well. I think I'm flunking at doctor-patient communication. Give me something, anything,' he says, and I'm starting to feel like I'm being mean to someone's grandfather. Something in me *thaws*. Just a little.

I shrug. 'Look, it really doesn't matter. She said some unkind things, but her opinion isn't important to me. I shouldn't let it bother me.' All true, but somehow, it still does.

'That is a very rational approach. Speaking of which, how are you feeling about the RQ test?'

'Nervous,' I admit.

'Listen. Anyone who did as well as you at the IQ should have nothing to worry about. Unless you're stark raving bonkers. And you don't seem bonkers to me. A little defensive, maybe, so watch that doesn't colour your judgement.'

'*Not bonkers*: finally, a medical diagnosis I like. But I thought IQ and RQ were independent: that you can be clever, and stupid.'

'By stupid, you mean irrational?' I nod. 'You can. This is called dysrationalia, commonly shortened to dys: irrational decisions and behaviour despite more than adequate intelligence. But that is the more unusual result.'

'What happens to people who are clever-stupid? I mean, dysrationalic.'

'What happens to them?' He looks surprised. 'Nothing *happens* to them.'

'But history has shown that they're dangerous. You couldn't just leave them loose on the world.'

'They're monitored in case they need help. True, they shouldn't have their fingers on any triggers; suitable occupations are found for them. But they're not hauled away and locked in a padded room, if that's what you mean. Is that the sort of nonsense that is going around?'

I stay silent. That is the sort of nonsense Goodwin at my school planted in my mind.

'Listen to me, Luna. You should do fine on the RQ, but if you don't, nothing bad is going to happen. Either way, you'll be absolutely fine.'

And the band of worry in my chest loosens. Just a little. 'About the IQ test—'

'Ah yes. Your IQ results were kind of a surprise.'

'Were they?'

'There had been some questions raised by your school—'

'Goodwin.'

'Yes. By your head teacher, about your suitability for a test appointment. She was obviously wrong.'

'So how did I get the appointment, then? No one seems to know.'

'I do.'

'You do?' I look at him, truly surprised now. 'Are you going to tell me?'

'I might. Maybe you could answer some of my questions a bit more, first.'

I raise an eyebrow. 'Ah, a deal. I see. Who goes first?'

He laughs out loud. 'Oh my dear, you are a treat. Now, I have a suspicion. That the answer to both questions might be the same. You go first: what did this Jezzamine say about your family to upset you so much?'

'I never said she said anything about my family.'

'Whoops…!' He claps a hand over his mouth.

I raise an eyebrow. 'If you already know, why do you ask?'

'You need to say it, Luna. To take the power away from hurtful words, you need to be able to acknowledge them, confront them, then dismiss them.'

I stare back at him. His eyes are so sincere, and maybe I'm paranoid because of Gecko, and stuff he said about PareCo manipulating things, but Dr Rafferty is with HealthCo – he doesn't work for PareCo.

'OK,' I say. 'It was just the usual. About me being crazy

99

because of my genes. 'Because...' And I hesitate. 'Because of my mother.' *And my grandmother*, I add silently.

'And there is your double answer.'

'What do you mean?'

'The reason you were given a Test appointment, Luna, was because of your mother. She had one of the highest IQ ratings ever measured by PareCo. It was felt your school grades were probably not reflective of your ability. There are people behind these decisions, not just computers. And they felt you deserved a chance.

'However your mother died, Luna, she's given you a gift now. Don't let being defensive, or scared of failure, take it away from you. She'd want you to have an amazing future, full of opportunity. Wouldn't she?'

Despite myself my eyes are welling up. I blink, hard. 'Can I go now?'

'Yes,' he says, and I head for the door. 'But Luna?' I pause. 'If you need someone to talk to, my door is always open.'

'OK. Thank you,' I say. And this time I mean it.

It isn't until later that I put a few other things together. Gecko thought his high IQ test result was proof that PareCo were manipulating the tests for their own nefarious purposes – even though he didn't know what those purposes might be. But Rafferty said there were people, not just computers, behind things, making the decisions. Maybe it was the same in his case – that they felt he deserved a chance. Or maybe deliberately answering every question wrong was proof of a high IQ in any event?

I go sit in the sun near the tree where Gecko and I were before. If he shows up, I'll tell him my theory.

The trees are in blossom; other students are dotted about on the grass of the quad. With the wind shielded by the buildings, it's a suntrap. I'm lying back, skin soaking up the warmth. Feeling more calm than I have in a long time. Rafferty said he was there to stop students stressing out: he's good at his job.

But finally I sigh, sit up, and face what comes next: the folder I was given earlier.

Inside is a dinner table assignment – we're back in the hall for tonight. My stomach twists: groups are really *so* not my thing.

And another instruction: not under any circumstances to communicate what I perceive with any of my senses. It is followed by a warning: *Any failure to follow this instruction will result in automatic failure in the RQ test.*

12

The tables in the hall are mostly full when I arrive. I scan along the room for table six, and anxiously check the faces when I find it: *relief*. No Jezzamine, no Melrose. No Gecko, either, which gives a weird mix of disappointment and uncertainty at why I feel that way. There is a girl I recognise from my room: was her name Anne? The one who pushed her bed as far away as possible from mine.

Bet they'll be pleased when I join them. I stand straight, smile, and head for the last empty seat at the table. 'Hi, everyone!' I say, and sit down.

Eyes swivel in my direction. It is a mixed group of boys and girls, two from each school, going by what they are wearing; in their midst is a boy I vaguely recognise but have never spoken to from mine. Judging by the looks of dismay, they know who I am. The taint of crazy is upon them.

Anne manages to curve her lips in something resembling a smile. 'Hello, Luna,' she says, and gets everyone to introduce themselves. The unknown boy from my school is Ravi; I'm so uncomfortable that most of the other names slip past me without registering.

Dinner is brought in. Conversations start up and lag now and then. There are curious questions about what we're doing together, and why. How they picked the groups, with a few glances at me. I look around at the other groups. Unlike the night of the formal dinner when we were all clustered together, tonight the tables are spread far around the edges of the hall, not close enough to easily overhear each other. I spot Hex at a table on the other side, Gecko on another, then look around again.

'There is a Hacker at every table. Except ours,' I say, voluntarily speaking without being spoken to for the first time. The others look around the hall.

'I wonder if group make-up has anything to do with IQ test ranking,' Ravi says. 'What ranking was everyone in?'

They start calling them out until I'm the only one who hasn't. 'I was in the top group,' I admit. There are a few looks of surprise; others' reactions, like Anne's, suggest they already knew. So it turns out Ravi was right: now that the bottom two groups have left, our group of eight has one person from each of the remaining ranked groups.

So that is why our group is the only one without a Hacker: like Gecko said, I really was the only one in the top group who wasn't one of them.

Pudding is served, and I can't get the instruction in my folder out of my mind: to not tell anyone what I perceive with any of my senses. Does everyone have instructions in their folder? If they do, are they the same, or different? Unease swirls in my stomach. Why can't I say what I can see, feel, hear, smell or taste? Lucky nobody asks me what I thought of dinner.

Then a test official comes in with a pile of folders in his arms, hands one to each group, and leaves.

Ravi holds up our folder. 'Shall I?' he says. He draws out a sheet of paper, clears his throat, and reads. 'Your task is to devise a test for one of the cognitive biases that prevent rationality. Begin this evening with choosing a bias that you, as a group, share and must guard against, and discuss the dangers it presents. Tomorrow you will continue with formulating a test for the bias.'

He puts it down and we exchange glances.

Anne takes the sheet. 'A bias that we share? What if we don't share the same biases?' Just what I'd been thinking. 'How about we all say what we think is our worst bias? You go first, Luna.' She looks at me, an eyebrow raised.

I might have been stumped, but my chat with Rafferty earlier brings it to mind. 'Negativity bias – paying more attention to bad news.'

Others say theirs. We have a few with projection bias: assuming others think as we do; a few confirmation bias: referencing only perspectives that agree with our own views; some in-group bias: over-valuing opinions of those we know over those we don't.

'How are we going to pick one over the others?' Ravi asks.

'Let's list them all,' suggests a girl with a notebook. 'And then everyone give their top three, and whichever carries the most votes we pick?' They start going through them while she writes them down. There are fifteen officially recognised biases; even in my class of Refusers they'd been hammered in enough to know what they are. They can all be bars to rational thought and decisions.

Everyone is looking at the list, fiddling with which ones they think they will admit they suffer from to see if there is a common element between us all. My eyes wander around the room, at the bent heads and heated discussions going on around us.

'Maybe it'd be more *rational* to pick one that is easier to test for than the others,' I say. 'Since it is a test we're supposed to—'

The lights go out, and I don't finish my sentence. They don't flicker or stage down – the room goes from brightly lit to pitch dark in an instant.

'Who didn't pay the electrics?' someone calls out from another table. A few boys start making ghost noises, and there is nervous laughter.

'Has anyone got a torch?' another voice says. No one answers.

The switches are by the doors we came in through. 'I'll try the switches,' I say, get up and with hands in front of me, reach out blindly until I hit the wall, then follow it around to the doors.

It is so dark I keep opening my eyes wider and wider as if that'll help, but can see *nothing*. I reach the door, and flick the switches up and down. 'The switches aren't working,' I call out. I grasp the door handle, thinking I'll see if the power is cut outside the hall as well, but it doesn't turn. A sense of disquiet strengthens inside. The doors are locked? We're locked in here, in the dark?

'Luna?' a voice says softly, close by. Gecko's voice.

'Yeah?'

'I thought that was you.'

'We're locked in,' I say, making my voice low. Shouting that one out might cause panic.

'What?' I hear a rattling noise – his hands trying the doors? 'That's weird. I don't like this.'

Across the room a voice calls out, 'We had candles at dinner the other night. I'll see if they're in the serving area.' There are footsteps, a thud, and muffled curses. More footsteps.

'I wonder if the doors upstairs to the balcony are open?' I say.

'Good thought.' Gecko takes my hand and we feel our way along the wall until we find the stairs. I grip the handrail and start up them just as some candles are lit below; there are a few bobbing lights, then the light level goes up as some candelabras on the walls are lit, and tea lights passed around.

Gecko tries the first set of doors at the top: locked. We exchange a glance.

'Try the others?' I say, and walk along to the next set of doors. 'Locked,' I call out, and head for the doors at the end. I glance back; Gecko is leaning over the waist-high parapet, looking down at the ground floor of the hall. Has he given up, deciding that if someone has decided to lock us in they'll all be locked? I'm too stubborn not to try each of them. I reach for the last door handle.

'Locked,' I say, just as the night is split by an ear-piercing scream.

13

'Get down!' Gecko says, and we both duck below the parapet. There is more screaming, shouting, running footsteps. Crashes and cries.

'What the hell is going on?' I say.

'There are two men below, shooting into the crowd, and – and – people. Bleeding, on the floor, not moving.'

I shrink down even more, horrified, shocked, freaked out, and...*listening*. There's mass hysteria – that I can hear. But no gunshots.

'Are they shooting at people? Right now?'

But he is peeking over the top of the parapet, and doesn't answer. 'Stay here, keep out of sight. I'm going down the stairs; they shouldn't see me if I go down low, under the height of the handrail. We have to get everyone to put out the candles, then we can tackle them in the dark.' He slips away, down the stairs.

Once he is gone I cautiously peer over the parapet.

People are running, screaming. Some are sprawled awkwardly on the ground. The light is dim, true, but there isn't any blood I can see. No gunmen, either. No sound of gunshots. I shake my head, stand up and look properly. It's chaos and hysteria, but I can't see a cause for any of it.

Then it hits me, and I sag back down on the floor.

Don't say anything you perceive with your senses – my

instruction. I'm the only one here without an Implant. This is all fake, is that it? Like the wall Gecko could see and I couldn't. And I'm not supposed to tell anyone?

Thinking you've been shot might not make you bleed, but it's a bloody rotten thing to do to somebody, just the same. I'm gripped with fury. If I can't tell them it isn't real, I'll show them.

I head down the stairs.

Jezzamine stands at the bottom of the stairs; she turns when she hears my footsteps.

'It's finally happened,' she says. 'Your crazy has rubbed off on me.'

'What?'

'I've gone mad, haven't I?' She stares back at me, eyes round and uncertain, and very un-Jezzamine-like. Is she in some kind of shock?

'It's OK, Jezzamine; this isn't real. It'll be over soon and everybody will be fine,' I say, pausing to reassure even though it is *her*, but trying to choose my words so I'm not breaching my instructions.

'Of course it isn't real.'

'You can tell?'

Her face is puzzled. 'I can see Implant images – obviously superimposed, not real. But everyone else thinks they're real. I thought I was going nuts, but you can tell they're fake, too?'

'Jezzamine, I haven't got an Implant.'

Realisation strikes her eyes. 'So they really are just Implant images, like how I see them. But why does everyone else seem to see things different from me?' She is horrified; she's not the sort to like *different* anything.

'Look,' I say, and I point to the shadows along the wall. There is a boy there, not hiding or trying to get away. Instead he stands there, puzzled shock on his face. We walk across.

'You just see what is happening as Implant images, right?' Jezzamine says to him. He nods. Relief floods her face; she's not the only one.

'We have to put a stop to this,' the boy says.

I nod. 'Right. I'm going to knock the guns out of the fake gunmen's hands, but I can't see where they are. Give me directions?'

'We'll do it together,' he says. 'Come on.'

The candles have started going out one by one, darkness beginning to return. Gecko's picking the wrong moment: we need everyone to see what we do.

We walk hurriedly across the room. There are students huddled behind upturned tables, others lying on the floor, eyes closed.

'They think they're dead?' I say.

'They've got fake blood all over them,' the boy says. 'Looks fake to me, anyhow.'

'Where are the gunmen?'

'There are two of them, in the centre. I'll guide you,' he says.

We start to walk forward, but then there is an anguished cry: Gecko? And then I'm knocked off my feet, and pulled away.

'Luna, Luna,' he says, running his hands over me.

'Stop it!' I snap. 'This isn't real. I'm not shot. Stop it!' I slap him across the face.

'Ouch!'

By telling Jezzamine and that boy I couldn't see what they could I've *so* broken the tell-no-one-what-you-can-perceive rule now, it seems pointless to hold back any longer. 'Listen to me, Gecko. It's like the wall you could see, but I couldn't.'

'What? But you're bleeding, covered in blood—'

'Implant images: there is no blood.'

Understanding – and relief – start to cross his face. 'But why—'

'Listen up, everybody, and listen good!' It's Jezzamine? 'This is all total bullshit. Stop screaming, stop bleeding, stop whatever you're doing. This is like a virtual game. It isn't real, it isn't happening. You're fine.' She shakes someone who is lying still on the floor, a girl from her group of friends who always does exactly what she says when she says it. The girl sits up, a dazed look on her face, and looks around her.

'See?' Jezzamine says. 'It's not real. Stop being a bunch of follow-the-crowd cognitively-biased sissies. You're all right. *Be rational.*'

Everyone looks at each other, then back to Jezzamine. By sheer force of her dominant will – and the threat of being labelled irrational, and all that goes with that – they are overcoming what they can see and hear. One by one the crying, the hiding and the dead stand up, and face her.

The lights come back on; the doors click unlocked.

'The gunmen have vanished,' Gecko says.

There are no gunshot wounds, but there are a few injuries. A sprained ankle; cuts and bruises from all the hysteria, but nothing serious. There could have been, though, couldn't there? Why'd they do something so cruel, so crazy?

Everyone is looking at Jezzamine, me, and the other boy who helped – Danny, he introduces himself as – in some kind of awe that we were the only ones rational enough to see through the Implant simulation. But it wasn't superior brainpower, was it? Just me not having an Implant, and them, for whatever reason, being able to see Implant images for what they were when the others couldn't.

What was the whole point of it? I can't grasp why they'd do something that awful.

But no matter the reason, when I told Jezzamine and Gecko what I could see, I broke the only rule they gave me. Consequence? I've failed the RQ test. Dysrationalia, here I come.

Gecko sticks close to my side, so close that when I turn I walk straight into him.

'What's with the puppy dog impression?'

He looks abashed. 'Sorry. It's just...'

'What?'

'I know it wasn't real. But I saw it. I saw you walk up to that guy – he shot you point blank in front of me. I saw it all, and I can't shake it off.' He slips his arms around me

111

in a tight hug, then abruptly leaves to help lift tables back to their places.

Well.

'Looks like you've made a conquest.' It's Jezzamine, and she's not even sneering.

'Still talking to me?'

'Don't worry, I won't make a habit of it.' She looks uncomfortable. 'Thanks for before. I owe you one, and I don't like it. So I'm paying you back now.'

'With what?'

'Melrose didn't tell me about your nutzoid grandmother, all right? It was my brother. He goes to school with your brother.'

I stare at her, shocked. *Jason* is the one who told?

'Are we even?' she says.

'Sure. Whatever.'

And she turns, walks off. People have started trickling out, back to their rooms; I scan faces, but can't see Melrose. I sigh. Something else I've got wrong. Was that my negativity bias again – expecting the worst of people? I deserve to fail.

14

I stand in the door to the hall, not sure I can bring myself to go in. They want us to work in *here* today, after what happened last night? I can't stop myself: I wedge a chair in the door.

I sit with my group. Anne raises an eyebrow. 'Feeling a bit claustrophobic today, are you, Luna? That's not very rational.'

I stare back at her. 'Are you serious? After last night I didn't want to risk getting locked in here again.'

They all turn and give me odd looks; no one answers.

'Locked in here *again*?' Anne finally says. 'What are you talking about?'

There are footsteps behind, and I turn. Danny?

'Can I borrow Luna for a sec?' he says, and I get up, walk with him away from the others.

'Do you remember what happened last night?' he asks.

'You mean lights out, locked in, panic and fake gunmen? Yep. You too?'

'Yes. So does Jezzamine. She denies it, but she's lying.'

'She kind of likes going with the crowd. From the front, of course.'

'The others just remember it as if it were a proposed test of a crowd bias that we all talked through. They don't think it actually happened. What does it mean?'

'No idea,' I say, but then there is a noise by the door – the chair stuck in the door is being pulled out of the way, and in steps Dr Rafferty. He looks at the table where I should be, then around until he spots me. Gestures for me to come to him. 'But somehow I think I'm about to find out.'

'I've been asked to interview you about last night.' Dr Rafferty gestures at a chair opposite his desk. I sit down.

'That sounds serious.'

'It is. Serious. Very serious, actually, Luna.' His face is grave. 'First I need you to tell me exactly what happened.'

I consider giving him the fake version that Danny alluded to, the one everyone except us and Jezzamine believes to be true. But what is the point? They'll know it all. So I do; I tell him the whole story.

'So you were given a direct instruction to not tell anyone what you could perceive with your senses. You were told that breaching this instruction would result in automatic failure of the RQ test, yet you did it, anyhow. A very irrational decision in view of your instructions and the consequences specified. Can you explain why?'

'You weren't there. It was horrible! Everyone was scared. People thought they were dead or dying.'

'So, would you say it was compassion for others that made you act as you did?'

I nod. It was that, and *fury* at what was being done to everyone. But I don't say that out loud.

'I'll make a case for you, Luna. But I'm not sure they'll

listen.' He sighs. 'You can go. Back to your group.'

'I have a question, too. Why'd they do it? It was cruel.'

He tilts his head. 'The testing means are within the purview of PareCo under their contract. But whatever you may think of their methods, Luna, they are designed to filter the rational from the dysrational. This is of vital importance to the safety and future of this country and everyone else around the world. It isn't taken lightly.' He smiles. 'Go. Try not to worry too much. Remember what I told you the last time: what happens to you if you fail the RQ?'

'Nothing happens to me. I'll be monitored, an appropriate job chosen.' But now this doesn't feel reassuring like it did the other day: a job where I can't make decisions that could harm anyone. One where I'll always be watched, to make sure my dysrationalia doesn't manifest. My skin crawls.

I step out of his office, back across the quad. I start to walk towards the hall but then think, stuff it. There is no doubt this is a do not pass go, do not collect two thousand pounds moment. I'm not going back in there.

First: rattle the chains of my prison. I head down one of the passageways between two buildings: is the force field on this time of day? A shimmering light in the air greets me. I try again to push through it, but like the last time I get a bit of the way in and then it's like it pushes me back out again. There is no escape.

I slip back to the side of the hall, look around: no one is in sight. Climb up to the balcony, curl up on the bench where Gecko and I sat in darkness the night we were both trying to escape. Where I saw the silver swirls in his skin, so like Astra's that the rush of memory made me run. Does he remember what really happened last night? How upset he was when he thought I was shot? That he put his arms around me.

Somehow it is important that he remembers.

Late that night I return to the balcony. Just as I'm starting to wonder if Gecko ignored the note I slipped him at dinner, I hear quiet steps, below. He climbs up.

'Heh. You came.'

'How could I resist?' He smiles in the moonlight, and moves with more of the swagger he had that first night, when he thought I was staring at him because he was so gorgeous. I flush. I was, then, but this is now, and there is something more important to deal with.

'Shut up, sit down, and listen.'

He's startled. Sits down. 'OK. What is it? I'm listening.'

'Right. You remember the wall you can see but I can't – the force field?'

'Of course.'

'It is a false image. Put there by Implants. Right?'

'Yes, but—'

'So how do you know you aren't seeing false images from your Implant all the time?'

He shrugs, uneasy. 'I don't *know*. Though there'd need to be a good reason for doing it on a large scale – the force field being a wall is a simple, static image that serves a definite purpose. I don't know that they even *can* do more complex images convincingly.'

'They can, and they do.'

'Tell me.'

So, I do. All of it: the lights out, the screaming, people being shot. The instructions I breached. How Gecko thought I was shot in front of him; how Jezzamine could see through the Implant images, and got everyone to overcome them. How only those who could see through the images seemed to remember it as it actually happened the next day. He gets me to describe it over and over again, every detail I can remember, to see if it brings any of it back, but then gets a terribly pained look on his face.

'Dammit. This is freaky. Who knows when they use our Implants to make us see what they want, when they want? Or even if they don't, worse: to change what we remember about things that happened, afterwards. The really weird thing is that if I try to remember what really happened last night, it's like my head hurts, my thoughts slide away from it. I can't. But I can think about what you told me about it.' He shakes his head. 'And what was the point of that whole thing?'

'I don't know. I was thinking it was some sort of rationality test, but it was so random and violent. I can't see how it tests anything useful.' I pull my arms in tight around myself. 'I'm sorry.'

'Why are you apologising?'

'You were happier not knowing all of this, right?'

'No. Thank you for telling me the truth.' He grips my hand tight, but it's not flirty Gecko now. 'Now, what am I going to do with it?'

'What do you mean?'

'Nothing. Everything.' He shakes his head, and turns back to me. 'And what about you, Luna? The RQ test is tomorrow morning. Take the test, go home, go to university and live happily ever after. Put all this out of your mind.'

I bristle. 'That is *so* not happening. Besides, I've got *dysrationalia reject* stamped in invisible ink on my forehead right now.'

'I can't see it.' He grins. It is a cloudy night, no stars – no silver around his eye tonight, but I know it's there. Just like the stamp put on me. I sigh. Lean back into the bench, and he slips an arm around my shoulders.

'I thought I was so lucky to get this Test appointment. Even though I was scared of flunking. Rafferty told me they were giving me a chance, because of how smart my mother was.'

I feel rather than see him shake his head. 'Giving you a chance out of the goodness of PareCo's black corporate hearts?' He snorts.

'Well, it sounded good at the time.'

'It is probably more like this: they are scared of you, Luna.'

'What? Scared of *me*? What nonsense.'

'They don't know who you are or anything about you, because you haven't got an Implant. That, together with

Astra being your mother, made you a risk they needed to investigate.'

'Oh yes, I'm very frightening to *them*.'

'Maybe your RQ test will be like my IQ.'

'What do you mean?'

'I failed the IQ; they said I passed. They said you are failing your RQ. What if it is all smoke and mirrors, and no matter what, we're both through? Because we're too dangerous to leave alone.'

'There go your delusions of grandeur again,' I say, but this time he laughs. He takes his arm off my shoulders, turns to face me. His smile is a sexy ghost in the darkness.

He leans forward and my breath catches in my throat. His lips brush my forehead, warm and soft.

'I'm the one who should be apologising.'

'What for?'

'I didn't take you seriously the other day. I should have told you how to get through a force field, but now it's too late. You're marked.'

A shiver runs down my spine. 'So, how do you get through a force field?'

'Don't push. As soon as you apply pressure, it pushes back. Just close your eyes and very, very gently become one with it until you get through to the other side.'

'Become one with a force field? Now you're making fun.' But even if I could get through it, is there any point to running away now? Could I get away before they label me, officially? And monitor me for the rest of my life.

'Tempted to run?'

'Very. But where would I go?'

'Already more rational than when I first met you.' I hit him on the arm. 'Ouch. But just as violent. Go, get some sleep. *Try* on that RQ test tomorrow, and who knows? Anything may happen. Whether you want it to, or not.'

The next morning we all report to the hall as instructed. Langdon is there.

'Good morning, everyone! You are probably expecting to do your RQ test now. But I've got news for you. You've already done it.'

Murmuring quickly spreads through the crowd.

'Listen, and I'll explain. We've found in the past that some of the very intelligent dysrationalic are adept at giving the answers we want to hear on an RQ test, and some were slipping through our attempts to catch them out. The solution? Reality tests. That has been what has been going on the last few days. All week we've being keeping an eye on each and every one of you, how you react in group tasks, to each other, to challenges. This data will be analysed to reach your RQ results.'

Everyone is exchanging glances, nervous thoughts ticking over behind their eyes as they sift through their words and actions over the last few days.

'Once you leave here today, speaking to anyone about the conduct of the RQ this year breaches the rules and will result in failure. An Implant block will be put in place to prevent inadvertent slips. So now it is time to go and pack your things; transport home has been arranged for everyone. Be ready to leave in an hour. Final test results and placements will be sent through to all of you next week.

'Good luck!'

We trickle out, go back to our rooms to pack, then wait out front for transport. Gecko's school is the first to go. He runs over, gives me a quick hug, and is gone. The loss at his absence is sharp. I've only known him for what: three days? It feels longer.

Everyone is talking about the RQ while we wait. Many are incredulous that they aren't being given an actual test; more are nervous how they've done, evaluated when they weren't even aware of what was going on.

Was that gunmen episode all part of this test by stealth?

At least *they* were all where they were supposed to be yesterday, not hiding out on a balcony. At least *they* didn't breach an instruction with the express penalty being RQ test failure. Rafferty may be trying his best to convince them my reasoning was good.

But I don't need luck. I need a miracle.

3
DEATHS

Refusal to believe until proof is given is a rational position;
denial of all outside of our own limited experience is absurd.

Annie Besant

15

The door opens as I walk up to it.

'There you are! How did it all go?' Sally says.

'Let me in, and I'll tell you,' I say, and she moves out of the way. I come in, dump my bag on the floor and pull the door shut behind me.

'You've not looking happy.'

'I don't think I did very well. Results are coming next week. All right?'

She shakes her head, arms crossed. A look on her face that says she expected nothing better. 'I hope you did everything you could to do well, I really do.'

'But you don't believe it, do you? So what does it matter?' I look around the room and realise what is missing. She's usually here this time of day, humming in a chair in front of the vid.

'Where's Nanna?'

'In her room. She's not been that bright while you were away.'

Before she finishes the sentence I'm already halfway up the stairs to Nanna's door. It's locked? I grit my teeth and enter the code. She's in bed, eyes closed.

'Nanna, Nanna – it's me, it's Luna.'

She stirs, doesn't open her eyes.

Sally follows me in.

'I'm sorry, Luna. The doctor isn't happy with how she's doing. She really needs care all the time now. Your father and I feel that—'

'No. You are not putting her in an institution.'

'But Luna—'

'No. I'll look after her. I shouldn't have left her to you.'

Sally shakes her head, and leaves.

I stay with Nanna all afternoon. She stirs a few times; her eyes open and look at me at one point, and she smiles, but doesn't really wake up.

It's early evening when Jason opens the door. 'Mum says to tell you dinner in five.'

'That gives us time to talk. Did you miss me, monkey?' He comes in a few steps but then stops, hesitant. 'It's OK. Come in. She won't bite. But I might!' I grab him in a headlock, twist him around, and he giggles.

'We need to have a serious word,' I say, and let him go. 'Do you go to school with a boy, second name Taylor? Older sister Jezzamine?'

'Yeah. That's Ollie. Why?'

'Did you tell him about Nanna? About how she freaked out the day Melrose was here for lunch?'

He doesn't say anything, but his face says it all. I sigh. In a twisted kind of way, I'd almost hoped that Jezzamine was lying. Now I know how wrong I had things with Melrose, and it really hurts to think how awful I was to her. I should have believed her, shouldn't I?

'Jason, it's not good to talk about family to other people

like that, OK? He told his sister, who made a big deal about it and told loads of people. In a not nice way.'

'I'm sorry.'

'No dramas. Just don't do it again. Deal?'

'Deal.'

Some things are best not put off. Sally's plugged in and Jason is asleep: it's time.

I stare dubiously at the small box in my hand, *Anti-nausea Drugs* printed across the front. I'm scared to try them, scared not to. Could it *really* be this simple?

My PareCo PIP is emblazoned, like they all are, with the source of the company name: *Parasensory Artificial Reality Enhancement*. The big breakthrough so many lifetimes ago that made perfect virtual experiences possible for the first time. *Realtime is just like reality, but better! Be who you want to be; go where you want to go. With PareCo.* So the advertising went. But never for me. The dizziness and nausea have always pulled me away, made me feel separated from myself – inhuman.

I swallow two with water, then wait a while in case they take time to kick in. I'd eaten as little as I could at dinner without arousing Sally's wrath, and I'm nervous. I'm not anxious to repeat how sick I was the last time.

I turn out all the lights in my room, and block the hall light from coming in under the door with a jumper. I feel my way to the PIP. Right, this is it. I settle back into the sofa, feel the warm fuzz of the neural net reaching out, reaching in, enclosing me.

The Realtime hallway appears at my feet as always. I step forwards. I should visit Dad, but this has to come first.

Melrose's door is still unlocked to me: at least that is something. I stand outside it for a while, staring at the door. I'm not feeling nauseous? It is all kind of weird still, in that I am standing here, and lying there in my room, and aware of both. But I'm not having to breathe in and out to calm my stomach the whole time. Could these tablets actually be working?

I hear low voices and laughter through the door. She's there, and she's not alone. Maybe I should message her to meet me on her own?

No; she might ignore a message. Just get it over with.

I knock, open the door. Look in.

Melrose is curled up on a huge beanbag with Hex, arms wrapped around each other. I don't think they're expecting company. They jump and start to spring apart, and I turn away and talk to the wall.

'Sorry. I'll…um…come back later.' I start backing out.

'Luna? Is that really you?' Melrose says.

'Yes. It's me.'

'You're *plugged in*?'

'Apparently so.'

'Don't go. What do you want?'

'I just wanted to apologise. I should have believed you when you said it wasn't you who told Jezzamine. I'm really sorry.'

She's standing up, facing me now. Hands on hips. 'I heard Jezzamine told you it wasn't me. So you believed her, but you wouldn't believe me.'

'No. Not really. I mean, Jason backed her up. But either way, I'm really, truly sorry.'

'Wow.' She looks at Hex, still on the beanbag.

'Double wow,' he says.

'What?'

'Not only have you apologised multiple times, you've done it *here*. You must be really sorry to come here to say it.'

'I am,' I say miserably. 'Sorry, that is. I'll go now.' I start backing towards the door, convinced she'll change the locks the second I'm gone.

'Don't be such a dys,' she says. 'Stay.'

'You're sure? I mean,' I look between them, 'you want to be alone, don't you?'

'Yes,' says Hex, and she gives him a look. 'I mean, no! Please stay. Here, make yourself comfortable.' And he gets up and pulls a sofa out of nowhere and plonks it down. Advantages of dating a Hacker? Instant furniture upgrades. I look around me more now and realise there is no ceiling– it is a night sky, but not like the real thing. The stars are so huge and bright it's like we're out there, in space.

'How'd you do with the RQ this week?' Hex asks. Someone had to ask, didn't they?

I slump back into the sofa. 'Totally rubbish.'

'Don't always think the worst,' Melrose admonishes. I raise an eyebrow. 'You do!' She throws a pillow at me. 'You never change. You even look exactly like you always do here,' she observes.

'Damn. I'm not magically virtually pretty?'

'You don't need to be, you already are,' she says, but *yeah right*.

Melrose and Hex are both themselves, but like turned up a few factors. His shoulders are broader; her waist is narrower. And her skin has the most incredible glow. Or maybe that is just from the serious stuff going on on that beanbag I interrupted.

'Do I really look just the same?' I say, and Hex pulls a mirror out of the air. 'It is most disconcerting when you do things like that,' I say. I look into the mirror, and do a double take. I am me, exactly as always, but there is silver swirling around my left eye. Silver Hacker marks, like my mother had. Like Gecko.

'Hex, *how* do people look different here than they do in real life?'

'Without getting too technical? It's keyed into how you want to look, the things you want to be different about yourself in the real world. So you must be self-satisfyingly smug about your appearance.'

I glare at him, then look back at the mirror. So, no surprises there: I want to look like the most beautiful woman I've ever seen – my mother. And they obviously can't see the silver swirls that I can see, or they would have said so. I stare at the mirror, resisting the urge to trace them around my eye.

'Give it a rest,' Melrose says. She takes the mirror, hands it to Hex and it disappears.

'Lemonade?' Hex says, and hands me one out of thin air.

'It's not cold, Hex.'

'Damn. I'm slipping.' He takes it and hands it back again. Ice cold.

'*How* do you do that stuff?'

'I'm magic,' Hex says. Melrose smacks him with a pillow, and it turns into a cloud of feathers that then vanish.

'Show-off,' she says. 'Answer the question.'

'OK, you asked for it. In real terms I'm hacking PareCo. I'm manipulating infinite strands of virtual time and space, changing what you can feel and see. Kind of like spinning a sensory web with code.'

'So none of it is really here. Kind of like we're not really here, in a physical sense.'

'Exactly.'

'Sure. Thanks for clearing that up. Since you're so clever, how do you think *you* did on the RQ?' I ask.

Hex shrugs. 'OK, I think. I—' And he stops, a kind of pained look on his face, then shrugs again.

'Can't you talk about it?'

'It's weird. We sort of can, but can't,' Melrose says.

'They said they put an Implant block on it. Can you hack around it?' I say to Hex.

'Haven't tried,' he answers, and frowns. 'Focusing on it gives me a headache; it's like when I try, my thoughts slide away from it.'

'Does you being here mean you're not a Refuser any more?' Melrose asks.

'I don't know what it means. But I'm not changing anything at school. Not when the year is nearly over.' Not when it would make Goodwin so happy to think she finally crushed Refusing out of me.

'Time check?' Melrose says.

'Five minutes,' Hex answers.

'Till what?'

'There's a midnight party tonight: celebrating the tests being over.'

'At midnight? Don't you ever sleep?'

They exchange a look. 'Don't need to,' Hex says. 'Your body is suspended in the PIP, right? More restful than sleep.'

Not sure that'll work for me, since my body is most definitely not asleep, and my PIP is a basic model: no life support. I'm doing my best to ignore my body, but the awareness is there all the time. Even though I'm not nauseous with these tablets in my system, if I don't concentrate on being *here* and deliberately block out *there*, it still feels all wrong.

'You must come to the party,' Melrose says. Somehow they convince me, and we time ourselves to be twenty minutes fashionably late. My stomach feels funny and I'm starting to worry, wondering how long it'll be before the ANDs wear off and I start spewing all over them. Maybe it is just nervousness bubbling in my stomach and nothing worse.

132

We head down Melrose's Realtime hallway. She's a group admin of the school party, and sends me an invite so the door will let me in. On the way, she has so many doors: friends, groups, games. The trail of her life since we stopped hanging out. The other side of things I know nothing about. There is an ache inside at all the things I've missed. What if all I needed was these tablets, and I could have been one of them?

We reach the door at the end of her hall. Hex pulls it open, holds it as Melrose and I step through. There is a sea breeze, fresh on our faces; surf crashes on the shore of an endless stretch of the *most* beautiful sandy beach. A virtual beach party? It might be midnight in the real world, but here the sun is shining, and feels good on my skin. Bare skin? I look down; there's been a wardrobe change as we stepped through – Melrose and I are now in bathing suits, colourful sarongs tied around our waists. Flowers around our necks. Hex is in wild rainbow board shorts. He frowns and they change to black.

'Come on; I need a drink,' he says, and we start walking across the sand towards everyone at a beach bar.

'Something's wrong; it's too quiet,' Melrose says. When we get there, a huge crowd from school are huddled together, but no one is in party mode, no one is happy. Some of them are crying.

'What is it? What's going on?' Melrose says.

One of her friends comes over to us. Her eyes are red.

'I can't believe it, I just can't. She was there just this

morning, and – and—' Her words catch.

'Who? What's happened?' Melrose says.

Another girl looks up. 'It's Jezzamine. She's died in a car accident.'

16

Jezzamine is the talk of school Monday morning before class. She wasn't universally liked but everybody knew her, and she was a *presence*. It is as if something immutable has been taken from the landscape. Like when Jason described the skyline of London with the dome of St Paul's Cathedral missing.

The midnight party ended soon after we arrived, but not before curious eyes noted I was there. It twists weirdly inside that the one person who'd have been in my face about it – Jezzamine – isn't here. Like a ghostly echo, half-heard whispers of others follow me down the hall.

Even Goodwin seems saddened by the news about Jezzamine, but that doesn't stop her from dragging me into her office just as the bell goes for first class. And I'm nervous she's heard about me plugging in. That someone told her, and she'll be at me now to leave the Refusers class.

'So, dear Luna, how did the tests go?'

I stay silent. So, she doesn't know; this is some other sport.

She smiles, a grin of pure evil even though her clown face and snakes are completely gone now from her red face. She must have spent the whole week scrubbing them off.

'I can read you quite easily, you know,' she says. 'So transparent. Poor Luna. Don't worry; if you didn't pass the tests, we'll find you something to do after graduation. I'm sure there are toilets somewhere that need cleaning. I'll make it my personal mission to ensure you get a *suitable* work placement.'

I make myself smile widely. 'Thank you so much! I really appreciate that. Should I go to class now, so I can learn as much as possible to prepare for my shiny new career in porcelain?'

Her smile slips a little, then comes back. 'Ah, I will miss our chats. But have no fear: I'm sure your new *career* will crush the attitude out of you in no time. Now, go.'

Out in the now silent hallway I pass the doors to the PIPs where Melrose and all the others will be plugged in by now. Hex, too, his exclusion having been lifted at last. I wonder what virtual school is like? There is some part of me that wants to find out. There is more that doesn't. If Hex can make me see and feel things that aren't there so easily, who knows what PareCo educational programmes do? Even Implants have more effect than I ever realised.

Rachel smiles when I sit next to her in class. After all that has happened in a week, it feels like aeons since I've been in this classroom. Counting down the minutes, and wishing I was somewhere – *anywhere* – else.

The test results are out tonight. Is there any chance of escape? Some little part *hopes*, inside.

As arranged, I've plugged in, and am with Melrose and Hex in Melrose's space. Waiting for the results. The second they're released he's hacked the list onto a virtual wall. Not paper, nothing as normal as that. It is like a thin screen, names in green for passed, red for failed. Details follow of placements.

Melrose finds her name first. 'I passed! And I'm going to London University!'

Then Hex whoops. 'Oh my God! Think Tank for me.'

And they're scanning down the list, all the names, noting how friends have done. No Luna Iverson.

'Maybe they forgot me?' I say, almost hopefully. Neither a pass nor a fail; somehow I'm OK with vanishing.

'No. Wait – you're last,' Hex says. 'There you are.'

I can't look; can't make myself. They're both silent. I finally turn and meet their eyes. Despite having taken the recommended two ANDs and a spare, just in case, my stomach is churning. But they're smiling?

'Did I pass?'

'Look for yourself. Look, Luna.' I follow Melrose's finger to the pulsing entry.

Luna Iverson: in green. 'I passed!'

'That's not all,' Melrose says.

'I really can't believe this.' Hex is shaking his head.

'What?' I focus back on the screen. *Placement: Think Tank.* 'What does that mean?'

'You don't know? It's like the top-notch best possible amazeballs with awesome sauce PareCo ultimate: off solving the problems of the world on some tropical island or something. Awesome benefits, pay, the works. I don't get how you got it.'

'Gee, thanks. But neither do I.'

'Will you be together?' Melrose finally registers that we're going away, and she isn't. 'Where is it?'

Hex does something weird with his hands, and calls up an information screen. He reads it out: 'Think Tank placements – report for transport to Heathrow in seven days' time to begin journey to Inaccessible Island. Prepare for an extended time away. Clothes and essentials will be provided.'

'Is there seriously a place called Inaccessible Island?' I say. 'Where is it?'

More hand waving, and a world map appears around us. A pulsing light marks an island in the *middle of nowhere*.

'It's like fifteen hundred miles from the coast of South Africa,' Hex says. 'Other than a few uninhabited islands, nothing else is closer.'

'Why so isolated?' I ask. 'What is PareCo hiding away there?'

'Don't be a dys.' Hex scans info tracks on Inaccessible Island, then looks up. 'It's because it's a world heritage site, so it's neutral. Not part of any country, so none have control or influence over PareCo.'

'Just fifteen hundred miles from SA, is that all? So I can come and visit on weekends, then.' Melrose's eyes are filling up.

I stand up. 'Three's a crowd; I'm going. Bye.' I'm not sure they even notice, doing the girl crying/boy comforting thing, murmuring that they can always meet in Realtime. I back out of Melrose's space and go through the door. It shuts behind me and I stand in my hallway, stunned.

Did Rafferty pull off my needed miracle, and somehow

get them to accept my reason for breaking the rules with the RQ test? Was it my high IQ result that got me this placement? What on earth is a Think Tank?

Distracted, I pace up and down my hallway. Absently hit 'no' to an Astra Remembered club as I pass a pulsing invitation; a door disappears. I lean on the wall.

A flicker above catches my eye. I look up. A silver line is moving across the ceiling; it becomes a square. The square solidifies into something that swings down, leaving an opening to a space above. A ladder drops through it.

What the hell?

I'm peering into the shadows above when feet appear, and someone starts climbing down the ladder. I jump back.

'Gecko?'

'Luna!' He grins and reaches to give me a hug, but I pull back, startled, freaked out and a little annoyed.

'How'd you do that?'

'The hatch and ladder? S'hacking one-oh-one.'

'Shacking?'

'Sorry: silver hacking. Easier to say as *S'hacking*. Just like silver Hackers are S'hackers.'

'But how can you get into my hall without an invitation from me? It's against all the rules of Realtime.'

'But I sent you one.' He grins, and gestures at the wall where I'd nixed the Astra group invite moments ago.

'That was you?'

'Yep. I didn't expect you to accept it, though it would have made things easier; I just used it to trace where you were when you rejected it.'

'Sure. I see.' So Gecko is in Astra Remembered: he really *is* a weird fan clubber like I suspected, isn't he? But some part of me has still gone warm at all this effort just to see me. I smile.

'Aren't you surprised to see me here?' I say. 'You know, given that I'm a Refuser and all.'

He grins back. 'You tried the ANDs, right? I traced that you were plugged in last night, but couldn't get a fix on location.'

'So, now that you've tracked me down…?'

'It's time for an adventure.'

'An adventure?'

'This way,' he says, and starts climbing back up the ladder. He looks back when I don't follow. 'Come on: escape with me for a while.'

Sounds good to me.

17

At the top of the ladder is darkness and nothing, and lots of both.

'What is this place?' I ask as I step from the ladder, and stare around me. Not complete darkness, after all: as my eyes adjust, pinpoints of light whistle past in all directions, adding to the sense of vastness of the space where we stand. My hair whips around, first one way, then another, as we're buffeted by strange winds, without pattern – up, down, from one side, then another.

'This is the virtual void. It is what all virtual spaces and worlds are made from.'

The darkness intensifies, and I spin round: the hatch and ladder are gone.

'Whoa. How do we get back down from here?'

'Don't worry. I can make another exit when you need it.'

There is a vague sense of rising panic inside mixed with excitement, and I involuntarily step closer to Gecko. He grins. Takes my hand. 'Stay close,' he says.

'Why?' I say, and peer all around for danger.

'The void is a big place. If you get lost, I could look for you forever and never find you.'

'Getting lost sounds like an adventure, but one I could do without.'

He laughs. 'Exactly. We've got more interesting things to

do. Come on.' He tugs on my hand, and we start walking into the void.

I'm holding my hair with my free hand to keep it out of my eyes. Gecko notices, stops. Gathers my hair in his hands behind my head, lets go. It stays there. I touch the back of my head: it's in a ponytail, a clasp around it.

'Neat trick,' I say, and we continue on. 'Where are we going?'

'It's a surprise. A new world I've come across recently.'

'How do you know the way?'

'It's one of my S'hacker things. I think about where I want to go, and see?' He points ahead; some of the pinpoints of light are not so random. They're forming a series of shadowy arrows.

'How do you do that? Is it like how Hex can make furniture and stuff in Realtime?'

'Hackers are different. They work in existing virtual worlds, and play with the world's code; they're all very logical and scientific. With S'hackers it is more like magic.'

'Sure. If you don't understand it well enough to explain it to me, fine.'

He laughs. 'I do, it's just not something we talk about it with outsiders. It's hard to find words that will make sense. But I'll try. It is logical and scientific too, but at a deeper instinctive level, so I'm not thinking code in my head even if that's what I'm doing. It's more like...well, how do you walk? Do you think about raising one foot, shifting your weight to step forward, keeping your balance, all that stuff?

142

It's more like that. I just kind of do it now, without consciously thinking of all that's involved.'

'When you were learning did you fall over all the time like when you were learning to walk?'

He laughs again; it's a good sound – it is so silent here that it seems to fill my mind. 'Very much so. I was dangerous. I made stuff accidentally sometimes from my nightmares, too – like snakes. I really hate snakes.'

'Not any more though, right? As far as being dangerous goes. I mean, you know what you're doing.'

'Most of the time. Ah, here we are!' He stops, and faint silver lines appear in front of us. They move across empty space to outline a rectangle, then silver spreads inside the lines to become a door.

He reaches for the door handle. 'Ready?'

'For what?'

He raises both eyebrows, says nothing. Holds the door open. I peer through. Bright sunlight. A lush green space: a high waterfall surrounded by tropical-looking plants. A gleaming turquoise pool under the waterfall.

'Any snakes?'

'No. I promise,' he says. I step through, Gecko close behind me. Like at the beach party that wasn't, there's an instant wardrobe change: a bikini? The pool beckons, and it's *hot*.

But this suit is *way* too skimpy to swim in without risk of swimming out of it, and Gecko is grinning at me in it in a way that says he knows it, standing there safe in his respectable swim shorts.

'Why don't you cool off a bit,' I say, and give him a push; he splashes into the pool, and starts swimming across to the waterfall. I wish my suit was more like the one-piece I had at the school beach party, and suddenly, it is.

I dive in after him, and follow him to the other side.

'Check this out,' he says, and pulls himself out of the pool. He climbs steps along the side of the waterfall to the top, waves, and dives: straight through the centre of the waterfall.

My stomach lurches as he hurtles down. But he slows as he nears the bottom of the waterfall, then leisurely splashes into the pool. 'It's anti-grav,' he says. 'Pretty much impossible to hurt yourself here, anyhow. It's good fun: try it.'

I go up the stone steps, stand at the top of the waterfall. Hesitate. It is *so* high: what – ten metres? Rocks to the sides, at the bottom. They *look* hurty. But this is virtual. Even if the anti-grav fails, I'll be all right. Won't I?

'Go on. It's a blast,' Gecko calls up.

I step off the rock above the waterfall into the water. It swirls all around me as I plummet down, in a rush of fear and adrenaline – then slows as I near the pool, splash gently into it. I swim across to the steps: I'm doing that again. Soon I'm jumping as high as I can, and diving into the waterfall; Gecko is doing somersaults.

'Were we gymnasts in another life?' I ask him when we pause for a rest.

'Taking fear away makes you go for it. But the world enhances your coordination and motor skills; it's part of it.'

144

'Damn. I thought it was me.' I laugh. 'This is seriously the most fun, ever. What is this place exactly?'

'It's like a holiday camp for the rich and famous. This is just one room; there's deep sea diving, skiing, mountain climbing, everything you could think of, and all in infinite multiples so we can be on our own whichever we choose. Or, if you'd rather company, there are themed parties going on all the time.'

'One problem with that. Last I checked we're neither rich, nor famous. Why'd they let us in?'

'Well. Most people buy a door in their Realtime hallway. We came in the back way; they don't exactly know we're here.'

My mouth hangs open. 'We're *trespassing*?'

'I didn't see any Keep Out signs. Did you?'

'Well, no, but—'

'Trust me. No one knows we're here. Besides – they like S'hackers. We're cheaper than PareCo if they want enhancements. Want to try skiing next? You're guaranteed to be good at it here.'

I'm yawning, suddenly aware of the passage of time. 'No, I don't think so.' And I'm tired; properly tired, to the bone. My body back in the PIP is aching as if it has been along for all the diving and swimming.

'Are you nervous about getting arrested or something? I promise: we're good.'

'No. It's not that. I just – I need to get back.'

'OK. No problem,' he says, disappointment lurking in his

eyes, and I want to tell him *why*, but I can't, can I? He'll think I'm a freak.

He climbs out of the pool, turns and offers me a hand. I take it, climb out. His eyes are dark, staring at me. I stand next to him, mouth suddenly dry. 'What? Bad hair day, is that it?' I say, and wring it out in my hands.

'Your hair is fine. But wish it dry if you want to.'

'Really? I can do that here?'

'Give it a try.'

I wish for dry hair, and not just dry but loose about my shoulders, gorgeously styled and wavy and soft, as if I'd just spent hours at a hairdresser I could never afford.

And...it is.

He reaches out a hand, touches it. 'Nice,' he says, something serious and undefined in his eyes.

'I could get used to this place. Maybe I should become rich and famous?'

'Or maybe there is another way?' He smiles as silver appears in the air in front of us, gradually solidifies, forms a door. We step through it into the void.

I'm back in my own clothes. It's neither hot or cold in the void, but after the heat of the waterfall world I *feel* cold, goose bumps on my arms.

We walk silently. My hair is still loose but so soft I don't mind it moving around my face in the strange winds of the void.

He stops. 'Here we are,' he says, and a silver square forms near our feet. When it is solid he pulls it open, and a silver ladder drops down. I turn back to Gecko.

'Thanks for the adventure,' I say, feeling suddenly shy. 'It's been fun.'

'Before you go, I need your help with something,' he says.

'What's that?'

'I need to find Jezzamine Taylor from your school. For some reason her space is blocked. I've tried some invites to trace her, but she hasn't responded.'

The warm feeling left from our adventure disappears. Jezzamine is – *was* – one of the most gorgeous girls in our school, no question. But, still: I somehow didn't expect this of Gecko. Not any time, but especially not after today. Does he want to take her to the waterfall, too?

'I can't help you there,' I say. I start down the ladder, and Gecko follows me into my hallway. I reach out back in my PIP, ready to unplug to get away.

'It's important,' he says, and his voice is *so* earnest. He must have it bad.

I sigh and turn back, leaving the PIP connection alone.

'I'm really sorry to have to tell you this, Gecko. Jezzamine died in a car accident a few days ago.'

'What? How? Tell me how it happened.' His eyes are wide with shock.

'This is what I heard. She was driving on her own. She'd only just got her electric licence, but for some reason she turned off the motorway automatic system, lost control, and crashed into a barrier. Paramedics couldn't save her; she was too badly injured.'

147

He leans against the wall as if his legs can't support him any longer. 'It's even worse than we thought,' he says, as if to himself.

'What is? Than who thought?'

'I've got to go.' He grips my shoulders, hard, and stares at me. His eyes are weird and fierce. 'Take care, Luna.'

He lets go, climbs the ladder in a flash, and then both he and it are gone: the ladder, the hatch, the outline, all vanished. Smooth ceiling restored.

I look up, wave. 'I'm fine, thanks for asking. And I found out I passed the RQ today.' I walk away, and look back before I unplug. 'And I'm going away to Inaccessible Island. Nice knowing you.'

I sit up in my dark room, stretch. My hair: it still feels lovely, bouncy, soft. It even *smells* good. I'm bemused: how can a virtual hairstyle still be with me? Gecko must have done it for me. But good hair isn't enough to cheer me up now.

I stand, feel the way to the light switch. Put it on, turn.

Jump out of my skin.

'Nanna?'

She's sitting on my bed. Staring. Eyes wide and scared. She looks at the PIP; back to me. Shakes her head. 'Danger, Luna. Danger,' she whispers.

18

'I'm not going. That's it.'

Dad rubs his eyes, still bleary from the emergency unplug Sally has subjected him to.

'You. Talk sense into your daughter!' Sally says, and leaves the room, slams the door.

'Well. She's kind of annoyed,' Dad says.

'Ha! Nothing unusual there.'

'Congratulations on passing the Test.'

'Thanks.'

'And I hear you've got this amazing offer from PareCo: a Think Tank placement, with all the bells and whistles?'

'Yeah.'

'Why don't you want to go? And tell me the *real* reason.'

I stare back at him. I could manufacture a list again like I did for Sally, searching for a reason she'd accept, but no. I sigh, sit down next to him. He puts an arm over my shoulders. 'What is it, Loony-Tunes?'

'I don't want to leave Nanna.'

'Ah. I see.'

'Even when I was only away for days for the Test, she was worse.'

'And she took a turn last night, didn't she?'

I nod. After I'd unplugged and found her in my room, she just collapsed. I had to wake Sally to help me get her back to her room. It was my fault, Sally had hissed, for not keeping Nanna's room locked.

'As soon as I'm gone, Sally will have her taken away. I know she will.'

'I won't let her. I promise.'

I believe he means it. I also believe Sally would wear him down, baffle him with false sympathy, with how it would be better for Nanna, and somehow get him to go along with what she wants. There is precedent. And who's to say that with me gone she really wouldn't be better off somewhere else?

I shake my head. 'That's not the only thing. It says I'll be gone for *an extended time*, whatever that means. Thousands of miles away. What if something happens to her or you or Jason, and I'm not here?'

'That'd really suck,' he says. 'But you can't stop stuff happening sometimes, even to people you love. Whether you're there or not. ' A shadow of pain crosses his eyes. 'But you don't have to go. It's your choice.'

'It is? Not according to Sally.'

'Don't worry about Sally; I can handle her,' he says, but his voice lacks conviction. 'Anyhow, they can't take you away to—' and he unfocuses a moment, comes back again '—Inaccessible Island, unless I sign some endless consent form. It just pinged in a while ago.'

'But what do I do if I stay?' Despite wanting – *needing* – to stay, visions of Goodwin finding me a suitable-in-her-opinion work placement gives me spine spiders: shivers from an army of invisible little feet.

'Let's see if we can get you swapped to university in London. That you got a Think Tank placement shows you passed their flipping tests with flying colours, right? They've got to want you at the university, too.'

'Really: do you think that will work?'

He shrugs. 'I don't know. But I'll try.'

His eyes unfocus, then come back again. 'There. I've just sent a refusal to sign the form, and requested a transfer. Let's see what they make of that.'

'Thanks, Dad.'

'Now let's go and visit your nanna. Don't forget she's my mum; I care about her, too.'

I don't forget it. I just know you're almost never here, and the harder it is to be with her, the less you will be. But out loud all I say is, *yes.*

Sally corners me later, after Dad is back in fantasyland. 'How could you be so selfish?'

'Excuse me?'

'Have you noticed lately that the house is falling down around our ears? That expenses keep going up and income down? It's getting harder and harder for your dad to find paying clients that need games guides: kids start with Implants so young they've got it all figured out before they've got a good allowance. And did it occur to you that university here will *cost*? By the time Jason is that age there'll be no chance he can go. You could help your family for once, Luna. The

151

signing fee alone would get us out of trouble. Would pay for your nanna's care – get her in somewhere they can do everything for her, not a state institution where she'll be headed no matter what we want if her doctor decides to commit her.'

'Signing fee? What are you talking about?'

'Didn't your dad tell you? When he signs the consent forms, PareCo pays your family a signing fee. And after that, a regular stipend. Think about it, Luna.'

I stare back at her, the reason she was so freaked I didn't want to go finally clear. She'd spent hours going on about this great opportunity, my future, the only chance I might ever have to make something of myself. But the whole time she wanted to sell me.

'Someone is here to see you, Luna,' Sally calls up the next afternoon. The first words she has spoken to me since Dad took my side.

Downstairs, on the sofa in our front room? Dr Rafferty.

My mouth hangs open. 'Uh, hi,' I manage to say.

'Hi, Luna, nice to see you.'

Sally hovers by the door. 'Can I get you anything?' Curiosity all over her face.

'Tea would be nice,' he says, and she goes to the kitchen. No doubt she will make it in record time.

He smiles, gestures at a chair, and I sit in it. 'So, you're probably wondering why I'm here.'

'You could say that.'

'I went to considerable trouble to convince PareCo that you should pass the RQ. That it was rational to consider the welfare of others when you took part in disrupting that phase of the testing.'

'Uh…thanks. I guess.'

He raises an eyebrow. 'But it looks like it might have been in vain. I understand that your father has refused consent to your PareCo placement, and requested a university transfer. Transfers can only be approved with an assessment by HealthCo, which is why I was notified. So why did your father refuse consent?'

'I asked him to.'

'Oh. I see. I was wondering if a court order to circumvent parental consent might be helpful. But they won't grant it if you are saying no also.' He shakes his head. 'Why, Luna?'

Sally brings in a tray of tea. 'Sorry, I couldn't help but overhear,' she says, smiling sweetly. 'I'm afraid Luna's… *compassion* for others is the cause.' The glance she gives me is exuding warmth and concern, very unlike the way she's looked at me lately. I'm glaring daggers at her, but she ignores me. 'Luna doesn't want to leave her poorly grandmother. She's not expected to last the winter, poor dear.'

I stare at Sally. No one has told me this, and despite myself, tears are welling up in my eyes. I blink furiously.

Dr Rafferty clucks. 'Oh dear. That is hard. I can understand why you don't want to go away right now.'

'Thank you.'

'Look, I'll recommend that you get a transfer to London

153

University on compassionate grounds. Given your test results, I'll recommend a scholarship.'

'You can do that?' I can feel my smile returning. If I can get a scholarship, even Sally should be happy. Ish.

'Oh yes. PareCo can't overrule any decisions we make based on student welfare.' He unfocuses, comes back a few moments later. Smiles. 'I've said your continued good health requires a placement you can reach from home, and recommended that you be considered for a scholarship to London University. They will likely make it contingent on you taking the original placement if circumstances change. All agreed?'

'Of course! Thank you.'

'One sec.' He's gone again. 'I've filled your dad in, and sent him the revised consents to sign. And…he's signed them. All done. All sorted.'

After he's gone, Sally gives me a weird look. 'You're looking pleased with yourself. You think you've got what you wanted?'

'I guess.'

'I really hope so,' she says. 'I really hope it works out for you, Luna.'

Her words *feel* sincere, and a worried frown lurks between her eyes. I'm filled with disquiet.

19

Late that night, I take a few ANDs, plug in and knock on Melrose's door. This time I wait for her to call out *come in* before stepping into her virtual space, to make sure I'm not going to interrupt anything.

But she's alone. 'Heh,' she says.

'Heh. Guess what?'

'What?'

'I'm not going away; I'm getting a transfer to London University!'

'Totally BB,' she says, but her reaction is muted.

'What is it? Is something wrong?'

She sighs, crosses her arms. 'Hex told me placements can't be changed, that he has no choice but to go where they've told him to go.'

'I don't think you usually can. It's like a health exemption, because I don't want to go because of Nanna being ill.' I explain to her what happened with Rafferty, but I'm not sure she believes me – or more, believes Hex.

'I've gotta go,' I say finally.

'Why?' She's surprised. 'Stay. Hex *should* be here any minute; we're going to Jezzamine's wake. Come with us! It'll probably go all night.'

I can't. My body is yawning in the PIP – I need some sleep. I make apologies, back out into my Realtime hallway.

I'm about to unplug when a door pops up on the wall in front of me. An invitation on it to Astra Remembered. Again? There is a rush at the thought of seeing Gecko, and pain at the memory of last time, when after everything all he wanted was Jezzamine. I sigh.

Choices: accept it, and go through the door. See if Gecko is in there. Run the risk of other Astra stalker weirdos clocking me. Or reject it. See if Gecko drops out of the ceiling like the last time. Or the final choice, last of all: ignore it, and walk away.

I'm pretty sure I *should* just walk away, but my hand seems to raise of its own accord, hesitates, then hits *reject*.

Silver lines form a hatch above me almost at once; it solidifies, opens. A ladder drops down.

Seconds pass: no Gecko.

I peer upwards; the space through the hatch is dark.

'Gecko?' I call out. No answer.

Going up there on my own might not be the smartest thing to do, but my feet start up the ladder.

I peer through the hatch at the top, still on the ladder. As before, it is dark, and winds whistle past strangely, in bursts and starts. As my eyes adapt I see faint lights streaking around me, crackling, almost like static.

'Gecko?' I say, tentatively, but my voice seems ripped away by the wind so I hardly hear it myself.

There is a faint trace of silver leading from the hatch that suddenly moves, changes into words: *This way, Luna*, and then forms an arrow.

I climb the rest of the way through the hatch and step off the ladder with one foot, tentative as the floor looks more like nothingness than a solid thing. But it feels firm enough, and I step forward with the other foot, off the ladder.

I sense rather than see movement, and turn back just in time to see the hatch and ladder vanish.

There is fear clutching at my insides, saying I could get lost and be trapped up here forever. But it is pushed down by excitement.

The arrow at my feet pulses a little brighter and I start towards it. It keeps pace with me, just in front all the while, and focusing on it helps me not freak out in the huge dimensionlessness of this place. The static lights snap around me still; the wind is at times gentle and almost seems to caress my skin; other times it is fierce, like a slap, whipping my hair around. I wish I'd tied it up and then, all at once, it is: pulled back in a ponytail. Then the arrow stops, and a faint silver line appears in the blackness before me, stretches out to form a large rectangle. Solidifies into a door.

I reach to open it. Inside there is dim light from silver-etched walls; after the darkness outside, it seems overly bright. I blink and step through.

'You came!' Gecko grips tight to my hand, warm and solid. And the weirdness of the walls fades away; the room seems to solidify more with him in it, with his dark eyes staring at mine.

'Hard to resist an invitation like that: what girl doesn't like to climb a ladder into all that weirdness?'

'Sorry about that; the void can be unsettling if you're not used to it. I would have come myself, but there are tracers looking for me everywhere. It's a bit needle-haystack, but just in case they pin my location, I didn't want to lead them to you.'

'What's going on?'

'Come.' He pulls me to a bench against the wall, and we sit down. 'This may be a shock, but I had to warn you.'

'About what?'

'Jezzamine's death wasn't an accident.'

'What?'

'She didn't turn off the automatic system; it was tampered with.'

I stare at him, shocked. 'Who'd want to kill Jezzamine? She wasn't the warmest person in the world, but… No, wait. That can't be true. I haven't heard anything. Everybody would know if it was being investigated.'

'It's not being investigated.'

'I don't understand.'

'Officially, it was an accident. The original report was suppressed and altered.'

'How would you know this?'

'I have…ways. Of tracing records.'

'But why'd you say you had to warn *me*?'

'Think about it. Jezzamine, the one who could see the Implant images weren't real, dies in an accident. You knew they weren't real, too.'

'But what about Danny?'

'Who?'

'The boy next to me when you thought I was shot. He could tell the images weren't real, too. Like Jezzamine.'

'Do you know what school he went to?'

'I'm not sure.' I frown, concentrating. 'He was in white at the party – I think he was. But this is crazy. Why would they be targeted? Who by? I don't get it.'

'I haven't figured it out yet, but I'm going to. Be careful, Luna.'

'Why? It's different for me. I haven't got an Implant, so I couldn't see the images at all.'

'But you *know*. Knowledge can be dangerous.' He takes my hand. 'I also wanted to say goodbye.'

'Goodbye? What do you mean?'

'I'm in hiding. Not just here,' he says, and gestures at the virtual space. 'But my body as well: I'm going away, far away. *Nobody* is going to hold me against my will, ever again.' His words and eyes are fierce, and I remember what he said on the dark balcony at the test centre: that the one thing he wants, more than anything, is freedom.

'You don't just mean when we were trapped at the test centre, do you?'

He doesn't answer at first, then shakes his head. 'I'm a bit messed up. Sure you want to know?'

'Only if you want to tell me. We all have our secrets.'

'Mine is ancient history.' He shrugs, as if that means it shouldn't be important. 'My parents were both S'hackers, as was my grandfather. But he refused it; he was convinced it was evil, and that if he stole me from them and kept me under lock and key, he could knock the evil out of me. He tried, I'll give him that.'

I look at him in horror – the boy he was still lurks in the pain in his eyes, then hides away.

'My parents had disappeared by the time I escaped years later. I was thirteen.'

'They *disappeared*?'

'Another long story,' he says, and shutters are closing in his eyes. One he doesn't want to tell.

'So you were locked up all those years: that's why you said freedom was your one thing.'

'Exactly. And that's why I have to say goodbye. There's no way I'm going to PareCo's Think Tank. I'm going away where they'll never find me.'

'You got that placement, too?'

He holds still. 'Tell me you're not assigned to the Think Tank.'

'I was, but I got a transfer.' And I explain all that happened.

His eyes are anxious, worried. 'I'm concerned about you, Luna. You mustn't go to PareCo.'

'I'm not, as I've just told you. But *why*? Hex is excited beyond belief; it's meant to be the greatest thing ever, if you believe him. Or Sally. What's wrong with it?'

'I don't know exactly. It just is. Wrong. People who go there don't come back.'

'Well, maybe that is because it's so brilliant they never want to leave. You'd have to do better than that to put me off if I wanted to go. But I'm not going, anyhow.'

'I'd be surprised if it was that easy to get out of.'

'It's been agreed. I'm staying put.'

He still looks worried.

'What is this place, anyway?' I look around me. Shifting, pulsing lights define the walls of a small square room. The bench we are sitting on feels solid, but again its dark shape is defined by pulsing silver.

He grins. 'It's my S'hack; I made it. It's kind of like my panic room.'

'Panic room?'

'You know, like rich people have to hide out in if someone breaks into their house.'

I look around. 'Not sure about your choice of décor. And the furnishings are a bit minimalistic. This bench is positively uncomfortable.'

'Sorry, I don't entertain much.' He grins again, and suddenly the bench is soft, yielding. I stroke it with my hands: like warm velvet.

I tilt my head back, stare into his eyes. He smiles, shakes his head. 'I'm trying to say goodbye, not hello. You should probably go.'

'Sure. Just as I was getting comfortable.'

'I'll send a silver arrow to guide you back, and make another hatch above your Realtime hallway.'

Back in my bedroom I sneeze, and automatically raise my hand to my nose in this virtual place, even though no sneeze happened here. Gecko looks at me strangely. I'd been so distracted by all this that I'd almost stopped noticing my double existence.

'How about I go the easy way, instead?'

'What do you mean?'

'I'll just unplug.'

He shakes his head. 'You can't do that when you're in the void. You lose that connection here.'

'Really? What if I'd stopped following your arrow, and got lost?'

'That'd be bad. If you stare into the void too long you can lose your way. Lose yourself, and be lost from your body forever. Until your body dies, of course. A long time if it is on life support.'

The spine spiders are back. That could be a long time to wander, alone, in nothing. 'Thanks for the warning!'

'I figured you could handle it.'

I stare back at him, not sure whether to be angry at the risk he thought I took, or flattered that he figured it wasn't a problem for me. Anyhow, he's wrong. I still have the double awareness I always have when plugged in. I can unplug to leave here whenever I want.

But I won't say goodbye. For reasons I'm not sure I want to look at too closely, I don't want to. I can't. 'See you later, Gecko,' I say, instead. I reach to unplug back in my room. I pause, uncertain, stare back at him. His eyes kind of hold mine, and it is hard to breathe. I do it: pull out of the neural net, just as he leans forward, brushes my cheek with his lips. He vanishes, but not before I see the startled look on his face.

I sit up in my bedroom.

All that happened – what he said, what I said – runs through my mind, and I'm left with one inescapable conclusion: I'm completely *mental*. Starting with rejecting that invitation when I thought it would make him appear, then going up that ladder when he didn't.

And the virtual void? It should have been terrifying, but somehow, it wasn't. It was more freaky, exciting. Of course I didn't know *then* that if people lose their way, they could be stuck there, wandering in the vast darkness until their bodies die. Not that the usual rules seem to apply to me: I can still unplug when I want to from the void. I shake my head.

And, messed up by his own admission, does Gecko really think somebody *killed* Jezzamine, just because she could tell the Implant images weren't real? Maybe all the horrible things that happened to him as a child colour how he sees the world. And now he's hiding out so PareCo won't take him to their Think Tank? When I was there, his eyes holding mine, it all seemed real. But now?

My cheek tingles, and I only half felt it – his lips brushing across my skin as I unplugged.

I shake my head, finally get into bed. My hair is still tied back, and I reach behind, pull at it. A silver clasp comes away in my hand. Did Gecko make it for me when my hair was whipping around in the void? I frown. Then how is it here, back in the real world? If it was virtual, it should vanish as soon as I leave that place.

This is all completely, totally, crazy.

I'm warm, happy, safe. I wriggle against Mummy's shoulder, her long hair a blanket around me as she adjusts me higher on her hip, and climbs the ladder.

Through the hatch little lights dance around us, friendly whispers against the darkness. They swirl around Mummy in a silvery blur as she lowers me down, her hair whipping about her in the wind that goes every which way at once. She gestures impatiently and it is tied back like mine.

'Playtime, Luna?' she says, and laughs. She spreads her arms wide, and gathers silver sparkles together; she throws them at me, and I catch the ball of light in my hands.

'What will it be today, little love?' she asks, mischief in her eyes.

I laugh and throw it above us, turn the blackness into a night sky of stars. The full moon is so huge and close I could reach and touch it, and I do: jump into the sky and sit on the warm white disc. I pull it bigger and Mummy jumps up to sit next to me.

She wraps her arms tight around me. 'You're so special, Luna. Only you can do what you can do. That's why I made you.'

I pull away from the cuddle so I can look at her eyes. They are bright in the darkness, pale grey shot with silver, and silver dances all around her eye in her skin. That is why I made her the stars.

Rat-a-tat-tat.

'Luna?' A voice is calling, and I stir, groggy, not wanting

to leave the dream. Of Astra and me. We were in the virtual void? Did being there today bring on the dream – did we really go there together, or is it a trick of my imagination? And me, making the moon and the stars: *that* I definitely made up.

'Luna?' It's Sally. She's opened the door now, and the hall light floods my room. Her face is white.

I sit up in a rush. 'What is it?'

'I'm so sorry, Luna.' And her face and her voice *are* sorry, genuinely so, and there is no one else here to make a performance worthwhile.

'What? What's happened?'

'It's your nanna. She…' Her voice trails away, and she shakes her head.

Then I'm up and running down the hall; the door to Nanna's room is open. The doctor is there, but he's standing back, and Dad is there, too, and he's holding her hand. Nanna's hand.

'What's happened?'

Sally follows in behind. She puts an arm over my shoulders, and for once I don't pull away. 'She died in her sleep. The medic alarm woke me and brought the doctor, and I got your dad. He wanted a moment before we woke you.'

No. It can't be. Can it? And I'm next to Dad, next to Nanna. Her face is calm, peaceful. Her eyes are closed.

'She's just asleep, isn't she? Dad?'

He shakes his head.

20

There is a blur of days that lead to this one. People are talking, saying nice things. Not many people, though. Not many watch as the coffin goes into the back of the crematorium; friends she had years ago have long deserted. I'm touched that Melrose is here, her father also. This couldn't do him any good if anyone notices.

After, Sally steers us away, back home. For once I appreciate how good she is at organising us. That she's somehow even bossed Dad into staying in reality for so long.

Rachel from school visits, and I'm surprised: REs don't get out much. And then I think about it some more, and I'm not surprised. People dying is kind of her thing – trying to make you feel there is a reason for it, or to make you feel better. It isn't working, exactly, but it's nice that she tries.

Religious beliefs are irrational by definition: not subject to proof. Freedom of religion is protected by NUN, but Religious Exemptions like Rachel are marginalised, their lives limited so they can't infect others with their views, with the conflict and wars that always follow when religion dominates society. These are all things we've been taught, but sometimes it feels like Rachel has a secret, one I'd like to share. If it made this feel any better, it'd be worth it.

Something inside *yearns*. For what? For infinity: for things that go on and on, forever.

*

Late that night, I pull my hair up in the silver clip from the void. While I plug in I *hope, hope, hope* that the hatch will be there, that I can climb up.

In my hallway there is no invitation from Astra Remembered this time, but I look up, and *there*: silver is reaching across. It doesn't start with an outline like before, more a stream of silver that rushes across to form a hatch. It opens, and a ladder drops down. I climb up, and step into nothingness.

There is no silver message from Gecko like before. The hatch vanishes, and I'm alone in the dark emptiness of the void. The twinkling blur of static lights rushes past in all directions; the strange wind is as before – at times fierce, at times gentle, changing direction. I lie down and stare upwards.

Rachel said she'd pray for Nanna's soul. That life is fleeting, but her soul is forever. I sigh. I see life more as one of these bright lights, shooting in a brief flare across infinite space and darkness.

Rachel also said I should remember Nanna as she was, not the way her illness changed her. But it's hard. For a long time she's not been the woman who was everything to me – mother, father, friend – after Astra died. Dad was even more useless then than he is now. Astra's death really derailed him to the point I'm not sure he even knew I existed. Nanna's illness seemed to come so gradually, so bit by bit that it crept up on me without my noticing, until suddenly it was a giant, overwhelming thing. So when did it start, really? Were all her warnings to me about not letting anyone know how I was different, not getting an Implant, not telling anyone how plugging in made me sick – did that start before she was ill, or was it part of the delusions that came after? And how about her obsession with numbers – was that part of her illness, too?

And here I am. Plugged in, not sick. A few ANDs was all it would have taken to make me like everybody else. All the things I missed with friends, school. She was terrified about me taking the Test, but I did fine – nothing bad happened from taking it, did it?

But one thing I *do* know: even if it was part of her delusions, she always loved me. Whatever she did, she did because she thought she was keeping me safe, that she was protecting me. Even if the monsters were all in her mind, to her, they were real.

A particularly bright light rushes towards me. Without thinking I reach up, grab it in my hands. I cup them around it: it pulses silver inside. *Goodbye, Nanna*, I whisper, and throw it into the sky. It turns into a star. A falling star that streaks across the sky, then is gone.

Spine spiders creep across my back. Did I really just do *that*?

I've barely thought of that dream with my mother, with everything that followed when I woke from it. Is that what *really* drew me out here now? I close my eyes and try to put myself *back, back*. Into that feeling of joy, warmth, security. And playfulness, too. The lights: she gathered them together into her arms, threw them at me. When I released them they became what I wanted, like the star I just threw into the void.

I stand up. Feeling foolish, I hold my arms out wide like Astra did, and try to scoop the lights towards me. It doesn't work.

I try to grab just one light in my hands like I did before. But now that I'm thinking about it, it isn't working. Overactive imagination, that's what I have. I probably drifted off and dreamed the whole thing.

The vast darkness and the lights whistling past are starting to creep me out. Time to unplug? But although I don't really want to go back, I don't want to be alone, either.

Where is Gecko? He said goodbye; is he really gone? He can't be; he must have put the hatch and ladder there so I could get into the void. I wish for him, and as if he is reading my mind, a silver arrow appears at my feet.

I smile, follow along until it stops. A sheet of silver rushes across and solidifies, forming a door. I open it, and step through.

The square room is like the last time – darkness defined by silver pulses of light. But it is empty. No Gecko. I bite my lip in disappointment. Why'd he bring me here if he isn't here himself? I've barely formed the thought when he appears next to me.

His eyes are wide in shock. 'Luna? How'd you get here?'

'I followed the arrow. Same as last time.'

'What?' He shakes his head. 'I don't understand. Though I *was* thinking of you. Did I lay a trace without doing it on purpose?' He shakes his head. 'If I did, I'm more addled than I thought. And how did you leave the last time you were here?'

'No biggie. I just unplugged.'

'That should be impossible. How'd you even still have connection to your body through the void?'

I shrug, uncomfortable. 'I don't know. I just *do*,' I say, and then my mind skips back to what he said before. 'Addled? What's wrong?'

'They found me.'

'Who did?'

'PareCo, of course. They've got me in a locked house prior to transport to Inaccessible Island. I can't get out.'

'What? But that's illegal.'

He laughs: not a happy sound. 'What planet do you live on? Don't answer that. As you're here, I've got something to tell you. It's important.'

'I'm listening.'

'I found Danny.'

'So he's OK, then.'

'No. He's not. He died of STDS – Sudden Teenage Death Syndrome.'

'*What*? Seriously?' I stare at him in shock.

'I'm afraid so. Somehow they must have worked out he could see through the Implant simulation.'

'Wait a minute. You must be wrong. A girl died of STDS at my school last year: they only call it that when somebody spontaneously dies when they're plugged in, and they don't know why. So there is no discernible cause of death.'

He raises an eyebrow. 'Usually. But this is PareCo we're talking about. They could fake it. But that's not all.'

I turn away, afraid to hear any more.

'I looked into Jezzamine and Danny to see if they had anything in common, anything I could have missed. Hacked into shopping records, and there it was: both of them regularly bought ANDs.'

Danny I didn't know well, but *Jezzamine*? She was a girl who did not like to be different; at least, not like that. She'd have hidden that secret to the grave. A sense of disquiet prickles inside: *she did*.

I shake my head. 'But what has that got to with anything?'

'I don't know. It must be something about needing ANDs to plug in that affects how you perceive things with your Implant, and whether they can plant blocks to stop you from talking about it. Haven't worked out what it is yet.'

'But I haven't got an Implant.'

'Don't get one, Luna. If you do – don't let anyone know you use ANDs. Have you bought them on credit?'

'No. Cash only, but—'

'Just buy them from different places, different times – don't establish a pattern, right? Then hope they don't find out.'

'Who is this *they*? Why does it matter?'

'Luna, listen to me. Your life could be in danger.'

I fight the tears, and the fear. Nanna, Jezzamine and Danny: three deaths in such a short time. Nanna whispers in my mind: *Three are the triangles: mind, body, soul; past, present, future*. But none of them has a future. Not any more.

I'm shaking my head, pulling away from his warm hand on my arm. I don't want to hear what he is saying; I don't want to even be here. A whole long list of *too much to handle* is crashing in on me.

And I run. Straight through the silver-etched wall of his room – it parts to let me through and out into the void. I hear a few shouts behind but they fade and vanish.

I run blindly. What is it with me? First Nanna has delusions; now Gecko? Maybe I really do bring out the crazy in people. He can't be right; *he can't be*. And he said that they found him, that they locked him up to force him to take that placement, but *why* would they do that? What would be the point of an uncooperative employee, anyhow?

I'm running so fast there is a streak of light around me – my legs, my arms – a silver blur.

Why am I running? There's an easier way out of here. I stop. The silver lights are still all around me, almost like they are clinging to my skin. Now *I'm* the crazy one. I breathe in and out, try to calm the panic. Back in my bedroom I reach to unplug, and slip out of the neural net.

I sit up in the PIP in my dark room, heart still thudding as if I really had been running. Clothes sticking to my skin.

I get up, open the curtains, the window, and lean out and breathe deeply, trying to calm down. It's a clear night. Silver traces from the stars above seem to cling to the air around me, the skin on my hands and arms. I pull back from the window and slam it shut.

Now *I'm* the one with delusions.

Wide awake, I wander downstairs. Put the kettle on. There is an elaborate bunch of white flowers in a vase on the kitchen table – lilies and roses. They weren't here earlier, were they? Beautiful, but something about lilies leaves me cold, and the roses' perfume hangs too heavy in this confined space. It catches in my throat. A card sticks out, unopened, and I look closer. It's got my name on it?

I frown. Who could have sent them? I reach for the card, then curse when I catch my finger on a thorn. A drop of blood smears on the envelope when I open it, and I try to rub it off, then suck on my finger.

More lilies on the card. It says the usual *Sympathy for your loss*, and is signed – by Dr Rafferty. And inside the card is a folded sheet of paper.

I unfold it and scan the printed words quickly, but can't seem to take them in. Then I read slower, but still the words jumble and dance.

Until two jump out stark and clear: *Changed circumstances*.

I needed the transfer to London University because of my grandmother's illness. No grandmother, no transfer.

We agreed to that, didn't we? And Dad signed the form.

I'm going to Inaccessible Island.

Tomorrow night.

21

Sally being nice is pushing me over the edge.

I finally snap when she insists she must refold my clothes neater in my suitcase so more will fit. 'Stop fussing! I've got plenty. It says they'll provide clothes anyhow, so I shouldn't need that much stuff.'

She folds her arms. 'Fine. Just trying to help,' she says, and stomps off.

Dad gives me a look, and I sigh. 'I know, I know. I'll apologise before I go.'

I shut the case, zip it up. The real reason for not wanting a complete refold in her war against wrinkled clothing? The ANDs tucked away in odd corners of my case. There are more in my bag: who knows if they'll be accessible on Inaccessible Island. And who knows what Sally'd make of *them*. Or is it Gecko's warnings echoing in my ears that make me want to keep it secret?

'Wish you didn't have to go so soon,' Dad says.

'I know. Me, too.'

'I've got something I want you to have.' He reaches into a pocket, and takes out a silver necklace. 'It was your mother's.'

I hesitate, then take it, wanting to cradle it close and push it away at the same time. The cool, slippery feel of the beads in my fingers brings a rush of memories. She always wore it. She'd let me play with it, get me to count the interlocking silver beads, and trace their intricate patterns. 'Are you sure?'

'Of course. She always said she wanted you to have it, to give it to you when you were older if anything ever happened to her. Shall I?' he says. I nod and hold my hair out of the way while he does up the clasp. He lets go, and the silver slips cool on my skin.

Jason comes in. His imaginatively named soft toy dog is tucked under one arm. 'Mr Dog wants to come with you,' he announces.

'Does he?' I take him in my hands, hold him to my ear, and listen. 'I don't know. He says he likes looking after you.'

'Well, I don't need looking after any more.'

'And I do?'

'Course. Since you won't have your brother there.' He suddenly launches at me for a hug; as my arms go around him and tighten, so does my throat.

He pulls away. 'That's settled then,' he says, and shoves Mr Dog unceremoniously in the already full bag I'm wearing across my body. His nose and paws peek out over the top. *Great*: Lunatic Luna is guaranteed to make a good impression, once again.

The electric transport pulls away from the drop-off point. I stare at Dad, Sally and Jason through the window, all waving in our version of happy families. Unable to take this in, and I'm fighting not to cry: *an extended time away*. How long is that? I'm shocked to think I'll even miss *Sally*.

175

There are excited voices around me: all happy to be going, to be joining PareCo's Think Tank. Hackers, every one of them. A few curious glances are cast my way but I avoid eye contact, and keep quiet.

Then we stop, and Hex gets on. 'Luna! You're coming, after all?' He sits next to me, gives me a hug. 'Sorry to hear about your grandmother,' he adds, voice lowered.

'Thanks.'

'I didn't know you were back on for this.'

'They cancelled my transfer.'

'You haven't told Melrose?'

'No. I just found out, late last night.' I stare back at him, dismayed I hadn't thought to call her. She won't take this well. 'I've been caught up with family today. Is she all right?'

'Not happy about me going. She'll be less happy when she knows you won't be at uni with her, either.'

I sigh; mentally add: *And that I'll be with you instead of her.* Best not put it off. 'Can you tell her for me, and that I'm sorry I didn't tell her but I only found out last night? Can you be tactful about it?'

'Tough assignment. But I'll try.' He unfocuses, and is gone for so long that I know a heated conversation is being had.

He comes back. 'She's OK. Just bent she didn't know. But then apologised for said bent-ness. You've got a dead grandmother free pass on things still.'

I wince. 'You really need to work on the tact thing.'

We make more stops, and at every one I watch for Gecko.

176

The transport is nearly full now. Maybe he really *is* crazy; maybe he never was locked up and told he had to come whether he wanted to or not.

Maybe he made it all up.

But then we make one more stop. The door opens, and there he is. Two men stand behind him while he goes through the door.

His eyes are defiant. He walks down the aisle as the door swings shut and locks, and scans the seats. When he sees me, his whole body stiffens. He walks over, nods to Hex. 'Is it OK if I sit with Luna?'

Hex looks to me. Not sure if it is wise or not, I nod yes.

Hex gets up, moves a few rows back. Gecko takes his seat, a deep frown between his eyes.

I raise an eyebrow. 'I'm happy to see you, too.'

'Luna, why are you here?'

'I didn't get a chance to tell you last night: my grandmother died. So I don't get the transfer to London Uni any more.'

He looks so appalled I almost start to wonder if he knew her. He shakes his head. 'I'm so sorry.'

'Thanks. So now I'm off to explore strange new worlds with PareCo; what the hell. It's not like I was doing anything useful or interesting around here.'

'We really need to talk. There are too many ears here,' he says, his voice so low I can barely pick out the words.

'Don't worry; we'll have plenty of time to talk. We're off for an extended time, remember?'

'Maybe,' he says, eyes watchful, body tense.

Then the transport lurches, hard, to the left. It *slams* – did it hit something, or just stop? – and there are screams. Everything seems caught in a strange slow motion, as arms and legs and the people they're attached to appear to fly and almost hang suspended in the air. Crash protection kicks in: giant air bags activate to stop people from slamming into each other or the walls.

But I've not flown out of my seat. A vice grip is around me; there is pain in my arm, my ribs. Gecko: he's braced us both into this seat. He *knew* this was going to happen?

Then the emergency exits activate. Before anyone else can react he's pushed me through the one next to our seat. He follows me out, and pulls me further into the night.

There is crying, shouting, sirens. Others are crawling out of the wreckage and I scan them anxiously until I see Hex emerge. 'Run!' Gecko says, still pulling my arm, almost dragging me away from the electric track.

'What?'

'I said, *run*. Run as if your life depends on it.'

But I'm stuck as if in syrup; in shock, confusion; my feet aren't working, and I'm not sure I want them to. 'Run? Why? What's happening?'

He turns back. 'You have to come with me: you're one of us. Save yourself!' The night is cold, clear; the stars are out, and show the silver etched on his skin, so like my mother that a different sort of pain catches inside.

'I don't understand. What are you talking about? I'm one of what?'

'You're one of us! That's how you found me in the void. How you left through the wall of my S'hack.' He reaches out his fingers, lightly touches around my left eye. His touch makes me shiver. 'The marks, Luna. They're here, part of your skin. Silver, like Astra, like me. I knew you must have them: only S'hackers can see them, and you saw mine.'

'No. NO! This is crazy!'

And he turns me around violently to face the crashed transport, a broken glass window. Jagged glass reflects the moon, the stars – and distorts my white face. With pale grey eyes. Shot with silver, and silver winds around my left eye. Silver, like my mother? Like Gecko.

I'm shaking my head, denying what I can see. Am I injured; is some sort of concussion affecting my vision?

'This can't be right. How can I have marks on my skin that I didn't even know about? They're tattoos, aren't they?'

'Run now, talk later.'

'No! I'm not going anywhere until I understand.' And I struggle to pull away from his grip on my shoulders.

He lets go. 'How old were you when your mother died?' he says, words fast and desperate.

'Four.'

'You must have been a S'hacker even that young: they appear and grow as you manipulate the void. Can't you remember anything about it?'

'No!' I deny his words, even as my mind sees the stars, the moon. *We sat on the moon.* But that was just a dream. Wasn't it?

Sirens are closer now; Gecko whips round at the sound.

'Run. You must! *Please*,' he says. Somehow the desperation in his voice dislodges the shock just enough to make my feet start moving forwards, Gecko half pulling me along.

But as we reach the next junction my feet slow as reason returns. 'Wait. Where we are going?'

He turns, pulls me close in the briefest of hugs. 'Please, Luna. You *have* to stay safe. We need you. *I* need you.' He looks back the way we came, and curses. 'Trust me,' he says, and leans down, and lightly kisses me so fast I don't have time to work out whether to pull away or kiss him back. He points me to a dark lane, slaps something cold on my wrist. 'Meet me in my S'hack when you can. Now, run to the end. A van will come. Get into it. Go!'

And I stumble down the lane in the darkness, mind reeling, not even sure why I'm doing what he says. I look back: he's going the other way? And there are running footsteps, chasing after him. I stop, unsure what to do, when a dark van rips around the corner at the end of the lane, pulls in next to me, and a door opens. Arms grab and drag me inside. The door slams shut.

A man – twenty-something – stares back at me.

'Who are you?' I demand, caught halfway between anger and fear.

'You've got Gecko's tracker,' he says. 'Who the hell are you?' An angry voice. Gecko's tracker? And he reaches across and pulls the ring of metal Gecko put on me off my wrist.

'I… I…he put it on me, told me to come here. I don't understand. What's going on?'

'Where's Gecko?' another voice says. A girl. I turn to face her and despite everything else, almost gasp. Her hair is so white-blond it almost glows in the darkness, her skin even paler. 'Where is he?' she demands, panic in her voice.

'Some people were chasing him; he ran the other way. *Who* was chasing him? Why?'

They look at each other.

The man curses. 'We've got to get out of here. There's nothing we can do for him now.' The girl starts to argue, but he gets behind the wheel, and soon the van is pulling away, away.

I plaster my face to the window, but can see nothing following in the dark night. What is happening? Who are these people?

Where are you, Gecko?

4 QUESTIONS

There are four questions of value in life . . .
What is sacred? Of what is the spirit made?
What is worth living for and what is worth dying for?

Lord Byron

22

I'm shaking.

'She may be in shock,' the man says, and hands me a blanket. When I just stare back at him, he tucks it around me. Heywood: he said his name was Heywood. And the girl so pale she doesn't look quite human is Crystal. She's a silver Hacker: she got out of the van first, and I glimpsed her silver tattoos, different from any I've seen before – like interlocking snowflakes in her skin.

The look she gives me is colder than ice as they argue what to do with me. 'You shouldn't have brought her here,' she hisses, and Heywood draws her further away. Their voices go lower and I can't hear them any more.

I pull the blanket tighter around and try to stop shaking, to quell the panic inside. Despite Gecko bracing us before the transport crashed, pain has settled into my ribs and chest, and it hurts to breathe. That was no accident, was it?

What is this place? The van drove down unrecognisable dark streets for an age, then through a back gate. Once the gates clanged shut, Heywood pulled me out of the van, not unkindly, down a long garden and through a back door. Outside, under the stars, I kept my face turned away from Crystal, to hide the silver in my own skin. Heywood couldn't see them; his face is devoid of Hacker marks of either kind, and Gecko said only S'hackers could see them. S'hackers...

like *me*? No, it can't be, it can't. My thoughts veer away from *that* and back to here.

We went down a flight of stairs; we're in a basement. It's sparsely furnished, dimly lit. No windows. Crystal locked the door after us, tucking keys away in her pocket. The air is cold, damp. I sneeze.

Crystal stomps out of the room, and Heywood comes over to the sofa I'm on, pulls up a chair. Gives back my bag that he took earlier. I'd been wearing it across my body so it came with me. Mr Dog is still sticking out of the top, but hind legs up this time: hiding his head in the sand? Good idea.

'Sorry about that,' Heywood says. 'Just had to check for communication devices. Crystal has volunteered to make us some tea,' he adds. I can hear loud clattering noises as cups are slammed about in the next room. He grins wryly. 'Well, not so much *volunteered*, exactly. Now. Who are you? Why are you here?'

I stare back at him. 'I'm here because you kidnapped me.'

An eyebrow goes up. 'Oh, I see. And here I thought we rescued you. You were wearing our tracker; it was activated, sending a "please rescue me" signal straight to us, you see.'

'OK, then; perhaps this is all a simple misunderstanding. Just unlock the door, and I'll be on my way.'

'I'm afraid things aren't quite as simple as that.'

Crystal stomps back in, puts a tray of tea things on a table. She perches on the sofa next to me, and I shrink away.

Heywood holds out a mug. 'Go on. It'll make you feel better.' But I don't take it.

He shrugs, puts it down again.

'What have you done to Gecko?' Crystal demands. I turn to look at her: palest blue eyes, white, almost translucent skin, but despite that, oddly beautiful. The cold fury in her eyes hides something else; some fear and feeling for Gecko. Ah. Is she a girlfriend? It twists oddly inside to think so.

'What have *I* done to Gecko? What has he done to me?! I didn't ask to come here.'

She shrugs impatiently, looks to Heywood. 'She's obviously an idiot.'

Heywood shakes his head. 'Don't be so fast to judge. Gecko must have sent her to us for a reason; we just have to work out what it is.' He turns back to me. 'As soon as we do that, you're free to go. If you want to,' he says to me, smiling kindly.

So, it's good cop, bad cop, is that it? I can play along.

I let my face soften, just a little, and look back at him. 'I don't know why I'm here. Perhaps if I knew who you were, I might have a better idea?'

They exchange a glance.

'Fair comment,' Heywood says, and when Crystal starts to sputter he raises a hand. 'You trust Gecko, don't you?' he says to her. 'So trust who he sends to us.' He turns back to me. 'I'll answer your questions if you answer a few of mine, first,' he says. 'Deal?'

'Depends what you ask me.'

He grins. 'Smart answer, and an honest one. First question: who are you?'

No reason to hold back what he can easily discover. Once the fact that I'm missing hits the news, it'll be everywhere. 'I'm Luna Iverson.'

He tilts his head. 'That name is somehow familiar. Why?'

I shrug. 'How should I know?'

He unfocuses a moment, comes back. 'Ah, I see. Daughter of Astra; correct?'

I nod, and Crystal looks at me with something like awe, but it vanishes so fast I'm not sure I saw it.

'Well. Nice to meet you, Luna. I'm Roy Heywood – generally known as Heywood, as you know. And Crystal you met earlier. Now, how do you know Gecko?' he asks.

'We were at the PareCo test centre together. We're sort of friends.'

Heywood raises an eyebrow. 'You must be more than just friends to have been sent to us.'

Crystal bristles, and I can feel pink rising in my cheeks. He held me, he kissed me; he said he needed me. Wait: what were his exact words? He said *we need you; I need you*. Is this the 'we'?

'Look, I don't understand why I ended up here. Gecko told me he was a prisoner, that he was being forced to go to Inaccessible Island. I gather that crash tonight was no accident; that you were meant to be his getaway. So why did he send me in his place?'

'Exactly: that is the question. Gecko hasn't been able to

report to us in detail for some time; his Implant is being monitored. So he used code to activate an emergency plan, but couldn't tell us everything that has been going on. You must know more than you are letting on, Luna,' he says.

'Enough questions; you said you'd answer mine. Who are you? What is this place? What is Gecko involved in?'

'We're investigating PareCo.'

'Who are "we"?'

'We are…a collection of concerned citizens.'

'But *why* are you investigating PareCo? Who are you working for?'

'For the people of the world.'

'Funny, I don't remember electing you to look out for everyone. What is your organisation called?'

He half smiles. 'Not the nicest of names, but we generally call ourselves the Worms. We're biting the pear that is PareCo, tunnelling into their deceptions, you see.'

'They're just a corporation. If you've got a problem with them, complain to a consumer watchdog or something.'

'It's not that simple. PareCo controls almost every avenue of our lives now, whether you've noticed it or not.'

I shift in my seat, wince as I do so.

'Are you all right?'

I shrug. 'Just bruises, I think. From the crash.'

'Look, it's late. How about you get some sleep? And we'll talk more tomorrow. Try to work things out.'

I shake my head. 'No. I don't want to be here; let me go.'

'I'm sorry, Luna. We have to figure things out a bit more

before we can do that.' His eyes hold mine, steady, and there is nothing threatening there. He *feels* like a good guy. But if they can't let me go now, when will they?

'I want to go home.' My voice is small, and pathetic, and I hate it. But I *am* tired, hurt, freaked out. Overwhelmed. I just want *home*. Even Sally's fury and fussing would beat this.

'I'm sorry, Luna. Really. But even if we did let you go, you'd never make it there. PareCo will be after you now.'

His words sink in, settle. PareCo will think I'm one of them, one of these *Worms*, won't they? That I was involved in causing that accident; that I disappeared on purpose. No matter that I haven't done anything.

This is the PareCo that Gecko thinks murdered Jezzamine and Danny. If he's right, what would they do to me?

Crystal takes me to an adjoining room, a small bed in the corner. Points me to the bathroom when I ask.

I shut the door behind me. There's a window, high and narrow. No good for escape, but as I splash water on my face, stare in the mirror, I wonder: is there enough starshine leaking in for a hint of silver? I lock the door, and pull the cord to turn off the light. With shaking fingers, I trace the pattern of swirls around my eye.

S'hacker marks. *You're one of us*, Gecko had said. Spun me around to show me my reflection in broken glass. How could this be? How could I be a S'hacker, like Gecko, like my mother, and not even know it?

There's a knock on the door, and I jump. How long have I been staring at myself in the mirror?

'Is everything all right?' Heywood.

'I'm fine,' I say, and put the light back on, and open the door.

He hands me some painkillers, water. I take them, go to the bedroom, lie down, pull the blankets up. There is a click as the door is locked.

Gecko said all he ever wanted was freedom, but he's led me straight into a prison.

I touch my face in the darkness: *silver*, like Astra? There is pain inside that Gecko kept this from me. How long did he know? I think back to that first night on the balcony with him at the test centre, when the clouds pulled back and stars revealed the silver in his skin. I had his hoodie on, pulled low so he wouldn't see my tears. That could have hidden the marks; if he did see them then, he didn't let on. But if only S'hackers can see the silver, he knew when I asked about his the next day. But he didn't react, didn't tell me what my seeing them meant.

Why did I let him convince me to run? *That's* what got me into this mess; I went along. I didn't have to, but I did. At least part of it was the shock – of seeing the silver in my own skin – but that wasn't all of it. I'd wanted to do what he wanted. The realisation makes me angry: angry at myself.

And tonight, Gecko slapped his tracker on my wrist; had me so-called *rescued* in his place. Did he think he was being all heroic and saving me from some danger he sees with PareCo, or is this something else? Unless they are very good actors, Heywood and Crystal didn't know this was going to happen. They were shocked when it was me instead of Gecko.

And Gecko held me; he kissed me, though so quickly the feel and memory of it is like something I imagined. He said he needs me. Instinct says to trust him; brain says I'm a total dys. What has he got me into? They're some sort of rebels, aren't they? Even if they're wrong about PareCo being after me, I know them now; they can't just let me go. If I want to get out of here, I have to find another way.

Despite the crazy evening and my twisting, dancing thoughts, the painkillers make sleep draw in fast.

Mummy is next to me on the moon. 'It's time to go now, Luna. Spin it all away. You remember how, don't you?'

I shake my head no. I don't want to leave, not yet. Not for the falling place.

'Now, Luna. I know you know how. It's important. Do you remember why?'

Not waiting for an answer, she puts her arms around me, and jumps off the moon, taking me with her. She sets me down and takes both of my hands in hers, starts spinning me around, faster and faster. When she lets go, my stomach lurches, but I do as she wants – hands outstretched now. Spinning ever faster.

The moon and stars I cast into the sky start to spin, too; they collapse into themselves, smaller and smaller until they spin into the space between my hands. The floor disappears next, and I'm falling, falling, falling...

23

'Nice. Is he your only friend?'

I open one eye, head heavy, confused, then sit up fast. Crystal stands in the doorway and holds Mr Dog between her hands.

'Give him back!' I get up and lunge for her, but she dances lightly away and out of the room. The pain in my chest stops me, makes me want to crumple back into bed. I guess a sudden stop at two hundred miles an hour can do that to a girl.

Heywood looks in and tosses Mr Dog towards me; I catch him.

'Breakfast will be ready soon,' he says, and backs out.

When I emerge, Crystal wrinkles her nose. 'Please shower. There are towels in the bathroom cupboard. Clothes on the chair.' She points at the door she took me through last night to go to the bathroom.

I notice what I was in too much of a state to register last night. The hall is lined with doors. Four have glass windows, three with a red light over the door: PIPs, occupied. The last PIP is empty. If I plug in, I could find Dad, ask him what to do. I glance back at the door I came through, and try the handle to the empty one. Locked. It was never going to be that easy, was it?

A shower, hot, is very welcome; it eases the soreness

enough that I can stand up straighter. But the longer I stay under the jets of hot water, the angrier I get.

My garbled thoughts from last night are starting to take shape. Who do these people think they are, keeping me prisoner? I'm sure they're wrong about PareCo being after me, but even if they're right, I could go to the police. Tell them I had nothing to do with that crash; that I wasn't trying to escape, I was kidnapped. It's the truth: they'd have to believe me, wouldn't they? I've got to find a way to get out of here.

And Gecko is the worst of them all. I thought he was my friend. *I thought he might be more than a friend*, honesty whispers inside, and that makes me even angrier. *Friends* don't get you in this much trouble, do they?

I towel myself, rough and fast, and the pain makes the anger sharpen: that is his fault, too. I shrug ill-fitting borrowed clothes on, and head into the hall.

The PIPs are empty now. Are they all locked? I grip a door handle to another one, and it starts to turn. But then the door to the main room opens.

Crystal raises an eyebrow. 'They're ID keyed, so if you try to use one you'll get zapped.' She smiles and makes a shooting motion at her head. I hold mine high, walk down the hall towards her. She doesn't move, just stands there blocking the door, staring at me with her weird, pale eyes. I shoulder her out of the way to enter the room. She staggers back and then spins round, fists clenched.

'Heh there,' Heywood says, voice mild, but there is a

warning look in his eyes aimed at Crystal. She focuses beyond him – at a woman, and two boys about our age, all sat at the table with Heywood – and visibly, reluctantly, relaxes her stance and her fists.

'Join us?' Heywood says to me, gestures at an empty chair next to him and opposite the woman: a Hacker, I see now. Extensive black swirls around her eye say of high standing, and that's not all: she's old. Older than my dad, maybe. Gecko said you never see old Hackers, and here is one at breakfast.

I hesitate, torn between hunger and wanting to tell them all exactly what I think of things. But if I believe Crystal, the PIPs are ID keyed. The only way to use one is to persuade them to programme it so I can. I force myself to smile, to sit down. Crystal takes a chair at the other end.

'Some introductions?' Heywood says, and calls out names, but the only one I hear is Tempo. I can't tear my eyes away from her, this Hacker across from me: there is something about her. *Silver*: I blink. For a split second I imagined silver all around her black tattoos, as if I've seen it there before. Is she a S'hacker, too?

Tempo smiles: a kind smile, somehow familiar. Something about her makes me want to smile back. 'Luna, I'm *so* happy to see you again,' she says.

'Again?'

'I was a friend of your mother's. She used to bring you to visit. Do you remember me?'

I'm staring at her and there is something, some tickle of

memory inside: a happy memory? But nothing definite. 'I'm not sure.'

'Ah, you were very small. Now, have your breakfast. We'll catch up after.'

There are platters of eggs, bacon, toast passed around, and somehow I'm starving. I busy myself with eating, and watch the others.

Tempo is in charge; that is very clear. Heywood is next, almost like a big brother chiding the others now and then. Crystal and the two boys are about my age; the boys are both Hackers – black tattoo swirls in their skin. Silver hacking status unknown without starshine. They seem uncomfortable at Tempo's presence.

When breakfast is finished, Heywood sends Crystal and the boys away with the dishes, to a flurry of protests.

Tempo is smiling again as they leave. Like before there is some whisper of memory that says I like her, that she is a friend. 'Time for talk,' she says. 'Come.'

We get up from the table, move to the sofa, Heywood to a chair.

'Luna, I can't believe how beautiful you've grown. You're so like your mother: you've got her eyes. I was so happy when Heywood called last night to say you were here.'

I shrug, uncomfortable. 'I'm glad somebody is happy.'

'Ah, yes. I gather you'd like to go home, but that isn't possible. I'm sorry, Luna. But if you weren't here, you'd be off to Inaccessible Island, anyhow – not home.'

'But I was going there of my own free will,' I say, stetching the truth. 'No one asked me if I wanted to come here.' Despite my best intentions, despite knowing I may need these people on side to ever get out of here, I can't stop the bitterness in my voice.

'But did you *really* choose to go there? There are some things you need to know about PareCo, Luna.'

I shrug. 'They're just a corporation.'

'However they started, they're so much more than that now. They control education; Implants; health care. Every government of the world uses their translation and communications. Their systems control every aspect of society, whether you have noticed it or not. Almost all social interaction these days is virtual and takes place in PareCo-controlled Realtime; everyone holidays in PareCo's virtual worlds, and plays PareCo virtual games. And the side effects this can have – well... How about the rise in so-called Sudden Teenage Death Syndrome? Teens who plug in at school all day, and play online all night, sometimes die for no apparent reason. It actually results from lack of natural sleep.'

'But if they knew that, surely they'd stop it.' I stare at her, shocked. 'There's been research into it and stuff; they don't know what causes it.'

She shrugs. 'There are recommended plug-in times, but who follows them? Adults are more resilient; younger brains need sleep to rest, recuperate, and grow. Without it they sometimes die. The authorities won't admit what the cause is for fear of panic, with most of the population of this country and others spending all the time they can in

197

Realtime and games. All run by PareCo.'

'You could die crossing the road; virtual has got to be safer. And they say street crime is at an all-time low.'

'Perhaps so, with most of the population plugged in, but what of other crimes? Have you noticed the dying neighbourhoods, the closing schools?'

'There is a primary that closed near where I live.'

'Birth rates are dropping. Nobody could be bothered having sex the usual way when virtual is available. Whole areas of the city are dying, then annexed to make bigger gardens for ever-bigger houses: bribes for those who are supposed to be looking out for us.'

And I remember the dark areas around Melrose's neighbourhood; how hers has grown.

'And paranoia and psychotic delusions are on the rise. A significant proportion of the population goes mad from prolonged virtual exposure.'

'But they're screening them out as MEs now.'

'Are they, really? Or is that just another way to control people they want to keep an eye on? And what about the increase in Implant addiction? PareCo claims that is from illegal programmes, made by Hackers. But strangely, it seems to happen to anyone who does or says anything PareCo finds . . . awkward. But leave that aside for the moment; we can't prove it. Yet. All I've said so far is that PareCo has great *opportunity* for misuse of power, happily handed over to PareCo by the governments of the world, to make life easier. To make people placid; to make governing easier. But if people are happy with how things are, if they want them that way, who are we to argue?'

'I get the feeling there's more?'

'Indeed. Implants have been changed without consultation. The newer ones have more capabilities. Not just allowing quicker, better PIP integration, virtual conversations, map apps and so on, which are all known and accepted. Much more than that.'

I stay silent. This I know about: from personal experience at the test centre.

'It appears to involve the last five years of Implants, so everyone seventeen or under – like Gecko, like Crystal – has the new version. Your year at school was the first affected. Anyone eighteen or older has Implants as they are meant to be, as publicly known. You see, Luna, how PareCo will gain more and more control over everyone, as more and more of the population have the new Implants? Not just in this country. This is global. Somehow we need to be able to show that they are misusing these new Implants, that it isn't just some equipment upgrade.'

Heywood clears his throat. 'I'm not sure we're answering the question we need to answer: why is Luna here?' And he is looking at Tempo as he says it, but now, suddenly, I think I understand Gecko's *we need you*.

I don't want to focus on it, don't want to say anything: as if words said out loud will make it more real. But somehow they drag themselves out of me. 'I think I may know why Gecko sent me.'

They're both looking at me now. I swallow. 'When Gecko and I were at the test centre, they did a horrible test using Implants. Where everyone – almost everyone, that is – saw gunmen shooting at people; people thought they were shot, that they were dying. Gecko thought it was real. I'm a Refuser so haven't got an Implant; I couldn't see any of it. There were just two others that somehow could tell they weren't real, that they were Implant images. And then, after we all went home, they both died.'

And I tell them about Jezzamine and Danny. As I say the words, I realise how foolish I'd been to deny Gecko's conclusions. I didn't want to believe it, but their deaths *couldn't* be coincidence.

Heywood's eyes mirror the shock in mine. He turns to Tempo. 'So: some are resistant, and they're being eliminated. And we have the only witness who can talk about it.' They both turn to me. 'And that is why Gecko saved you, and sent you here,' he says.

'That was the real reason for the test we had, wasn't it?' I say. 'To screen out those who could somehow withstand the new Implants. And get rid of them.'

'Luna, why do you think you were going to Inaccessible Island in the first place?' Tempo says. 'You have dangerous knowledge. They know it. They were never going to let you go.'

'So let's go to the police. Murder was still a crime last time I checked. Tell them what PareCo are doing, let them – and the government – handle it.'

'If only it were that easy. They're not playing by the rules, Luna, so neither can we. And what about Gecko? He may have given up his freedom for yours.'

'What will they do to him if they catch him?' I ask, voice small.

'We don't know for sure. They seem to want him for something; if they wanted to make him disappear, they could have done that by now.' But there is worry in her eyes. 'We don't even know where he is. He's not answering messages. He may not be able to, or he may be avoiding using his Implant as it'll allow PareCo to trace his location. Another bonus in the new generation of Implants.'

He may not be able to: another accident? The anger I had against Gecko before is gone. Maybe he really did save me. And if I hadn't resisted, if we'd got away faster, he might be here now, too.

'And you say you are a Refuser, Luna, but you've been in the void recently. It's in your eyes.'

'Gecko took me.' But is that the whole truth? Gecko wondered if he'd sent the ladder and arrows the last time just by thinking about me, but maybe he was wrong. Maybe I did it myself, because I'm a *S'hacker*. The word sounds funny connected to me, even not said out loud.

Tempo raises an eyebrow as if she knows there is more, but says nothing.

'Wait a minute. Why don't I go and look for him, see if he is all right?'

'Look for him? Where?' Heywood says.

'About the last thing Gecko said to me was to meet him in the void,' I say. 'Let me plug in, and I'll go and ask him.'

'I could get you into the void, but it is infinite. How would you find him?' Tempo says.

I hesitate. *Does she know what I am?* 'I've done it before,' I say.

'We'd have to know you won't contact anyone through Realtime,' Heywood says. 'If you do, PareCo will know you are there and try to trace you. Can we trust you?'

Tempo shrugs. 'I'd accept a promise not to.'

'Let me plug in and see if I can find him. I won't try to contact anyone else,' I say, unsure as I say it if this is a lie or the truth.

Her head tilts to one side; thinking? Then she shakes her head. 'We'll think this through and discuss our options, tonight.'

It's a quiet afternoon for me and Crystal. Everyone is busy, and she is assigned the task of watching me. She isn't happy about it.

'Just lock me in the bedroom already. I don't care.'

She shakes her head. 'Tempo might. For some reason she felt it necessary to tell me to not be mean to you.' She sighs, and scowls. 'Also to answer any questions you may have.'

'Really? *Any* questions?' I think for a moment, and then *all* the questions start tumbling out. 'What is this place, this house? Who is here, why are they here? What does everyone do? What—'

'Slow down. It's Heywood's house; his family owns it.

202

The basement is used as a safe house. For runaway Hackers, who don't want to work for PareCo. We're—' and she hesitates '—sort of doing advanced Hacker training. With Tempo and others. We're trying to break into PareCo inner systems, and to find out what they're doing on Inaccessible Island. Haven't managed it so far.'

'Those boys at breakfast – and you – are young enough to all have the new Implants. How come you're not traced by them?'

'It's a right pain, but we don't use them. If you don't use your Implant, you can't be traced. Tempo has been trying to find a way to hack the new Implants like we can hack the old ones, to block PareCo from tracing them when they're used. So far it hasn't worked.'

'Can't you just have the Implants taken out?'

'Removal surgery has been tried on Implant Addicts: they rarely survive, and if they do, well…' She shudders, and there is real distress in her eyes.

'Do you know someone that happened to?'

'None of your business,' she snaps. 'Let's just say it's not a good option.'

'Sorry. But wouldn't you get found out when you plug in, anyhow?'

'Only if you use Realtime.'

That information settles. Hackers like Hex have to use Realtime to get into existing worlds and muck with them. Only S'hackers can get around that by going straight to the void.

'So, that means you must all be S'hackers; you don't have to use Realtime because you go to the void. So by advanced Hacker training you mean S'hacker training in void manipulation, is that it?'

Her mouth hangs open. 'How do you know about the void, and S'hackers? Did Gecko tell you?' She looks shocked, angry, and I remember Gecko saying he was sworn not to. Some urge to protect him makes me lie.

'No. My mother was Astra, remember? She was both a Hacker and a S'hacker. Like Tempo.' I venture the latter, and Crystal doesn't object: so Tempo *is* a S'hacker too, as I'd half remembered – half guessed.

'Of course.' She shakes her head. 'Silly me. I should have realised Gecko would never tell *you* anything really important.' She sits forward in her chair. 'You haven't asked me the one thing you really want to know, have you?'

'Oh? What's that?'

'You want to ask about me and Gecko, don't you?' She grins, and I say nothing. *Yes*, I am curious, but I would never ask. Is it because I don't want to give her the satisfaction, or because I'm afraid of what she might say? 'Heywood told me, by the way. The real reason Gecko saved you – that you're some sort of witness. Don't feel bad.'

'About what?'

'It's part of Gecko's job, you know. He's, like, the best spy. The best at getting information from people, especially girls. By whatever means necessary. You're not the first to be taken in.'

I stare back at her, a denial on its way, but I bite it back. 'Whatever,' I say, and stretch out on the sofa, my back to Crystal. Eyes shut, breathing even, I pretend to fall asleep.

Could it be true: Gecko and Crystal? There is some part of me that knows at least some of what she said is true – that he *is* good at getting information from people. He had me opening up about getting sick in Realtime almost as soon as we met, something I've never told anyone, apart from Nanna. Did he target me from the beginning; did he somehow know there was something different about me? And all that stuff he told me about PareCo: he was so open that at the time I wondered *why*. If he really thought PareCo was as rotten and dangerous as he said, shouldn't he have been more cautious of me, a stranger? How'd he know I wouldn't go and tell on him?

I try to push thoughts of Gecko away and nap for real, but even without him to obsess over, my mind can't stop spinning with everything that has happened, all that was said today. Something is troubling me beyond all the other mega-troubling stuff, and I shuffle through it all, trying to work out what it is. When it hits me I sit up and gasp.

Crystal looks up from a book vid.

'What is it? You look like you've seen a ghost.'

'Is Tempo still here? I want to ask her something.'

'She's plugged in. Not worth my life to disturb her. What is it? Maybe I can help. Not that I can believe I just said that.' She rolls her eyes.

'It's just something she said before. I'd said that I'd chosen to go to Inaccessible Island, and she said, had I really? That PareCo were never going to let me go anywhere else.'

'And?'

I swallow. 'The reason I was on the transport to go there is because my grandmother died.' I explain to her about the contract Dad signed to get my transfer; the clause about changed circumstances. 'Could they have had something to do with her death?'

'If they were interested in you for some reason – hard to imagine, but if they were – it's possible. Knowing PareCo, it's maybe even likely.'

'If they did, then it's my fault she died.' I'm stricken. 'I have to know.'

She hesitates. 'I'm rather good at hacking government records; I could see what cause of death is given. Though if PareCo did it, they've probably faked the records anyhow.'

'Please.'

She stares back at me, coolly. 'I'll think about it. But you'd owe me one. So, *so* much.'

24

Crystal unlocks my door late that night. 'Come on,' she says.

I get up, rub sleep from my eyes. Follow her into the other room. She unlocks another door: narrow, dark stairs up. Servants' stairs? They lead into a kitchen, then through to a really grand dining room with a massive wooden table and eight carved chairs. Floor to ceiling plush curtains line one wall. Heywood must be minted.

He's there, and Tempo. I glance at a grandfather clock in the corner. 2 a.m.?

'Nice time for a meeting. What's up?'

'Sit down,' Tempo says. 'Would you like some hot chocolate?' She pushes a steaming mug towards me, with marshmallows and sprinkles on top.

A twig of memory pulls inside. I reach for it and take a sip, then another. *Nice.* 'You used to make this for me, just like this. Didn't you?'

She smiles right into her eyes. 'Almost the same. I couldn't get quite the right chocolate.'

Another memory tickles inside. Hot chocolate is for stubbed toes, skinned knees. Lost puppies. 'Is something wrong?'

'I'm afraid so.' Her face is grave. 'I hate to have to tell you this. I wouldn't have, but Crystal told me you worked it out.'

'Tell me what?' I say, but a yawning pit in my stomach *knows*, doesn't it?

'PareCo tricked your father into signing the consent for the university transfer with all its fine print. They were never going to allow you to go anywhere but where they wanted you to be.'

I shake my head, wanting to deny it, to stop her from saying the words. Don't let it be my fault. 'Nanna died. They said it was her heart. The doctor said—'

Her eyes are kind, but she shakes her head. 'No, Luna. Not natural causes. Her Implant was geared up to cause a heart attack. Not difficult in someone of that age.'

'But she was just a helpless old woman.'

'It's hard to hear, but you have to know the truth. Crystal managed to hack the medical report. It was classified, but she cracked the code and copied it so I could show you.' She holds out a tablet. At the top of the screen it says *Official Coroner's report of Amelia Iverson*. Nanna. I look up at Tempo. 'Go on. Read it,' she says.

I take it and scan through. Much of it is medical mumbo jumbo that makes little sense, but the conclusion at the bottom is stark and clear:

Cause of death: heart failure due to Implant acceleration.

Only PareCo makes Implants; only PareCo controls them. They did this, they must have. Could they really have done it just to make me go to Inaccessible Island?

It's my fault. I blink back tears, struggle for control. How could they?

Tempo puts her hand on mine. For once Crystal looks almost human. 'We've all lost people to PareCo,' Crystal says, and there are shadows in her eyes. Past pain, or fear for Gecko? Maybe both.

'And my mother?' I ask, almost whispering the words. 'How about her?'

I look at Tempo, and the answer is there, in her eyes, the gentle shake of her head. Gecko had hinted as much. I'd pushed it away, unable to even consider the possibility.

'How? I was told she deliberately set her life support to fail if she died in the Game. To prove she was the best, she gambled with her life, and lost.' *She left me.*

'No, not true. She would never have done that – all lies, spread by PareCo to cover their tracks. Her PIP was sabotaged.'

The pain slams into me, wants to take me under. And I fight to push it away, save it for later, when I'm alone.

'I know you didn't want to come here, Luna. But we had to keep you safe. PareCo were never going to leave you alone, let you live your own life.'

'Why? Why me?' I stare back at her. At her eye, black tattoos surrounding it. Silver that hides. She *knows*, doesn't she? 'It isn't just what I witnessed at the test centre.'

'You know, don't you, Luna? At least somewhere inside, you must feel it.'

Heywood and Crystal exchange puzzled glances. They have no idea what's coming, do they?

It isn't just making hot chocolate that brought us upstairs.

And Tempo isn't just a night owl who likes her meetings in the middle of the night. There are no windows downstairs, other than the narrow high one in the small bathroom. Here there are floor to ceiling curtains: is it a clear night? I stand up. Flick the light switch by the door to plunge the room in darkness. I walk to the window, stroke the curtains: heavy velvet. They'd block every bit of sunlight. Or starshine. I grip them in my hands, and sweep them open.

It's a slender new moon tonight. It casts little light, but it is clear, and with all the light pollution laws these days the surrounding houses are dark. The stars shine brightly.

I turn back to the others. A brilliant dazzle of silver surrounds the black marks around Tempo's eye. Delicate snowflakes reappear on Crystal.

Crystal gasps, stares at me, eyes wide. 'You're one of us?' she says, echoing Gecko's words just days before, but hers are said with dismay.

Heywood looks between us, unable to see the silver markings himself. 'Is Luna a S'hacker?' he says, surprise in his voice.

Tempo nods yes, turns to me. She smiles; are her eyes misting with tears? 'I wanted you to be the one to acknowledge it. Welcome back to us, Luna.'

I shake my head. 'I really don't know what this means. I'm not a Hacker, silver kind or otherwise. I didn't even know I *had* these marks like my mother until just before I got here.'

Tempo draws the curtains, and the silver marks around

210

her eyes vanish. She puts the lights back on.

'I find that hard to believe,' she says.

I shrug. 'Believe what you want. But there is a reason I haven't got an Implant, y'know. I'm a Refuser.'

Tempo sighs, shakes her head. 'If only your father—'

'What about him?'

'Luna, darling. He wouldn't let me see you after Astra died, out of some misguided attempt to keep you from your birthright. If only he had, you'd understand, you'd be prepared for what is coming. As it is I'm not sure you even *can* be prepared any more, without having trained all these years.'

'What on earth are you talking about?'

Tempo looks at Heywood. 'Luna and I need to talk on our own for a while now, about her family. We'll go to the office downstairs.'

She gets up, and I stand, follow her downstairs and into an office, surprised my feet can still move when everything inside feels so numb. She shuts the door.

'What is it? What more could there possibly be about my family?'

'I caught a glimpse of your necklace yesterday. Your mother's. I'm so glad your dad gave it to you like she asked.'

My hand moves towards my neck where the necklace hides under my clothes, and covers it protectively.

'It's a memory string, Luna. Memories your mother made for you. She always knew she was at risk; she was too visible. She made it for you to have if she wasn't here to tell you herself. It's been waiting for you all this time. It'll explain much.'

She was at risk. This echoes Gecko's words: what did he say – that he couldn't believe they left her alone for so long?

Hot tears are forcing their way through no matter how I fight them.

'Show me her necklace, Luna.'

I hesitate, pull it out of my clothes. Struggle to undo the clasp with shaking hands, then study it closely. A memory string? It is made of interlocking silver beads; delicately, intricately carved. I peer closer: the swirls in the silver are very like S'hacker tattoos. *No.* Not just very like – they are exactly like, and not just any. They are miniature reproductions of Astra's. 'What are they?'

'She programmed her memories inside silver from the void, and trapped them in these beads: an act of incredible power. You have to go to the void alone to release the memories.'

'You'll let me plug in?'

'Of course. I understand your anger at being here not through your own choice. But it was the only way I could reach you. What happened to your grandmother, and your mother, could easily happen to you if PareCo discovers your abilities. We need you to be safe until your time comes. I trust you to do what is right when you know the truth.'

She stands, walks to the door that leads to the PIPs. Looks back. 'Are you coming?'

'I don't understand. *Why* do you need me to be safe? Until what time comes?'

'We'll let Astra tell you, in her own words. Come.'

My head throbs. Is this for real? I stare at the door: an ordinary rectangular door. An ordinary office, with a desk and a few chairs. No windows. But everything feels *slanted*. The words she has spoken between these walls are so unreal, it's like this place must be, too. I swallow. Stand, walk around the desk, as if moving, breathing, will make me feel more ordinary in my skin. It doesn't work.

Where before it was comforting, now the necklace feels hot, a weight around my neck. Memories from my mother, stored here for me, all this time? I divert to the room I sleep in to fish some ANDs out of my bag, swallow them and then follow Tempo to one of the PIPs.

She enters an override password so it'll allow me to plug in. I settle back on the sofa, listen to her instructions and wait for the connections to begin.

The warm neural net takes over, but Tempo's last words echo in my mind: *This will only work once. Don't waste them; the memories can only be released once, and then they're gone, forever.*

25

The silver hatch appears as soon as I enter my Realtime hallway, a solid sheet that spreads in seconds, then opens. The ladder drops down.

But I pause. Tempo warned me not to respond to anything in Realtime, or use any Realtime doors; that it'd signal my presence to PareCo. But she didn't say I couldn't *look*.

Messages? Two. One from Melrose, one from Dad, and neither is flashing urgent. I'm stunned. Doesn't your only daughter disappearing after a dramatic transport crash rate some attention? Some panic, even? Frequent pleas to make contact at the very least?

They don't know. That's it, isn't it? PareCo hasn't told anyone I'm missing. Disquiet ripples through me. As far as everyone knows, I'm on my way to Inaccessible Island for an extended stay. Only PareCo knows I'm missing, and if they don't tell, no one else will. Though Hex was there; he knows. Wouldn't he say something to Melrose, and she to my family? I push it aside to think about later, and reach for the ladder.

I climb the rungs into the void. As always the hatch and ladder vanish as soon as I step away from them. Twinkling lights rush past on the strange winds of the void, off on some mission of their own. I breathe in deep. There is an odd, comforting smell in the air, in my lungs. It tastes like forever.

My hair whips around until I wish it not to. This time, a long braid twists down my back. I smile. I did that, didn't I? The first time I was alone in the void, I wished my hair tied back; I thought Gecko did it. But was it me all along?

I lie down on what passes for ground here; while it holds me, it also feels insubstantial. The collapsing void spun in my dream fills my thoughts. I'd dreamt of falling in the void many times, with no idea what it was. But it wasn't just a dream: it was a memory, wasn't it?

I close my eyes, turn the necklace around to the first bead by the clasp, as instructed. *Cast your light into it*, Tempo said, as if that would be perfectly clear.

I hold the bead between my fingers, try to trace the carving on its surface by feel. Nothing. *Think like a bead*, I tell myself, and laugh. Maybe Tempo is crazy and this doesn't work; maybe she got me into the void to try to trap me here. She doesn't know I can just unplug to get out any time I want – or does she? I don't really know *what* she knows about me, about what I can do. More than I do, maybe. I sigh, longing for Astra's memories, and scared of them at the same time. My emotions rise into a swirling silver maelstrom above me, growing larger and larger.

Spin the light…?

I stand, hold out my hands, and spin like I do in my dreams. But not to collapse the void and fall this time. Instead, I fling my arms out and gather and spin the silver, then concentrate the swirl of light by drawing my hands together, closer and closer. To form a brilliant point of light. And

215

inside, I start to panic. What am I doing? *Incredible power*, Tempo said. What if this goes wrong?

I fight the fear, and focus: on the necklace; on the bead by the clasp. The silver light rushes from my fingertips through my body, a flash of dazzling heat.

Then…everything changes.

Warmth, soft light and joy suffuse my senses. I'm looking down at a tiny, tiny baby in my arms, overwhelmed by the swell of feelings inside me. Dad, very young, without all the worry lines, is gazing into my eyes in a way that isn't for his daughter. With shock, I realise: I'm experiencing Astra's memory, reliving it like I'm her. The baby is me? I gaze down at my chubby face, long dark lashes curling on soft cheeks.

A blur of memories follow, all of baby me: sleeping, playing, even crying. My first steps. And every strand of memory tastes of love and joy. *She loved me.*

Mostly I can only half remember my mother. Sometimes I can't even bring her face to mind, and when I can the feeling often isn't there, as if the memory is more from her photos than anything real. But she loved me. It's in her memories, imprinted into them. Tears are wet on my cheeks. Both here, in the void, and back in the PIP. Hope I don't short circuit anything.

And then…it changes. Now I'm Astra, looking at myself in a mirror. I stare hungrily. This is Astra as I remember her when the memories will come; it must have been not long before she died.

She smiles. 'Luna, is that you? It must be you. Darling.'

216

Her face is sad. 'If you're sharing this memory with me now, it must mean I've left you. I'm sorry, Luna, so sorry.' She holds out a hand, reaches it towards the mirror, and I can't stop my hand reaching out in the void, as if I could touch hers. Goosebumps rise as I understand: she spoke to her reflection in a mirror as if I were listening, then stored it as a memory – a message just for me.

'Darling girl, be strong. I will tell you everything I can.'

Her face changes, to serious, and cold. 'Trust no one. Trust only yourself. Now listen to me very carefully: much of what you will have been told and taught is wrong.

'NUN has idolised rationality over intelligence, as the way to keep the world safe from the human race. For many years, we – S'hackers, scientists, thinkers, all marginalised in the cult of RQ – have known the dangers. The cost of the loss of intuition, of creative leaps to advance thought, science, the human race. You *must* think outside the box, Luna. Listen to your inner voice; trust your intuition. Things are going wrong. And they are getting worse. PareCo is growing stronger; they're using their technology to manipulate NUN and the governments of the world. And under the guise of the tests, they are stealing the brightest minds away to work for them. People, many of them our own, vanish, and we don't know where they go. PareCo is false. The emperor has no clothes.

'But we, the Council of Scientists, are fighting back. And you, dear Luna, are part of the fight. Always remember that no matter how or why you are here, I love you, Luna. You *must* always know this. But you were planned. There are special characteristics we've been mixing S'hackers with for generations, trying to achieve your perfect self: a S'hacker still, but, like your Nanna, able to perceive real and virtual together. Who can overcome the restrictions of the void, and resist PareCo.

'Trust no one. Trust only yourself. You're special; you can change things.'

She stops, smiles, sadness in her eyes. 'Your dad doesn't know. He does know you have S'hacker capabilities; he doesn't know the rest of it.' Astra blows a kiss at the mirror. 'Be brave, special girl. I love you.'

The light fades. She's gone. I'm alone in the empty and lifeless void.

'No! Come back!' And I'm yelling into the void. What the hell was all that about? What did she even tell me? It was almost like she was afraid to say too much, afraid of who might be listening.

What did that mean – that they've been mixing S'hackers for generations? Did Nanna have the same ability as me to be both virtual and aware of her body at the same time? She never said – I never knew. I shake my head. Is that why she always warned me to not tell anyone, told me to avoid getting an Implant – did Nanna somehow know the danger? But she had this characteristic that the S'hackers wanted, and then—

Shock makes my thoughts stop as if they've run into a wall. What – am I some sort of genetic *experiment*? They were trying to come up with somebody with certain abilities.

Like crossing flowers to get the most desired colour, or vegetables with disease resistance, or apple trees that give more apples. And Dad didn't know…did Astra target him to make me? Did she conduct some sort of survey of the population, and come up with him as good genetic daddy material because of Nanna? I feel sick inside. And now I'm somehow supposed to resist PareCo and change things, is that it?

I sit up, heart pounding wildly, with fear, fury, and loss: emotions so strong and tangled I can barely work out what they are.

How do I figure out what's what?

Gecko. I need to see him. Or is that I just *want* to see him? To know he's OK first and foremost, but even more: to hear from him exactly what role he played in all of this. I shake my head. Astra said to trust my intuition, and for whatever reason, I want to see him.

Where are you, Gecko? I focus my thoughts on his face, and just like the last time I wanted to find him in the void, a silver arrow appears at my feet. I start to walk, then think, *no – go faster*. I run through the void, silver clinging to me like the last time I ran in this place. I flick it out and away, sending trails in all directions.

There: a dark shape in the void. I slow and stop as silver outlines a door, then step through.

'Gecko?'

He's across the room, and whips around at the sound of his name. But then he dives for the door; it disappears as he reaches it and he slams, hard, into the wall.

'Heh, nice to see you, too. OK if we talk for a moment before you run out on me?'

He groans, and rubs his shoulder. 'Sorry, but I'm distracted by being trapped. Can you make another door?'

'Can't you?'

'No. I don't know what they've done or how they've done it, but I'm a prisoner. In my own S'hack!' He punches the wall in fury. 'Let me out!' he yells.

'Calm down! I'll help you if I can, but you have to help me first.'

He turns and really looks at me now. 'Is everything all right? Are you safe?'

'If you call being locked up in a basement with a bunch of loons "safe".'

He half grins. 'That sounds about right; Heywood got you, then?'

'Yes. How about you? Did they catch you, or did you get away? What happened that night?'

He frowns, sits on the bench; I sit next to him.

'Well?'

'They caught me. Took me to Inaccessible Island: nice place, by the way, if you don't mind being in the freaking middle of nowhere. They gave me some drug or another, and next thing I know, I'm here.'

'Where's your body?'

'Must be plugged in somewhere on the island, but I don't remember plugging in. I've been going completely mental.

220

I've tried everything I can think of to get out, but nothing works!'

Gecko positively radiates tension; being locked in this small space in the void would be bad enough for anyone, but for Gecko? It's his worst nightmare. *Is it my fault?* a small voice whispers, inside.

'I'm sorry. But you shouldn't have dragged me along with you; you should have run.'

He shakes his head. 'I'm not blaming you. But I couldn't leave you behind.'

'Why?'

'So many reasons,' he says, his voice light. He takes my hand, weaves our fingers together. A glimmer of Gecko the flirt is back.

'Try to stay serious, if you can. I need to know some stuff. Please be honest with me.'

'I'm always honest! Well, almost always. Fire away.'

He stares back at me and now that he's next to me, so close, his hand warm in mine, I'm feeling more and more reluctant to ask what I need to know. Some of the things Crystal said – about Gecko manipulating me because I was a witness – might have started this, but there is more. Tempo knew who I was, what I am: did Gecko?

'All right, here goes. Were you instructed to seek me out at the test centre?'

His eyes open wider. 'No, of course not!'

'Well, maybe not directly. Was there something that led you to me?'

He's thinking, and I don't interrupt. 'Well, no; not *specifically* you,' he says, finally. 'Why does it matter?'

'It just does. Not me, specifically? What do you mean?'

'You've met Tempo?'

I nod. 'She's the one who let me plug in.'

'When it became apparent PareCo was taking me to the test centre whether I wanted to go or not, Tempo asked me to seek out anyone without an Implant. We were suspicious the new Implants weren't what they were supposed to be, and that something was up with the tests. To be around someone without an Implant was the best way to assess this.'

Someone without an Implant, at the test centre? That'd be me with a big shiny 'pick this girl' sign pointing at my forehead. I was the only one there that fit the bill.

'And how about later? Were you told to find me after the tests?'

'Nobody tells me what to do, Luna,' he says mildly, but his eyes flash annoyance. 'S'hackers aren't like that. We're all equal in the void.'

'Suggested it to you, then.'

He frowns. 'I told Tempo I'd met Astra's daughter. That you could see S'hacker marks. That you didn't have an Implant and were a Refuser, but that I'd told you about ANDs. She said we should keep an eye out for you, and if you plugged in, to assess what you could do in the void.'

'So that day you took me to the waterfall: that was why, wasn't it?' It hurts inside to think so, but I shrug it away, not wanting to look too closely at *why* it hurts so much.

'I didn't have to take you to my favourite place and spend half the night with you there, did I? I *wanted* to. And you did it, there, without even knowing: manipulated the void.'

'What on earth are you talking about?'

'Your swimsuit. You changed it. That was a fairly simple unconscious manipulation. But then there was your hair.'

'My hair?'

'When you dried it, styled it, the works. Not an easy thing to do.'

I stare back at him, surprised. 'I thought the world did that.'

'No. It was all you, Luna. That was when I knew for sure you really were a S'hacker. Tempo wasn't convinced; she wanted proof you could navigate the void.'

'So you slipped a ladder down to get me up there on my own.'

'Just so. I did argue against that. It was risky. Of course, then I thought you could have got lost in the void if you lost your nerve. I didn't know you could just unplug if you wanted to.'

'So I've been some sort of project you've been checking out, is that it?'

'It's not like that, Luna. I was happy to spend any time with you that I could.' Something in his eyes is warm, says, *Yes, this is the truth*. I shrug it away.

'Whatever. And the crash. Were you supposed to pull me with you out of the wreckage, get me to Heywood?'

'No. I didn't even know you'd be there! But –' and he

pauses – 'Tempo had stressed how important you were. When I got caught and thrown on the transport myself, I didn't know you were going to be there. What does this matter now, anyhow?'

'I don't know, but it matters. I think Tempo has got some sort of plans for me, something to do with PareCo.' *Tempo and Astra*, I add silently. Were they planning this before I was even born? 'I don't know what. I think she set things up so you'd rescue me.'

'That's crazy.' He says the words, but I can see he's thinking about what I said. He takes both my hands between his. 'Listen to me, Luna. Keep away from PareCo. Stay out of sight, stay with Heywood and his loons. They'll look after you.'

'I don't need looking after.'

And I don't, not in the usual sort of way. I've mostly raised myself, relied on myself. It doesn't mean I wouldn't like it if someone I trusted was there for the job. I sigh, lean my head against his shoulder and close my eyes. Not tired as in wanting to sleep, but emotionally drained; so much so that I feel almost empty.

'What's happened, Luna?'

'Tempo thinks PareCo killed my grandmother to get me on that transport.'

His hand strokes my hair. 'I'm sorry. I thought that was likely.'

'She also said they…' My voice wavers. 'That they killed my mother all those years ago. That they sabotaged her PIP.'

'That is believed to be true. We can't prove it, though.'

And I think of all the hidden and not-so-hidden barbs and slights aimed at me, at my family, because of how Astra died. Deep inside, something eases at the thought that it wasn't her fault; something else hardens.

'Did my dad know?'

'I don't know. Ask Tempo; they were friends then. She should know the answer.'

His arms slip around me, but the emptiness inside has begun to fill – with hot molten fury. I pull away.

'I can't stay away from PareCo. Not after what they've done to my family.'

'PareCo is dangerous. Believe me, Luna, you don't want them to take you.'

'Why should I listen to anything you say? You haven't been honest with me.'

'I've never lied to you. There may be stuff I never told you, but—'

'That's as good as.' I shrug, and stand up. 'Anyhow. It's a door you want, isn't it?' I focus on the wall; the silver appears as I will it to make a door. I walk towards it, pull the handle, step through. Hold it open.

He walks forwards, but as soon as he reaches it the door vanishes.

That's weird. I make another door, and step back through.

He's holding his head. 'Ouch. That hurt.'

'Sorry. So you can't make a door; you can't go through one that I make. You really *are* trapped.'

'Yeah. Thanks. I think I worked that one out.'

'There is something else I could try. Though I really, really hate doing it, and I'm not quite sure what will happen.'

'What's that?'

'I could spin and collapse this part of the void.'

'You can do that?'

'I think so. At least, I could. Not sure I still know how.'

'Go ahead. I'm not sure where I'll end up, but anywhere has got to be better than here.'

'Are you sure?'

'Yeah. But before you do…'

'What?'

'I'm sorry. You're right, I should have told you what I knew. It was about you, and what you are, and you had the right to know. Forgive me?'

I pause, turn away, trying to work things out. But finally turn back to Gecko, shake my head. 'I'm not sure I can right now. I'm too muddled up with everything. Maybe later?'

He stares back at me, and despite everything he's been through – being caught, drugged, and trapped in the void – he looks like this one thing is at the centre of his mind. And something relents, a little, inside.

I smile, and he grins back.

'If a smile is the best I can get, it'll do. For now.'

'Shall we give this a try?'

He nods.

'Give me a moment,' I say, and close my eyes again.

Cast myself *back, back, back*...to standing under the moon with Astra.

I open my eyes and start spinning, hands held up. Sparks of silver run through the walls into my hands and swirl around me, faster and faster, more and more silver, gathered and spun and stretched.

Then I slowly bring my hands together. Start to collapse the walls of Gecko's S'hack.

I stop when the screaming starts.

26

I sit up abruptly in the PIP. I didn't unplug. At least, I didn't mean to. How am I back here?

The door is ripped open: Tempo. 'What's happened? Were you screaming?' She comes in.

'I…I don't know. I have to go back. It's Gecko; he's trapped, and I tried to get him out. But it didn't work.'

Now Crystal is in the doorway, staring at me. 'You let *her* plug in?' She stares at Tempo in outrage. 'What's she done?' she demands.

Tempo gives Crystal a quelling look, but she stands her ground. 'Tell us about Gecko,' Tempo says, with slight stress on his name as if saying not to mention the memory beads. As if I was going to. As if I can concentrate on anything now but the sound of his voice still ringing out in pain inside my head.

'We were talking, and—'

'But I told you not to message anyone.' Tempo's face is coldly furious.

'I didn't! He's in his S'hack.'

They exchange a look of disbelief. 'You went to his S'hack?' Crystal says. 'How on earth did you find it?'

'Can't you do that? I just thought of Gecko, and an arrow appeared that led me to him. Let me go back, and…'

Tempo shakes her head. 'Not until you explain.'

'Shut up and I'll try,' I snap. Anger crosses Tempo's face but she keeps her lips pressed together, silent.

'He said he was caught; that they gave him some drugs, and then he was in the void. He's in his S'hack but can't get out. I made a door I could get in and out of, but when he tried, it disappeared, and he slammed into the wall. I went back in, and—' I hesitate, with a glance at Crystal, but her stance says she's not going anywhere, and time may be important. So I continue in a rush '—I spun the void to see if collapsing his room could get him out.'

'You did *what*?' Crystal says, jaw dropping.

'Spun the silver, then folded it in.'

There is an odd look on Tempo's face, a trace of *satisfaction*, almost, that is quickly replaced by coldness. 'So, let's see if we have this straight. He was trapped in a room, and you collapsed the room while you were both in it. Doesn't sound too clever. And then?'

'I stopped before it collapsed completely, when he started calling out. And somehow what happened made me unplug here, pull myself from there to here – I didn't decide to do it, it just *happened*. Let me go back and see if he is OK.'

'You unplugged from the void?' Crystal says, shock on her face. Despite everything else some small part of me notices Tempo isn't reacting, not to that; not that way.

'You dys!' Crystal pushes her hands into my shoulders. 'Don't you know what will happen to him if his virtual self is destroyed in the void, and can't go back to his body? He'll be a shell, like he's in a coma, for the rest of his life.'

'But I thought people died in games all the time. It doesn't do anything to them!'

Tempo shakes her head. 'It's not the same. Places created by PareCo have escape code; this is what allows you to unplug from Realtime or games at will, or if something happens to you. The void and S'hacker spaces do not.'

I stare at her, shocked and terrified at what might have happened. 'I have to go back.'

'I'm coming with you,' Crystal says.

'No,' Tempo says. 'You know this is one for me. Stay here, Crystal,' she says, her voice gentle this time, then turns to me. 'Plug in. Climb into the void and find me. I can help.'

I lie back into the PIP, and will the connection to be quick. It almost slams into me, and I gasp; circles spin in front of my eyes but soon vanish. The Realtime hallway is there, the silver ladder. I race up into the void, then focus on finding Tempo. The arrows are instant and bright, and I run.

She's just emerging from her hatch when I find her. She looks different in the void – younger – her hair is loose, but doesn't whip around like mine. It behaves, hanging all around her head weirdly, as if suspended in midair.

'Ah, there you are,' she says. 'Now, can you find Gecko?'

I concentrate on his face, and the arrow appears.

'Clever,' she says. We follow the arrow, and as always time in the void seems different; I can't tell if we run for a minute or an hour, and then…

We're there. His room is distorted, misshapen, flattened. 'Gecko?' I call out, and can hear the panic in my voice.

'Stand back, Luna,' Tempo says. 'I'll take time back.'

I do as she says. After, when I think about it, I can't work out what happened next. There was some sort of swirl, a vortex, about Tempo, but not like when I do it.

And the next thing I know I'm back in his S'hack, staring at Gecko. No sign of Tempo. He's standing there; the room is upright and square. As it was when I first arrived. Has Tempo really spun us back in time?

'What is it?' he says. 'Isn't it working?'

I don't answer, and just stand there, looking at him. Struggling not to rush over, to check if everything is still where it should be.

'The spinning and collapsing the room thing. Can't do it?' he prompts.

'I...no. I can't do it. I'm sorry.'

He shrugs. 'I was hoping. But never really believed it was possible. Don't worry about me; I'll find a way out of here. There'd be no point to them leaving me in here forever. Whatever it is they want from me, I'll find out when they're ready.'

'Right.'

'You better get going. Tempo's kind of impatient; she'll wonder what you're getting up to, plugged in for so long.'

She knows. Can she hear us, out there? But out loud all I say is, 'OK'. And then – 'Before I go, there is one other thing.'

'What's that?'

'I'm sorry for what I said before. I forgive you. For not telling me stuff.'

I take a step towards him; he takes one towards me. He hesitates, unsure, and I reach out my hands, pull him closer. His arms encircle my shoulders, mine go around his waist. I turn my head and nestle against his chest. His breath is warm in my hair; his heart beats under my cheek. Virtual this may be, but it feels close, warm, real. I breathe in and hold this moment, this memory, and fill myself with it. To make it take away the one before of him screaming in pain, pain that I caused. Stuff that I'll never tell, so how can I hold anything he never told me against him?

We obliterate and erase it until it never was.

Once we unplug, Tempo takes me back to the room where I sleep, tells me to rest, that the timing she did in the void with me in the centre of it is like I lived extra days. She actually gets me to lie down and tucks the blankets around me. I'm so tired that I let her, eyes already closing.

'We'll talk tonight,' she says.

As I drift off I hear her on the other side of the door, reassuring Crystal that Gecko is all right. It must make Crystal furious that I saw him in his prison and she didn't, but there is no comfort in that. I almost killed his virtual self, didn't I? Without that part of him there would have been no Gecko, none of what makes him who he is. If we'd thought it through a little more, collapsing his S'hack with him and me in it when he couldn't escape wasn't going to do anything good, was it?

And I feel lost, drifting, as if my anchor has been cut. The questions are too many, almost as if I can't focus through them all to the ones that are most important, and the answers are things I can't face or understand. Nanna would have said this day was a four: that I need to *centre, endure and persist.* But the stability is elusive.

I slip into uneasy dreams: of liquid power rushing through my veins, bleeding out and covering the world in beautiful, glistening silver. Opaque, smothering the land and blocking the sun.

27

'You must have questions,' Tempo says. We are in a back office, alone, and I'm fixed in her eyes. They're an odd colour: the silver-grey, like Astra's, like my own eyes, is there, but mixed with some indefinable *other* that seems to shift in the light. The same eyes that can unravel time in the void? Undo things that have been done. I shiver. What is she? What am I?

'I don't know where to start,' I say, feeling subdued, quiet, and still all wrong in the head from Tempo timing the void; not like myself, at all. *And who am I, really?*

'With everything else that happened, I didn't get a chance to ask how you got on with the memory beads. Did you manage to access them?'

I nod. The rush of Astra's warmth, and love. The shock revelations. 'So I'm some sort of genetic experiment, is that it?''

She doesn't deny it. 'I wouldn't put it that way,' she says, eventually.

'How did my parents end up together?'

'There were a number of possible male candidates with the desired trait present in their own mothers. This was important as it is linked to the X chromosome, so a man, who has only one X chromosome, will pass a copy of the genes involved to all of his daughters. Women have two X chromosomes, and your mother was already known to carry one copy of the gene, so in this match any daughter would have a fifty-fifty chance of having the trait. We managed to get DNA samples in various ways. Your dad was the most likely candidate: his mother had the strongest desired trait.'

'Stop with the genetics lesson. So what happened is this: she checked out his genes not his jeans, and then targeted him.' He didn't stand a chance. Astra was beautiful, poised, smart. Everything my bumbling dad wasn't. A swirl of anger on his behalf brings me out of this trance. 'This is so wrong! Nobody asked him what he wanted. Nobody asked *me*.'

'A little hard to do before you were born.' She hesitates. 'No matter how things started, Astra loved you, Luna. She came to care for your dad very much also.'

I shrug. Too little, too late, to make up for what she did? But I know she loved me. I felt it, all tied into her memories from years ago. Is that why those memories were placed there with the others? Emotional manipulation from beyond. I'm tired: I don't want this. *I want to go home.*

'And what about your grandmother, Luna? She wasn't involved in any of this, and she has paid the ultimate price.'

The anger comes back in a rush. I slam a fist on the desk. 'But what is it you think I can do about any of this? Look what happened when I tried to help Gecko. I don't know what I can do, what I can't. I could have as good as killed him.'

'What you did was dangerous.'

'I know that now.'

'Luna, if you are going to go to the void you have to learn

235

what you can control and what you can't. If you are with us, I can teach you.'

Part of me sings *yes*; more says *no*. And there is so much that I don't know. 'You haven't told me everything about who you are, what you are, have you?'

She smiles, pleased. 'About our organisation? Heywood and friends – the Worms—' she smiles again '—are a small offshoot of something far greater that he knows nothing about. It is COS – the Council of Scientists. I've been on the board for many years; your mother used to be the chair.'

'Astra mentioned it in her memory, but apart from that, I've never heard of it before. What is it?'

'The NUN cult of rationality is stifling all human advances. Without imagination – and intuition – there can be no progress, in science or any other areas for that matter. And PareCo has exploited this weakness, and manipulated NUN for their own ends. COS formed to stop them: we need you. Join us, Luna. We can train you.'

I shake my head. 'I don't want to go back to the void.'

'You may be the only one who can find Gecko again. He's invisible to me when he's in his S'hack. I've no idea how PareCo imprisoned him there; we have to work out how to get him out.'

'But I don't understand any of this! I don't even get what the void *is*, or how I can manipulate it. Stuff just happens. It scares me.' True, but it is also exhilarating. I've never felt more *alive* than with the power rush of gathering and using silver; everything in the real world feels dull, colourless, in comparison.

'I know,' Tempo says, as if she acknowledges what I said and what I didn't say at the same time. And her eyes are both sad and angry – a strange mix. She shakes her head. 'All these are things your mother was starting to teach you. And your father stopped me from seeing you, or you would know all of it and not be in this sea of confusion. He seemed to think you'd be safer if you didn't know, but he was wrong. I can help you understand.'

I say nothing. Even though Astra said he knew I was a S'hacker, I'm still stunned to think that *Dad* could have known any of this. And he didn't tell me?

'The virtual world everyone knows – Realtime hallways, personal and group spaces, holiday worlds, games – are all constructed out of the void by PareCo. Coded computer language creates three-dimensional places that are completely real to our virtual selves. Ordinary Hackers can manipulate the places built out of the void by PareCo by mentally tapping into the code.'

'Gecko told me that. That PareCo allows this, uses it to monitor Hackers. To keep tabs on them and what they can do. But what about S'hackers?'

'S'hackers can use the void themselves and create their own spaces, like Gecko's S'hack, and even whole worlds. This is what Astra did with her space game worlds, so famous even now.'

'But *how* do S'hackers manipulate the void?'

'How do you do it?'

'I have no idea. It was more random to start with; I didn't even *know* I made things, or the arrow that led me to Gecko the first time I did it, or the hatches and doors. How do I do it?'

'Because you are of the void.'

'But what does that mean?'

'The void runs in you; in your DNA. It is programmed to be part of you, like the S'hacker marks in your skin. Hacker tattoos are ink in flesh tattoos; yours are of the void.'

'I don't understand. *How* can the void be programmed to be part of me?'

'Early Hackers worked with scientists to find ways to get around PareCo's control. They needed to be able to manipulate the void themselves. They engineered this into their DNA; now this ability is passed from parent to child. It's running in your veins. It's part of you, like your name.'

'My name? But Luna was from a character in Virtual Harry Potter World. My parents met there.'

She shakes her head. 'Not that name. What is your S'hacker name?'

'What do you mean?'

'Think about it. I'm Tempo – time. Astra – the stars. Crystal – ice.'

'What about Gecko? Isn't a gecko a lizard?'

'Yes. One that can walk on ceilings, unnoticed. Gecko – the spy. He has been our best spy on PareCo. Insinuates himself into their worlds without notice. Or so we always thought. What is your S'hacker name?'

'I don't have one.'

'You must choose it yourself. Most S'hackers do so when they are much younger, by ten at the latest. Once they know what skills they have in the void.'

'I have none.'

'Is that so? What you could do hadn't fully manifested when Astra died, but I know she thought your abilities could be crucial, especially combined with the double awareness you indeed inherited from your grandmother, as was hoped. And the ability to unplug from within the void that seems to have come with it.'

'But what do you—'

'Enough questions for now, Luna. I have one for you. What are you going to do?'

'What do you mean?'

'Your mother and I were both committed – and I still am – to stopping PareCo's relentless manipulation and control of the worlds, virtual and otherwise. You've seen with your own eyes how PareCo has used the tests to their own ends; how they're willing to go to any lengths – even murder – to keep their secrets. Your mother died in this quest; your grandmother was a victim of it. Where do you stand?'

Anger struggles with *caution*. Gecko said to keep away from PareCo. And Tempo's words don't quite jive with Astra's: something is troubling me, deep inside, about Astra and Tempo. Astra was against the RQ tests and PareCo manipulating them for their own purposes. She said I could change things. What about Tempo? 'What is it that *you* want?' I ask her.

She smiles, pleased. 'Power can't vanish, only change form. If PareCo isn't in control there will be a power vacuum that must be filled. With our abilities, S'hackers are the logical replacement.'

'Astra never said anything about taking over.'

'Your mother was an idealist. I'm more . . . practical. But if she knew what they've done with the new Implants, she'd agree with me. And our goals were always the same: unmask PareCo. The emperor has no clothes.' Prickles run up my back: the same words Astra used in her memory.

'But I don't understand what you want from me!'

Her eyebrows go up. 'That is for you to determine. What can you do for us? Why? Think about these things, Luna. These things will become obvious when you choose your name.'

I *am* thinking about it. But I just want to go home. I want none of this to have happened. I stare at my hand, turn it over. The veins faintly visible in my wrist look the same as anyone else's – a faint blue-green under the skin – but I know different now. Silver runs through my body, whether I want it to or not.

Wanting things to be as they were won't bring Nanna back, won't change that everything I thought I knew about my mother, about my parents' relationship, was wrong.

Won't help Gecko.

*

Late that night I wake as the door to my room is unlocked, and watch as it opens: Crystal is silhouetted in the darkness.

I sit up fast. 'What is it with you: have you got something against sleep?'

'I can help you. Teach you how to control the void so it doesn't control you.'

I stare at her suspiciously. 'What's in it for you?'

'There is a price. Take me to see Gecko.'

'Why?'

'I have to see him. Look, you don't know him like I do. He'll be going crazy locked up like that. He can't take it.'

I stare back at her, somehow hurt that he's told his secrets to her, too.

'Please, just take me to him.'

'So you can't find people in the void on your own.'

She scowls. 'If I could, would I be here? No, I can't. It's not a common S'hacker skill. Actually Tempo is the only other S'hacker I know of who can do it, but even she can't find someone if they're in their S'hack. Gecko can find places, but not people.'

Part of me is sure I should say no, and not just out of wanting to keep her away from Gecko. There is nothing in Crystal that says she has my interests at heart; quite the opposite. Yet…here is a chance to find out more about the void without Tempo's control, without her insisting I commit to helping when I don't even know what that could entail. Despite what I said to Tempo, I'm gripped by curiosity. Just thinking about it makes my blood feels

241

hot, as if it is calling me to the void.

'Well?' she says, an impatient edge in her voice. 'You owe me for getting that report on your grandmother.'

'Is this just between us?'

'Tempo'd have a fit; I'm not going to tell her.'

'All right, then. Let's do it,' I say.

We creep down the dark hallway. She opens one of the PIP doors, enters a passcode. I lean back in the PIP; she watches me plug in before going to do so herself.

It is somehow reassuring that she can't find me. My skill at finding people is useful, given that I can't use Realtime the usual way to friend her and go to her space so we can go up a ladder together. Not when PareCo will be alert to any use of Realtime by me while I'm missing.

I head up the ladder, through the hatch, and step into the void. For all its strangeness it is becoming more familiar now. I look at the veins in my wrist again: is it a trick of the strange light? They're silver.

I focus on Crystal, on her face; nothing happens.

It's not working.

I sigh, then try again, and again. Why? As if from nowhere the thought comes. Is it because I don't really *want* to find her, is that it? She'll be angry by now.

I focus on wanting to be with Crystal, and finally, an arrow. It wavers as if it knows I'm not really sure, then strengthens until I find her.

'Where've you been?' she snaps. Voice brittle like the ice cloud that surrounds her.

'Sorry, it seems to be fallible. I was having trouble convincing myself I really wanted to find you.'

She laughs. 'That is an excuse I can understand and accept. All right then. Tell me what you can and can't do.'

'Er…OK. I can find people. As you know.'

'Useful.'

'If I really want to.'

'Fair. Anything else?'

'I can make doors into the void, out of my Realtime hallway. And into things, like Gecko's S'hack.'

She shakes her head. 'That should be impossible; it's trespassing of the worst kind.'

'He doesn't seem to mind.'

Her eyes grow colder, if that is possible. 'Wonderful. Is that it?'

'Once I did my hair. And I can spin and collapse the void.'

'Interesting – if you're not trapped in it at the time. Anything else?'

'I don't think so.'

'The main S'hacker skill you haven't mentioned is creation. What can you make?'

'Make?' I frown. 'I made a falling star recently. I think… when I was very small, I made a night sky: stars and a moon.'

'How?'

'I don't know. I sort of wanted them, threw silver, and there they were.'

'What would you like to make now? Desire is important

here. Something you desperately want. Half-hearted doesn't cut it.'

The only thing I can think of that I want is my family. Dad. Jason. Home. My room, at home? It wasn't anything special, but it was *mine*. Even Sally wouldn't generally invade it when I was in residence.

'I've got something. What next?'

'It sounds like when you've been spinning before you've gathered power, then collapsed it. This is the opposite. Gather power and thrust it out to create.'

'Yeah, sure. That's helpful.'

She crosses her arms. 'Just try it, you dys.'

I walk away from Crystal. Stand in the void, in the darkness, the comfort of little lights, whistling winds. I picture everything I can of my room from home, every detail, the battered shelves, the photo of Astra. Then raise my hands and spin.

Silver rushes to me from all directions. It clings to my skin, and my blood rushes to the surface in a wave of heat. The silver in me and around me longs to embrace; one calls for more and more of the other, in perfect harmony – a duet of growing power.

Vaguely I hear Crystal's voice calling through the vortex that has started to swirl above me: *You need more control!* And I try to calm it, to steady the rush, but there is so much, too much.

Not just my room then, no. Our house, too. The garden. It spreads out around me and is more than it ever has been.

244

Fragrant blossoms fill the air as if a mad hyperactive spring has taken over.

'Rein it in,' Crystal yells. 'Or it'll implode in on itself.'

I slow, calm, pull in the borders. Breathing deeply, but not air – silver. It is me, of me, around me. My hands: I stare at them. Beautiful silver.

'Luna, Luna.' A distant voice calls my name, but I ignore it now. Lie on the warm grass, a sunny day. As I calm, the silver breathes out until I'm more the *me* that I usually am. But the other is me, too? The orange and black of a butterfly flutters past, and I smile.

'Luna, please!'

I frown. Is that Crystal?

I make a door in the edges of blue sky and open it. Outside in the blackness of the void is Crystal. She stares through the door, eyes wide. 'That was a bit of a wow.' She hesitates. 'Can I come in?'

'Of course.'

She walks in, looks around her in wonder. 'Nice S'hack,' she says, finally. 'Show-off.'

'You told me to make something I wanted, so I did.'

'What is this place?'

'Home,' I say, simply.

'It's your S'hack now. No one but you can find it. No one but you can get in or out unless you let them.'

'Did I do all right?'

She rolls her eyes. 'You pass creation. Next lesson would be new worlds, but by the looks of this that won't be too much for you. Only thing is you took in too much power. If you overwhelm what you are trying to create with more than it needs, it might get away from you, and tear you apart with it.'

'Spinning power…it's intoxicating. I wanted more and more.'

'That's the danger you must guard against.' She shakes her head. 'Most of us don't have that problem; most of us struggle to make something small and plain.' Envy is stark in her eyes.

'Come on; let's find Gecko.'

I make another door in the sky; we step through. As soon as we do the door vanishes. No sign my own S'hack is even there unless I think of it: then, much like with Gecko's S'hack, a faint outline appears.

I hold Gecko in my mind, and we follow silver arrows until we get to his S'hack. I stop. 'Here we are.'

'Where?' she says, looking around her.

'You can't see it?'

She frowns, shakes her head no.

I wish for a door, and as the silver spreads, she nods. 'I can see the door.'

I open it, step through.

Crystal doesn't follow.

'Luna?' Gecko is lying down on his bench. He sits up but doesn't stand. There are stark black circles under his eyes, but he smiles to see me.

'What's wrong?'

A pained look crosses his face. 'I don't…I can't…'

'What is it?' I stare at the struggle on his face; it's like it was when he was trying to talk about what happened at the test centre. 'Is your Implant stopping you from telling me something?'

He nods, then winces as if that simple movement caused a backlash inside.

'Crystal is with me; she wants to see you. But she couldn't seem to come in. Can you do anything? Like, give her permission or whatever?'

He nods. 'Try again,' he says.

I make a door, look through it. Crystal scowls on the other side.

'What game you playing at?' she snaps.

'Nothing. You didn't follow me.'

'You just vanished. I couldn't see where you went.'

'All right. How about if I pull you through?' I hold out a hand. She hesitates, comes up, takes my hand. Hers is so cold hairs rise on my arm. I start to pull her through the door but she lets go, cries out. I turn back, and she is cradling her hand against her.

'Sorry. Looks like you can't come in.'

Her eyes are filling with tears that spill and freeze to crystals on her cheeks. She blinks furiously.

'Is there anything you want me to tell him?'

'I don't know. Just say…I miss him. And hope he's all right.'

'OK. Wait here.'

I go back through to Gecko. 'She can't come in.' I relay her message, watching his face. Is she really his girlfriend?

As if he reads my thoughts he shakes her head. 'We used to be together. Not for a while. It didn't work out.'

'Oh. Does she know that?'

'She should. She's not always good at processing stuff she doesn't like, though.' He hesitates. 'We've been friends for years. I know she's difficult, but she's had a tough time. Her mum was an Implant Addict; Crystal had been selling her S'hacking abilities to dodgy customers to feed them since she could walk.'

I stare at him, horrified.

'But she is a friend, nothing more. And it's good to see you. What's happening out there?'

I relay a summary of Crystal and me in the void; Tempo's words last night.

'Don't listen to Tempo; don't let them use you like they've used me.'

'What do you mean?'

He shakes his head. 'Just suspicions. But keep away from PareCo.'

'I can't. I have to make PareCo pay for what they've done to my family.' I spit the words out. The words I'd been holding back from Tempo, wanting to think things through before I give her what she wants to hear. But no matter what her reasons are, our ultimate goal is the same.

'Don't let them get you, too, Luna.' A note of fear, of warning.

'What has happened to you? What's wrong?'

He visibly struggles. 'You don't want to be where I am,' he finally manages to get out. Then breathes heavily, as if he fought hard just to say that.

'Are you still at Inaccessible Island?'

He nods. So his physical location isn't blocked; something else is.

'I need to go there.'

'No, Luna. Don't do it.'

'You think I can't do anything useful!'

'No, that's not it. It's too dangerous. Do you want to be trapped like me?'

'Listen to me, Gecko. They can't trap *me* in the void, can they? I can always just unplug at will, even if I'm in the void. So that can't happen to me. I'll go to Inaccessible Island. I'll find out what they're up to, and I'll find you. Do an emergency unplug on your body, and set you free.'

'No, Luna. Don't go there. It's too dangerous. Nothing can happen to you; it's too important. *You're* too important.'

I stare back into his dark eyes. 'Why?'

'Isn't it obvious?' He smiles and a trace of his swagger comes back. 'You haven't completely fallen under my spell yet. It's ruining my track record.'

I smile, but shake my head. 'You can't stop me. Gecko, I'll find you, wherever you are.'

He wraps his arms around me, and I can feel him shaking. He's still fighting the Implant, fighting to find a way to tell me what has happened. He finally sags and shakes his

249

head. Murmurs into my hair. 'I can't help you. You'd be on your own.'

'I know. It's OK; I'm used to it.'

After unplugging, Crystal and I head up the dark hallway, and through the door at the end. Then the lights suddenly go on. Tempo and Heywood stare back at us.

'What have you done?' Tempo demands, staring at Crystal.

She straightens her shoulders. 'What you should have done in the first place. Start teaching her, so she isn't a danger to others.'

'Or herself,' Heywood adds mildly.

Tempo turns her glare on Heywood. 'You knew about this?'

'No. But it was a good idea. The right thing to do.'

They all start winding up for an argument, ignoring the one they're arguing about. I sit on the sofa for the show, but then suddenly feel tired of it all.

'Listen up,' I yell out when there is a pause. 'Remember me? I've decided where I stand. What I'm doing. That's what you wanted, isn't it?'

Silence falls. Three sets of eyes swivel towards me.

'I'm going to Inaccessible Island.'

Later that night I lie in bed, unable to sleep.

Heywood and Tempo argue outside my door. He thinks I need more training. That I'm dangerous. Tempo's voice is cold, condescending; how could *he* possibly know anything about it when he's not a S'hacker, or even a Hacker? That every virtual means to find out what is happening at Inaccessible Island has failed: the only way forward is for someone to go there in person. That from what Crystal told her I did in the void tonight, I'm more than ready. And she says that is exactly why I should go there, and go there now: that I'm dangerous, unpredictable. PareCo won't know what I'm going to do.

They're not the only ones.

And me: *dangerous*? If only they could see me now. I hug Mr Dog close, curled into a ball, with pillows either side of me at the edges of the bed like I used to do when I was a child – convinced it'd stop the scary creatures under the bed from climbing up and getting me.

But this time I'm going under the bed.

28

Tempo takes me to her office the next morning. She shuts the door; we are alone. 'Tell me what you want to do,' she says.

'I'll go to Inaccessible Island. I'll find out what PareCo is up to there. And I'll find Gecko.' I say the words like all that will be easy to accomplish, but inside, I'm scared.

She's pleased, though she doesn't say. There is a gleam of triumph in her eyes. Am I doing exactly what she wants? That grates for some reason, but I shrug it away. *It's what I want, too.* It's what I must do.

'There is a catch. You can't just walk out of here as if nothing ever happened. How do you explain where you've been? Even if you can come up with a good story, they'll never believe it. A few truth drugs and they'll know everything.'

'So what can I do?'

'Memory beads, like your mother's. We'll put your memories of here in beads. I can take time back to the last time you were in the void before you came here.'

Shivers go up my spine. Take my memories, and hide them away in beads? Like Astra did. Shock hits me hard when I see the implications: memories aren't just copied, they are taken. And they are taken out of time: only Tempo could do this.

'You did that for Astra, too, didn't you? You made this necklace.' I touch it where it hangs around my neck.

'Yes,' she admits.

That isn't quite what she told me before, but I push that thought away as tears prickle in my eyes. 'So when Astra put memories in these beads – of when I was born, my first steps – she didn't remember those moments herself any more.'

'It's the only way it can be done.'

'So she took early memories of me as a baby, and put them in beads?' I shake my head. 'How could she do that, strip her own memories for me? And *why*? Did I really need them more than she did?' It hurts to think she could just walk away from them like that.

'If she'd survived she could have restored them to herself, just like you will do later on – restore the memories we place in the beads.'

'But how will I know to access them later if I can't remember anything?'

'When the time is right, you'll know.'

That isn't good enough for me. Later when we plug in to go to the void for memory shenanigans, I race to my S'hack first, write myself a note, and pin it to the front door of the house. I won't remember my S'hack, or making it. But won't I be drawn to it? It's my home away from home, the one place I'd want to run to in the void. I hope so; it's all I can come up with now.

I try to hurry to meet Tempo, picturing her face: forcing the silver arrows to show me the way. It's even harder than that last time with Crystal. I *really* don't want to find Tempo, do I?

But I must.

It's fear, that's all it is: fear of having my memories mucked with. But it has to be done; it's the only way. I push it away, focus.

When at last the arrows take me to her she is facing the other way, and I pause, study her. There is something about her that is calm and almost regal, while everything in and outside of me is a swirling storm. Even her hair flutters gently about her face, hanging in the void. Mine whips against the constraints of its ponytail, fighting to be free.

Then she turns, smiles to see me. 'There you are. Did you have trouble finding me?'

'A bit. It took a while to make myself do it this time.'

She inclines her head. 'Taming your will in the void is one of the first challenges a S'hacker must face.'

Now that her eyes are on me here I feel her power like a physical thing, one that makes me aware of all that I lack. 'I don't understand why you're not training me.'

'Luna, you are of the elements. Training wouldn't enhance your skills, it would curtail them.'

'Heywood doesn't agree with you.'

She raises an eyebrow. 'His opinion is of no consequence. He's not one of us.' Her shoulders rise in a shrug, dismissive, and it needles: he's not a S'hacker and so can't manipulate the void, but so what? It makes me remember all the slights from my classmates because I didn't plug in at school. I'm still the same person I was then.

'Isn't he part of your organisation?'

'He is useful; he will continue to be useful. He will never be in charge.' She smiles. 'But this is a diversion from what we are here for. Are you ready?' she asks.

'No. But do it anyway.'

'It won't hurt. I promise.'

As before when she timed Gecko's S'hack, power swirls about her in a vortex. But this time there is more power, so much more, and I'm inside the vortex with her. We're spinning in a swirl of silver so fast that everything about me is a blur, and I have to fight myself to not pull away, to not resist.

And then, all at once, we are *back*. Back in time to when I last plugged into the void before I left home for the transport to Inaccessible Island. To when I threw a star into the void for Nanna, and watched it fall. To when I ran out on Gecko for telling me his crazy theories about PareCo. Not so crazy, after all.

Tempo winds time forwards from then to now, more slowly, and the memories unwind with time. She is spinning them away – wisps of thought, feeling and sensation that are part of me now become part of the vortex swirling around us. As she does so, everything is relived in a strange fast-forward:

The note on the flowers sent by Dr Rafferty: my transfer cancelled.

Saying goodbye to my family; Dad giving me Astra's silver necklace, on which so much depended.

The transport. Hex. Gecko appearing; his strange words.

The crash, coming to this place, the fear.

The void; collapsing it, and Gecko's pain.

And Astra's memories. If I don't manage to restore my own memories, these will be lost forever. It hurts to relive the joy she felt when I was born, knowing as I do now that she gave up the memories she stored for me. That Tempo did this to her all those years ago like she is doing to me now.

And Astra's words to me as she stared in the mirror. Listening to them a second time I'm struck again by all she doesn't say. And by *trust no one; trust only yourself*. Repeated twice with more emphasis on the words than I noticed the first time.

All she doesn't say?

The first time I experienced her memories, I thought she was afraid of someone listening in. Tempo was listening! She was there to unwind Astra's memories, to store them away. She was there the whole time.

My memories are swirling up in silver, and I struggle to focus my thoughts, to pull them back.

Tempo had said bringing me to Heywood's house was the only way she could reach me. That they needed me to be safe until my time came: that she trusts me to do what is right when I know the truth.

But what is the truth?

Part of Tempo's truth is that she wants power, to take over from PareCo. For some reason I don't understand, she thinks she needs me to do that.

Horror is dawning inside. I should have listened to Gecko. He said *don't let them use you like they've used me*. I'd thought he was in on things with Tempo, but was he? He'd said his S'hacker status had been betrayed by someone – that he'd been forced to go to the test centre by PareCo. The same test centre as me. Who betrayed him? Then later he was in hiding, but somehow PareCo found him again, and threw him on that transport. The same transport as me. But *how* did they find him? Did Tempo betray him in both instances, so he could first check me out for her, then later rescue me?

But more: how did *I* get on that transport? Nanna's death. But PareCo did that, didn't they?

But something about that isn't right, doesn't *feel* right, and I struggle to focus on what. When it hits me, I gasp: Crystal said *if PareCo did it, they've probably faked the records*. But they weren't faked.

According to official PareCo records, Nanna died of Implant acceleration. Would they have had it there, bold, in print on an official report, if they'd done it themselves?

I feel cold, sick, inside. Tempo must have hacked PareCo records and found out I got a university transfer because of Nanna being ill, and the fine print – that a change of circumstances with Nanna would have me going to Inaccessible Island, instead. Crystal told me S'hackers could hack old-style Implants like Nanna would've had. And Tempo said she wasn't going to tell me how Nanna died; not until she knew from Crystal that I suspected it wasn't natural causes.

Not until she realised she could blame PareCo, and give me another reason to hate them.

But this can't be true. Why go to all that trouble to have me put on the transport and rescued from it? It would have been much easier to snatch me on the way home from school.

Because she still needs me to go to Inaccessible Island. Only PareCo can get me there. By deciding to leave this place so they'll take me there, I've done exactly what she wanted.

'Stop!' I scream, and struggle to pull my memories back from the vortex. 'It was you Astra was afraid of; it's you she tried to warn me not to trust.' Rage fills me, and I fight to pull the memories back to myself, to stop time as it swirls between us.

Tempo turns and smiles, ghostly in the swirl of power that surrounds her. 'Yes, I suppose that's true. Your mother was misguided. She thought it wasn't enough to topple PareCo and for S'hackers to silently take over. But she soon forgot she wanted proper democracy to decide what happens next. As if *that* could ever do anything but go wrong.'

'And Nanna? Gecko, too?' I gasp to even say their names, full of pain at what happened to both of them, and with struggling to hold onto the memory of it.

Memories are drifting into silver beads.

Why did I say their names?

She smiles, and I fight to pull my memories back to myself, unsure even why, but I'm desperate to get them back, to hold onto them. But Tempo is too strong. Another memory whips away in the air, drifts into a bead.

'But don't let that trouble you, dear Luna.' She holds my necklace in her hands. It's longer now, with eight shiny new memory beads, my S'hacker marks on each one. Then she smiles and pinches the last two off the necklace: the ones with my last memories. The ones of me realising what she's done.

They float away, to be lost in the void forever.

I fight to hold these last thoughts, to keep them. And she said *Astra forgot*? No! Some of her memories must have been stolen: Tempo didn't keep them all on the necklace with the others. Some were pinched off and lost in the void, like mine.

Could I call a silver arrow to find the missing memory beads?

But how would I know to do so?

I *focus* as much, and as hard, as I can: on silver beads. Floating in the void. Imprinting – engraving – the image in my mind.

Silver beads. With my S'hacker marks; every swirl, every detail. Floating in the void.

Trust your intuition, Astra said. Every fibre of my being said to stay away from Tempo today, but I didn't.

I'm filled with sadness. *I'm sorry, Mum. I didn't do what you asked.*

Silver beads in the void. *Fight.*

Beads. In…in…the void? *See them.*

The void?

Nothing.

5

WORLDS

*For there is a single general space, a single vast immensity
which we may freely call Void; in it are innumerable globes
like this one on which we live and grow. This space we
declare to be infinite, since neither reason, convenience,
possibility, sense-perception nor nature assign to it a limit. In
it are an infinity of worlds of the same kind as our own.*

Giordano Bruno, burned at the stake in 1600

29

Sunlight streams through the window next to me, and I blink, confused. It's night, isn't it? I look around. I'm sitting at a table on my own; there are other tables around me. A waitress bustles about with plates of food. I'm in a café, is that it?

But where am I? How did I get here?

People stream past the window, and I stare out. A busy street; could be anywhere in London but I don't recognise it, and panic is rising inside. This is it: I've finally completely lost it.

OK. Breathe deep, calm down. What is the last thing I can remember?

I try to concentrate, but my head feels so *wrong*. But I was in the void: I'm sure of that at least. I'd been with Gecko. He'd freaked me out, talking about how Danny and Jezzamine died. He'd said he was being held by PareCo and forced to go to Inaccessible Island. And I'd panicked, and run out of his S'hack. Straight through the wall.

And then...? No idea.

I'm not plugged in now; that I'm sure of. There is no double awareness, no body lying in my PIP at home. So no matter how I got here, it's real.

Check surroundings? Next to me on the table: a menu screen; a half-drunk cup of tea, gone cold. My bag is on an empty chair next to me, Jason's dog peering out from the top of it. Is Jason here? I search the café: tables about half full, more people coming in the door, no sign of Jason or anyone else I know. My tummy rumbles and a clock on the wall tells me it has gone noon. Lunchtime.

A waitress walks up. 'Have you decided yet?' she asks, a wary look on her face.

When in doubt, eat. I scan the menu fast, order sandwiches, more tea. Scrabble through my bag for a credit token, panicking when it isn't there, but then realise it is already in the table slot. I frown. Did I put it there? She punches my order in, starts to walk away.

'Wait,' I say. Swallow. She turns back and I try to think of a way to get information without looking a complete dys, but then give up and just ask. 'How long have I been sitting here? Did anyone come in with me?'

She keeps her distance. 'The same as the last time you asked me,' she says, speaking very slowly. 'You got here by yourself, just after eleven.' And she walks away, fast.

I've definitely lost it.

Tea comes, hot, and I wrap my shaking hands around the cup. Sandwiches next. I eat, mechanically at first, then with more attention, and somehow start to feel better. The light glares less, my head spins less. Have I been drugged?

Dad. *I should call Dad*, I realise, finally forming a useful thought. But before I can wonder if my phone is in my bag and, if not, where I can find one, the door opens. A man with a familiar smile, a white coat: the HealthCo doctor from the test centre? Dr Rafferty.

He scans the room until he spots me at the table in the window, and walks over.

'Luna? There you are,' he says, pauses by the other chair and I move my bag from it to the table. He sits down.

'Hi,' I say. Staring at him with relief: a face I know, even if not top choice.

'Where've you been, Luna? We've been looking for you. Everybody has been very worried.'

'I...I don't know.' And now I'm shaking again, wanting to cry, and beyond working out if I should or shouldn't tell him the truth, but I'm not up to coming up with a useful or believable lie, so it is the only option. 'I don't know. One minute I was plugged in at home; it was the evening after Nanna's funeral.' Pain twists inside. 'The next minute... I'm here. I don't know what's happened!' And I can hear the panic in my voice, feel tears wet on my cheeks.

His eyes are concerned. 'Oh, dear. There, there, Luna.' He pats my hand awkwardly. 'Everything will be fine. Don't worry. We'll work out what has happened to you. Come on.'

He stands, and I get up, tuck my bag around my arm. He nods reassuringly and we head for the door. The waitress looks relieved.

Outside the café is a van. A door opens from inside; Dr Rafferty has a quick word with someone, then turns back. 'Come on, Luna. Get in. I think a trip to hospital is in order.'

A stark white room. There is someone outside my door all the time, fuzzy but visible through the obscured glass pane: a guard? Who am I being guarded from? Or maybe he is here to keep an eye on me. I consider trying to leave to see what happens, but then dismiss it. I'm in the right place to figure out what is wrong.

There are scans, tests. Dr Rafferty comes in and out. Then there are drugs, and I drift away, dream of questions. *Who am I? Where was I?* But I can't answer them any more than I can when I'm awake.

Later I open my eyes, and Dr Rafferty is in the chair next to me, reading a patient chart. Mine? He looks up. 'Ah, hello, Luna. Back with us, I see.'

'So, have you worked out what is wrong with me? Have I lost it?'

He grins. 'No, you're completely sane. That's not it.'

'Tell me what's going on. Please.'

'I will as much as I can. When I found you in the café yesterday, it was actually six days later than you thought it was.'

'Six *days*?'

'Yes. Your transport crashed, and you were seen being pulled away from the wreckage. Then you disappeared.'

'A transport? What transport?'

'The one taking you for travel to Inaccessible Island. That was the day after your nanna's funeral.'

'I was going there? But I had a transfer to London Uni.'

'You did, but due to changed circumstances, the transfer was cancelled.'

I stare back at him, confused, then the pound drops. I had

the transfer because of Nanna. When she died, circumstances changed: no Nanna, no transfer.

'The transport crashed, and then I disappeared?'

'Yes.'

'People can't just disappear.'

'No. But we couldn't find you. When you used your credit token at that café, that flagged your location on the system, and I came to see if you were all right.'

'What about my family? When can I see them? They must have been so freaked.'

He shakes his head. 'They didn't know. We felt it best to spare them until we knew what happened to you.'

'But where have I been?'

'All I can do is speculate. It's being looked into, but you may have been taken by a group of rebels.'

My jaw literally drops. 'There are rebels? In *London*?'

'Regrettably, there are always the disaffected, the deluded, the mentally deficient. Not just here; in countries all around the world. Marginalised and wanting attention for some lost cause, most usually.' He shrugs dismissively.

'But why was I in that café? What's happened to my memory?'

He shrugs. 'Perhaps whatever it was they thought they wanted you for didn't work out? Perhaps you resisted their plans, or they decided you were of no use, wiped your memory and let you go. We know your memories of this time are truly gone from the tests we carried out, not just suppressed, but as for why, or how – again, this is just speculation at this point.'

There's a knock on the door, and an orderly brings a suitcase into the room. I recognise it: it's mine. The one I used when I went to the test centre. But why is it here?

'Ah, your things have arrived,' Dr Rafferty says.

I look at him blankly.

'The bag you packed to go to Inaccessible Island. It was recovered from the transport after the accident. Perhaps your own clothes will make you feel better? I'll leave you a moment; get dressed. Soon it will be time to go.'

'Am I going home now?'

'I'm afraid not. You have to catch up to your cohort at Inaccessible Island. They'll be ahead of you in training now.' He stands, walks to the door. 'Get ready and I'll be back in twenty minutes.'

He leaves and the door swings shut.

Well. I wheel my suitcase across the room, put it on the bed. At least I can get out of this terribly attractive hospital gown. But I feel like I'm trespassing on my own life. Did I pack this bag? I don't remember, and suddenly am desperate to go through all my stuff, to see if it helps things come back.

Inside are neatly folded clothes, neater than I'd do. Maybe Sally packed it for me, though it isn't like me to let her do that. ANDs are tucked in corners, and I remember I'd started using them to plug in, that Gecko had told me about them.

Gecko said he was being taken to Inaccessible Island, too. Will he be there? Is he crazy, or isn't he? If he's there, then maybe he isn't. Maybe he was right about PareCo causing Jezzamine and Danny's deaths. Spine spiders walk up my backbone: he warned me not to go to the PareCo Think Tank.

But it's not like I have a choice.

Bemused, I get dressed, then go through my handbag also. No phone, but whether I didn't take it, or it went missing either when I did or later, here at the hospital, I have no way of knowing. And why've I got Jason's toy dog with me? Generally called Mr Dog; full name Mr Dodgy D Dog. I hold him in my hands.

Something glints, and I look closer: silver is double-wrapped around his furry neck. Astra's old necklace? What on earth is it doing here? I undo it and put it around my own neck under my clothes. The silver is cool against my skin, but somehow it zings, like electricity.

30

I glance at the ticket stamp, faint on my wrist: 49B – then back
at the number on the seatback. It's my seat, but it's occupied.
I clear my throat. 'Excuse me, I think you're in the wrong
seat.' A face that is pale even for a Hacker turns towards me,
dark eyes wide under a shock of green-streaked hair.

'Would you mind taking the window seat, instead?'
she says.

I shrug. 'Sure. Whatever.'

She stands so I can get in, and she's tiny: I tower over her
by a foot at least. It's an exit row, and for a moment, something
about that twinges uneasily. I shrug it aside. Extra foot room
– what's not to like?

I sit down, and elbow the button on the seat arm for the
automatic seat belt. Glance back at the girl next to me. Her
hands are laced together, knuckles going white.

'Are you OK?'

She jumps, turns to look at me. 'Fine. Only…do you mind
if we talk while the plane takes off?'

After being ignored by the tight group of twelve smug
and happy Hackers in the airport departure lounge that I'd
been herded into by Dr Rafferty, I'm about to return the
favour and ignore her, but then I really look at her again.
She's breathing is short, sharp gasps. Her pupils are dilated.
The engines rev up, and she jumps so much if her seatbelt

wasn't on I'm pretty sure she'd have hit the overhead lockers.

She's completely freaked out.

'Don't like flying?'

'I hate it. Please don't tell anyone; it's totally dys.'

I'm shocked. A Hacker who is afraid to fly? Fear is not allowed in Hackerville. A trace of sympathy registers inside. The others in our group are up and down this side of the plane in a cluster, Dr Rafferty and a PareCo official at the front; none of them are in our eye line. She might get away with it.

'OK, sure. What do you want to talk about?'

'Anything that doesn't involve being *here*. Who are you, anyhow? Speculation as to why you joined us has been rife.'

'So I didn't just imagine that everyone was talking about me.' Their tattooed eyes had all swivelled in my direction when I got to the airport, and real conversation had died. Vacant looks followed, indicating virtual conversation had taken over. Not possible now as Implants are blocked during flights; something about interfering with communication and navigation systems. So she has to make do with me.

She almost manages to grin. 'No, it wasn't all in your mind. We'd been in the same group together since we boarded the transport yesterday; then you appeared through a special door into departures, and you're not even a Hacker. If that wasn't enough you had a doctor in tow, and didn't respond to Implant hellos. We were understandably a little curious.'

I raise an eyebrow. 'I'm Luna. I haven't got an Implant, so

271

sorry if I ignored anyone earlier. And I was supposed to be in the previous group, but got delayed.'

'You haven't got an Implant?' The shock on her face is as severe as if I'd just said I haven't got a brain, or a heart, yet somehow still manage to walk and talk all by myself. 'And you were delayed, and they still let you come? What happened?'

I'm uneasy. What I just said was the Dr Rafferty-approved line; he didn't say what to do if people ask questions, and they are bound to, aren't they? Saying as little as possible sounds like a good idea. 'There was an accident.' No worries about getting into too much detail; kind of hard when I don't remember a thing about it.

'What sort of accident?' Her eyes are more curious now, less scared, but then we start hitting speed for takeoff, and the fear comes back. She grips the arms of the seat hard, her eyes clenched shut tight as we lift off and the G-force pushes us back into our seats.

'Flying is supposed to be safer than walking, you know,' I say, trying to think of something helpful.

'I'd rather fall over when I'm walking on the ground than drop like a stone from the sky,' she hisses through gritted teeth.

'Good point.' I'd always liked the feeling of speed, and the *boom* when we break the sound barrier, but tend to not think of being in the sky and hurtling from said sky – it is more the rush of going faster and faster that I like.

'Talk? Please,' she says, eyes still shut. 'About anything.'

'What's your name?'

'Marina.'

'OK, Marina.' I scan my memory banks for something that'll distract her. It's an obvious answer, really, and they'll find out anyhow, won't they? Somehow, Hackers always do. 'How about we each say one surprising thing about ourselves?'

'You go first,' she says, her voice gaspy and not quite right.

'My mother was Astra.'

Her eyes snap open. 'What? Really? I love her interpretation of black holes. Is that why you're coming even though you haven't got an Implant?'

I shrug. 'Probably. I don't know. I did rather well on the IQ test also. Now it's your turn,' I prompt.

'You've already got the only surprising fact about me. The flying thing. The rest is pretty boring. I'm just a Hacker.'

'Obviously,' I say, glancing again at the waves of black swirls around her left eye. 'But is that all you are – a Hacker?'

She gives me a look, one that says – what else is there?

'What's your Hacker kick?' I ask.

'I'm into Atlantis mostly. Mermaids, too. Anything to do with the sea.'

We've levelled off now. Her colour is starting to come back, but she keeps her eyes turned carefully away from the window, from a London rapidly receding from view. I try not to visibly stare out of the window, wanting to reach out and touch *home*, one last time. My throat feels tight and it is nothing to do with fear of flying: we're hurtling towards the unknown.

I turn back to her. 'Do you know anything about where we're going?'

'You missed the info dump, didn't you? We all got it through our Implants when we arrived in departures. About the trip and the island.'

'Tell me about it.'

She starts going over what I've missed, and both her voice and her colour continue to improve. Is it just a taking off thing? Or maybe talking does help. She explains how we're flying to South Africa, that Inaccessible Island – nicknamed Inac – is hundreds of miles from there. It is an extinct volcano, only about fourteen square kilometres. That we're getting a boat from SA because air space is restricted above Inac, as part of a world heritage site.

'But why is it a no-fly zone?'

'It's part of being a reserve: no unnecessary tech is allowed. So no flying.'

'What about PareCo being there? They're all tech, tech, tech.'

She shrugs. 'They're PareCo.' As if that says it all.

And I wonder why PareCo are out in the middle of nowhere like this: are they up to things they don't want anyone to see? It's got to cost loads to transport people, equipment and supplies. Hex said it was part of them staying neutral, not being under any one country's control, which makes sense. But there has got to be an easier way to do that.

But I'm excited just the same to see this remote place. 'This island thing should be just right for you,' I say.

'What do you mean?'

'Mermaids – an island – the sea…?' She looks at me blankly. 'Shouldn't where we're going be perfect for all of that?'

She shakes her head a little. 'Where we're going, that stuff is real.'

'Except for the mermaids. So?'

'Virtual is better, Luna.' She gives me a pitying look.

'How so?'

'Last I checked, I can't breathe underwater in a real ocean; last I checked, I couldn't be a mermaid, either. And I've heard that swimming at real beaches is awful. You get sand *everywhere*, and salt is horrible in your hair.' There is a sense of repetition, as if she is parroting things she has been told. Her wistful face goes against the words, and the green streaks in her golden hair, like sun on seaweed, say she yearns for it to be real.

Now I give her a pitying look. 'Try the real world some time. Have you ever been to a real beach?'

She shakes her head. 'Have you?'

I nod. 'Astra took me to Brighton once. I couldn't have been more than four years old, but I still remember.' And I describe chasing waves on the sand.

She frowns. 'That isn't much better than virtual, you know. That beach wasn't naturally sandy – it was all shingle. They brought the sand in decades ago, before the Preservation Act.'

'To four-year-old me it felt pretty real.'

'You could go there again in virtual. At any point in history you want: a sandy beach, or a stony one; even before the new piers were destroyed in the war.'

I shake my head. 'It wouldn't be the same. I prefer my own memories.' My words smart, inside. Whatever happened to me before and after that transport crash, I've lost *six days*. Who knows what might be in the missing bits? It feels like something vital has been stolen, leaving a dull ache behind.

'Memory is notoriously unreliable: why not see what it was really like?'

'Who is to say that what is in Virtual Brighton is any more real than my memories? Isn't it constructed based on someone else's memories?'

She shakes her head. 'There's more to it than that,' she says, an impatient look in her eyes; one that says *if you were a Hacker, you'd understand*. 'Anyhow, you'll have to find out more about how VeeDubs work if you're going to work for PareCo.'

'VeeDubs? What does that mean?'

'Virtual Worlds, V-W: VeeDubs.'

I sit back again and look out the window, but all there is now is darkness. As if I could do anything useful for PareCo. Until seconds ago I didn't even know what a VeeDub was. I don't even know what Hackers really *do*, apart from the very little Hex has told me, about manipulating code in virtual spaces. VeeDubs, that is.

When we finally get to the approach at Cape Town, Marina goes through the whole panic thing again as the plane lands, and I try to keep her talking until we're down.

We taxi to the gates, and the *No Implants* light goes off before the doors open. Marina's face switches to blank, then comes back again.

'Thank you, Luna. I really owe you one.' Her eyes are anxious.

'Don't worry about it. I won't tell anybody.'

But Marina seems to take discharging a debt seriously. Later she introduces me around to the others while we wait for transport to the boat. Hackers every one, and they can't seem to believe I'm there, without a Hacker mark in sight. That I could possibly be a PareCo intern, like them. So that is what we are now: I'm a *PareCo intern*. Sounds weird. Why should they believe it when I can't?

Including Marina and me there are seven girls and six boys; all look about the same age, seventeen or so. Marina also seems to have told them I don't have an Implant, so now and then one of them talks to me out loud. Slowly, like I'm not quite there.

And she summarises the latest info dump they get on the boat. Over 1500 miles to Inac, so even on the latest and greatest high-speed skimmer it'll take hours.

When the island finally appears in the distance, our eyes are eager. Inaccessible it is, and not just because of its isolated location. Steep cliffs rise out of the water. As we get nearer there is one narrow strip of beach we can see in the rocky coastline; sheer cliffs above. Marina gasps. 'Beautiful,' she whispers.

A smaller boat takes Dr Rafferty and us interns to the beach. We are tossed so on the sea that some of the others are sick, but I'm exhilarated. A tricky approach through rocks, and soon we are standing on the sand, salt in the air, and I breathe in deep to taste it. Surf thunders against the rocks. That and bird cries are all there is to hear. There is no traffic, no buildings or structures of any kind, no pollution. Nothing man-made in sight.

'So. How is the real thing measuring up?' I say to Marina, but she doesn't answer. Her eyes are shining.

'Luna!' a voice calls out, and I turn in time to get crushed into an enthusiastic hug, nose crunched against shoulder: Hex's shoulder. He lets go, holds me at arm's length. Studies my face as if checking every detail is as it should be, then grins widely. 'I'm so glad you're all right.' He pulls me close again, not so tight this time, and holds me. A warm hug, and I cling to him. My only friend from home in this strange place.

There are footsteps, a throat-clearing sound. 'Time to go up,' Dr Rafferty says. He walks towards the cliff, and the air shimmers. Changes. He pushes a button, and doors swing open. 'Come along then.'

'A lift? There's a lift in the cliff?' I say.

'Of course there is,' Hex answers. 'Did you fancy climbing it instead?'

At a gesture from Dr Rafferty, I get into the lift with Hex.

It only takes half a dozen at a time; Marina and some of the others get in with us. She raises an appraising eyebrow at Hex, and winks at me when he's not looking, and I look at him again. Something is different. Is it just his clothes? He isn't wearing his usual black jeans and weird scrawled T-shirt, he's in some sort of soft green tunic that felt good when he hugged me, but looks even better. He's somehow standing straighter, taller; his eyes are different, too; not so full of humour. More serious. And they're looking back at mine. He grins and I jump, realise I've been staring. I turn away.

The lift zooms up so fast that my stomach lurches; then it swings sideways. Not just a lift, then? Marina is pale and keeps one hand on the side rail, but otherwise seems all right. The lift finally slows, and stops. The doors open.

We step out, blinking, into the light.

31

'Welcome to Inac, PareCo's premier Think Tank facility!' A woman in a white coat beams at us. 'If you find the Centre uncomfortable in daylight, there are sunglasses available.' She gestures to a stand, and I and most of the others put them on and stare at the massive open space around us.

We're in a glass dome, but the walls aren't smooth: the glass bends and twists in angles, forms prisms that snake together to enclose a football pitch-sized space. They join maybe a few hundred metres above us, and every twist and bend of the glass reflects the sunny sky over and over, blazing sun and cool blue in an endless kaleidoscopic pattern. And underneath it all? Water splashes in an elaborate, statued and carved fountain that even my eyes recognise. 'The Trevi Fountain? That's an amazing copy.'

'Not a copy,' Hex says.

I frown, turn to him. 'I'm sure it was destroyed during the third world war.'

He shakes his head. 'It was taken into protective custody, and re-homed here. You could say it went *missing*.'

My jaw does that hanging open thing again. I shut it. 'Serious?'

His eyes twinkle and I don't know if he is for real, or not.

The white-jacketed beamer must have heard; she walks over, the rest of our group off the next lift in tow, wide smile firmly in place. 'Yes, that really is the Trevi Fountain! Hidden, as Hex said, and gifted to PareCo by the Vatican for their assistance in rebuilding after the war. Not generally known.' She winks. 'Now, Hex: as you're here, could you take the new interns to check in, please?'

'Aye aye,' he says, and swings an arm. 'This way.'

We follow him across the shining marble floor. As we get closer to a wall we can see that the dazzling glass actually juts out in mirrored panels at the lower levels, hiding doors from sight.

We go through a door that leads to a more ordinary hallway, then up stairs to a check-in desk.

'Gotta go,' Hex says. 'My free pass this afternoon to greet you is over. See you at dinner!' And he's gone.

We get our room assignments, and head up more stairs. I find my room and open the door to the biggest, most beautiful bedroom I've ever seen, but I head straight across to the window. To call it a window is wrong – the entire expansive far wall is glass. And beyond it? The island. We're at the heart of Inac; PareCo has built on the centre of the extinct volcano that formed the island.

And beyond the PareCo compound is…nothing. Nothing by London eyes, that is – no people, no roads, no buildings. Wild green places stretch on and on to reach the sea, a distant shimmering blue that curves around the island. I'm transfixed. It's beautiful, and more than anything I want *out*: to walk to the sea.

Then there is a low beep and the view is gone. Replaced by

Marina's giant smiling face, and I jump out of my skin. Or I would have if it were detachable.

'Whoa! How'd you do that?'

She laughs. 'Can I come over?'

'Sure.'

Her face disappears and a moment later she comes through the door.

'What the heck was that?' I ask.

'It's an interface screen.'

When I look at her blankly, she walks over and touches the window, and the view vanishes once again. 'It's like a giant touch screen. You can put up anything you want on it, too. See?' And her hands move rapidly, changing the outside view for other scenes: tropical; snowy; a jungle complete with monkeys. 'Or put up your own photo or photo stream. Or, like I just did, use it to call other rooms or departments. Though most of the time I'd just message an Implant if I want to talk to somebody.' She shows me how to call up the intern directory, and a list of names appears. 'Like your friend Hex,' she says, and points out his name. 'Isn't it awesome tech?' She shuts it down and puts it back to the view of Inac.

I gesture. '*Outside* is awesome. How do we go there?'

She frowns. 'I'm not sure we can. It's a reserve, remember?'

'How much of a reserve can it be with a giant glass dome and the Trevi Fountain plonked in the middle of it? Besides, look: the sea. It's all around. I bet you can see if from every room around the edges of this place.'

'Give me a sec,' she says, and her face goes blank. She's

gone longer than a sec. I start lugging my bag across the room and onto a sofa to unpack it.

'There,' she says, finally, and a map appears on my window. It shows the whole PareCo complex. The place is actually an octagon, an eight-sided figure. 'That took a little digging. There aren't any official exits apart from the lifts we came up in. But there are emergency exits.' She points them out on the map, eight spaced around the compound at the bottom of each of the main stairwells, then shows me how to minimise the map on my interface so I can find it again.

'Did you see what's in the wardrobes?' she asks, and when I shake my head, touches a panel on a side wall. It opens, and inside? Clothes.

I run my hand across a row of tunics, beautifully soft, all the same but in different colours. Trousers and skirts to go with. Soft shoes in matching colours.

'They just give us all this stuff?'

'Yep. It's part of the joy of working here, apparently. And I checked mine; they're exactly my size,' she says. 'I'm going to unpack; dinner is in an hour. Not that I'll ever wear my own stuff with all *that* to choose from.'

Once I'm on my own I can't resist. I pull on a soft blue tunic. It looks plain, simple, but somehow it just hangs *right*. Feels like wearing a warm hug, as do the matching trousers. All of the stuff is in pale and muted colours, not what I'd usually go for, but when I work out how to change my window wall into a mirror, they don't just feel good. They look kind of *wow*.

Next I tap the window and hunt for the intern directory Marina'd had up before. It had come and gone on the screen too fast for my eyes to scan.

Directories listed include Virtual World Support, General Computing, Catering, Logistics, Staff Housing. Medical departments by the score. Think Tanks number 1 to 430? That's a lot of thinking. Finally I find it: intern directory.

I scroll it up and down and scan the names, then do it again more slowly. I'm here; Marina; Hex. Most are names I don't recognise: thirty interns in total. Is that all? Who works in the Think Tanks?

But no matter how many times I look, Gecko's name simply isn't there. Disappointment pulls, inside. And what does it mean? Either he's here under another name, he lied when he said they were bringing him here, or he really *is* bonkers. So that is a win-win situation, right? If he's somehow still here, good. If he's not here, he's bonkers, so just as well.

But I can't ignore a sinking feeling, one that says it could be lose-lose, instead. He'd said he was being held by PareCo, that he was being brought here against his will. If he was telling the truth and he's not listed on the directory, what does that mean? What if something has happened to him?

At dinner we're in a glass-sided dining hall on the outside wall of the Centre. We watch the sun go down in awe while quiet servers bring course after course of some of the best food I've ever tasted.

We're at a long table, thirty of us: the twelve plus one – me – that arrived today, and the rest including Hex are the previous arrivals. The group I should have been with. But no Gecko.

And all of us have been into our magic wardrobes, and are wearing tunics like mine, with soft trousers or skirts. It doesn't even look too samey; somehow they're a little different on everyone. How'd they get all our sizes exactly right? It feels a little weird, like someone has been busily measuring me while I sleep.

Afterwards, Marina and I wander back to our rooms with the rest of the girls, and say goodnight. The boys are on a different floor. My room still has the outside screen on: the stars somehow look bigger here, more beautiful. Like they're happier to shine on this wild, remote place than London. Part of me feels uncomfortable with this huge open wall, like I should have curtains across it, but there is *nobody* out there on this island. That, in itself, feels strange. In London it always felt like other people were inches away.

My room has everything you could want, with one glaring exception: no PIP. I want to see Dad, make sure everything is good at home. It seems an aeon since I was there. Tomorrow I have to find one.

I have a long shower in a bathroom so high-tech it takes me five minutes just to work out how to turn the water on. Wrap a towel around my body while I hunt through the wardrobe for a robe I'm sure I spotted earlier.

Ding.

The room light changes, and I swing back around to the window.

Hex grins on the interface screen.

I dive behind the sofa, put the robe on: it's really short. Stand up cautiously, pulling it down with one hand and holding it closed with the other.

He whistles. 'Nice outfit!'

'I wasn't expecting you to appear all giant-sized on the wall of my bedroom!'

He laughs. 'There's a privacy lock. If you're asleep or wandering about *naked*. Not that I mind. Just tap either no calls, or no visual.' He explains how to do it while I mentally address Marina for missing out this crucial bit of info.

'So what's up?'

'Meet me by the fountain? We need to talk. And the dome is awesome at night; you need to see it. Do you remember the way?'

'I'll work it out. Give me ten.'

He signs off and I throw on some fresh clothes from the endless wardrobe, work out the high-tech high-speed hairdryer, and am sorted in minutes. I slip out of my room, down the hall to the stairs. Are there detectors? None that I can see.

I take the stairs down and soon find the right door, and step out under the glass.

It's still dazzling, but not like this afternoon when sunglasses were needed. Hex isn't here yet. The vast space is empty and quiet, and I walk carefully across the floor, somehow wanting each step to be silent, to not disturb what my eyes are drinking in. The night sky is clear; stars are endlessly reflected over and over in the glass, on the shiny floor, in the clear water of the fountain. The swishing and splashing of the water is the only sound. The stars reflect everywhere – patterns of silvery light on my skin, my clothes. I stare at my reflection in the star-speckled water, and almost imagine I see silver winding around my eye.

I hear a distant door open, and turn. Hex waves and crosses the floor.

'Alone at last. I've been dying to talk to you,' Hex says, points at the steps by the fountain. I sit next to him. 'Where've you been, Luna?'

I know what I'm supposed to say. But nobody else is here, and this is Hex.

I sigh. 'I don't know. You probably know more about it than I do.'

'What do you mean?'

'I don't remember anything since the day before the transport left. One moment it was the night before; the next, I was in this café in London. Dr Rafferty came and got me. They did scans and all sorts of tests; I found out I'd lost six days. They said my memories aren't suppressed, they're actually missing – like they never existed, as if somebody cut them out of my brain.'

'Wow.' He ruffles his hair, shock in his eyes.

'Now tell me everything you know about it. Please.'

'Of course. You were on the transport. I was surprised to

see you, thought you were transferred to London Uni?'

'The transfer was revoked when my nanna died.'

'Right. That's what you told me. And then Gecko got on the transport—'

'He was on the transport? Then why isn't he here?'

'He asked to sit with you. I switched seats with him.' He swears under his breath. 'I kept thinking back to that moment, and thinking, if only I hadn't.'

'I don't understand. What happened?'

'There was a crash; the transport crashed. People flying through the air. Lucky no one was seriously hurt. Then Gecko pushed you out through an emergency exit.'

A shiver goes up my back. Is that why the sight of that emergency exit on the plane freaked me out?

'I'm really sorry, Luna. Will you forgive me?'

'What for?'

Hex looks miserable. 'Back when we first got to the test centre, Gecko asked me to introduce you to him, to get you to sit with us at dinner that first night. I should have told you. I just figured he fancied you; I didn't think he was planning to kidnap you.'

'He *kidnapped* me?'

'He dragged you away after the crash. I could see you were struggling but couldn't get to you in time to help. He must be a total nutter, Luna. A psycho. Thank God he's not here and you're all right.'

I look away, to the water splashing in the fountain.

So is Gecko completely bonkersville after all? Did he

288

really *kidnap* me? He must have; Hex saw it happen. Where did he take me? My stomach twists. If he really has lost it, then all that stuff he said about PareCo, and how Jezzamine and Danny died, could be delusions. Or even worse: lies.

I'm relieved that their deaths may have been acccidents after all. But being right doesn't feel good. It feels sad. A blue wave of loss, of solitude, washes over me, and I sigh, head in hands. Gecko with the crazy, warm glint in his eyes, and that adventure we had together: the magical trip to the waterfall world. But not again. He's not here; not now, not ever.

'Luna? Do you forgive me?'

I look up at Hex. His tattooed face is tortured in the starlight, black swirls twisting and broken on white skin where the frown wrinkles his brow. Not like Gecko. Gecko would be beautiful in starshine, dark skin warm with S'hacker silver winding around his eye. Like Astra.

I try to push away tears that want to splash on marble, to join the fountain. 'Of course I do. You didn't know; neither did I.'

His arms encircle me for a hug, even more crushing than the beach one. 'Don't worry about Gecko or anyone else, Luna. Nothing like that is ever going to happen again, not with me here. You couldn't be safer.'

I wriggle away. 'Don't worry. I'm not planning on getting kidnapped again any time soon. And I'll try to keep away from emergency exits at all times.'

His dark eyes are serious, way too serious. This isn't the Hex I know.

I punch him in the arm. 'Chill out, mate. How's Melrose?'

He shrugs. 'She's fine; she loves university except for the homework. She's the same, but I'm not. This place changes you. It changes what you think you want.' His eyes, still not laughing, hold mine, and for a moment I can't breathe. The black swirls around his eyes have multiplied: there are more Hacker marks there now than there used to be. What has he been up to to earn them? My curious hand wants to reach up and trace them, and starts to move of its own accord.

I pull my hand back to my side, and stand up. 'Right. OK. Good night, Hex.' I practically run out of the place, this time not careful to silence my footsteps, but the clattering doesn't hang loud in the stillness. Instead it is almost muffled, as if this austere space doesn't allow it, doesn't like messy people with their messy feelings and sounds. Behind me I hear Hex laugh.

32

'Good morning! Today we begin phase one: Exploration. Also known as exploring strange new worlds!' We've assembled as instructed in a meeting room, and the Beamer who greeted us on arrival is back: her smile is so wide and her teeth so sparkling, it's almost hard to look at her.

'We're trying to find out where you are best suited to fit in PareCo's organisation. There are many branches: from technicians all the way up to VeeDub controllers, or even working here at the Centre itself. Don't worry about any of that today, just have some fun. You'll have free access to all PareCo worlds, so knock yourselves out. See how many you can visit.'

Where you fit best? *Nowhere* has to be the answer for me. Unless it is working at the Centre: they must have cooks and cleaners here. Imagine if I ended up as chief Think Tank toilet scrubber? That'd make Goodwin from school *so* happy.

'There are advanced MD-PIP stations here at the Centre: MD stands for multi-dimensional. They bypass Realtime and take you straight to PareCo's Multi-dimensional Gateway to all the virtual worlds. For now, just explore as you like, but stay in pairs. Be back by eight for dinner tonight; after dinner, your time is your own.

'The MD-PIPs run on Implant technology. Which one of you is Luna?'

Eyes turn towards me; I raise a hand.

'For now, you'll have to use an old-style PIP without an Implant interface. A senior intern will escort you to the Gateway.' There's a knock on the door; Hex peeks in. 'And there is our volunteer now.'

We head down the hall as a group. I hang back and slip a few ANDs into my mouth behind my hand. The others disappear one by one into rooms with MD-PIPs on the way, until Hex and I are alone.

It feels a bit weird after running out on him last night. Why'd I do that? He's just *Hex*. This is mental.

'Sorry I dashed last night. All that stuff we talked about was a bit much.'

He grins. 'Oh, really? I thought you were just overcome by my charms, and ran away.'

I roll my eyes, relieved he's back to joking. 'Sure, that's it. So you got the short straw this morning?'

Hex shrugs. 'You can't use the MD-PIP so have to go through the void. The void is kind of the stuff PareCo makes all the worlds from – exciting!'

I look at him curiously. 'Is this void thing new?'

He raises an eyebrow. 'It's been there *forever*.'

'New to you I mean, idiot.'

'There were rumours about it, but I'd never seen it until I came to Inac. It was part of the info dump you get when you arrive here. Which you've missed. Anyhow, best way to learn is to step out into it. But the void can be disorienting; I wanted to take you there myself.'

He's looking all protective; I wonder what he'd say if he knew I've already been there with Gecko, and by myself? My smile falls away. I sigh. It's lucky I can get out of the void by myself; maybe Gecko would have left me there, lost and wandering in the void forever.

'What is it? Is something wrong?'

'No, I'm fine. What are the MD-PIPs like? Are they better?'

'They're awesome. Instant connection to the MD Gateway to the worlds. We'll still get you there now, it's just more of a faff.'

He shows me to an empty room with a conventional PIP. 'Meet you in your hallway in a tick?'

'Sure.'

I settle into the PIP. It's way, way grander than the one in my bedroom at home, with full life support for extended use. It's plush, instantly responsive to my body. Even the neural net feels softer – warm, not jarring.

The hallway appears. I may have taken the tablets a little late; my stomach is twisting. I breathe, in, out, in, out, and it subsides, just as Hex appears through a *friends* door.

'Hex, before we go, can I say hello to my dad?'

He hesitates.

'Please? I haven't been able to plug in since I left home. They didn't tell my family I was missing; they must think I'm ignoring them.'

'OK. But be quick, and I have to come with you.'

'Why?'

'I promised I'd see you to the Gateway, and not let you out of my sight.'

I roll my eyes. 'If you must.'

I hit *respond* to Dad's message. Answer with *are you there?*

Moments later he answers back with a *yes.*

I open his door, and there he is: today he is Sherlock, complete with silly hat.

'Dad!' And this time it is me that runs to him, hugs him. 'I miss you. Is everyone OK at home?'

He pulls away a little, looks in my eyes. A little disconcerting when he is rather gorgeous as Sherlock no. 27. 'Everyone is fine. And just starting to wonder how you've been getting on. Is everything all right?'

Hex coughs.

'Sorry. Dad, have you met Hex? We're on our way to some training thing, but he's snuck me in for a minute to see you.'

They shake hands. 'Thanks for bringing her by,' Dad says. He turns back to me. 'Listen, you: I know trouble is your middle name, but try to stay out of it.'

I roll my eyes. 'I'll try.' But trying doesn't always help.

He winks, as if he heard my thought. 'Do what you can.'

'We should probably go. Sorry,' Hex says.

Dad reaches out a hand to my cheek, then touches my necklace. 'That looks good on you, but somehow different.' He shakes his head. 'I'm taking my super-sleuthing too far. I imagined it looks longer than it used to. Must be because Astra was taller. Take care.'

Hex and I step back through the door to my hallway, and I wave goodbye as the door shuts. 'Can I answer Melrose's messages?'

'Only if you're very, very fast. I'm going to be late for my session.'

There are three from Melrose now. All a variation of *are you OK, how are you doing over there?* Hidden in the words: *how is Hex?* I sigh. Quickly answer: *I'm fine, I'll call to chat as soon as I can.* Hit *send*.

'Done. Now what?' I say, expecting a silver hatch and a ladder to appear in the roof.

'Your Realtime has been upgraded. You've got a void access door.' He gestures down the end of the hall, but it's a proper door. It's not even silver. I'm sort of disappointed.

We step through it and straight into the void. The door swings shut behind us, but doesn't vanish like the hatches. It's outlined in darkness.

The void is as always: a limitless space. Darkness that becomes lighter as eyes adjust, lit by whistling silver static that rushes in all directions. Strange winds that whip my hair around. I breathe in deep, reach back to hold my hair and find it is tied. I have a strange sense of familiarity and belonging.

'You're calm,' Hex says.

'Am I?'

'It usually freaks people out the first time.'

'Where are we going?'

'Follow the yellow brick road,' he says, and gestures. I look down at our feet and see there are vague outlined rectangles, linked together. We walk along it a few moments until we reach another door, one that looks much like the new one to the void in my hallway.

'Here we are!' Hex opens it, peeks in and waves to whoever is there. 'This is where I say goodbye. Wait here at the end of the day and I'll come get you and take you back.'

'I can follow the yellow brick road quite all right by myself, you know.'

'Sure. Of course you can. I'll see you then.'

I roll my eyes, step through, and there is Marina.

'Sorry,' I say. 'Have you been waiting for me?'

'Yes. I was about to raise the alarm that you were lost in the void! Then I thought maybe you and Hex wanted to get lost together for a while.' She smirks.

'No, thanks.'

She raises an eyebrow.

'Seriously! He's a mate. He's dating my friend. At least, I think he still is.' Mental note: visit Melrose at first opportunity. 'How'd you get here?'

'Easy. Plugged in, and here I was. I volunteered to wait for you.' She looks aggrieved.

'You know you don't have to keep doing things for me. I won't tell anyone about the flying thing.'

'I know. I wanted to.' And she smiles.

'Thank you. So what do we do now?'

'Pick a door, check things out, come back and do it again.'

I look around properly now. We're in a strange sort of room, full of doors. It looks ordinary enough, but when you focus closer you see that the sides curve up from where we stand. There are doors everywhere: all sides, floors, ceiling. The room is deceptive; bigger than it looks at first, as everywhere I look the doors seem to multiply.

'What are the options? Go for random, or what?'

'If you walk up to one, it reveals itself. Kind of like a flasher.'

I'm intrigued. We walk up to a door together: an image appears on it. Snow. Ice. 'Brrrrr. Next?' I say.

A circus.

Then a cocktail party – maybe later?

'If *all* VeeDubs can be accessed from here, it can't just be random,' I say. 'If you wanted to find somewhere in particular, there'd have to be a way to find it or you'd be here for years.'

'Good point.'

I concentrate on Gecko's waterfall world: I can't stop myself. Probably a *very* bad idea to go down that particular memory lane. My eyes skip across the room, and *there*. One of the doors is brighter than the others. It's on the floor. I walk backwards, away from it; Marina makes a funny face, then does the same. And the room is like a giant hamster wheel. It revolves as we walk, until the bright door is in front of us. With a vision of pool and waterfall on its surface.

'Nice,' Marina says. 'Shall we?'

With all sorts of reasons to say no, I nod, and she opens the door.

Like before, it's hot, and we're in instant swimsuits. Marina dives in the pool. I follow, but she swims underwater so fast I can't keep up. She doesn't surface, and I lose sight of her. Just when I start to get worried, something taps on my shoulder from behind. I spin around and there she is, laughing. Marina, but not Marina. Her hair is longer, greener, and her eyes also, but that isn't the surprising part. She's got a long shimmering tail that she slaps lazily on the surface of the water, a beautiful half girl, half fish. She's a mermaid.

'That is *so* cool. How do you do it?'

She shrugs. 'It's code, but it's kind of my thing. I can do it without thinking now.'

'Can you breathe underwater too?'

She nods, plunges under and swims circles around me, jumps up again.

'But you'll need legs for the waterfall,' I say, and I climb out of the pool, up the steps alongside the waterfall. I reach the top, and dive down.

'That does look like fun!' Marina half frowns like she is concentrating really hard, then climbs out of the pool and onto the steps. She has legs again but they've got shimmery scales on them, like she couldn't be bothered with a complete change. She dives down from the top and changes to tail halfway down the waterfall, swims underwater to the other side of the pool and back again.

'I wish I could do that.'

'It's not the most useful skill. God knows what they'll have me doing here. Sorry,' she adds, hastily, like she just realised who she said that to: the one intern with *no* skills, useful or otherwise.

'I don't understand why they've brought me here. I can't do stuff. I'll probably end up serving dinner.'

She tilts her head to one side. 'I think there's more to you than meets the eye.'

'Huh. How would you know?'

'Why would you be here otherwise? But if you don't want to end up serving dinner, you should get an Implant. Why haven't you got one?'

I stare back at her, and for once, I haven't got an answer that makes any sense. All that stuff from Nanna about avoiding plugging in and not getting an Implant – was it part of her delusions? Maybe it's time to leave them behind. They didn't do Nanna any good. 'It's kind of a long story. I was a Refuser at school.'

'So you don't really know what you could do here if you had an Implant. You might be an awesome Hacker, if you tried. Maybe PareCo has somehow sussed that out, and that's why you're here.'

'I doubt it.'

'Listen to me; I'm good at picking things up about people. Like you and Hex.'

'There is no *me and Hex*. He's a friend.'

'There is definitely some intensity in the way he looks at you.'

I shake my head. 'No way. Not interested, can't happen. Don't want to go there and even if I did, wouldn't do that to my friend. He's hers.' But despite my words, there is an uneasy feeling inside that says Marina is right. Something *is* different with Hex. OK, I kind of stared at him a little, but I was just trying to suss out what it was. No matter how confusing it felt last night, I really, really hope he hasn't gone all dough-brained on me. I want to keep my friends, both him and Melrose. I don't have that many of them.

We swim for a while longer, and I think about what she said. Hex has advantages over Gecko: he's here. He's not, generally, bonkers, and I've never noticed him kidnapping anyone. But the eyes that haunt me aren't his. They're Gecko's.

When Marina surfaces again, I call her over. 'Shall we go, try another door?' I say, suddenly impatient to leave this place and my thoughts behind.

'Sure.'

We climb out of the pool, Marina more slowly as she has to morph from tail back to legs. While she does that I wish my hair dry and gorgeous like the last time, and – *hey presto!* – it is.

Marina is startled. 'How'd you do that?'

I shrug. 'I don't know. Can't you?'

She pulls a face. 'No. There you go, I know what you'll be!'

'What?'

'Chief hairdresser.'

We go back to the Gateway, and it's Marina's turn to pick a world. She concentrates on Atlantis, one she's visited before, but can't find the door. She describes it and I soon find it. She gives me a strange look. 'Another thing you can do that I can't.'

We hang out in the underwater kingdom for a while, and then head back to the Gateway: it's time for dinner. Marina goes ahead while I wait for Hex.

But all that stuff she said about him has made me uneasy, and then annoyed. I do *not* need help walking out a door and down a clearly defined path: this is stupid.

I don't need to even go down the path, do I? Back in the PIP I reach to unplug.

When I emerge, everyone from my group is already there, waiting for the straggler. We're told we can come back to plug in after dinner, stay until tomorrow morning if we want to. Then we'll move on to something else. But I'm too tired to be hungry; weary to my bones. I head for my room.

33

'I hear you skipped dinner, and didn't plug in with the rest of the interns last night.' Dr Rafferty smiles back at me, giant-sized on my interface screen. He's not in a white coat now, he's in a tunic similar to mine, and something hits me that should have done a long time ago. He's still here: he works here. He doesn't work for HealthCo, does he? He probably never did. He's PareCo, through and through.

I shrug. 'They didn't say we had to; they just said we could.'

'Yet the rest of them did. I'm worried about you, Luna.'

'Oh?'

'Without an Implant, you can't keep up with the others. This is a competition, make no mistake about that. You are all competing for the best places. Don't get left behind.'

'But they're all Hackers. How can I possibly compete with them in virtual?'

'How do you know what you could do if you had an Implant? And that's not all. With an Implant you could be in constant contact with your family back home, whenever you want. Think about it, Luna.'

His face fades away from my interface wall, and the island view comes back again. It was locked on *no calls*, so he has the ability to override that. Which basically means he can appear on the wall of my bedroom whenever he wants.

Nice.

And now he's openly promoting getting an Implant. He hasn't done that before, though I'd wondered how long it would be before someone raised it in this place. But is there really any reason not to any more? And I could be in contact with my family, too.

Everything inside screams *no, don't do it*. But whether that is reasonable or is from years of resistance and fear, I don't know.

I meet the others in the meeting room, ANDs already swallowed and more in my pockets. I'm last in.

Marina frowns. 'Are you all right? I tried your interface last night when you didn't come to dinner, but it was blocked.'

'Sorry. I switched it off so I could sleep. I wasn't feeling that great,' I say, kind of a lie and kind of the truth.

'Hex asked where you were at dinner; he seemed really worried about you. Asked whether you got back OK from the void. Weren't you supposed to wait for him?'

Guilt registers inside. But before I can come up with anything to say about it, the Beamer is back.

'Today we begin the next phase: boundaries. We want you to push boundaries, do things you can't do. Things you are afraid of. To make it interesting, we're having a little competition. Two groups, with leaders I will choose.' She points at a tall girl, Sparky, whose skin is so dark that she's chosen to have her Hacker tattoos in white instead of black so they can be seen. Then she chooses one of the boys, Blood. I wonder what his Hacker name means, then decide I probably don't want to know. 'Team leaders, you will take turns picking your teams. Blood, you begin.'

He picks someone, then it is Sparky's turn. They continue, back and forth, until the room is down to just me and one boy. It's Sparky's pick; Marina is on her team, and judging by the blank looks on their faces they're having an Implant conversation. Sparky finally says, 'Luna,' and then winces: was there an Implant backlash from her team? Our team, that is, and if me being on it isn't bad enough, there are seven of them and six of us.

'We're taking you to test-run a new world that is under development. It's great fun; kind of urban warfare in a ruined city!'

Marina and I exchange glances. Not my idea of great fun, and judging by her eyes, not hers, either.

'So today one group are hunters, the other are hunted. You can use any means at your disposal in the world to achieve a kill, and you can code any changes in the world to assist you that you can, and use any weapons you find or create.'

I stare at her. A *kill*? We're going to kill each other?

Blood raises a hand. 'Which group is which?'

Beamer beams. Flips a coin. 'Call it?' she says to Sparky.

'Heads!' she says.

It flies through the air, lands. Tails. The sense of dread deep in my gut that started with the word *kill* deepens.

'Your choice,' Beamer says to Blood.

'We'll hunt.' He smiles, but there is no warmth in thin lips pulled across teeth.

'Hunted, you get a head start: meet in Sparky's hallway. Quickly friend anyone you need to in order to get them in. The door to world 5691 will be there. Sixty minutes later the hunters will be allowed in at the opposite side of the city. Escape code will return any kills automatically to a virtual meeting place where they are to wait for the others. The team with the most left standing after twenty-four hours wins. Any questions?'

I have a load of questions. Like what will the Hunters do to us when they catch us? What does being killed virtually actually feel like? What does *any means necessary* really mean – guns, knives, explosives, ritual eviscerations? But none of them are questions I'm prepared to ask out loud, not when everyone else stays silent. Not when most of their faces are like they've been asked to a party, not a fight to the death.

Beamer takes out two timers, and gives one to Blood and one to Sparky. 'The sixty minute countdown has begun.' Beamer glances at me. 'To make things a level playing field, all Implant communications will be blocked as soon as you plug in. Away you go!'

I plug in fast. With the speed, the neural net isn't soft like yesterday – it slams in and makes my head spin.

Sparky's friend invite is already in my hallway. I hit *accept* and her door appears; I rush through. Even with hurrying I'm still the last one there. Not used to non-Implant aided discussion, they're all talking at once.

Sparky raises a hand. 'To summarise for Luna, we feel there are two possible game strategies: separate and hide, or combine and defend. Let's get out there now, and see what's what before we decide. Come on.' Sparky opens the door to VeeDub 5691. It actually has *in development* scrawled across it. We step through.

Purple sky? Nice. There is a haze of smoke hanging in the air, with an odd smell. Bombed-out buildings mix with still standing structures in various stages of falling down. It's hot and humid, and beads of sweat instantly form and trickle down my back. We're on a hill, the door behind us. I feel to the side of the door. It looks to my eyes like the city carries on, but when I touch it, no. There is a barrier. This place has edges.

Below us the ruined city is bisected by a wide river. Even from here the water looks and smells evil: is it polluted, poisoned? The air makes me cough. There is one bridge across the river. A hill on the other side.

'Bet that's where they'll appear,' a boy says, pointing at the other hill.

Sparky glances at the stopwatch. 'In fifty-four minutes.'

'There are lots of hiding places. They could take forever going through buildings looking for us if we separate,' he says.

'Boring. We should destroy the bridge and defend the river,' Sparky suggests.

Eyes turn to her. 'Can you do that?' Marina asks.

She nods. 'Yep. Easy. Let's vote: who wants to destroy the bridge?'

Five hands go up, including mine. Anything that has us hiding on our own scares me more.

We hurry down the city streets as a group. It's slow going with debris and bombed-out vehicles to get around. With all the lovely places and things they could make in a VeeDub, why this? Why a fake war zone? I don't get it. Sparky stops at a burnt-out car near the bridge, rips something out of the engine. She and another boy do some weird Hacker thing and start pulling wires and charges out of stone, running them to bridge supports.

'Ready,' Sparky says. 'Has anyone got a watch?' One is volunteered. Another weird Hacker thing and she's changed it into a timer. 'Let's make sure they know who did this. I've set it on a delay for when they arrive in five minutes. Come on; let's get out of here.'

'No, wait!' I say, an idea forming, and Sparky hesitates.

'What is it?'

'They'll expect us to hide, to defend. If they see the bridge explode, they'll know we destroyed it, and expect us to be over here.'

'And?'

'Why don't we go to the other side of the bridge? They won't expect that.'

'But then we'll be on the same side as the hunters,' Marina says. 'Four minutes left. We need to run one way or the other soon.'

'Wait a minute,' Sparky says. 'Luna is right. They'll use all their efforts to get across the river. They won't expect us to be on the same side. How about instead of sitting back and hiding or defending, we hunt the hunters?'

Startled looks are exchanged.

'Three minutes,' Marina says.

'Let's do it! Run!' We follow Sparky over the bridge at full speed, and dive behind a burnt-out building.

'Twenty seconds,' Marina says.

'Wait,' I say. 'Stop the countdown! Wait until they're *on* the bridge.'

Sparky does something frantic in the air with her hands, then smiles. 'Good idea. But without enough time to reset it, I've disabled the timer. I'll need to have the bridge in sight to set it off now. Somewhere they won't see me. There's not enough cover around here.'

Marina points: a few streets up the hill. 'There's a clock tower. How about up there?'

Sparky nods. 'Assuming it's intact enough to get up. Let's try it. But there's no easy way out if they track us there. We need to split up.' She points down a street that winds along the foul river. 'Find a defensive position. Keep your fingers crossed, and keep a look out for us.' Sparky's eyes settle on me. 'This was your bright idea, Luna. You can come with me.'

The others vanish and we run for the clock tower.

Sparky glances at me. 'You look pale.'

'You look like you're having fun.'

'I am. I love combat games. Don't you?'

'Er…I've never actually been in a combat world.'

'No way. Not ever?'

I shake my head. 'Sorry.'

'You had some good ideas, and maybe that is why. You're not trying to recreate the same old scenarios from *Zombie Wars* or *Last Combat*.'

'But I can't fight.'

'This isn't about slogging it out in a punch-up, and it isn't real. It's about strategy and outthinking their manoeuvres. Think of it like a chess game, and you'll be fine.'

The tower door is locked with a padlock. 'Damn. I'm rubbish at hacking physical locks,' she says, and looks at me with an eyebrow raised.

I shake my head. 'I'm no Hacker.' Then I look at it more closely – damaged and rusty. 'But I'm good at breaking things.'

I find a rock and smash it into the lock. No dice. I do it again and then again, and it falls to the ground.

She grins. 'Knew I brought you for a reason.'

I open the door; we peer in. It's dark, musty. We sneeze.

'A simul-sneeze,' she says. 'Nice bonding moment. Come on.' We go in, she pulls the door shut. 'Wait a sec while I set a charge. If they try to come up here, the door will blow.'

Nice touch.

We find the stairs, and I go first, slow and tentative. The stairs are wooden, uneven, some missing. Half rotten. 'Be careful, they're rubbish,' I say, and hang onto the handrail.

Halfway up the next flight a step gives way under my foot. I grasp for the rail but it breaks, and I start to fall, foot slipping through the broken step. There is a sharp pain in my calf, and I almost scream.

I scramble, pull myself back up.

'All right?' she calls from below.

'A step is missing, and I've hurt my leg. Be careful.'

One more level and I'm at the top. The clock is dislodged, hanging at an angle. The space is flooded with light.

I stagger, sit down. There is *pain*: something warm and red running down my leg.

Sparky catches up. She curses when she sees what I've done to my calf. 'That's too much blood.' She rips a strip off her tunic and ties it around my leg. 'Blood'll be onto us now.'

'Blood? You mean the Hacker?'

'He can smell the stuff. He'll follow it right to us, I bet.'

She peers out the tower. 'Got one thing right: there's a perfect view of the bridge. I hope they separate and we can knock off a few of them before he finds us.'

My vision is fuzzy, and it's all I can do to not reach out to unplug back in the PIP.

'Why does it hurt so much? This is virtual! It's not supposed to hurt, is it?'

'Depends on the world. In most of them when you get killed you don't really even feel it. You bounce back to your hallway, can go straight back in to try again. But I've heard some of the eighteen-plus ones are more real. You feel pain like real pain. This must be like that.'

'So if they kill us, it'll be like we're really dying.'

'I guess.'

'This is a sick and twisted version of fun.'

'Just gives you more reason to want to win.'

I'm focusing on her words, struggling not to unplug. Double awareness, double pain.

Double pain? Back in the PIP, careful not to disturb the neural connection, I reach a hand down my leg. Warm. Wet. Pain. My leg is bleeding, in the PIP? This makes no sense.

My head is spinning. My leg isn't tied up to slow the blood loss in the PIP. It's bleeding there too?

'Company below,' Sparky says, voice low. 'Approaching now: Blood and one other. Here's hoping the charge—'

Boom!

'Damn. Blood is OK. Got the other one, though, that's one for us. Blood looks unhurt, but really, really pissed off. He's gone through the door. The others are still heading for the bridge.' There's a creak below.

We exchange a look. 'How near are they to the bridge?'

'Not near enough; a few minutes from it still. Thank heavens there's no Implant communications, or he'd call them here. There's two of us and one of him, right?'

'I'm sorry,' I whisper.

'Not your fault. Could have been my leg, not yours. But is there anything you can do to slow him down? The others are nearing the bridge. I need them to get there before Blood gets up here.'

'Right.'

I stand up, swaying on my feet, and look around for weapons. A piece of wood?

I grasp it and stagger down the steps. Will myself to move quietly, and hide round the top of the stairs. I should be out of sight here.

Slow careful movements sound below me, and I feel sick. I could vomit on him; that might gross him out enough to make him run away. It's hot, I know it is, but I'm cold, bone cold, and clammy.

Hands gripped tight to wood.

Step. Creak, below.

I can do this, can't I? It's just timing and luck.

Another step. He's nearly here—

I jump around and swing the piece of wood.

But I have no timing, and no luck. He catches it easily in one hand, then throws it down the stairs and laughs.

'What have we here?' he says.

I shrug. *I need to delay him.* 'Just me.'

He has a knife in one hand, a smile on his face. 'It's the blood that called me to you, you see. I love it: the smell, the feel, the taste. Only in VeeDubs, don't look so shocked. I'm not a monster, just a gamer.' He hefts the knife in his other hand. 'But why are you up here?'

'Hiding.'

He shakes his head. 'So predictable. But it's a rubbish place to hide. No exit. No way to escape.' He comes closer. 'And you: you're half dead already. Not so much fun. Still. I'll have to make do, somehow.'

I wish I wasn't here. I wish I was *anywhere* else. I wish none of this existed, especially not his eyes, his knife, a knife that is closer now. I'm too weak from blood loss, from fear. There is nothing left to resist the knife. I think of unplugging but even that is too difficult, too remote. My body back in the PIP can't move any more than this one can.

The blade touches my skin. Not at my neck. Nothing quick. It caresses my arm, flat at first, then it bites. More red wells up on skin: beads; a trickle. Pain, but remote, as if I'm pulling away from it. And then—

Things happen. All at once.

There is a massive explosion. Not here, no – the bridge?

Fury on Blood's face as he turns away, turns to the sound.

But most of all there is silver, a rush of beautiful, glorious silver. And a door. I fall through the door, and into the void.

34

I'm warm now. The void holds me close, the lights whistle past. The wind buffets my hair, my body, as if saying *wake up*, but I want to sleep.

Why am I so sleepy?

I try to focus, but all I can see are beads. Silver beads, with swirls of intricate carving. Floating in the void like spots in front of my eyes. I blink, but they're still there.

Warm. Sleepy…

Wet. Blood, is that it? Draining life away.

Stop. Stop the blood. *Please…*

Silver from the void gathers all around me, then on my leg and arm. It feels warm.

Time passes. I don't know how long, but slowly, gradually, things stop swirling. I come back to myself.

I sit up.

Something glints next to me, and I frown. A knife. Blood's knife? It's smeared with dark red. Is that my blood from when he cut my arm? Both my arm and leg are whole now, but there is a sheen of silver on my skin.

Was it escape code that brought me here – does this mean I died in the game?

I shake my head. If that happened, I should have gone straight to the virtual meeting place. I think I was close to dying. But I didn't die.

How did I get here? And apart from how, that was a VeeDub game world. It might have been programmed to hurt when you get hurt, but it was still *virtual*. As soon as I left it, I should have been all right.

But I wasn't, was I?

Back in the PIP, I reach to check my leg like I did before. It's not bleeding; there is no wound.

Did I imagine that before?

What the hell is going on here?

Sparky. Is she all right? When I left, Blood was furious. The bridge had blown up. She was there, alone.

And Marina; the others.

I have to go back to that place, don't I?

Silver coalesces in front of me. A sheet of it forms a door, a handle.

Blood's knife is there on the ground. I could take it with me; it might be useful. Instead I pick it up and throw it as far as I can into the void.

A deep breath. I'm shaking; I want to run.

I reach out a hand, and open the door. I stand there, still in the void, door open, looking through.

It's the tower, on the stairs. Just where I was when I left before.

I can't see anyone.

If Blood…if he killed Sparky, he'd have left, wouldn't he? She'd still be there. He wouldn't be. I have to check.

I force myself through the door. It shuts and vanishes behind me.

315

There's blood on the steps where I'd been lying before. I step over it and into the clock tower room. It's dark now, night, but there is moonlight. No sign of Sparky, and I swell with relief. Step cautiously forwards and peer out into the night.

That's when I see her.

A broken body on the ground far below.

I stare, look away, then look back again. She's still there.

It's like a chess game, she said. It's not real, she said. It might have been different for me, because I'm different, right?

Panic is swelling up inside, and I start to shake.

This isn't real. I chant the words over and over again as I force myself down the tower stairs. Every step I take, I repeat: *This isn't real.*

Another step gives way but this time I spring back, don't fall. It's real enough that I nearly bled to death for stepping on a rotten step on the way up; I take more care.

Outside now, the air isn't any better. It still smells foul.

I have to check, don't I? I hesitate, walk over to Sparky, but don't have to go much further. Even in moonlight she is very clearly dead. *This isn't real.* It looks real, final, over. *This isn't real.*

What now? Find Marina and the others. If they're still alive. But how?

The next street loops down to the river. That is where she told them to go, and to set a lookout. But going by the light, that was hours ago. Would they still be waiting, or have they given up?

I creep down the street. Ducking down, hugging buildings, cars. My heart is thudding so loud I'm convinced if Blood is out here, he'll hear it, that he'll taste the fear thundering through my veins.

But I reach the end of the road. It's a dead end by the river; the water is sick, foul. A mist rises from it like blood.

I stumble backwards.

'Luna?' A whisper.

I spin round.

'Marina! Thank God.'

'They thought I was mad for still waiting. Where's Sparky?'

'She's…she's…' I shake my head.

'OK. That's only one of us gone; the rest of us are still together. The bridge blew – how many went with it?'

'I don't know, I couldn't see. One of them died as Sparky booby-trapped the door, but then Blood came up the tower. And—' I hesitate. 'I tried to delay him. She'd said they were approaching the bridge, but I don't know for sure if they made it.'

'You got away from Blood? Impressed.' She frowns. 'So maybe no one was on the bridge, and she blew it while she still could instead of when they got on it.'

The night passes. We decide to stay on the same road until morning, but in two groups. Marina and I are together in a shed in a garden that is mostly intact. The other three hide over the road in a half-destroyed house. I'm exhausted; I need to sleep, desperately.

'Don't you get tired?' I ask.

Marina looks at me curiously. 'No. We're hooked up and asleep back in the PIPs, remember? You don't look so good.'

It's not just exhaustion, it's ANDs. They're wearing off. Back in the PIP I wriggle around, careful to not break the neural connection. There are ANDs in my pocket. I reach down and find them, manage to chew some dry and swallow without moving my head too much. Slowly I start to feel less like vomiting on her. I close my eyes to see if I can sleep, but no: is it the waiting, the uncertainty? Or maybe it is just impossible to sleep when I'm half here, half with my body.

The sun starts to come up, but the sky is a dirty smudge.

'Luna, what do you make of this?' Marina is standing in the door, pointing to a cloud that seems to be almost oozing towards us.

I cough. The air is worse than before; there is an unpleasant, metallic smell. Familiar, yet what is it?

'Blood. It's blood!' I say

Marina looks at me. 'Run!' We bolt out of the shed and through the house to the street; Marina throws a rock at the window where the others are hiding. 'Run!' she yells. They stumble out, see the cloud that is growing, starting to fill the sky, and run.

I glance back; it's moving faster.

Did he wait until daylight so we could see his creation? It's impressive. Different colours of blood: bright red, smudges of brown, like dried blood, fading to black.

It reaches one of the boys behind us first. He screams, drops to the ground.

Any thought of being quiet now gone, we run blindly up the road, and then we see him. Blood. He's wearing a gas mask, a protective suit from head to toe. The cloud is gaining on us, faster than we can run.

Marina falls; I pull her up but she gasps with pain. A twisted ankle? 'Go without me.' She looks back. 'It's just us left now.'

'No!' I try to help her walk, but fingers of red are close, closer. Reaching for us, and then—

RRRRRing!

A bell?

The red cloud disappears. The world disappears.

35

Sparky and I are stretched out on towels on the beach, and not just any beach: it is seriously the most beautiful sandy cove I've even seen: our team prize for winning the combat world. Turns out the rest of Blood's team died on the bridge, so there were two left on our team and only one on his when the time was up. Marina's in the sea, doing the mermaid thing, and the others are surfing.

Sparky lifts herself up on her elbows. 'You have to tell me. How'd you get away from Blood?'

'Honest answer? No idea.'

She raises an eyebrow. 'Hmmph. Strangely enough, that's pretty much what he said. So keep your secrets, then.'

'And you, how'd you end up over the side of the tower?'

She shrugs, sheepish. 'You saw my body?'

I nod.

'Not proud to say this, but I jumped. Blood came howling up the stairs for me, said you vanished and he was going to have all his fun with me. Jumping seemed like the best plan.'

She frowns. 'Are you OK? You don't look so good.'

'Fine. Tired. And I know! I'm not supposed to be tired here.'

I reach out back in the PIP to have more ANDs. How long can I keep this up? I feel *stretched*. I close my eyes again, soaking the beautiful sunshine into my skin. I long for sleep, but somehow can't with my body awake in the PIP. I long to unplug, but how can I with everybody watching?

There are footsteps. Echoing, like on a hard floor. I jump, sit up, and look around. Sparky has gone for a swim with the others. I'm alone, no one is nearby, and there is no hard floor for footsteps to sound on even if there were.

Then I hear a creak; a door.

It's in the PIP.

I open my eyes to a slit. Dr Rafferty? He's checking my life support screens. Whistling to himself, taking notes on a tablet. I will myself to be still. He starts to turn towards me and I close my eyes. A moment later there are more footsteps, the sounds of a door opening, shutting. I open my eyes. I'm alone in the PIP; I'm alone on the beach.

Everything is weird and wired.

Playtime over, Blood's team eventually join us in the beach world. Now we're instructed to combine what we love with what we fear. So Marina becomes a flying fish – well, sort of a mermaid, but with wings – soaring out of the water. First with fear, then joy.

Sparky is making a giant electrical monster – interesting.

Blood's fear appears to be a giant soft toy teddy bear, but the teddy is also a vampire – kind of a Count Cuddles.

I play around with ideas – of fears, and loves – and all I can come up with is a giant spider with Jason's face. Creepy-weird, but more funny than scary. And even with that I need

Marina's help to make it, since even if silver doors seem to appear magically to save me at awkward moments, I can't code stuff. But I can't focus on anything long enough to come up with a strong feeling one way or the other.

Things go vague. I can see lips moving, know they are talking to me, but I can't hear what people are saying. Marina shakes me a little, splashes me with her wings. She takes me for a spin across the bright blue cove.

'What's wrong, Luna?'

'I don't know. I'm losing it.' I struggle to hold onto her, but give up and spill into the water and sputter in the waves. It'd be so nice to lie still, to float away…

She drags me out onto the beach. Frowning. 'Something's not right with you.'

'Tell me something I don't know.'

We move on to another world: can it really be my fifth? *Five is for travel and adventure.* Too right. *Instability, change and unpredictability.* That, too.

More wired. More weirdness…

I'm unplugged. I didn't do it. I blink wearily, eyelids like sandpaper. It's Dr Rafferty? I swallow. 'What's up?' I say, a whisper the most I can manage.

'You tell me.'

I shake my head, thoughts thick and heavy like syrup. Did he emergency unplug me?

'You're not well, are you? Poor Luna.' He leans in close. 'Would you like us to make you better? Make it so you don't have to take ANDs any more, and so you can keep up with your friends in virtual?'

I nod. He knows about the ANDs? Tears are slipping out of my eyes. 'I'm dying; I know I am. Nothing is right.'

'I can help you, Luna. An Implant is all you need to fix everything.'

'OK,' I whisper.

He opens a screen on a tablet. Takes my thumbprint; records my voice consent.

He'll fix me, and then I can sleep.

I'm moving; they're moving me. There's a pinprick in my arm.

Everything goes dark and blissful.

There is no truth. There is only perception.

Gustave Flaubert

36

Ding.

I jump, open my eyes. My head aches with the light and I shut them again.

Where am I? Pillows, blankets. Softness and warmth. I'm in bed. Where?

I open my eyes more cautiously, and peer through my lashes. It's my bedroom at the PareCo Centre. Inac. That's where I am. The wall window is set to outside view, and it is a dazzling sunny day.

I want to get up and tap the window, change the view. Or dim it down at least. But I feel weak, too weak to stand.

A screen appears in front of my face.

What? I blink; it's still there. It's a mini version of the interface window. Can I dim the screen from here? A rocker dimmer switch lights up.

I reach out a shaking hand towards it, but there is nothing there – my hand passes through the screen. But I can still see it. I think *dim* at the switch. It taps a few times and the room darkens.

What the hell?

I fall back against my pillows.

My memories are a mixed-up daze. The combat world. The tower. My cut leg, blood running down it; the silver door; going back. We won. The beach world that followed;

the love/fear exercise. It felt like days. Weeks, even.

Then Dr Rafferty unplugged me.

He said I needed an Implant.

I sit up fast, and my head whirls. Do I have…an Implant?

Yes flashes in front of my eyes.

Ohmygod.

Did I agree to that? **Yes** again. Not good enough; I struggle to remember for myself. I did give consent, didn't I? I was so completely exhausted, I'd thought I was dying, that it was the only way. Can you die from lack of sleep?

As soon as I think the question an encyclopedia entry scrolls past my eyes. Yes. You can, apparently.

Wow.

Will an Implant stop all that? Will I be able to plug in all the time like everybody else now?

No data.

Before I can absorb that, there's a sort of *ding* in my head again. Is that what woke me up before?

Luna?

I jump. Was that Hex? I look around the room. I'm still alone.

'Er…yes?' I say.

He appears in front of me. Sort of. Like, he's not there, but I can still see him. I realise he can most probably see me as well, and hurriedly pull the blankets up.

'Luna! Hurrah, you've got an Implant!'

'Yeah. It's spinning me out.'

'That'll only last a few days, until you get used to

integrating everything. Are you all right?'

'I don't know. Yes. I think so. Maybe.'

'Dinner is in an hour. Get up, you're coming. I'll knock just before.'

'OK. Sure.'

He says bye, and vanishes.

That is super *weird*.

I get up slowly, cautiously. I can stand, but feel all out of balance. I manage to shower. Find a clean soft tunic and trousers, and pull them on. Everything feels wonky, like my body and brain are not quite in sync.

I'm ready early, and take a deep breath. Can I work out how to do this? Do I just think it, or is there something else I need to do?

Dad?

Seconds later he *pings*, and appears in front of me.

'Wow! Luna! You've got an Implant?' His current face is Doctor Who no. 46, but astonished just the same.

'Yeah, apparently. Seemed like the thing to do at the time.'

'You look well.'

'Er...I do?' I stand as I'm speaking to him, walk to the wardrobe. There's a mirror on the inside of it. I touch the door to open, and stare at myself in shock. I'm *tanned*. How'd that happen?

The beach. I was sun-baking forever on that beach with Sparky.

But that was *virtual*. I wasn't really there. But I'm... tanned?

'Luna? Are you all right?'

'Sure. Fine, sorry. Feeling a bit dazed with the Implant still.'

'Don't worry, that'll pass quickly.'

'I've got to go to dinner soon. Is everything all right at home?'

'Yes, everything's good. Though Jason got some school detentions. Something to do with freeing frogs from the virtual science lab. And Sally's been doing a little home renovating.' A pained look.

'Sure, is she turning my bedroom into a gym or something?' I say, kidding, but a look on his face says *nail on the head*. 'Oh. I see. She is.'

'Not a gym, but, well...'

'No worries. It's not like I'm using it.'

'Sorry, Loony-Tunes.'

There's a knock on the door, and I plaster a smile on my face. 'Gotta go, Dad. Hex is here. Byee!' I sign off.

The smile slips away. No room at home? It's not like I thought I was going back, necessarily, but – I shrug. Anyhow, this room is a hundred times better than that one. This is my life now. Here. There is no going back to what I was, not any more.

Not now that I've got an Implant.

37

This time I'm not last.

Marina is here; a few others. One by one the rest of them pile directly into the Multi-dimensional Gateway from their fancy MD-PIPs, and for the first time, so do I. Though it's not that exciting. Once plugged in I go straight to the Gateway, no trip via hallway and void. Is that the only difference? There's a vague disappointment inside at not going through the void.

Marina gives me a high five, and I smile and try not to look how I feel, because Dr Rafferty totally lied. Nausea rips through me, and I concentrate on breathing, trying to keep my face blank, while back in the PIP I reach for the ANDs I'd put in my pocket just in case. Lucky I did. So I still need to take them, even with an Implant: figures.

Are you OK? Marina, via Implant whisper. A whisper is different from talking – it's private, so no one else can hear it. I'm getting more used to the distinctions and uses of the thing but say 'Yes' out loud, and then realise the mistake. She laughs.

Today is skills-sharing day. We're going to a blank world, and everyone is going to do their hacking thing, and see if anyone else can learn how to do what the others can. And we're meeting the other group – Hex's group – there also. We're to pair off until a bell goes, then swap along to someone else, and all along the way there will be points for learning new skills, and points for teaching well enough that others can learn yours.

Pity I haven't got any.

A door opens; Hex peers through. 'Step right up!' he says, and we go through the door.

'I thought a blank world would be, well, blank,' I say to Marina, as I look around at the varied landscape. It's like a world in miniature – and there is a little of everything. A seascape, a hill, a forest, a desert, a village, a meadow, a ski slope, and more – but all small and ridiculously close to each other, like sections of a pie with the door we just came through in the middle.

'No. It just means lacking in unusual code. Everything is simple here. There are no druids in the trees, no wine in the water, no talking birds. It's normal stuff. It won't be by the time we leave, though.'

Sure. It's normal to have a miniature world divided into sections.

We pair off as instructed, head in different directions. Hex came towards us but I had Marina's arm already, and no surprises: we're heading for the sea.

'Can you show me how to be a mermaid?' I ask.

'I'll try. But that's changing your own living tissue: it's complicated. Let's try something easy, first.'

'Like what?'

She pauses, thinking. We've reached the beach. She takes

my hand, pulls me to the water's edge. 'Swimsuits would be handy as a starting point,' she says.

'So what do I do?'

'I'm not sure. This is weird.'

'How so?'

'Hackers generally start when they're really young, first by joining with a teacher, often a parent. They go it alone once it becomes instinctive, once they can start tapping into code without thought. Like once you learn to tie your shoelaces, you don't have to think about it any more. But I'm not sure if you can learn this stuff at your age. Or if you can, by what method.'

'Maybe I can't.'

She tilts her head to one side, considering, then shakes her head. 'I'm sure you *can* learn. You were the one who could find doors to worlds you wanted in the Gateway, weren't you? I can't do that.'

And escape through silver into the void, my thoughts add, but I'm not sure anyone but me knows I did that. Blood turned his head when the bridge exploded: did he see, or not? If he did, he never said.

She shrugs. 'But we might as well try to join Implants and see if it works.'

'OK. How do we do that?'

'Close your eyes; let your mind go blank. You should be able to see the Implant grid inside you. It's like a three-dimensional working space in your mind.'

I try. Eyes closed, mind blank…but it won't go blank.

There are too many things cluttering it up inside. Fear I can do this; fear I can't. I sigh, and try to let it go, imagine as I'm breathing out that the fear is washing away on the water that is lapping at our feet.

Then it happens: I'm there. My eyes are still closed, but the reality – virtual reality, anyhow – of my closed eyes fades away, and I'm standing in a grid space, like some sort of weird 3-D map.

Somehow I'm *aware* of Marina. She's there, a calm presence, one that is coming closer. Another grid, separate to mine. Then for a moment there are two grids superimposed on each other. Then they snap together.

I open my eyes. I can see out of Marina's eyes, and out of my own; everything in a curious extra dimension. *Weird.*

Yes, isn't it? she thinks, responding to my tendrils of thought. *To me also. This isn't something we usually do; I haven't done this for many years. You have to really trust somebody; they could mess with you like this. I just couldn't see any other way to show you.*

Show me what?

Watch. Don't break the connection, even if it feels alarming. It isn't real, remember?

I swallow. *All right. Do it.* I'm nervous; they said the combat world wasn't real, and it nearly killed me.

The world around us changes – into a grid space like the one I saw inside. Everything: our bodies, the sand, the sea. Like lines drawn on an integration map in maths class. Colour isn't perceived as colour, but as variations in code – the blue of the sea is a number, the sand a range. Marina's green hair and my grey eyes. She's talking inside me and I'm trying to listen, but all I see are the beautiful, elegant numbers – *everywhere* – and there is some place inside me that chimes, that *opens*. That says, *yes – 42.83.22 is that shade of blue*, as if I could see it. I pull the strands of the graph: a little more aquamarine would be nice? And it shifts – the numbers change. Nanna would have loved this.

Heh, I thought I was showing you stuff here? Marina murmurs in my mind. She pulls strands of her own and our tunics change and dance with precision: two-piece swimsuits. I change mine to blue, Marina's to green, deep green that matches the streaks in her hair.

Colours are your thing, aren't they? she whispers inside me.

Mermaid? I ask, the word not a word but a collection of numbers that code to mermaid. And we're still joined and stepping further into the sea – the warm sea that is more aquamarine than it used to be, through both my eyes and Marina's.

Legs are numbers; skin, bones and muscle also. Legs can join together, bones change; skin skews to scales, to iridescence. Green, like Marina's? No. I make mine deepest blue. I flop into the water and cough until I remember: gills. We float underwater. I see her with my eyes, me with her eyes.

Our grids still joined, there is a murmur of chatter from the others, but distant, detached; all there is, is Marina. I can feel her heart beating; it beats with my heart, the same *th-thump, th-thump*, in rhythm. Her thoughts wind around mine. *Curiosity*: she's curious how I managed to do this so quickly. A little good-natured annoyance when it took her so long to learn. She's looking inside me now like I looked inside her. There's a ghost of another grid, a shadow superimposed on the one we both see when we look at the world's code. A silver grid?

What is that? Marina's linked emotions overlay her words – surprise, wonder, curiosity. *I've never seen anything like it.*

My feelings echo hers, so how can I answer? Before I can try, a wave catches me wrong and I flip over, gasp when I slap into the sand. The connection is wrenched away. An empty loss left behind. One heart that beats; one pair of eyes.

Marina looks at me. 'Holy, Luna. You're beautiful as a mermaid, but not very graceful,' she says, as I flail in the water. She puts an arm around my waist, steadies me.

I look at my tail through the water. 'Not bad,' I admit. 'But I can't seem to work out how to swim without legs.'

A swimming lesson follows, and after a while I get it: how to use my tail as a single entity instead of fighting it. The joy of swimming deep underwater, no need to come up to breathe; eyes changed so they stay open comfortably underwater.

Time is nearly up, Marina Implant-whispers. *Do you want to try to restore your legs by yourself, or should we connect again?*

I hesitate. Part of me longs to connect, part says no. *Tell me how to do it myself.*

Go to your Implant grid. Return all the code to the way it was before. Can you remember?

I'll try. But I have no idea, none. It was instinctive, isn't that the word she used before? Can I do it without Marina there?

I find the grid. The world fades away – colours and substance gone, replaced by elegant numbers once again. And I panic: how were things before? And then, I know what to do. Use the second grid, the silver one – the wild one that hides inside me. It bends to my thoughts. It regrets my beautiful tail, but does as I ask. I open my eyes, and I'm standing on the beach. Legs as usual, two of them, and they seem to work as they should.

There is a *ding*.

'Time to change,' Marina says. She is looking at me, green eyes wide. She hesitates. 'Luna – if you link Implants with someone, you'll learn quicker. But only do it if you trust them completely.'

'Why's that?'

'It's dangerous if you have secrets. They might find them out.'

Silver secrets.

Next I'm with Hex – in a castle.

'Nice digs,' I say.

'Thanks! I built it in the first round. From a rock.'

337

My jaw drops. He built a castle? From a *rock*?

'But I wasn't so busy that I didn't have time for a quick peek to see how you were doing with Marina.'

'And?'

He whistles. 'You appeared to have a fishy sort of tail.'

'It wasn't fishy! It was beautiful. And great for swimming, once I worked out how.'

'How did you manage that?' He shakes his head. 'Luna, whatever you thought before – you're a Hacker. No one who isn't a Hacker could do that. And few Hackers can easily master skills outside of their own area. Who knew you were a fish?'

I shrug. 'So I'm a Hacker. Big deal.' The words, said out loud, send a shiver down my back. A Hacker? *Me*?

He reaches out, lightly touches the skin around my left eye, tracing a slow circle that makes me shiver. 'Just here: I'll tattoo you myself when we're done.' He leaves his hand on my cheek. His eyes are intense, and I pull away.

'Is that actually required?'

He's surprised. 'Well, no. You don't have to. But it's kind of a badge of honour.'

'I'll think about it,' I say, uneasy at the thought of black tattoos in my skin. I can't picture them; it'd seem somehow *wrong*.

'OK, let's try this. Find your Implant grid,' he says, and I close my eyes. This time it is instantly there. Then his is there, also; it bumps into mine. I push it away. Not before I feel an echo of hurt.

You must have joined with Marina, he Implant-whispers.

Just for the first time. I want to try to do things myself, I answer the same way. And I wonder, in a closed-off place: is this because of what Marina said, that I should only do this with somebody I really trust? But I trust Hex. Don't I? But he's been weird since I've been here. Something – *someone* – makes me hold myself back: Melrose. Guilt stirs inside. I don't know quite what is happening with them, but I can't do anything as *intimate* as that with my friend's boyfriend.

Well, let's see if you can cast a few spells.

He explains, and I start to see: spells are just code changes, cast outwards, and concentrated on the object or person subject to the spell. And like the aquamarine sea, once I know how to work the numbers, it's there.

Colours are the easiest for me: a spell cast out that changes colour. Blue, once again. I change a pebble; Hex's shirt; a chair.

'I wonder if I could change the entire castle?' I ask him.

'Doubt it. But give it a try.'

As it turns out it's not any harder with something big than something small. Instead of concentrating the spell on a point, a single object, I set a chain reaction. It starts at my feet and fans out – the floor, the walls, accelerating as it goes.

'Thanks a lot!'

'What?' I turn back to Hex. He's blue from head to toe, clothes and skin – bright, deep blue, like a Smurf. I can't help it: I laugh. 'Sorry, mate. I didn't do it on purpose. Was it because I cast it into the castle while you were standing in it?'

'It was like a multiplying spell. I wonder if…? Come on,' he says, and we step out of the castle and look around, and – as far as we can see? *Blue*. Landscape, trees, sea, people: all the same shade of blue, all sending Implant protests in our direction.

'Whoops.' I turn back to Hex. 'How do I fix this?'

'No idea. I've never seen anything like it.' He's not happy, and it's nothing to do with being blue. Is it because I've taken his thing – casting spells – and somehow done something different with it, something he can't do?

'I'm sorry, Hex. I don't know what to do!'

He shrugs. 'Working on it,' he says. After a while he returns to his usual self, then Implant-explains to the others how to de-Smurf themselves and their surroundings. Gradually the world returns to normal.

There's a *ding*.

Time for someone else.

And so Sparky shows me how to blow things up. Blood tries to show me how to smell the blood of the living, the blood of the dead, but when we get to the latter it so nauseates me that I refuse. Other skills follow: I learn how to hack doors and computer defences; and one of my favourites – how to fly.

My tiring body back in the PIP is always there, a separate awareness. It reminds me to take ANDs now and then to prevent nausea from returning. It is getting weaker and weaker, sending protests, but I'm pushing them away. I don't want to stop. Each change brings something new to learn, to master, and I don't want to miss a single moment.

Not everyone gets everything. I'm the only one so far who has managed to be a full mermaid; more have managed Hex's spells, at a basic level at least. We keep vague track of our successes and failures via Implants. And the only one who has done it all – apart from Blood's skills, and that is because I didn't want to – is me.

And somehow this new joy – manipulating the grids, the beautiful numbers, the things I can do that others can't – is like a drug. Another one to add to all the ANDs I'm taking.

I'm wired up to something amazing, and I never, ever want it to stop.

38

A hand pushes at my shoulder. 'Luna?'

I ignore it.

It pushes again. *LUNA!* Via Implant shout, and that you can't ignore. I jump and open my eyes. It's Marina? Her eyes are anxious.

'What is it?'

'Are you OK?'

'Sure. Fine. Why?'

'You've been sitting there, rocking back and forth and humming. You freaked Zippy out and he whispered a message to me.'

'I... I...' I look between Marina and a boy whose vaguely familiar face is as anxious as hers. Is he Zippy? Yes. He's in Hex's class. My latest pairing in the skills-sharing world, he was supposed to be teaching me...it was something about... I can't remember what it was. I've been in my grid, lost in it. With the numbers, beautiful numbers...

LUNA!

I open my eyes again.

'You were doing it again: humming.'

'Really, I'm fine.' I'm lying. I'm the opposite of fine, unfine, so lacking in fine that my mind can't even come up with a word that fits. I stand and I'm shaking, my hands are shaking. I've been zoning out, humming, rocking back and forth, and—

The shock slams into me, and I gasp. 'That's what Nanna used to do.'

'Your grandmother? What did she do?'

I look at Marina and realise I said it out loud. I didn't mean to, but I did.

My head is pounding and the double awareness – of here, of my body in the PIP – is slipping back and forth. It's exhausted – my body. *I'm* completely exhausted.

I've got to get out of here.

The void is in my mind: the vast darkness. *Peace.* Away from all the clamouring numbers; the strands of the grid.

I start walking away, up the hill. Marina follows.

'What is it, Luna?'

'I don't know. I think maybe I need a break from here.'

'Yes. Good idea. I'll come with you.'

'No, don't miss out. I'll just unplug for a bit.'

'I'm coming.'

'No. I want to be alone!' I snap, and her face is hurt. 'Sorry. Really, I'll be fine. I'm going to turn my Implant to no messages, so don't worry if I don't answer.'

I do it as I say the words: *Implant off.* No messages. I even find the emergency message override function and disable it. As I do, I spot tendrils, a data trail: where does it lead? I follow the trail from my Implant to PareCo, along a hidden channel, and soon puzzle it out. It has tracking functions: every time I use my Implant they track what I do, and where I am. I disable that as well, and hide my interference:

343

all the hacking practice here has honed my skills.

We get to the door.

'It's only a few hours to dinner,' she says. 'I'll see you there?'

'Sure. OK.'

I pull the door open and step straight into the void.

The void? That's weird. I struggle to focus on *why* it's weird, thoughts slippery. Ah: this door should have gone to the MD Gateway, not the void? At least, it did when we came through it the other way.

I'd been thinking I wanted the void, and here I am. Hackers can't do that; I've learned a lot about what they can and can't do lately. They can manipulate code in worlds and spaces built out of the void. They can't control the void. Access to the void and creating new worlds within it are completely up to PareCo and their infinite memory and processing speed. Humans can't do that.

So how did I get here?

Who cares? I'm happy to be here. I stand still, breathe deeply. There is a peace here that is nowhere else. Infinity. Nothingness. Contradictory, yet both are here at the same time.

I wander about. Wouldn't it be wonderful to be here forever? It's supposed to be terrifying to be lost in the void. But it's so tranquil, so beautiful. All the tumult inside me quiets down.

I swat in front of my eyes. A bead – I saw a silver bead? Like it was following me around. I don't want it to; I want peace.

I lie down. It's so soothing, so lovely.

Back in the PIP, my heart feels fluttery.

There are footsteps there, voices. I don't want voices; I want silence. My body is annoying with its complaints, its senses.

'Not much longer, I should think.' A cheerful voice. 'She'll be ready soon.'

With a huge effort, I open my eyes in the PIP to a slit. Dr Rafferty is there, and a woman in a white coat. They're checking screens. Murmuring words that aren't making it through any more, to ears full of fuzzy cotton confusion.

Listen, I tell myself, and I try, but it's hard. I sit up in the void, open my eyes, willing myself to concentrate back in the PIP.

...the beta Implant scheme...drug interaction... harvesting...

They leave, and I'm relieved. All those troubling words worry at my thoughts, and like the phantom beads I swat away, I want them to leave me alone. I want to sleep in the void.

But something pricks and prods inside. I stay sitting up, and look around me: at the unending darkness, the little silver lights that dance. At forever.

They're pretty, the flickering points of silver light. They seem completely random most of the time. But not now.

Phantom spine spiders run down my back.

They're forming letters, spidery silver letters. Too vague and insubstantial at first to read, then coming together, bit by bit.

345

Luna.

I smile. Yes, that's who I am.

It's time to go.

Go where? I frown.

Go back to your body. You need each other.

Yes, I should. Shouldn't I? Go back to my messy body with the fluttery heart and cotton ears.

But it's hard. I'm so weak.

Go back pulses in silver. *Do it now.*

All right. The easy way, this time. I tell myself to reach to unplug back in the PIP. It's not simple like it usually is; my hands feel weighted down. But at last I manage it. I push away the connection, and I'm *back*. Back in my body.

It's not a great reunion.

I go to sit up and don't quite make it, and have to push up with my arms. Finally I manage it, trembling from the effort.

Eyes like sandpaper, whole body weak. Like a newborn kitten is weak. How long have I been plugged in? I frown. We were unplugging for dinner, weren't we? But did we? Thinking back, I can't remember. It was like it was always about to be dinner. But was it ever?

I manage to stand on shaky legs, holding myself up against the PIP sofa, then take a few tentative steps to the PIP monitor. I used to check my dad's monitor all the time. This one is different, but enough alike that I can work it out.

Forty days. It's been forty days since I unplugged? There's been life support on, giving all the nutrients I need to survive.

But with the double awareness I always have when plugged in, my body never sleeps like the others do.

So: I haven't slept for forty days. That can't be good.

Bed. Sleep. Yes; that's what I need. I leave the PIP, head down the hall on wobbly legs, one hand on the wall, then make for the stairs that go up to my room. There are voices in the stairwell above.

I go down the stairs instead of up. Hiding, but why?

I feel kind of floaty, like I'm still not really in my body. It feels light, wrong. I pull at my tunic; these clothes feel wrong.

After footsteps disappear down the hall above, I climb the stairs, up and up to my floor, each step taking more effort than the last. I make it to my room, shut the door. Take off all the PareCo stuff, put on my own jeans, top, everything my own. They're heavier, but they're more *me*. I feel more anchored to the world in them somehow.

Time for bed?

But I stare out the window, at the island. The green plateau and sparkling sea beyond. It's another beautiful day, almost like PareCo programme the weather to ensure their giant domed entrance hall always reflects sunshine in an endless pattern as designed.

And I'm overwhelmed by feelings of enclosure – the glass, the walls, the soft, warm blankets and pillows that are calling for me, all in muted colours like the clothes I discarded – all closing in on me in a beautiful, plush, crushing PareCo embrace. Can I be claustrophobic, in this giant bedroom?

Yes. I want out of here, desperately.

I find the map of the building that Marina minimised the day we arrived on my interface. At the bottom of our stairs is an emergency exit.

Before I even finish the thought I'm out of my room, down the hall. I hear footsteps coming the other way, and duck into a doorway. I peek out. They stop at a door, and open it. Is that my door? Are they going in my room?

I don't want to be delayed. I need air, fresh air, *real air*. I wait until the door closes behind them, and change my plan. I won't go down the closest stairs in case they're looking for me; I'll carry on along here, and take the next ones.

I pass door after door – our wing of bedrooms, dining hall, kitchens, unlabelled places. I stop to rest now and then. There is strong temptation inside to curl up in a corner. Just here, on the floor. Sleep. Who'd know? Or lost in a corner of one of these endless rooms. I try a few door handles; all locked.

When I reach the next stairwell I'm feeling all light again, even in my jeans, and moving slower and slower. That's what saves me.

There are motion detector cameras here, like the ones in my school. The ones I outwitted so many times to cut class. Move in slow motion, no sudden sounds or movements, and they don't engage. Just as well my maximum speed right now is like syrup.

So many stairs down. Too many stairs: I stop, sit on the top of a flight, head in hands. I can't, I can't…

My chest tightens; I can't breathe. I have to get out of

here. I pull myself to my feet, slowly, using the banister. *Keep going, Luna, you can do this.*

And finally, I reach the bottom of the last set of stairs. And what is there? A dead end. A blank brick wall.

I almost scream in frustration. Did I get it wrong when I looked at that map? Wasn't there an emergency exit at the bottom of all the stairwells? Not a bloody brick wall. The mere thought of having to climb all those steps up again has tears leaking out and trickling down my cheeks, but I'm too tired to raise a hand to wipe them away. I could link to my interface screen with my Implant to check the map, see if there is another way, but if I use my Implant, the tracking functions will re-engage. They'll know what I'm doing, and where I am.

A brick wall. An Implant.

I stare at it: it looks like an ordinary brick wall, but why would there be a brick wall here? Why would stairs lead to a wall? It doesn't make sense.

What if it isn't real?

There were brick walls at the test centre – ones I couldn't see, but Gecko could, because he had an Implant and I didn't: the wall he saw was an Implant image. I've got an Implant now. Though Gecko said Jezzamine and Danny – who also had to take ANDs to plug in, like me – could tell Implant images weren't real. This brick wall looks real enough.

But Dr Rafferty said I've got a *beta* Implant – different from the ones Jezzamine and Danny would have had. Has PareCo managed to overcome the fault?

349

But how would they know I might try to escape, to modify my Implant to stop me with a fake wall? Though maybe they didn't. Maybe the emergency exits always have false brick walls, and they just disable them if there is a real emergency. Maybe this is coincidental, and they've given me other tests – fake walls, or fake people. Or fake anything, really. How can I even know what is and isn't real any more?

Gecko told me that the way to get through a force field was not to push. I struggle to remember exactly what he said. It was something like merging with it, to get through.

But Gecko tried, and he couldn't overcome what he could see with his eyes – couldn't push into the wall, like I could – even when he knew what it was. So how can I?

Wait. Can I see what surrounds me through my silver grid, even though I'm not in virtual now? I close my eyes, and *reach* for silver: it wavers, a ghostly shadow. I focus on it, pull the strands, and it strengthens. I stand in my grid. Open my eyes. As in the VeeDubs, the silver grid overlies all I can see. The Implant brick wall image is still there, but twinned with a strange pulsing light. It *is* a force field.

I place my hands against it gently. Like at the test centre, there is a little give, then it pushes back. Again and again I try, different ways, different approaches, but every time it pushes back.

I lean against the wall, and give up. I can't do it. All I want is to *rest*, not solve problems; not even move. The silver fades away, and my mind vagues out.

I slip into waking sleep. *It's warm*. Warm like that force

field at the test centre. *Warm…sleep…*and I fall.

What? Jerked awake, I spin around. I'm on the other side of the wall. Did I fall asleep against it, then pass through? Is that the secret of how to get through a force field without pushing: fall asleep? I touch the wall and my hand easily passes into it. So, it's a one-way problem: from this side, easy to get through. From the other side, difficult.

I turn away from the wall, and there is the door. To the outside.

I can't see any alarms. Perhaps they thought a fake brick wall was enough? I reach a shaking hand to push the door. It opens, and I step out into dazzling sunshine.

I close the door and lean against it, and *breathe*, deep into my lungs: fresh air, real air. The knots inside start to unwind, just a little.

I walk. Away from PareCo, out on the volcanic plateau. Although it looks almost flat from the windows above, close up it is rough walking, picking an uneven path through scrubby low trees, hopping between clumps of grasses to avoid wet ground between them. Bird calls, my hard breathing, and the ever-louder surf crashing into rocks are the only sounds, as I get closer and closer to the cliffs and the sea. I jump at a movement, and focus in time to see a small bird run across the ground like a mouse.

I stumble, last remains of energy fading. I don't know why I keep going. If I look back I can still see the glass eyes of PareCo staring at me: is that it?

I crawl. Stop and rest a moment, and crawl some more.

Now I can hear new music: water, running water? A splashing waterfall. Beautiful, like Gecko's waterfall.

But this one is real. It falls through rocks, here, to a pool, then over cliffs to find the sea. There is lush greenness all around – trees, ferns, grasses – unknown and exotic to London eyes. I kneel at the edge of the pool, and drink deep. Drops of cool water spray and soothe my skin. Trees block the glass eyes; fallen leaves and grass on the ground are soft. They welcome me.

I sleep.

39

Cold. Cold is reaching for me, deep inside – calling me back. I don't want it, but it keeps prodding at my awareness, until finally it can't be ignored. I stretch, yawn, and open my eyes.

It's dark. Night. How long have I been here? I sit up and rub cold hands on cold arms, then hug my knees in close.

What now, Einstein?

I have no answers. I'm freezing, and jump at weird rustling noises in the night. Are there snakes here? I fight the urge to switch my Implant on to check. I don't want to be traced to this place: it is mine. A secret I don't want to share.

Through trees, the distant PareCo glass dome shines, reflecting the full moon and starlight. It's beautiful, but what were they doing to me? My mind is groggy, still half caught between sleep and exhaustion. It doesn't want to think.

And it is miles away. I can't believe I got this far.

I'm hungry. There is water here but no food, and there is no one else on this island but PareCo. There is no way off this island without PareCo, even if I knew where to go.

There is no other option. Even as it makes my stomach twist with a confused mix of longing and fear, I have to go back.

But I'm not ready yet.

What was happening to me there? I was *loving* being a Hacker, playing with the grid and the numbers, pulling strands to change myself, the world around me. So obsessed with what I was doing virtually that I was ignoring my body. Could I have died if I hadn't left when I did? Something inside answers *yes*. I wasn't too far away from completely losing it, losing even the strength to unplug. Not sleeping made me feel like I was drugged.

Was I hallucinating? Those silver letters in the void, spelling out my name, telling me to go. I *must* have imagined that.

But is sleep deprivation the whole story? When I left Marina, I'd been rocking and humming, just like Nanna used to. I didn't even know I was doing it until she told me.

But Nanna used to sleep just fine – it wasn't caused by sleep deprivation in her case. As much as I don't want to think about it, maybe it *is* genetic. Maybe whatever was wrong with her is wrong with me, too, and no matter what I do I'm going to go that way: delusions. Fits. Death.

Still, it really felt like I was drugged.

Nanna was drugged; she was on so many meds it was hard to keep track of what and when.

But I was drugged too, wasn't I? I was taking ANDs by the handful.

I sit bolt upright when it hits me. What – *exactly* – did I overhear Dr Rafferty say in the PIP, when he thought I couldn't hear? I concentrate, really hard, but my mind was so fuzzy then. There was something about beta Implants, and drug interactions.

The only thing I've taken is ANDs. I never told anyone,

but either they were spying on me or searched my room, because Dr Rafferty knew: he'd told me that if I got an Implant, I wouldn't need them any more, so he knew about them then. He was wrong about that, but—

Wait: I was plugged in for *forty days*. The ANDs supply I had in my pocket would have run out in a fraction of that time. I had no idea it had been so long – must be something about hacking. Maybe when I'm in the grid it takes loads of time even though it feels like stuff happens really quickly. But I never got sick. I took ANDs from my pocket now and then because I thought I needed to – but not often enough to cover forty days.

There is only one possible answer. The PIP nutrient feed must have drugs added to it. Is that why Rafferty said I wouldn't need to take them any more? He made it sound like it was because of getting an Implant, but he lied. The drugs were built into my PIP; they must have been.

Have they been experimenting on me to see if they can change Implants and drugs so even those who take ANDs can't tell Implant images are false? Is that why I saw the brick wall at the bottom of the stairs as a wall, and could only see it as a force field through my silver grid?

They can't drug people or experiment on them without consent. It *must* be illegal. And if they're doing that, who knows what else they're doing. If I'm right, I can report them, but this is all complete guesswork. Maybe Melrose's dad could help. But I need proof.

Add that as another reason to all the others: no matter that everything inside screams *bad idea*, I have to go back.

I stand, and groan as I do so – stiff, sore, still tired – then turn to the pool for a drink. Stars reflect in the water. I kneel, move close to the water. Suddenly *another* is there, staring back at me:

Dark hair…pale skin…silver.

Astra?

Liquid fear runs through my veins; I jump back.

Am I hallucinating? Hesitant and trembling, I lean forward once again.

No. I'm not hallucinating – at least, it's not Astra, or her ghost. It's my own face reflected in the water, not hers looking up from it. But not my face at the same time. Goosebumps rise on my arms: I look like Astra. Silver winds around my left eye.

I look away, rub my eyes, and look back again.

Silver? Around my eye?

Am I still drugged, is that it?

No. My head is clearer now; still tired, but not exhausted and unable to think like before. All synapses are firing at top speed.

Silver: like my mother, Astra. Like Gecko. I raise a shaking hand to touch the marks, to trace them. The swirls and patterns: so beautiful. They don't rub off. They're part of my skin. That night at the fountain with Hex I thought I'd seen something on my face; I convinced myself it was just part of the starshine speckled on every surface in the dome from the endless reflecting glass, but I was wrong.

Gecko and Astra were S'hackers, the silver only visible to some, and only in starshine. A special type of Hackers – ones PareCo can't detect.

My thoughts are whirling, spinning. All those things I could do in the VeeDubs – I wasn't hacking, at least, not the way the others do. I was *S'hacking*. That's why I could learn to do stuff so fast. The silver grid inside me? It isn't part of the Implant; it is part of *me*. Once I knew how to use the Implant grid it was a simple step to the silver grid. That's how I did those things.

And Gecko took me into the void through a silver hatch, a silver ladder reaching down from it into my Realtime hallway. He did that as a S'hacker. But there have been other silver doors: like the one I fell through that rescued me from Blood in the combat world. And the door from the VeeDub that took me straight to the void.

Did I make them? I must have done. When I desperately wanted something, was I unconsciously accessing the silver S'hacker grid?

Hackers can't access the void without PareCo, or manipulate it. Somehow, I can.

I start walking back to PareCo, glad of the moonlight as I pick my way. The night air isn't so cold now I'm moving, and something inside is strangely energised.

So, I'm a S'hacker. Like Astra. How did I not see it? The silver grid; the things I can do. Like most lost things, the answer was blindingly obvious once I found it.

Maybe I'm not mad or going that way. Maybe Nanna

wasn't, either: maybe it was all those drugs her doctors kept giving her that did it, like the ones I've been given here that had me rocking and humming like she used to do.

Maybe Gecko wasn't, either. He didn't trust PareCo; he thought Jezzamine and Danny were killed by them. He said they'd captured him and were bringing him here, but I didn't believe him.

Maybe I should have.

Gecko, where are you?

40

Can they see me, walking in the moonlight? The closer I get to the PareCo dome the more there is nowhere to hide. I walk tall and straight. There's nothing else I can do.

I head for a door, a different one from where I left.

It opens; on the other side is a brick wall. I shrug and walk straight through it.

I head up the stairs to my level, and around to my room, half expecting someone to jump out and yell, *gotcha*! But it is quiet.

If it wasn't a sleepwalking induced nightmare, someone was in my room checking it just after I left yesterday. Now nothing seems disturbed, no one is here. First up? A long hot shower. Fresh clothes; Centre clothes again. I'm overwhelmingly sleepy; just sleepy this time, not like yesterday's trembling, fuzzy exhaustion.

Someone is bound to come, to ask questions. But until then?

I crawl into bed, close my eyes and am instantly asleep.

Rat-a-tat-tat.

Hmmph? I open one eye. Light is streaming through my room, and someone is knocking – loudly – on the door.

No point in putting this off: they'll just find keys. I get up, stretch, and open it.

'Marina!'

She hugs me. 'I'm so glad you're all right.'

'Of course I'm all right. I've just slept, like, a million hours.' My stomach audibly growls. 'And now I'm starving.'

'You're in luck. Dinner is in ten. They've got us all unplugged to meet the new lot of interns.'

'New interns?'

'Yep, the next intake is here.' She eyes me. 'Brush your hair or something. And turn your Implant back on. I think I broke a nail banging on your door.'

I brush my hair and teeth while Marina waits. Think *Implant on*, and a stream of unanswered messages flashes past: a few from Marina, one from Dad, and about a dozen from Hex.

And then – *ping*. It's Dr Rafferty, calling here and now. 'Hello, Luna.'

I can't ignore him, can I? 'Hi,' I say, and his image appears in front of me.

'There you are. Come see me after your dinner.' Dr Rafferty's face is calm, unruffled. Nothing on it says *where the hell have you been*? But not a meeting I'm looking forward to, just the same.

'Come on. Let's go,' Marina says, links an arm in mine and pulls me out the door.

I was wondering if they'd put us in a bigger room, or have more tables or something, but no: same dining room, same tables. Our group is here, and the new interns. No sign of

Hex or any of his lot. 'Where'd Hex's group go?'

'They've graduated,' Marina says.

'What? But where are they?'

Marina shrugs. 'I don't know; they all looked impossibly smug about their top-secret assignments, and said they couldn't tell us. They're off working now. We had a virtual farewell party last night. You missed it.'

I stare at her, appalled. All those messages from Hex that I haven't even looked at. 'But aren't they still here, on the island?'

'I don't know. Maybe not: they left around the same time as the new lot came this morning – there would have been boats here then.'

We sit down and get introduced all round to the newbies. Their eyes are wide. Were mine like that? All impressed with PareCo, the clothes, the rooms, the top of the line equipment. What you can learn to do and the competition against each other.

I zone out enough to check Hex's messages. They start out with *where are you, is everything OK?* Move on to an annoyed tone at lack of answer. End with a goodbye. I try messaging him back: no answer. And not because he's ignoring me: it pings back with *Implant not found*. Is his Implant offline like mine was before? Where is he?

And what am I going to tell Rafferty?

Dr Rafferty smiles when I come into his office. 'Have a seat,' he says. 'Tea?'

'No thanks.'

'I've been very worried about you, Luna.' He's so earnest, so genuine. 'Where have you been?'

'I'm not entirely sure. I was really exhausted, couldn't seem to think properly. I wandered off and fell asleep. Woke up and went back to sleep in my room. I didn't wake up until Marina banged on my door just before dinner.'

'And your Implant?'

'I switched it off. Didn't want to get woken up.'

'Impressive to see how much you've learned in the skills-sharing. Is that where you learned how to hack your own Implant?'

'Sort of.'

He leans back in his chair. 'Sure you don't want some tea? No?' He pours from a teapot into his cup. 'And how did you unplug from the training world?' He stirs milk into his tea, eyes not leaving me.

I shrug, and lie. 'Usual way. Out through the VeeDub door to the MD Gateway.'

'I see,' he says, and there is something behind the bland look on his face. Does he know there are things I'm not telling him?

He smiles. 'Don't look so worried. We at PareCo love a challenge. We also love rebels, even misguided ones. All the interesting material we get from them – well. Some of our most popular virtual worlds are run by happy PareCo Think Tank employees who used to be rebels.' His eyes are twinkling like they always do, but this time I'm not fooled.

'Once we find the right niche for them, they can be very creative, very useful. Don't worry, Luna. We'll find the right niche for you.'

That night I lie awake, eyes staring unseeing at the ceiling.

They want us to compete at their games, to learn, to get better and better at hacking. And then they want to use us to run more games, games that will hook in more players.

I don't want to play any more.

41

PareCo might like rebels, but only so long as they are punctual. I get the evils from the Beamer when I come in last for our next adventure. Dragged along by Blood, who they'd picked to chase down the straggler when I ignored an Implant summons.

This time Marina is one of the team leaders, and she picks me first. Because we're friends, or because after how well I did at skills-sharing I'm a Hacker to be reckoned with? I try not to care, but somewhere inside, I do.

Beamer beams. 'Today we're going to a fictional game world, Slated world 12.' She flips a coin; Marina calls it but loses. 'You can choose to be either Lorders or Slateds,' she says to the other team leader. After some consultation, they pick Lorders. Primarily based on wardrobe – apparently they'll be rather cool in black.

Our team meets in Marina's hallway. Nausea hits me straight away, but I resist slipping my hand to my pocket for some ANDs back in the PIP. Moments later it eases, then is completely gone. There is the proof: they *must* be giving me drugs through my PIP feed, just like I thought. But for once being right isn't a good feeling.

Everyone is here now; there is a new VeeDub door marked *Slated 12* at the end of Marina's hallway. *At least we're the good guys*, Marina Implant-whispers, and sighs.

'What is this fictional world, "Slated"? I've never heard of it,' I say, out loud.

'Didn't you study it in English?' Marina says. 'The novel was used as an example of what can happen when rulers govern irrationally in pursuit of their own interests, and how ends don't justify the means. That sort of stuff.'

I shrug. 'I fell asleep a lot in class.'

'The first few Slated worlds take you through the plot of the novels; Slated 4 onwards just use the world concept for some fun combat stuff. Slated 12 is new, but I assume it will follow that trend. Basically, as Slateds we were underage criminals who were caught, and our memories erased as punishment. Lorders are part of the evil government we want to overthrow, to stop Slating and reestablish free democracy.'

'What do we do: stage a rebellion?'

'Sort of, but there's a catch. We'll have Levos around our wrists. They're linked to emotions, so if you get upset or angry, you get zapped unconscious; too far and you die. So we can't commit any acts of violence. And if they catch us, they'll terminate us. And they've got all the nifty weapons.'

'Great. Sounds like a fair fight, then.'

We step through the new VeeDub door, and on the other side – instant wardrobe change. We're all dressed the same, in black trousers, white shirts under maroon jumpers with *Lord Williams' School* embroidered on them. Old style school uniforms? TACKY. And there they are: Levos around our wrists. They have digital readouts on them; mine says 5.1.

'What does the number mean?'

'It's like a mood ring – it says how happy you are. Five is kind of middling. You're in trouble if it drops below three.'

'Do these things actually do anything?'

'Try this,' Marina says. She mimes twisting it a little, and I twist it as hard as I can. *WHAM*. Pain in the skull, like being sledgehammered. There are spots in front of my eyes. Now there are numbers flashing into red on my Levo: 4.2...3.9...

'Do something! Get happy fast, or you'll get zapped and it hurts worse than that,' Marina says.

Stuff this. I close my eyes, find my grid. See myself through it, the device on my wrist. It is actually linked to a chip in my brain? *No way*. What sort of evil government would do this to teenagers? But it can't be hacked in this world; it's not accessible. No *normal* way, that is. I hack my Implant to block PareCo's monitoring. Then I reach for the silver shadow inside me. A few tweaks, twists, and they're gone: the Levo, the chip, the whole lot. It would have made a short story out of a novel if the characters could have done *that*.

I open my eyes. The others are staring at me, wide mouthed. At my bare wrist.

'How'd you do that?' a boy asks. 'That is a non-override world protocol.'

'We should make a move. They'll be tracking us by now,' Marina says, interrupting before I can try to work out what to say. There is an info dump to our Implants with directions to our camp, and known Lorder movements, maps.

'Split into pairs and see you there,' Marina says. She draws me into the woods with her.

'Wait a sec,' I say. 'Want me to take your Levo off?'

'Can you?'

'I think so. But we'd have to link grids. So I won't do the rest of them.'

'Go for it,' she says. We close our eyes. Find grids; link. It's like before – I can see out of her eyes, feel the beat of her heart synchronise with mine.

And I can feel yours.

This is a secret.

What is?

This time it isn't just the shadow she saw behind the other grid; the silver grid takes control. And within seconds her Levo and chip are gone.

She's full of wonder. *Don't worry, Luna. I won't tell anyone. I can't, because I haven't a clue what that was, or what you did, so how could I?* She hesitates. *PareCo might be monitoring your Implant grid, though I'm not sure they could see what you did. Since you didn't use that grid.*

It's OK. I blocked them.

You did what? Surprise. Envy. *Show me how?*

Another time. Let's get out of here. We unlink, and run through the trees, follow the map unfolding in our minds.

'This is so brilliant,' Marina says. 'We can blow the Lorders up now! They won't know what hit them.'

'Maybe we could go undercover? As Lorders.'

'I like that idea. Anything to get out of these horrible clothes.' And she starts planning, whispering to me via Implant, and it all sounds good, sounds doable.

367

And I want our team to win, but most of all... I want to win myself. There is a crazy surge running through me as we run, like when we were in the skills sharing world – I want to do more, and more. When we were in the combat world I didn't have the drive to win; I was too scared. Now things are different.

Or are they?

We're just doing what PareCo wants us to do. Every time. We compete, they observe by spying through our Implants; we learn things, they use what we can do. What's the point?

Gecko said PareCo uses Hackers. Pits them against each other to engage their competitive streak; that Hackers are encouraged to rebel and hack the system so they can be used by it. I discounted much of what he said as crazy, but isn't that what Dr Rafferty implied, too?

If Gecko was right about that...maybe he was right about everything else.

Though Hex said Gecko kidnapped me after the transport crash. Is he dangerous?

Maybe. But not to me. Now that I focus on it close, remember Gecko as he was – his smile, the firm feel of his hand, that day we spent together in the waterfall world – no.

So what am I doing? Why am I here? Apart from the lack of choice thing, I don't *have* to do as they want. I don't *have* to compete. I'd decided that last night, but as soon as we got here, I changed.

Is it the ANDs that are making me want to win at all costs, or is it something else? Maybe it is something in *me*.

My feet start to slow. I can't be sure; I have to stop taking the drugs. I can't be here without them though, can I? Without being sick.

I wish Gecko were here. I wish I could ask him about all of this again, now that I'm beginning to see he may have been right.

Marina is pulling away. I Implant-whisper: *Sorry, Marina, I've got to go for a while. Can you go on without me?*

She stops, and turns; looks back at me standing there. *Why, have you got something better to do?*

Not exactly, just something I have to do.

She pauses. *Are you OK?*

Yes.

And to think I picked you first.

Sorry.

She looks at me, curiosity in her eyes, but doesn't ask. *It's OK. Do what you have to do. Catcha later.*

She disappears through the trees.

I hide myself deep in undergrowth, away from any paths. I have to try this.

This time I don't even go near my Implant grid. I can't risk them logging *this*. I close my eyes, and the silver grid is there. If I can hack my Implant, why not my PIP? I'm hooked into it and it into me, right now.

I ignore the rustling trees, the cool air, the damp ground and rotting leaves underneath me here in the Slated world. I focus on my body back in the PIP. Find my silver grid *there*, then superimpose it on the PIP nutrient feeds. And hidden

369

amongst all of it is something that shouldn't be there. A drug feed. And I also see all the variations in constituents and dosages, and the tracking system linking back to my Implant log. They've been varying it, monitoring intake against my hacking performance in the VeeDubs.

Once I've found it, switching off both the drug feed and the linked tracking system is simple.

I sit up back in the Slated world. What will happen now the drugs are switched off? I have the answer almost instantly. When I take the tablets, they last a certain period of time; not so now. Nausea slams into me almost as soon as the drug feed is gone. I try to control it, to breathe in and out slowly. But it's awful. I nearly reach back to start it again; maybe if *I* control it, decrease it over time, I can wean myself off it, bit by bit?

No.

I don't want to be PareCo's puppet. I need to find Gecko, find out what he knows about all of this. I want out of here.

I want out of here *now*.

And almost before the thought is complete, there is a rush of silver: a door in the air next to me.

I pull the handle, and step through.

It closes behind me, and I'm in darkness, buffeted by the winds of the void. My eyes adjust; dancing lights are clinging to my skin. I spin around, and laugh. The second I came through that door? The nausea was gone. Gone! Take that, PareCo.

All I need now is to find Gecko.

A silver arrow pulses at my feet.

42

The arrow stops at a dark presence in front of me in the void – large in scale, much larger than Gecko's S'hack.

Let me in. A rush of silver outlines a door.

I peer through: it's a VeeDub, a whole world. An exotic city landscape set beside a harbour, with roads and cars and people. It's massive. How am I going to find Gecko?

The nausea is back in full force. If I'm going to stay here to find him, I have no real choice; I have to take something to control it. But I won't use their drugs. Back in the PIP I reach for the ANDs in my pocket, chew and swallow a few of them.

I concentrate on Gecko, on his smile, hoping somehow the void silver will find a way to lead me to him in here.

Nothing happens.

I start to walk down a steep hill past huge houses – mansions, really – towards the harbour. There are restaurants and casinos around the water's edge, and cafés and amusements on a pier. Everything – and everybody – is opulent. It all feels a bit overdone. The footpath is crowded, but space opens around me; odd looks are cast my way. I look down: *great*. I'm still in the totally lame Slated world school uniform. Just as I think I should try to do something about it, a black limo goes past, then stops. A window winds down, and the chauffeur peers out.

'Are you Luna?'

I pause. 'Who wants to know?'

'Get in,' he says, and an electric back door slides open.

Before I can decide if this is a good idea or a bad idea, two very large, burly, bodyguard-looking types appear, one either side of me.

'Get in,' one says.

'Please,' the other says, and smiles, but instead of that making him look less frightening, it has more the opposite effect.

I shrug. It's not like I know where I'm going. And I can always fall out of a silver door if I need to.

I get into the limo. Burly no. 1 gets in with me; Burly no. 2 sits next to the driver.

'So. Where are we going?'

No answer. We appear to be heading up, away from the harbour, the opposite side to where I came down.

I lean back on the plush seats. This is way cooler than Melrose's dad's limo. His was government functional. This one is more rock star.

We pull in and go down a ramp under a shiny black skyscraper. The car is parked, the door slides open. Burly no. 1 and Burly no. 2 flank me from the car and into a lift. The lift is glass and one wall faces out on the city. There is something weird about the buildings and gardens spreading out below, and then I see what it is: they all look angled for effect – as if arranged to look good from this one place.

The lift doors open. 'Get out,' Burly no. 1 says.

'Please,' Burly no. 2 says again. I don't wait to see that smile; I bolt. They don't follow, and the lift doors shut.

I'm in a massive room, glass windows all around, and my eyes are dazzled. I blink, and across the room a dark figure facing the other way is outlined in the light.

He turns. 'Where the hell have you been?'

'Gecko!' I start to run across the room to him, slowing and then stopping when his words sink in. He's not moving.

'Well. Lovely to see you, too,' I say.

'What took you so long?'

I stare back at him, baffled, not answering. Shake my head. 'I didn't exactly know where to find you.'

'Well, here I am.'

'How'd you know to send that car for me?'

He shrugs. 'It's my world; I made everything in it. I just *know* who is here, where they are.' He raises an eyebrow. 'You could've saved me the effort by coming straight here. But sorry, I'm being a bad host. Would you like a drink or anything?'

'No, thanks.'

'Thanks for stopping by.' He turns away again, looks out the window.

I'm trying to remember why I was so anxious to find Gecko, what I wanted to ask him, but all I do is stare out of the window along with him. This world is pretty amazing. Did he make it all? 'Nice place you've got here,' I venture.

'Do you think so? I'm getting bored with it. Come over here. Watch.'

I walk closer, stand next to him. He's staring at the harbour: pretty yachts bobbing in the water, pier lined with crowded cafes.

Then people start to run.

But not fast enough. There is a wall of water rising up almost vertically from the sea. It throws yachts, and people; slams them into buildings.

'Are you doing that? Stop it!'

'Why? I built it; I can knock it down again.'

'What is wrong with you? What about all those people?'

'Those people are having the time of their lives in an exclusive VeeDub world. They've paid PareCo a small fortune just to come here, and be surprised out of their stupid, bored little minds. They'll die a horrible death and be whisked out of here by escape code, then have it to dine out on for weeks. Why disappoint them?'

'What's happened to you?'

He turns to me, and there is a trace of the Gecko that I knew in his eyes. A confused, pained look crosses his face. 'I don't know, Luna,' he says, voice low. 'There's nothing you can do. Just get the hell out of here. Before it's too late.'

Below us the sea is still swelling, still rising. It's a cataclysmic scene, yet strangely silent. But it is heading straight for us. It slams into the building, the windows shatter, and the silence is broken. Glass flies everywhere, water starts rushing in.

Get me out of here!

A rush of silver forms a door behind me. I turn, and open

the door. Look back. Gecko hasn't moved from where he was standing, but a protective bubble surrounds him: the torrent of water, glass and debris just washes past. Nothing he's done can harm him.

He raises a hand in farewell, anguish in his eyes, just as a surge of water pushes me through the silver door.

I cough and sputter, choking on seawater. I should have turned into a mermaid; that would've surprised him, wouldn't it?

What is wrong with him? Why did I even *want* to find him?

I'm soaked through. I go to wring my hair out and recoil when something horrible touches my hand. I reach back again, and a slimy strand of green seaweed comes away. Really? Thanks, Gecko. Thanks a lot.

Then I remember, and reach for the silver grid inside. Change this ridiculous, soaking wet school uniform for some decent clothes – dry ones – and de-seaweed my hair.

But I don't feel better.

It was his eyes; the naked look in them when I was pushed through the door. The pain. He's not happy. Though did he really need to take it out on me and all the stupid, bored idiots?

What now?

I sigh. I don't know; I have no more ideas, nada, zilch. All I really want is to get out of here. I want to go *home*. Off Inac, away from everything and everybody associated with this place.

OK, it hasn't all been horrible. I've made some friends here, especially Marina. And so much of what we've done has been beyond awesome, other than nearly bleeding to death in the combat world. And almost dying from exhaustion.

But then Hex and his group disappeared.

And what has happened to Gecko? I don't understand what is going on here, but there is a deep ache inside, one that says something bad is coming.

I wish – *so much* – that I could just go home, and leave it all behind.

Silver swirls about me, almost seems to urge me to my feet.

I stand, and a silver arrow pulses in front of me.

Goosebumps trail up my arms. All I wished for...was home. Can it somehow take me there from here, in the void?

The arrow pulses brighter.

No matter how crazy, I start walking. The arrow stays bright, leading the way, and I walk faster.

Then I reach a dark space in the void – black, outlined by silver pulses. Smaller than Gecko's VeeDub; bigger – much bigger – than his S'hack.

What is this place?

I wish to go in; a sheet of silver forms, turns into a door. I push the door open, and peer through. Shock slams into me. I pull back and let the door shut again.

What the hell? Tears are pushing into the backs of my eyes. Is this some sort of PareCo joke, or what? If it is, it's a sick one.

But I can't stop myself. Hand shaking, I reach for the door again. Pull it open, and step through.

It's home. Our garden, our house. But not exactly like it; more like it'd be if you could wish it bigger and better. The garden is awesome – huge; brilliant green grass like velvet; flowers everywhere, but mixed seasons, as if spring blossom, summer roses and autumn camellias were tricked to come out at once.

Hesitant at first, I walk around, flinging my arms out and breathing in deep. It isn't *really* home, but it feels like it, even smells like it, somehow. But *who* would make this place? Why? Nobody but me would ever want to come here. I turn back to the house, and that is when I see it: on the door. There is an envelope taped to the door.

I walk towards it, look closer, and my skin crawls.

Luna is written on the front of it, but that isn't what is bringing out the spine spiders. It's written in *my* handwriting.

Hand shaking, I reach for the envelope. Rip it open. Inside is one sheet of paper: a letter. Again, it is in my handwriting.

Dear Luna,

Seems kind of weird to be writing a letter to myself! But here goes.

You're standing right now in your very own S'hack, which you made; seemed the best place to stash this letter as only you can find your S'hack.

You kind of did the unexpected, and joined up with Tempo, Gecko and some other anti-PareCo rebels called the Worms – charming name, or what?

I'm short on time as about to dash off and have my recent memories wiped so you can be the best undercover spy of all: because you don't know that is what you are. So instead of me telling you all about everything, what you need to do is recover your memories.

Astra's necklace is made of memory beads. Sounds weird, I know – but focus on the beads, cast silver into them, and your memories will come back.

Trust me on this one.

Luna xx

I stare at the letter, one hand drawn involuntarily to the necklace I've worn every day since I found it in my bag at the hospital. I pull it out from under my clothes, undo the clasp. Study it closely in my hands.

A string of interlocking silver beads; a pretty thing I've known since childhood. My mother always used to wear it. But have I ever really *looked* at it before?

There are marks on the beads – carvings. They look a lot like S'hacker marks, but they're not all the same. Some of the beads – six of them – shine with an intensity greater than the others. And they have marks *exactly* like the ones around my eye.

Dad said he thought Astra's necklace looked longer. Was that because my memory beads added to its length? And those beads I kept thinking I could see, floating in the void: maybe it's some trace of this that made me see them.

Is this for real?

Are my missing memories here, in my hands, right now?

I lost *six days* of my life. According to this note, written in my own handwriting, I *chose* to have this done to me. I did it on purpose, so I could be a spy. I'm some sort of anti-PareCo rebel, like Gecko and others I can't even remember?

One thing I do know: if I do this, if I get these memories back, everything will change.

I'm scared. Who knows what is in my missing memories? What could have made me agree to all this craziness? It must have been bad. Really bad.

But they were six days that were mine; I want them back. *Six is for enlightenment, seeking solutions.* How can I not?

I read the letter again: the instructions are so short as to be meaningless.

But I have to do it. I have to know.

I take a last look around me: I made this place? It's my very own S'hack. *Wow*. Part of me wants time out – to just stay here, and hide.

But what I have to do can't be done here. Silver forms a door at my command, and I step out into the void.

Blinding silver sears into the six beads in my hands, shedding light where all was darkness.

The transport crash.

Gecko; following him into the night. He kissed me, then led pursuit away, sacrificing his own freedom for mine.

The S'hacker marks around my eye: something I rediscovered here on Inac.

Being pulled into the van, alone. Heywood, Crystal and Tempo: the Worms.

Astra's memories, bathed in her love for me. Her warnings. *Trust your intuition, Luna.*

And most of all, the *anger*: PareCo caused Astra's death. Nanna's death. Jezzamine and Danny, too.

PareCo must pay.

And Gecko: is he still a prisoner? Is his body somewhere on Inac?

I'm coming for you, Gecko. This time I won't let you chase me away.

Now, I remember.

What it lies in our power to do,
it lies in our power not to do.

Aristotle

43

I have to fight to make the silver arrows take me to Tempo, when everything inside screams *Gecko*. But she'll know what to do – I hope it so much, it must be true.

When they finally stop they are pointing at something completely different: a void space, like S'hacks or worlds, but when I look at it directly I can't see it. A sideways glance shows curious silver patterns, like S'hacker marks; they vanish if I look straight at them. I try to form a door by wishing for it in the usual way. Nothing happens.

Tempo: I concentrate on finding her. An arrow points to the same place again. She *must* be in there.

I close my eyes, find my silver grid, and *focus* on the place she should be: it is slippery; a direct analysis yields nothing. But the area *around* where I'm trying to focus? There is something there, fuzzing it out, some sort of barrier to get through first. I wish for a door in the barrier instead. This time, it works.

Through the door is a narrow passage surrounding another dark space inside. Can I make a door into it from here? Caution says go small, first. I make a peephole, and peer through.

It's like some sort of city council chamber – a dozen men and women sit in a semicircle, facing a small woman in a formal chair. And Tempo is one of them. All have intricate

S'hackers marks around their left eyes, under a roof made of starshine. And they're having a furious argument.

'This is our best chance to find out what is happening on that island. Why are you being obstructionist?' Tempo.

'You know exactly why,' a man says, shaking with anger so much that his whiskers are twitching. 'The risks of activating this unknown power—'

'She's not a tool to be used or discarded, whatever her mother was thinking in her creation.' A mild, chiding voice; the small woman in the big chair the others face. She looks somehow familiar. 'She has the right to her own memories.'

Their words are percolating through; *the island. Her mother. Memories.*

Wait a minute. Are they talking about *me*?

'We should put this to a vote,' Tempo says.

'I think the time for that has passed.' The woman in the big chair gestures at the wall where I stand; a silver door forms in front of me, and opens. The others turn around in their seats, open-mouthed when they see me standing there.

The shock on Tempo's face is quickly replaced by delight. She jumps up and pulls me into the room for a hug. Lets go, but holds me at arm's length, searching my face.

'Darling girl! You're all right.'

There is furious sputtering behind her from Whiskers. 'You were pretending to take this to the council when all the time you'd already activated the girl?'

Tempo turns. 'I did not. Luna? If you're here, you must have retrieved your memories. How did this happen?'

'I left a note to myself explaining how. In my S'hack.'

'See?' Tempo looks around the room, daring them to deny what I said.

'But how did she find us, break through the barrier of nothing we set around the council?' Whiskers again. 'This has never been done. That is your proof: she is dangerous.'

'She may be merely curious.' This from the big chair. 'Let her tell her story.'

Thirteen pairs of eyes are looking at me for answers.

'Just one thing first. Who are all of you?'

The woman in the big chair smiles. 'Fair enough. We are COS, the Council of Scientists. I'm Media, the current chair. Your mother was the chair many years ago, and despite what she did, is greatly missed.'

'What do you mean – what she did?'

'There were disagreements on the ethics of certain genetic projects; she continued without sanction.' She looks uncomfortable.

'Certain genetic projects. You mean *me*, don't you?'

'This is old history; there are matters for today. Come, Luna.' She pulls a chair out of the air. 'Have a seat. Tell us your story.'

I look to Tempo; she nods. So I do: beginning with becoming aware in the café, and getting taken to the hospital in London. Then Inaccessible Island, and being tricked into agreeing to an Implant. The MD Gateway with doors to all the worlds; the combat and training worlds. Hex's group, gone. And Gecko, locked in a world he creates and destroys,

385

over and over again. And how I found the Council today.

'Thank you, Luna,' Media says. 'We need to consider what the next course of action should be. For now, continue as you were with PareCo. We'll come up with a plan.'

'What about Gecko?'

'That is very disturbing. We'll work out what we can do to help him. Leave him alone for now, Luna.'

I keep my mouth shut. But that *so* isn't happening.

Does Media read my face? 'Be patient, Luna. We'll do what we can. For now, go back to the game world you're supposed to be in with the other interns. Hopefully no one has noted your absence.'

Dismissed so they can argue some more about what to do with me? Anger is swelling inside, but when I glance at Tempo, she gives a small shake of her head.

'Come, Luna. I'll show you out,' Tempo says, and we go through the double doors to the void.

She squeezes my shoulder. 'So lovely to see you. I caught your trace in the void a few times, but you were always gone before I could find you.'

'But you sent the beads that were following me around to remind me about the necklace, didn't you? And the words that helped me in the void. Spelled in silver.'

She pauses. 'Just so.' She smiles. 'There have been rumours about the existence of the MD Gateway you mentioned. Tell me about it, every detail. How do you get into it?'

'If you plug in to an MD-PIP it can take you straight there, but it doesn't always. PareCo must control it. And before I had an Implant, there was a path to it through the void from my Realtime hallway.'

'And inside the Gateway? Describe it.'

'At first it seems an ordinary sort of room with lots of doors. But if you walk, the room spins and grows: there are doors on the walls, floor and ceiling, and it's immense.'

'Are there doors to *all* PareCo worlds through the Gateway?'

'So they said. Why's it important?'

She smiles. 'I'm not sure yet. I need to think about this some more.'

She says goodbye, promises to find a way to help Gecko, and rushes back to COS. She's excited by what she's learned from me, what she can do with the information.

What *we* can do with it.

I should do as she says. Go back to the Slated world, back to my group. To the competition we are trying to win against the Lorders. I struggle to control the silver arrows, to make them take me there, but it is hard when I don't really want to go. Flickering arrows form and I walk, dragging my feet.

Something is niggling inside, something skipped over as being of little interest to the council. What has happened to Hex and the rest of his group? It should have been my group. If it still had been, by now I'd know.

Isn't that part of the whole mystery of this place?

I've reached the dark shape that is the Slated world. I should go in; the less I make PareCo suspicious, the better.

But Hex's Implant was *not found* the last time I tried. He was so *on* – always. He'd never voluntarily turn his Implant off like I did. The worry inside is growing. The least I can do is try, one more time.

Implant on.

'Hex?'

A few seconds pass, and then—

Ding.

'Heh, Luna!' Hex appears in front of me. 'How're you doing?' His eyes look around. 'Tell me you're not lost in the void.'

'You can see where I'm calling from?'

'Of course.'

'Then why can't I see where you're calling from?' All I have is Hex, with a fuzzy outline around him. As if he is completely nowhere.

'No idea. Maybe because of my top secret assignment.'

'So what are you doing, then?'

He gives me a look. 'Didn't I just say *top secret*?'

'Tell me anyway.'

'I can't. But it's awesome with awesome sauce on.'

'So you're all right? Really?'

'Me? I'm absolutely fine. But where have you been? I was really worried when I couldn't get in touch with you before we left.'

'Where'd you go?'

'Don't try to be sneaky. Are you all right, Luna?' His eyes, so concerned, so familiar.

I sigh. 'Wish you were here.'

'Lost in the void? Thanks a lot!'

'I'm not lost. I'm standing by a door to the VeeDub I'm supposed to be in. I'm fine.'

'Hmm. Not buying the *everything is all right* line. Anything you can tell me? Maybe I can help.'

I hesitate. I want to tell him; to warn him about PareCo, if nothing else. But should I?

'Luna? Come on, this is me. Spill.'

'It's PareCo. They've been manipulating the tests for their own purposes. And I think they've been experimenting on me with drugs, through the PIP.'

'Heh, wait a minute. Is that how you turned me psychedelic blue?'

'I'm serious, Hex. Not just that. They kill people, too.' *Like my mother.*

'Wow. That's heavy. You need to talk to somebody.'

'Somebody, who – like a psychologist?'

He glares. 'No. If you really think all that is true, then NUN, or the police. Listen. Sit tight; don't say anything to anybody. I'll see if I can come up with something.'

I shake my head. 'Don't do anything. Don't make them notice you. I just wanted you to know, so *you* can be careful. I've got things under control.' Tempo and I have got things under control. I hope.

'What are you up to, Luna?'

I mime zipping my lips. 'You're on a top secret mission, aren't you? Well, so am I. That's all I'm going to say.'

'Fair, I suppose.'

'Gotta go, Hex.' He waves, and I sign off.

Maybe I shouldn't have said anything. I hope he won't get into trouble because of it.

44

Media's right. I should go back to the Slated world, but the arrows won't coopcrate. Every time I try, I think of Gecko.

When I finally stop fighting it, the arrows strengthen. That comforts me somehow. The arrows didn't want to take me to the Slated world, but silver approves of going to Gecko.

This time I concentrate very hard on being taken directly to Gecko, and not just to his world. And hope he's not still standing in a ruined, flooded building.

A silver door forms.

I open it, peer through: is it safe?

It's dark, quiet. Dry. Good enough. I step through; the door shuts behind me, and vanishes.

My eyes adjust; I'm in a house. Windows show it is night. And Gecko is lying on a sofa, hands behind his head, staring at the ceiling.

'Heh,' I say.

He turns, sits up. 'You came back?' Surprise in his voice.

'Well, yeah; I must enjoy near-death-by-tsunami.' I sit next to him. A window looks out on a scene of devastation. We're above it all – in a house on the hill? 'I like what you've done with the place. Will you rebuild?'

He shrugs. 'Eventually I'll get so bored and lonely that I'll have to: I'll make something lovely, so they'll send more people to be here when I knock it down again. What else is there to do?'

'So you're still trapped, like you were in your S'hack.'

'Yes. It was either stay alone in a small dark box forever, or this: build a world for PareCo. I hate that they've made me do what they want! But I couldn't take being locked in my S'hack alone any longer. But this—' and he raises his hands, 'this isn't freedom. I'm completely and thoroughly trapped. There's no way out. That's how I started out with the disasters. I kept trying something worse, kept hoping I'd die and get out on escape code. But none of it ever touches me.'

'Tempo said she'd try to find a way.'

'Somehow I don't think I'm top priority.' His voice is bitter.

'Maybe. But I don't agree.'

'Thanks for coming back. Sorry I was such an ass before. I regretted it the instant you left.'

'Yes, you were an ass. But I'll let it go. This time.'

'Now tell me your stuff. Tell me everything.'

So for the second time in a day I find myself recounting everything that has happened since I got to the island.

When I'm done he leans back. Shakes his head. 'I *so* wish you hadn't come to Inac, Luna. Nothing good happens here.'

'What has happened to you?'

A struggle – and *pain* – cross his face.

'Don't try to talk. Not if it hurts. You can't tell me anyway, can you?'

'No. Sorry. But there is more stuff you could tell me.'

'Like what?'

'How'd you know you needed to unplug from the training world; how did you know your body was in trouble?'

My biggest secret. I gaze back at Gecko: do I tell? Intuition says *yes*.

'All right. You know how I take ANDs. That's only part of the problem I have with plugging in. I've got double awareness.'

'What do you mean?'

'Like I'm here, but my body is fully aware all the time, too. That's why I get so exhausted if I don't take breaks from plugging in. I don't sleep. So it's like I'm awake all the time.'

Before he can reply, a door creaks. It opens.

I hold up a hand for Gecko to be quiet, and focus back on my body in the PIP.

'We're moving the schedule for this one up to today.' A voice. Dr Rafferty? I open one eye a fraction and look through my lashes. It's Rafferty, and two others. In white coats.

They're doing something to my PIP. I access my silver grid to watch through it: they're disconnecting stuff, but not unplugging me?

Gecko tugs my hair lightly. 'What's up?'

'Something's happening with my body.'

'Tell me.'

'They're disconnecting things. The main neural connector is still attached to me, but they're unhooking it from the room PIP and connecting it to something else. I'm not unplugged.'

'Clearly, as you're still here.'

'Shut up a minute.'

I concentrate back there. Hands are reaching around my body, lifting it, and it's really hard not to react – not to slap them away. I don't dare open my eyes with people so close, but feel them moving me onto something else. Straps are put across my shoulders and legs. Then there is movement. I risk a peek just as we're coming out of the door of the PIP. Rafferty is walking ahead, and one of them is controlling a remote, watching me – it must make the trolley I'm on move along.

'This is weird. It's like I'm still plugged in – yes, I know, as I'm still here – but my body is being moved. They've detached part of the PIP, hooked it into a mobile unit on a trolley. What the hell is going on?'

'Sit up and ask?'

'Don't tempt me. I can find out more stuff if they don't know I'm aware.' I glance at Gecko; his face is actually grey. 'What is it?'

'I…I…don't know. I can almost say something, then I can't.'

'Because of your Implant blocks?' He nods. 'Wait. Are they related to what is happening to me?'

A struggle crosses his face.

'Never mind. We'll guess that it is.'

I focus back on my body. We're going down a hall, through a security door and into a lift. Going down, down. I didn't know there were levels this far below; they must be underground. The lift stops, we get out and go through another security door.

Pristine white walls; a disinfectant smell. It's like a hospital or something?

I'm wheeled into a room. They move away, talking, and I risk more of a look around.

Definitely a hospital: equipment, monitors, instruments laid out on a cart. And tank-like things to the side.

They link my PIP into something else: I watch with the silver grid. Drugs. They're hooking me up to drugs? The second they turn away I stop it, but not before a woozy feeling hits. It soon subsides.

I'm cold with fear inside, but here, in his world, Gecko is warm next to me.

'What's happening?' he asks.

'I think they're preparing me for some sort of surgery. I've got to get out of there. I'm going to have to unplug.'

'Wait. Link grids with me.'

'Won't it tip them off if we use our Implant grids?'

'No. Not that way. Link silver grids.'

Only if you really trust somebody, Marina said. He reaches a hand to mine, holds it. I've fought, inside, for so long, against trusting *anyone*, let alone Gecko. A deluded kidnapper, or a friend? *Trust your intuition, Luna.*

A friend.

I'm scared, but I nod. 'Yes. Do it.'

Our eyes stay open and on each other in the VeeDub, not closed like with Marina. My silver grid is there, then his.

They come close together, and lock. He smiles, and I both see him smile and feel his lips smiling. He slips his arms around me, and I feel his body and *am* his body, curving against mine – a sensory overload that threatens to drown every other thought.

This is nice, he thinks, his words an understatement, his feelings echoing mine.

Stop distracting me. Can you see out of my real eyes?

Let's try.

I close my virtual eyes, and open the others a slit.

Back with my body one of the techs is looking at a screen. 'Monitor her until the next shift. All the surgical staff are exhausted; I don't want to risk any mistakes with this one. She's rather interesting,' Rafferty says. He and the other tech leave. The remaining tech leans over some equipment, facing the other way. I open my eyes wider, risk a little head movement and look around.

Get out of there, Luna. Get out of there, now. Panic runs all through Gecko: fear for me, and old fear, remembered fear? But as soon as I recognise it, it withdraws. *Pain*: Gecko's.

No time for that now, he thinks. *Get out of there now while there's only one of them.*

I'm going to have to unplug. We'll lose connection.

Gecko gives me the closest, most intimate hug imaginable. Every bit of me returns it.

He laughs low, inside. *I can imagine closer and more intimate. Go.*

I unplug from the PIP, keeping movement to a minimum.

Something beeps on a monitor, the tech rushes to it. While his back is turned I reach to undo the straps holding me on the trolley, but someone is still *here*, inside me.

Gecko? You're still with me!

Yes. Relief – his and mine – caresses my mind.

What is even stranger is that you're still here. He holds my other hand warm against his heart in the VeeDub. *Th-thump, th-thump.* It beats under my fingers.

I'm still there? Confusion washes over me.

Figure it out later.

Right. I tense muscles, ready to jump off this thing and run for the door.

No. He'll raise the alarm too quickly. Let me.

I see what he wants me to do. Somehow I let myself relax enough that Gecko can take control of my body. We spring off the trolley. The tech turns around, surprise on his face that soon disappears when we punch him, just so. He collapses, unconscious.

I wince, holding one hand with the other. *Good one. Maybe let me take over now?*

Take his security pass. Might come in handy.

Gecko's control eases, and I kneel, slip the pass out of the plastic case, turn it around so it isn't obvious it's missing.

Nice touch. Now push him out of sight of the door.

He's heavy, but somehow I manage to drag him around behind a bank of monitors.

Good. Now go, go!

I rip the door open, and run. Where is there to go? This

whole place is PareCo. Instinct says to go up to the above ground levels and try to get out, but is that what they'd expect me to do once they realise I'm missing?

I pause, try another door. It's locked, but a swipe of the stolen security pass and it opens. It leads to a dimly lit hall, with many doors; maybe there will be a quiet place to hide and think about what to do next. I start down the hall, and Gecko's emotions jolt.

Wait. I know this place. Pain.

Is your body here? If I can unplug you, maybe we can get out of here together.

I...I don't know.

If you can't tell me, can you take me there?

I'll try.

It's deathly quiet. Gecko is back in control; we walk, jerkily. Every step is *pain*. Not in my body, but in his hidden places. I cradle him, inside.

He stops, and starts. I stay silent, somehow knowing this is the right thing to do. Back in the VeeDub he's shaking and my arms are around him tighter.

Doors. There are numbers on the doors.

429.

428.

427.

We stop.

Gecko shudders inside, lets go of control of my body. I reach a hand to the door, but it's locked. I try a swipe of the security pass; it doesn't work. Whatever is in here, that tech wasn't cleared to get in.

We assess the door: gleaming solid metal, with an electronic locking system. *It's a dead end. We'll never break that down,* Gecko thinks.

I stare at the door. There must be a way. If we can't unlock it or break it down, we have to gain access to PareCo systems and hack it open, but how? And then it hits me.

Wait. I think there is a way!

Tell me.

I show him the channel I found before, between my Implant and PareCo. Part of my beta implant, there to monitor and track. I disabled those functions but the channel is still there. And it runs two ways.

This is something new.

They've been doing experiments on me – with drug feeds. I show him what I'd found. *They've been using it to monitor their experiments.*

He's angry.

Can we use it in reverse, to gain access to PareCo and hack the door open?

He pauses; assesses the channel and links. *I think so. But then they'll know where you are. There are alarms. I don't want anything to happen to you, Luna.*

Like beyond the current mess I'm in? There's no other way. Let's do it.

With our silver grids linked, hacking into the PareCo security system through their channel is relatively easy. *Red herrings first,* Gecko says, and hacks alarms in dozens of places around the entire Centre so they all go off at once. *That should keep them busy.*

Then we focus on door 427. The lock springs open, and Gecko flinches.

Gecko? Are you all right?

Gecko shakes his head *no* in the VeeDub. 'Do it, anyway,' he murmurs into my hair. Here he is motionless and frozen, a pain-filled presence hiding in my mind. I push the door open.

It's a lab. White. Sterile. There's a gentle hum of equipment. I walk in. *Gecko?* He's silent.

There's a huge bench in the middle with all sorts of wires and tubes and stuff going every which way. They lead from a central point to the four corners of the room, to more equipment. All of it is like nothing I've ever seen before.

What is it?

No answer.

I examine the equipment, both through my eyes and our linked grid. The central station is almost like a modified PIP life support. It feeds nutrients and chemicals, drugs, lots of it stuff I'm not familiar with, and all of it way, way more complicated than a PIP. To four tanks.

Biological support tanks?

Inside – *no.*

I recoil, stomach rising inside.

No.

Is it what I thought? Gecko is back in my mind, strangely calm.

He pulls me to the one in the back left corner. There's a viewing screen; my fingers move with his volition, tap at it. And together we see it – a grey mass, bathed in fluids, linked and fed by the central support. Linked into PareCo systems.

Is it...is it...

Yep. That's me, Luna. Or what's left of me. A brain in a Think Tank. Aren't I gorgeous? I think unplugging me isn't going to be quite like you thought.

45

Our link is suddenly broken. Is it the shock? Gecko is gone, and not only that, without the link I'm completely here now – not in the VeeDub any more. Frantic, I search for him inside, but nothing.

Tears are running down my face. I sit on the cold hard floor, arms wrapped around myself. Is this what happens to all the interns? Do they train us up in world manipulation, separate us from our bodies, and trap us in a game world to run...forever?

Has this happened to Hex, too? Is he in a tank in another one of these rooms, along with all the other interns in his group? I try to remember them, and can only get some of their faces and names linked together.

And my group: Marina, Sparky, all the others. Are we next?

I have to get word of what they're doing here out. I have to. This has to be stopped.

Tempo will know what to do. I need to find a PIP, and do it now. They'll still be busily checking all those alarms we set off, but sooner or later, they'll make it to this one.

Pull yourself together, Luna.

I wipe my face on my sleeves. Stand up. I push the door open a crack, and peer through. The hall is, as before, dimly lit, silent. I guess the occupants of these rooms don't need a lot of lighting.

I move as quick as silence allows to the end of the hall, where a door leads to a junction. There are stairs ahead, and doors to the left and right. Which way now? The left door is the one I came through to get here. I try the right one. It's locked, but a swipe of the staff ID, and it opens.

It leads to a large open room, with some sort of hulking technical equipment lined up in rows, and a massive lift on the opposite wall. I start to walk along a row, then hear voices in the far corner. I duck down behind one of the pieces of equipment. That's when I focus on it closer, and almost stop breathing.

No. It couldn't be. Could it? It's a tank? I glance around me. There is row after row of gleaming tanks, just like this one – and they're *all* biological support tanks. Not like Gecko's Think Tank. They're bigger, much bigger.

I should get out of here before someone sees me, but suspicion and dread are trickling through my gut. *I have to know what is inside these tanks.*

Footsteps echo across the floor. I scrunch down further, and risk a look down a row. There are two techs; their backs are towards me as they walk towards the lift. They reach it just as the lift doors open. They pull some of the tanks into it, and get in with them. The doors shut. The numbers start changing; it is going up.

Am I alone in here now? I stay very still, and listen. One minute, two – the only sound is my heart beating.

I move towards one of the tanks. I swallow; my head is

light. I tap the view screen, and struggle to make myself focus. Recoil when I see what is inside.

A body.

My feet want to run, but I rotate the view, and the face, the eyes, are all still there – the room spins when I recognise him. It's Zippy, from Hex's group. The back of his skull is missing; brain removed. He's all carefully hooked up, heart still beating, lungs still breathing. Kept alive without a brain. His eyes blink and I almost scream.

I stagger backwards into another tank, and jump forwards into yet another. Tanks, surrounded by tanks. All with... bodies? Without brains? Are they alive, or are they dead? Panic is rising inside. There are more of them than just Hex's group, many more. Were they all interns? Is this some sort of transplant bank; do they wait here until they're needed, then disappear into that lift?

There is a whirring sound. The lift – it's coming back down. The doors will open. I dash blindly across the room, out a door on the other side.

I'm not trying to be quiet any more. I'm running. It registers that this isn't part of the hospital. The hall looks like the one our rooms are in, but more lived in – pictures on walls, shoes in front of doors. I slow, stop. Try to control my breathing, and think.

Is this staff housing? It's very quiet. *The surgical staff are all exhausted*, Rafferty had said. Have they been busily separating Hex's graduation class from their brains?

Taking more care to be quiet now, I creep down the hall.

I continue past silent doors, then a dining hall, and – bingo. A recreation room.

And there they are, along the back wall: a row of PIPs. Some of them are occupied, with a red light over the door. Playing games while they sleep?

I find one that is green.

The door is locked, but I put the staff card in the slot – *beep*. It opens. Fingers crossed they haven't found him yet, or noticed his card is missing. But best not chance it. I access my silver grid, use the channel to PareCo to find this PIP, and scramble the ID code. Maybe that'll stop them from tracing it later. Just in case it doesn't work, I put a pingback on the general security logs. Anything unusual, and it will ping an alert to me.

The ANDs I took before must have worn off by now. I plug in, and dive out of my hallway and into the void so fast that the nausea doesn't have time to hit.

Tempo first. In case anything happens to me, I *have* to tell her what is going on here. *I'm sorry, Gecko: I'll be there soon.*

I call the silver arrows, start to follow them, and then—

'Luna?' Hex's voice. Via my Implant. But it's still off…?

I *can't* not answer. I can't. 'Hex?' He appears in front of me.

Tears rise in my eyes. 'Are you…have you…' My voice trails away; I can't make myself ask the question. Are you missing something, like, say, a body? Sounds harsh.

I force myself to keep walking, following the silver arrows to Tempo.

'Luna, are you all right? I had to commit a mighty hack to get around your Implant disabling and bring it back online.'

I'm warmed that he sounds impossibly smug, like he usually does. Just the same. It helps me try again.

'Hex, what are you?'

He raises an eyebrow. 'Let's see: an impossibly gifted Hacker. Extraordinarily handsome.'

'OK, given, and given. But *where* are you? The rest of you?'

His face is serious now. 'Ah. So you've worked it out, have you? What Think Tanks really are?'

'Has it...are you...'

'Yes.'

'Oh, Hex.'

'Don't look so appalled. It's the best thing *ever*. Think about it, Luna. It's like you control your entire world, forever. If you're trusted like I am you're not trapped in one world; you can roam the Gateway and do what you like. Forever.'

'Forever?'

'Sure. You live forever; you control as many worlds as you can manage. What's not to like?'

'You mean you *wanted* this?'

'Of course. Who wouldn't? Luna, this is a way to move beyond physical limits, to become *more*.'

I shake my head, still walking, still following the arrows: I see Tempo in the distance. 'I've got to go, Hex. Bye.' I disconnect.

Tempo waves; Crystal is with her. I wipe my tears away. It is time to be tough.

They start to say hello; I interrupt. 'Listen up. I've found out what happens at Inaccessible Island, what happens to the interns.' I explain it all, holding nothing back. Wanting to reach out to Crystal when I tell them about Gecko, but as if she knows my hand wants to creep up and find hers, she shakes her head, moves away.

Tempo nods. Not surprised? Somehow, she *knew*. So why did she need me to come here as a spy – to confirm suspicions?

Crystal's eyes are both bright and hard, like meltwater on ice.

'Is it legal if they consent?' I ask.

'No. Completely prohibited under NUN law,' Tempo says. 'Though there are jurisdictional issues on Inac.'

'Why would anyone consent?' The horror on Crystal's face echoes my own.

'You can live forever. In virtual.' *Like Hex*, I add silently.

Hex, who hacked my Implant to call. Hex, who said he is trusted by PareCo…? Did answering him make me traceable? The last time we spoke, I told him my suspicions about PareCo. Is that why Rafferty moved my surgery up?

How could I be so stupid! I curse inside, and look around us. While we've been talking, the flickering void lights have decreased without my noticing.

'We're in trouble,' I say. And it's not just the lights – the winds of the void are dying. This isn't void – this is becoming less than void. True emptiness.

'It's a trap,' Tempo says. 'Quick, Luna, spin. Spin before the silver is completely gone.'

I've started before she's finished the sentence: spinning, arms and hands outstretched over my head. There is so little silver left. I spin, and spin, and call it to me, bit by bit. The silver in my hands grows until it is bright.

'Don't collapse it,' Tempo calls out to me, her voice feeling light and distant. 'When you have enough, thrust it out.'

I spin faster, and want to take in more and more, not throw it away – but her voice is insistent.

Reluctantly, I let go. It spins out in a bright arc, and connects with something – I don't know what. For a second it is bright, defined by the silver – a sphere all around us. It's holding?

Crystal flings bolts of ice at the edges and the whole thing shatters.

We run, out into the void. Normal void.

'Listen to me, Luna. Go to the MD Gateway. Spin and collapse the Gateway – it's linked to all of the PareCo worlds. It will destroy them.'

'What about the Council of Scientists? What did Media say to do?'

'There's no time to go to COS over this. You have to do it now.'

'It will destroy the PareCo worlds? All of them?'

'It's the only way. The only way to stop them. Crystal? Go with her. Defend if necessary.'

'And you, Tempo?' Crystal says, looking at her strangely.

'I'll do what I can to stop them from following you. Go.'

I focus on the MD Gateway: *take me there*. Silver arrows waver. I focus, and they are stronger.

I run, Crystal by my side.

46

'It doesn't look that impressive,' Crystal says, as she surveys the inside of the MD Gateway.

'No? It is only a link to every PareCo world, ever. But what about everyone in the worlds?'

'Escape code. They'll get dropped back into their hallways. Do it, Luna. It's the only way to stop PareCo. Tempo is right: it has to be done.'

I try to spin, to gather power, but it's not working.

'What's wrong?'

'I think this only works properly in the void or S'hacker spaces. This is too closed off from it.'

Crystal throws ice at the wall between two doors: it coalesces into a sheet of silver. She flicks it, and it shatters. She smiles. 'How about if there are windows to the void? I'll make more. Keep trying.'

I raise my hands, close my eyes. Spin. This time it starts to work; silver starts to draw through Crystal's window, then another and another as she makes more of them.

Silver, and more silver. More than when we escaped from the PareCo trap. I'm pulsing with it. It's in me; it's part of me. Just a part, but becoming more and more. I'm growing. A wave of silver surrounds me now – like Gecko's tsunami.

Gecko? I frown. What about Gecko? He hasn't got escape code, and even if he did, he has no body to escape to.

What about Crystal? And everyone else in the void?

Like a distant fly buzzing, somewhere I can hear voices, blows, screams. Crystal? Some of the Gateway doors are opening. Monsters are coming out to try to stop us, and getting caught in Crystal's ice. But there are too many of them, coming from all sides. They can't get me; I'm too strong. I try to flick at them, to catch them in the silver wave to protect Crystal, but it is hard to do that and spin at the same time, to grow and grow in power.

This is what Tempo wanted all along. But is it what Astra wanted me to do? She was training me to spin, to fall with the void. I can destroy: is this why she said I was *special*?

I can return chaos, and claim my S'hacker name:

I could claim Anarchy.

A final scream. Crystal? She's fallen, then she is swept into the silver. Becomes part of it.

No.

Silver tears blur my vision. Tempo sent her. She knew she'd die, didn't she? Crystal did, too. She came anyway.

I sigh, breathe out silver. I'll die, too. I can only take in so much power before I'll die. Somehow I *know* this is true.

And it is comforting somehow. Dying is better than being a brain in a tank, a puppet of PareCo.

What about Tempo? She went somewhere safe. Crystal knew that, too. She meant for us to die, and for her to live?

I'm slowing now. Some of the silver is bleeding away, back to the void where it belongs. There is a jumble of doors and worlds all around me in what is left of the MD Gateway.

I leave for the void through one of Crystal's windows.

My hands are silver, beautiful silver. I stare at them in wonder. My body also. I'm still spinning, but slower – just enough to hold power now, neither growing nor diminishing. But I can't hold it in for long.

And then I realise the mistake: escape code won't work, not in a collapsing VeeDub. It was never designed for this scale of destruction. Anyone in a VeeDub that is destroyed will be spilled into the void. Everyone in the void will die if the void collapses, won't they?

Another tear drops from my eye, and splashes down: a silver tear.

Dr Rafferty appears in front of me. He smiles kindly.

'Luna, you are so very much more than you appeared. What are you going to do now?'

'I don't know.' I'm still spinning, slowly; somehow he is moving with me so his face is always straight ahead.

'Join us, Luna. You can help sort out this mess you've created. Then join your friend Gecko in his world. Be together forever there. You'd like that, wouldn't you?'

I sigh, silver bleeding out from my lungs. 'For a while, maybe. But not forever.'

'Poor Luna. You could have stayed safe at home if you were still a Refuser. But once you started coming to the void, you were far too dangerous to leave alone.'

I could have stayed at home? Nanna was right – about not plugging in, about everything. It was Gecko who told me about ANDs, but it was Tempo who pushed us together. He

412

didn't know what would happen.

I shake my head. 'But it's too late to go back to being a Refuser now.'

'Yes. And in case you need extra incentive to stop this crazy destruction, I have it.'

'What do you mean?'

'Listen. Listen very carefully.'

My silver ears listen: they can hear the entire void. A cacophony of cries of the lost, distressed and broken worlds. Hidden inside it, one little tug? *My name*. It's faint, but I focus, closer and closer.

Luna… A familiar voice, calling my name. *Luna?*

Jason's voice.

'Jason? Where is he?'

'I don't know. I'm not as good as you are at finding people in the void.'

'He's in the void?'

'Lost, and alone.'

I'm angry. I spin and reach for Rafferty, to pull him into the silver wave, but he laughs when my hands pass through him. He's a projection? From where?

Luna, help me! Jason's voice again. It's wavering; he's scared.

It's a trap. Isn't it? Even they wouldn't put a ten-year-old in the void, would they? But I can't risk it. I have to try to find him.

I sense rather than see them. Rafferty and others, camouflaged and waiting, in a ring all around me. They're waiting for me to stop spinning; then they'll have me.

One last thing:

One last spin:

I throw silver into the void above. It becomes a fiery meteor shower. It catches Rafferty and his friends by surprise; fending off the flames keeps them busy.

Silver words form in the sky:

Run, you clever girl, run.

47

I run and run.

I'm fractured. Parts of me are running; parts of me are crying. Some in the void, some in my hallway, some in every world I've ever visited.

Focus: what was I going to do? My memories are fuzzy, damaged: there are beads to fix that. Memory beads?

No: *Jason first. Find Jason.*

I concentrate on his smile, his laugh. To start with, there are silver arrows everywhere, pointing in all directions. The void is fractured, like me; but when I follow first one arrow and then another, they are pointing at beads. I ignore them, concentrating hard on Jason, on holding him first in my thoughts. And after a while it settles, and there are fewer, and finally just one arrow leading the way.

'Luna?' I hear his voice again. This time he is close. I can see him!

'Jason?'

But when he turns and sees me, he runs. In the other direction.

'Jason!' I call his name again. 'It's me, it's Luna.'

He pauses, looks back. He's crying. 'It looks like you, but not you.'

I look at myself, and frown: I'm beautiful silver, and I love it. But I will it to go. It starts to bleed off, bit by bit. First my lungs are clear; then deeper tissues; skin. But it stays in my blood, my eyes. I'm finally starting to accept that it is part of me, and always has been.

'Better?' I say, and hold out a hand. He hesitates, finally walks towards me.

'Is it really you?' he says.

'Yes, monkey. It's really me.' He launches himself, holds me tight. 'Come on. I'm going to take you somewhere safe.'

I take him to my S'hack for now. It is safer than anywhere else I can think of – I'm the only one who can get in there – but once again, the silver arrows are confusing, pointing in all directions. I have to focus hard on the S'hack to get there.

It hasn't escaped the spinning – the garden is jumbled and the house a bit sideways, but it is intact.

'Wait for me here. I've got to sort some things out.'

'You'll come back? You promise?'

'Of course.'

I kiss him and he doesn't fend me off like he usually would. I look back and wave from the silver door, and step back into the void.

What now?

Again there are arrows, multiple sets of them, and I can't ignore them any longer. One by one they take me to beads. I collect them in my hand. Seven in total: two are carved with my S'hacker marks, the other five with Astra's. Memory beads?

These ones weren't on the necklace, but they look just the same as the ones that were. I thought Tempo had sent phantom beads to remind me about the necklace; I thought they weren't real.

Yet here they are – seven beads in my hand. What do they mean?

Seven is the seeker of truth. I must do this: I have to know what they hide.

The silver comes to me easily now.

The memories are harder to bear.

I lie in the void. It is a while before I can make myself focus on what it all means, along with all I've learned since then. Silver is swirling into a message above me, but I ignore it, and look within.

In my beads were my realisations – too late – that Tempo manipulated Gecko; she manipulated me. Though I can't regret meeting Gecko, I'd never have known about ANDs and plugged in with them if it wasn't for her setting him up.

If Rafferty told the truth when he said they'd have left me alone if I'd stayed a Refuser, then Nanna was right, all along. She was the only one who always had my interests at heart. Even Astra made me for a reason, had plans for what I could do. Nanna was the only one who didn't want to use me for something.

And Tempo killed her.

And in Astra's beads?

Astra had been investigating Tempo. She'd found out that Tempo had betrayed S'hackers who stood against her in COS to PareCo, and worse: gave PareCo the means to trap them. Silver was extracted from inside the S'hackers when their brains were removed, and used as part of their virtual prison. One that could not be escaped. Like Gecko's.

The memories stop abruptly, but one thing is certain: whatever happened to Astra, Tempo must have been behind it.

The one person I thought could help me was the most dangerous. How could I have been so wrong?

I don't know how long I lie there, lost in the things I've learned. There is some fluttery movement out of the corner of my eye; I ignore it. It becomes more insistent. Finally I look up.

Silver coalesces to form letters and words that appear, vanish and reappear: *Go to your hallway.*

When it happened before, I thought they were from Tempo. But that can't be right, can it? They've helped me, whereas Tempo has done nothing but hurt and deceive Gecko, Crystal, me, Astra. Tempo, despite the double game she plays, wants PareCo destroyed so she can sweep in and take over – what happens to any of us is nothing to her.

So I go to my hallway. Take the last AND in my pocket, then drop down through a hatch.

I look around, and sigh. There's nothing out of the ordinary here, just the usual doors, the usual fan club invites. It's a dead end.

Would a message do any good? To Melrose. Just old-fashioned words, not in person – if she can see me it'll be hard to get away. But as soon as I send it PareCo will know I'm here, will come for me. I'll have to be quick.

I concentrate, but seem to be incapable of making sense.

M – please tell your dad. General weirdness on Inac. Bio body transports and brain Think Tanks. Pls send help. A helicopter would be nice. Love, L. Not Crazy.

That will have to do. I hit *send*, and run for the hatch out of my hallway, past a fan club invite.

Did it just pulse?

I pause, glance back. It's just the usual thing: *Astra Remembered*.

I look closer. No; wait. It's different.

The spine spiders are back. I blink, and look again.

It says *Astra Remembers*.

It feels like my heart *stops*. Just stops beating. Everything inside me is frozen. Remembers…? Present tense?

No.

It can't be.

Can it?

There is a faint *whoosh* behind me, then another. One by one the doors to my hall are disappearing: access withdrawn. PareCo knows I'm here. They're coming.

I hit *join*, and push the door open.

She's not as tall as I remember; barely taller than me. Of course I was much shorter the last time I saw her. But her dancing eyes and dark hair are just the same. She hasn't aged.

We stare at each other. We're in a clear dome, stars all around. Silver winds around her eye – even more than in my memory.

She holds out a hand, trembling.

'Luna? Oh, my darling girl. You're beautiful.'

I hesitate.

I want to demand to know *everything*: how she could deceive Dad, how she could engineer a daughter – me – to be some sort of weapon against PareCo. What am I, even? Part girl – part void? How she could let herself be trapped by Tempo. How she could leave us alone all these years.

But that can wait. I step forward. It feels good to hold each other, just the same.

We're in a space station in the midst of a galaxy-wide war. No real surprise that once Tempo gifted a captive Astra to PareCo, the world they would choose to incarcerate her in would be a space game.

She's like Hex, and Gecko. She exists only in virtual; a permanent prisoner of a Think Tank in reality.

Little did they know she's been working on manipulating wormholes all this time. It took her nine years to start spying on the world outside from here, and another four after that to work out how to get silver messages out to the void. She saw how Gecko manipulated a group invitation to trace me a while back, and only just worked out how to use one to provide a portal to her.

She never gave up trying to reach me. Not once.

48

Ping. What is that? Oh. The security pingback I set: I scan the logs. They've begun a PIP-by-PIP check of the entire Centre.

'I'm sorry, can we work a little faster?' I say.

Astra looks up, smiles. 'Just as patient as when you were three.' We've been S'hacking wormholes, trying to see if together we can find a way Astra can get out.

But nothing has worked so far.

'I should go soon. They've started checking all the PIPs to try to find me. And I've got to go to Gecko before I unplug.'

'Why didn't you say? Go, go!' She's distressed. Hugs me again, and despite everything, it is hard to let go.

I promise I'll be back, and wish for a door. It's not fair. Everyone else can go in and out at will, but those trapped by PareCo in a VeeDub – like Gecko, like Astra – no way. I told her everything that was in her missing memory beads, including that she, herself, is part of the fabric of this world. If it's part of her, how can she leave it? She said we had to try.

I start to step through the door, then turn back. 'Wait a minute. Crystal opened multiple windows to the void, so we could get many flights of silver into the Gateway for more power. Would that work here?'

'It might. But you need to go.'

421

I pause, and check the security logs again. 'They're nowhere near me. I've got some time. Don't waste it arguing!'

'All right.' She grins. 'But make it fast.'

I open dozens of windows, and we spin together. I draw silver in from the void – more and more flies in, more than I could command – and funnel it to Astra. She has more control than I do. She shapes and contains it, a massive ball of silver power – then flings it out to explode against the world's barrier.

It's like a million silver fireworks set off at once; for a moment I can't see, not anything.

When my vision clears, the world is gone. We're in the void.

She's pale, but all smiles. 'Are you all right?' I ask.

'Wonderful, lovely clever girl! Get back to your boy, and look after your body.'

'What are you going to do now? Go to COS?'

'No. Tempo would know; there's a risk she'd twist things and talk the Council around. I'm going straight to NUN.'

I check the Centre's security logs. They're concentrating the searches on intern PIPs and areas we frequented.

'I'm OK for a bit longer; I'm monitoring the situation. I'm coming with you.'

When we get to NUN's virtual towers, I find out that Astra is good at breaking into places. Even places that are supposed to be impossible to break into.

It's in full virtual session: there was an emergency meeting called in response to widespread void chaos – caused by *moi*. I scan the room; Melrose's dad is absent. My eyes stop on one of the representatives. That's why I thought Media looked familiar: she's in NUN?

The house falls silent when we appear in the midst of the floor. Astra has presence – or maybe it's the way we climbed from nothing through a silver door.

She addresses the Speaker.

'I'm Astra. I died thirteen years ago.'

He snorts. 'You're looking well for a dead person.' He motions for guards to remove us. She speaks fast while I try to erect a silver barrier between us and them, wondering why she's not helping. There is so little silver in this place that my efforts falter, but then, with a small gesture, Media bolsters the barrier. It strengthens and holds.

'PareCo faked my death, and extracted my brain from my body. My body is missing, presumed dead. My brain has been tanked and linked to a game world, where I've been incarcerated all these years, until my daughter helped me break out. Likewise, the PareCo interns on Inac are being brained – brains extracted and linked through bio tanks to run game worlds. Their bodies are stored in bio tanks until they're shipped out, presumably to be sold for organs and other parts on the black market. The NUN tests have been manipulated by PareCo to get the best brains for their so-called Think Tanks, providing games that keep the populations of the world sedated and compliant. NUN avoids acknowledging what is being done in their name!

423

Perhaps if you weren't so worried about being considered rational all the time you might have noticed what is going on under your noses.'

Cries of *irrational*, *preposterous* and other ruder things are called out around the house.

'There was a scientific resistance group I was part of – the Council of Scientists. Some of you will know about that.' Glances are exchanged here and there. 'But in my absence, it's been warped by one who is hungry for power – she was using my daughter to try to destroy the void.'

I wave. 'Yep, that was me. Sorry about that.'

Arguments break out, and I start backing towards the silver door before they decide to arrest me.

That's when it happens.

I don't see her come in. She's just suddenly there – in the midst of it all. Standing and spinning: Tempo.

I try to call out, to warn everyone. A few words escape, then are pushed back down my throat. She's spinning time.

Media spots the danger. She tries to stop her, but I don't see what happens next.

Time is jumbled, and swirling *back, back, back*...

Silver. I'm caught in silver, beautiful silver. Spinning faster and faster. The void with me, like the moon pulling the oceans. Soon it will be destroyed, all of it. And I'll fall.

But Tempo was wrong to think we could do this and just start over. I see that now. Our world is linked to the void, isn't it? Just like I exist both here and there at the same time;

424

like how my real body bled when I was injured in a game world. How can one continue without the other?

I'm sad, but I can't stop.

Faster, faster…

'Luna?'

I frown. Who is that?

'Luna, come back!'

Jason. He's in my S'hack.

My thoughts are muddy, confused. How is he in my S'hack? I concentrate, try to work out what is happening.

Tempo? She's taken me back in time. To when I was spinning. Why do I remember Jason being there if that is true? That came after.

It's the silver. That's how I know. She can't hide: the time vortex is part of the void's silver, part of me.

I have to stop. I have to make her take time forward to where it should be.

I cry. Silver tears. I can't stop; I can't…

So much beautiful power. It needs a place to go, or I'll implode and fall, taking the void and all its worlds with me.

I *must* stop, but how?

I concentrate, hard, on the cause of it all: on Tempo, and the time vortex she spins. I focus: and then, like she feels the scrutiny, she's in my mind.

Luna, don't fight me. This is your destiny.

Destroying everyone and everything?

Your S'hacker name IS Anarchy! This is what you've been searching for. Destroy, and then we can start again.

Our way. The S'hacker way.

No! I say, but even as I protest, I spin faster, overwhelmed with more and more power. It won't be long now.

You cannot deny it. You were made for this.

Luna, don't listen to her. Astra's voice? *Tempo is wrong. I was wrong. Join with me, Luna. Let me help you.*

She wants to link grids, and I'm scared. She made me to be this weapon. What will she do? Will she take control? She spent so many years, so much effort, to reach out to me from her prison. But was that for *me*, or the weapon she could use?

I struggle inside to find the answer to all my doubts; a reason to *trust* with all the reasons not to.

I've been in her memories. I know what she's done, but I also know how she *feels*. I don't know what she will do, and I'm terrified of that. But I can't stop on my own; I need help.

Please, Luna; let me help you. I love you.

Is that enough?

Her silver grid is there, next to mine.

A shift, inside me: to forgiveness. And a leap of faith.

We join.

Together, Tempo cannot resist us, Astra whispers. She lends me her strength to help dissipate the silver: it flies off me in sweeping arcs as my spinning slows. Tempo's dim protests are ignored. Most of the silver goes back to the void, where it belongs: some we hold between us. Astra uses more and more of her strength to do these things, even as I see that hers is failing.

She's sad – a three-letter word that doesn't begin to cover this agony of feeling as it washes through us both. *I'm sorry to leave you so soon, Luna. But I'm not really alive, am I? That prison I've been in all these years was made of me. Shattering it began this ending; my virtual self can't survive outside it, and I have no body to return to. Be strong.*

My pain turns to anger that wants to lash out, to destroy Tempo with the silver we've harnessed. But Astra has another idea, a better one. We make Tempo a S'hack, a small one. One made of Tempo's own silver essence so she'll never be able to escape. We extract it from her without needing PareCo surgery, using silver from the void. And we imprison her inside it.

As soon as Tempo is locked away, screaming, time unravels like a snapped elastic. Back to the way things were before.

With one difference. Astra is fading. She is pale, then translucent. Silver shines through her hair and eyes.

I give her what she wants, whispered inside with the name she most wants to hear. *I love you too, Mum.*

Was that what she was waiting for? She's gone.

Now NUN appear to be taking heed of all she said. Media takes over where Astra – *Mum* – left off. Is it what PareCo has done with the interns on Inac that has shocked them into opening their eyes and ears, or that PareCo had teamed up with that madwoman, Tempo, who nearly made me destroy us all?

Either way, I'm not sure how much good it will do. Does the world prefer fantasy to reality?

I leave them to it. First I deliver Jason, whole and well, to Dad.

Then I go to Gecko.

49

The second I'm through the silver door to Gecko's world, we join silver grids. Linked as we are, thoughts and emotions, he sees and feels it all – everything that has happened.

I'm sorry about your mother. He holds me. Gecko is full of wonder at all that Astra did, but not why. *She loved you, Luna.*

Yeah. She really did. And I'm sorry about Crystal.

We're full of sorrow, both of us, but I have no jealousy for Crystal. I see how he feels about her. How he feels about me. But my sorrow is edged with guilt.

It wasn't your fault. With either of them.

I'm dangerous. I was made to destroy. I even failed at that.

No. You're a S'hacker. No one tells you who you are, or what you're for. You choose your path, your name.

And I chose to stop.

Yes.

Your body, Luna? he reminds me. *You need to get out of there.*

Oh, yeah. I unplug back in the PIP, but like before, we're still linked. We're both here in my body, and in the VeeDub together. *What now?*

You know what I have to do. I can't do it without you.

I know. The only thing Gecko has ever wanted is freedom.

He doesn't want to be like this. But that doesn't make it any easier.

Gecko taps into PareCo security through my Implant channel. *There's a lot of fuss happening. They really want to find you. Let's see what we can do to confuse them.* He sets off alarms in a path leading away from where we're going. The one place I never want to go, ever again.

Door 427.

We hack the door again – but this time we unlock every door in the Centre. They won't know where to check first.

Gecko takes over my body so I don't have to do it. I could fight him, but it is his decision. His right. I stay weak, dormant.

Never, ever weak. His thoughts caress me. *You're the strongest person I've ever known.*

Is that why I'm crying?

No. That's because you're also the loveliest person I've ever known.

I stare at the gleaming equipment, the dark secrets contained in this room and many others like it. *This can't happen here, not in this nightmare place. Don't let this lab be the last thing we see together. Can you make it slow?*

He pauses, peeks into my thoughts. A mental smile. *OK.*

He does what he has to do.

We creep back to the room with the bio body tanks, and across it to the lift. We press the button; go in, and up, up, up.

It opens outside, away from the PareCo complex. There is an empty helipad – they must take bio tanks away by helicoptor. So much for the no-fly zone around Inac. Maybe that is just so no one spots body part-laden helicopters coming and going?

It's very early morning, the sky just starting to lighten.

We walk. Gecko is weakening, so I run. The nutrients he stopped from going into his Think Tank are starting to run out.

We hear the waterfall before we see it.

I lie down by the pool. We watch the sun come up together, glinting on the water.

What's that? he murmurs.

What?

The sound. Above.

I look up through the trees. A giant NUN helicopter is flying past, soon followed by another, then another. *Looks like PareCo is in trouble.*

All down to you. You did say to send one. You should probably flag them down.

It'll keep.

Back in his virtual world, he kisses me again. *Thank you, Luna,* he murmurs. Our arms are around each other, waiting for the end. A physical embrace, the kind he said was closer and more intimate than I could imagine.

He was right.

It finally happens: he slips away. My arms are empty. The instant our grid link is broken, I leave Gecko's world. I am utterly alone in my mind and my body, here, by the pool.

I cry.

EPILOGUE

*If you would be a real seeker after truth, it is
necessary that at least once in your life you doubt,
as far as possible, all things.*

René Descartes

It's a while before I can make myself return to the void. Even
as it calls to me, and sings in my blood. But there is something
I have to do.

At last I've chosen my S'hacker name. The search was
difficult, but like most lost things it was blindingly obvious
once I'd found it. And that's what I do, what I'm really for,
isn't it? Finding things. Seeking out truths. Never easily; not
without pain – but some things that you'd never miss for the
world *have* to hurt, don't they?

But never, ever, to destroy. That is easier to do, but I
choose not to.

Friends are here around me, Marina and Media amongst
them. With all the changes coming since PareCo was
discredited, the old secretive S'hacker ways and barriers are
coming down. I'd insisted on inviting non-S'hackers, too:
Jason, holding tight to Dad's hand, nervous to be in the void
again but determined to be here. Roy Heywood. Melrose and
her dad. Even Sally. They wait until I can turn to face them.

The meaning being found was only part of the search: the

name to represent it took thought as well. But in the end, the beauty was always in the numbers, wasn't it?

Seven: the seeker of truth.

When I finally turn and meet their eyes I smile for the first time in a long while. I may seek truth, but I still have my secrets.

'My name is Seven.'

ACKNOWLEDGEMENTS

One thing I get asked all the time is where ideas for my stories come from. I can't always trace the precise origins, but *Mind Games* was very much inspired by research into rationality and intelligence by Keith Stanovich, a professor at the University of Toronto. He proposed that the reason smart people can do stupid things is that intelligence and rationality are separate traits – that someone can be both intelligent, and irrational. And I thought, what would happen in a world where rationality was prized, much the way intelligence is today? One in which individuals who are intelligent but also irrational are considered dangerous to themselves and society? This is how *Mind Games* began.

The second source of inspiration was the quotation from George Berkeley at the beginning: *Truth is the cry of all, but game of the few.* I found it in an old edition of the *Oxford Dictionary of Quotations* that I often use for ideas – it was given by my mother-in-law, Joan, to her husband Eric, way back in 1969, and found its way to me many years later. I've dedicated *Mind Games* to their memory: I wish I could have got to know them better.

I have to mention Inaccessible Island! I had a very clear picture in my mind what PareCo's island should be like: very isolated, with sheer cliffs to make access or escape impossible. Convinced I'd have to make one up because none would fit the bill, I did an internet search on 'inaccessible islands', and there it was. A real place, and that is its real name. And it even has a waterfall.

Special thanks to Sharon Jones, who said *you must write this*, and to my agent, Caroline Sheldon, for agreeing with her; to my editor, Megan Larkin, for championing the story, and her insightful editing; and to editor Rosalind McIntosh, designer Thy Bui, and everyone at Orchard Books and Hachette Children's Books for their hard work and enthusiasm.

Thanks to Scoobie (SCBWI) pals Addy Farmer, Jo Wyton and Amy Butler Greenfield for reading early versions and giving invaluable feedback. Thanks also to Liz and Paul Medhurst from my SF pub night, and to Anne Rooney for the Giordano Bruno quotation.

Thanks to Christina Banach – a fellow author and Scoobie – for making the highest bid for a character name in the Authors for the Philippines Auction. I was very pleased to name a character for her father, Roy Heywood.

Thanks and all my love to Graham, Banrock, and muses everywhere – even Dodgy Dog. I couldn't do it without you.

And finally, the answer to Lord Byron's four questions. I didn't complete the quotation, as Luna was – and Seven is – still working on the answers:

There are four questions of value in life, Don Octavio. What is sacred? Of what is the spirit made? What is worth living for and what is worth dying for? The answer to each is the same. Only love.

Lord Byron

ABOUT THE AUTHOR

Teri Terry has lived in France, Canada, Australia and England at more addresses than she can count, acquiring four degrees, a selection of passports and an unusual name along the way. Past careers have included scientist, lawyer, optometrist and, in England, various jobs in schools, libraries and an audiobook charity. The footpaths and canal ways of the Buckinghamshire Chilterns where she now lives inspired much of the setting of Teri's first books, the internationally best-selling *Slated* trilogy. Teri has won twelve awards including the Leeds Book Award, the North East Teen Book Award and the Rotherham Children's Book Award (twice).

Teri hates broccoli, likes cats, and has finally worked out what she wants to do when she grows up.

Twitter: @TeriTerryWrites
Facebook page: TeriTerryAuthor
Website: teriterry.com

If you enjoyed *Mind Games*, you'll love
Book of Lies by Teri Terry, coming soon.

Who lies? Who tells the truth?
Death hangs on the answer.

Turn the page for a sneak peek…

CHAPTER ONE

There are things you know you shouldn't do. Like standing on the tracks when the train is getting too close. Or holding your hand over an open flame. You can wave it across fast and be fine, but something inside makes me hold it there a second longer, then another, and another. Train tracks and mothers are much the same as flames: too close, too long, risks pain.

If I sat and made a list of all the things I shouldn't do and put them in order, starting with the worst, being here today would be near the top. But I'm drawn to things I shouldn't do. Is it just to see what happens, who it will hurt? Maybe.

So no matter how much that inner voice of caution, of reason, says stay away; no matter how much I try to convince myself or hide the keys or deliberately don't wear anything even vaguely acceptable, I was never going to be anywhere else, was I?

How close, how long, is another matter. For now, I'm shivering under leafless trees on a hill above the crematorium, a splash of red in a colourless dark day. Considering my options.

It starts to rain, and I'm glad. She hated the rain. Not just how most people grumble if they're caught in a shower, or their garden party is ruined, or clothes soaked on the line – she proper *hated* it. Almost like she was made of something that would wash away, not sinew, muscle, and bone, all in hard angles.

Maybe she was afraid rain would wash away her mask. Like the one she wears in the newspapers, smiling with a man I've never seen before. *Smiling?* I wonder if she smiles in her coffin, if they arranged her features into a pleasant lie for the afterlife, in hope it'll persuade them to open the pearly gates instead of giving that final push for the long slide down. Or maybe there wasn't enough left of her face.

Cars start winding up the road. The first is long and black, a coffin in the back. When it pulls in front of the crematorium, it seems right that the rain goes from steady to *more*. It thunders down in sheets, and lightning splits the sky.

Even as I hang back and think about the things I should and shouldn't do, about how close to get to the flame, it is almost like the storm has made the decision for me. It says, *Quinn, you must step forward. You must seek shelter.*

But that's just the excuse. I'm really here to make sure she is really dead.